$\mathcal{L}$INEN SHROUD

Linen Shroud

Destiny Kinal

THE SECOND NOVEL IN
THE TEXTILE TRILOGY

sitio *tiempo*
press

TO VICTORIA KLEINSCHMIDT KINAL,
TAMARA LACEY DAVIS ADDESA & BILL SACKINGER

Cover art: Destiny, 1900 (oil on canvas),
Waterhouse, John William (1849-1917) / Towneley Hall Art Gallery and Museum,
Burnley, Lancashire / Bridgeman Images

sitio *tiempo*
press

An imprint of
REINHABITORY INSTITUTE
PO Box 10064, Berkeley, CA 94709

A collective publisher founded in 2009, sitio tiempo press brings home
the lessons of time and place to a diverse audience.

ACKNOWLEDGMENTS

Linen Shroud is dedicated to honoring two women in my contemporary family who died suddenly, just as they were launching into important life's work: Victoria Kleinschmidt Kinal and Tamara Lacey Davis Addesa. This is also for Bill Sackinger. He and I co-authored the genealogical story of our family following our female lineage. For more than a decade, we collaborated on this quest our mothers had requested. To everyone's shock, Bill died of pancreatic cancer before we could publish. The loss of that decade of work with Bill still feels like a missing molar in my jaw.

I want to acknowledge those of my female ancestors who reach out to me in gratitude for my work, in ensuring that they not disappear from the historical record, lost in the haze that comes from documenting lineage only through the patronymic. We feed off each other's energy reciprocally. My mother, Constance Davis Kinal, has, in the decades since her death, continued to reveal herself as a more and more dazzling star.

I dedicated my last book, *Burning Silk*, to my mother-in-law, Marian Skeist, who paid for my MFA, now twenty years ago. Her critical and early belief in me continues to be inestimable; her patronage made possible the research trips that provided the foundation for my fictional re-creations of nineteenth-century silk and linen cultures, both in the eastern United States as well as abroad.

My extraordinary editors, Lois Gilbert and Lisa K. Marietta, have worked with me through both *Burning Silk* and *Linen Shroud*; Raven DiSalvo-Hess added her millennial voice to both developmental and line editing of this book. Cecile Moochnek's weekly writing practicum midwifed me into some of the deranged sections of this book, essential to expressing the effects of war on sensitive spirits.

In particular, I thank my Native American sisters who have kindly read and edited this manuscript to provide me with insight into their way-of-life today. A larger group of Native American friends—too numerous to thank by name—have shared their thoughts about how contact between Native cultures and white people of European descent might have been occurred during the nineteenth century. Special thanks to Bernadette Zambrano, Joanne Grandstaff, and Kristen Lee for their editing and commentary. The teachings that the late Chief Paul Waterman of the Onondaga gave so generously contribute to my spiritual life and my books on a daily basis. Sally Roesch-Wagner's seminal book *Sisters in Spirit*, documenting the influence of Native American matrilineal women on the women's rights movement of the nineteenth century, underpinned both of the first two books in this series.

When it comes to insight into textiles and particularly linen, I can only mention a few, as it has been a journey of restoration many of us are making together. I cannot go forward without first asking my oldest granddaughter, Breanna Bayba, to take a bow; her work in historical costuming personifies what drove the women of Regina Coeli. My business partners in Sun Shine Down, Mollie Favour and Susan Logan, as well as my early career experience at Alvin Duskin Manufacturing in San Francisco in the sixties, gave me firsthand pleasure in garment design and production. Fibershed's prophetic mission in the textile industry and Planet Drum's sustained development of the concept of bioregionalism continue to be key formative philosophies in my life and my work. Rebecca and Dustin, Peter and Judy and all the salmon restoration people: deep bow! To Janice Langdon, whose devotion to my getting the technical parts of this book right, has honored this humble neophyte. The members of my Weaving a Life circle, led by Judith Thomas, animate what women have enjoyed in small communities creating textiles together, for millennia.

I thank all the men who have been willing to discuss the nature of warfare with me, over time. To Jeffrey Mosher, who can take my heat from my heart into his heart and cool it. To my father Murl Kinal whose silences about the war he served in, as a medic with Patton's Army, continue to illuminate the dark corners of his first-hand experience, including liberating concentration camps. To my great-great-grandfather Kilian Sechinger whose service during the U.S. Civil War resulted in his hospitalization for a year. Diagnosis: debilitas, the forerunner of shell shock and PTSD. To Karl, who complied, when the women of our family each told him, "Do not go. You are too beloved to lose." To Bradley/Chelsea Manning who was brutalized when jailed for his courageous patriotism speaking out against these unjust wars. To all the men who returned home from war with PTSD, their only route out of the experience of having to kill women, children and elders. In the immortal words of Pete Seeger, "When will it ever end?"

On a publishing level, it has been thrilling to have exactly the team at Sitio Tiempo Press contribute to *Linen Shroud* as they had *Burning Silk*, the first book in the Textile Trilogy: to my business partner, Judith Thomas, for both her friendship and for "being there," a creative sounding board, the spark. To our guiding Renaissance woman, Laura Greer; to project manager pro Susanna Tadlock; and to book designer Nancy Austin whose aesthetic so completely matches our own. Thanks to David Bullen for this gorgeous and lush series design.

On a personal level, I have deeply appreciated my husband, Barry Skeist, for providing me with the time and resources to write—a great privilege. Finally, my maternal line animates everything I write. I am especially grateful to the three women who set a new bar for that lineage in our contemporary times: my sister, Candace Hines, as well as my daughters, Gilian Handelman and Solange Gould.

To those not named here who nurtured this book and the Textile Trilogy, I thank the Mother every day that our paths crossed when they did.

I believe we are called to our subject matter as writers.

Contact between native, *métis*, and European characters in the nineteenth century, which has not been well explored in a literary form, fascinates me.

And yet I ask: Can I go there?

The imagination does not thrive within boundaries, by circumscribing what and who a writer can write about.

I have plumbed my family's deep experience as the indigenous people in several ancestral homelands where my family immigrated from one hundred years ago: Galicia in Ukraine, Ireland, and some hills north of Frankfurt. Older bloodlines fertilize my imagination.

All of the Native American characters to whom I give a point-of-view are *métis*, mixed blood, with European and Asian bloodlines to mediate their perspectives.

I take full responsibility for imagining what Contact might have been like. Having reached the limits of research, the spark must leap across the gap. Many native tribes, having lost much of their culture during the genocide, are engaged in similar processes of retrieval: solid research backed up by intuition and inspiration.

I truly hope I will not offend anyone.
Apologies in advance if I do.

Linen Shroud

Characters

THE DULADIER/SECHINGER FAMILY

Catherine Duladier, the first *maîtresse de la soie* in the New World; wife of Philip; mother of Kilian and Regina

Philip Sechinger, Catherine's second husband; stepfather of Kilian; father of Regina

Kilian, son of Catherine and stepson of Philip

Regina, daughter of Catherine and Philip

———————

THE DULADIER/SHAFER FAMILY

Elisabeth Duladier, steward to the *maîtresse de la soie*; Catherine's sister; mother of Kristiana

Wilhelm Shafer, Elisabeth's estranged husband; father of Kristiana

Kristiana, daughter of Elisabeth and Wilhelm; *maîtresse* after Catherine; mother of Threadneedle; partner of Turtle Dawn

Threadneedle, son of Kristiana Shafer Duladier and Lazarus Montour

———————

THE MONTOUR/LAZAR FAMILY

Marguerite Montour, elder of the Wolf Clan; Delphine's mother

Delphine Montour, daughter of Marguerite; mother of Turtle Dawn; wife of Blaise Lazar

Blaise Lazar, Delphine's husband

Turtle Dawn Montour, partner of Kristiana, and co-mother of their son, Threadneedle

Lazarus Montour, nephew of Marguerite and father of Threadneedle

Prologue

FIRST FOOD

Spring Equinox 1857,
Cattaraugus Reservation, New York

Lazarus pricked his ears, then hand-signaled to Threadneedle: *You circle to the right. I go left.*

The two men, father and son, moved quietly, in random patterns to avoid detection, starting and stopping as the leaf trembles in the wind and then falls still.

They rose on either side to flank the den that overlooked the small valley where Cattaraugus Creek went north to Lake Erie and meandered through willow, the color of acidic chartreuse, just before leafing out. Stands of red dogwood counterpointed maple buds swollen red against the sunset in the canopy. The wind, typical of March in these hardwood forests just off the Great Lakes, where cold and warm systems meet, had risen to choreograph a bare-limbed tree limbo, pruning off dead branches as the trees groaned and rubbed against each other, sap stirring in their roots. All this was lit by sunset's red spectrum, the illusion of warmth just before maple sugaring. Earlier, tiny silver fish the English speakers called smelt ran abundantly from the small streams into the Finger Lakes and Great Lakes.

For several years now, father and son had made a camping trip of it, north to where the westernmost Finger Lake was cut. Out with their torches, they joined both whites and natives helping each other fill their fine nets with the coin-sized fish that could be caught only at night. Their fellow *landsmen* hung their lanterns high on poles to light the darkness where the creek ran into the lake, a vestige of the great beast of ice a mile high who had raked its claw marks deep into the ground when it receded, its waters contained and tamed for a period, stasis between watersheds holding the larger stasis between ice ages, which their lore told them pulsed, and pulsed, throughout time.

Then and there, at that fish camp, they had made their first overtures to the Seneca who lived on Cattaraugus Reservation. Now, a couple of years later, could this *métis* family, with their Wolf Clan matron and a legendary lineage, move in permanently with these People who were related distantly through bloodlines? The Montours, it had been made clear, would be welcome. Their clan had given them this ritual to perform on behalf of this band of Seneca, who lived in one of the last places besides Akwesasne itself, in Canada, which hosted wolf dens within its protectorate.

When the principals of Regina Coeli, the family's popular fashion line, had moved to Cottage permanently, near Cattaraugus Reservation, Lazarus and Threadneedle had been offered a place at the fire in council. Now they had been given a ritualistic job, a great honor; they were each aware of how much hinged on doing it correctly. Primarily, the First Food was to bear no trace of human handling. The pups needed to know the elements of their world without having to sort out human scent and the information it bore: emotion, sexual development, and overall well-being, including a recent history of food consumption. Tobacco, corn, and all matter of cultivated crops were not to be even hinted at for the pups' First Food. Their clan had asked them: Could the Montours do this for both clan and tribe?

Father and son had camped deep in the woods near the stone cairns that marked important boundaries in the ley lines.

"Let me guess, Katarioniecha," Lazarus had said, as he and his son, who was still reaching manhood, sat rolling pemmican balls in parchment by a snapping fire, precisely following the instructions they had been given by their Wolf Clan chief. The trees sighed against each other as the warm spring wind met banks of cold snow and frozen ground.

"Guess what, Father?"

"Call me by my real name, son," his father said in a low voice.

The boy-man flushed. "My Father Kerioniakawida, what would you like to know?" He leapt up lightly and placed a small log across the fire, and then, after consideration, laid another by the side of the one that was burning well. He lifted the first log and placed it down across the second. He was rewarded both by the immediate sight of a gratified fire balanced between fuel and air and by his father's grunt. Threadneedle wore a headband to hold back his long hair, voluptuous as a river otter's pelt, to keep it from singeing in the fire.

Threadneedle had been raised in two communities: one, the Haudenosaunee and Lenape community of the Montour bloodline, the other the deeply Quaker family that his mother's side found themselves a part of when they had immigrated from Europe to establish their reputation as premier producers of silk thread. This enlightened European way-of-life (Quakers were staunchly against war as well as hierarchies of gender and skin color) was balanced uneasily against the traditions of the Montours, with whom the Duladiers had become increasingly involved.

But Christians of all sorts were indelibly missionary; just as the Moravians made inroads with the Lenni Lenape, so too did Quakers offer their liaison skills with an intractable federal government to the Haudenosaunee's Six Nations, thereby recasting the matrilineal people in lines more agreeable to the patrilineal European Americans. This policy alone almost broke the Haudenosaunee: to cut into the earth with steel plows and then plant in rows led inevitably to disrespecting women and their role as Earthkeepers. This single necessity of abandoning even the appearance of matrilineality—a shocking concept to white men—had been a difficult act to manage: traditional ways suffered. But to bend did not mean to break. This challenge had provided grist for a continuing discussion in both the men's and the women's councils since the Europeans had first come to their land.

As the two men sat rolling the balls of pemmican, they listened to the trees, studied the positions of the bright stars, monitored the fire. Lazarus had taught his son how to listen. An owl swooped by on furry wings, its flight punctuated by the squeak of its prey upon meeting those formidable claws.

Lazarus wanted to touch down on something delicate. Tomorrow they would crawl on their bellies to the threshold of a wolf den. Their approach would not go unnoticed. Finally Lazarus could see how to speak.

"I make fear my ally. My death sits on my right shoulder." He wanted to say his truth, to his son, his only child. "I believe that the hour of our death is written," he said quietly, making it clear by his tone that this was his belief alone, that he did not expect his son to share it unless Threadneedle's own experience delivered up a similar certainty.

But Threadneedle was not experienced. Lazarus and Grandmother Marguerite had brought him to the tribe frequently, to be accepted by their clan, to go with the other boys his age to be taught by the elders and chiefs of the Wolf Clan. Threadneedle approached the moment of acceptance into a warrior clan with humility. His native name, Katarioniecha, He Who Breaks to Heal, came with a history to live up to.

More than half of the time, the boy was raised by two women, both his mothers. One native. One white. It was not easy. Even in a progressive Quaker community, many of the inhabitants were strangers to this way-of-life, which was new to them, although the alliance between the two races had been forged for centuries on this continent. To them, Threadneedle was known by a loathsome word: half-breed. He might have been marginalized were it not for one detail: the boy himself. Every young man—Quaker, métis, or full-blood—wanted to emulate Threadneedle; every man and every woman wanted to have their son be like this lad who carried himself with natural grace, assurance, and, most importantly, humility.

Thread rose and unrolled their sleeping skins just so far from the fire. Everything was correct: a small pile of logs near his own sleeping mat for keeping the flame going until morning, moccasins by his head, knife in its sheath with the clasp undone and near his right hand. Next to him, Lazarus kept the fresh pemmican balls in a tin lined with parchment paper, the lid sealed tight with wax.

Thread cleaned up their work area and beat the ground with cedar boughs to erase the smell of meat and fat from their camp. He lit a braid of sweetgrass and smudged the air with its smoke. He banked the fire and then crawled in between his skins and a trade blanket. He calmed his breathing as he looked at the stars. He waited until he heard that his father was also in his bedroll, heard the relaxed circle of his breath.

"Father," he said. "Kerioniakawida." He could feel him, aware in the night. "My ancestors speak to me."

This apparently took Lazarus by surprise, for he made a sound that told his son it did not go without notice that Thread had said "my ancestors" rather than "our ancestors."

As Orion wheeled overhead, his sword hilt gleaming, Thread said (and both of them knew this would be his final word for the night), "They know me. And I know them. I am at peace with my fate . . . whatever it will be."

Lazarus allowed himself to slip into his dreams, content that his son was not afraid. His last conscious thought was to thank the Mother of All for the man his son was becoming.

The den was set into a hillock that had undoubtedly started as a great fallen tree, its roots a locus for rocks that worked their way to each other and the surface. Time did the rest. This wolf den was one of two packs within howling proximity of each other, related by blood through the maternal line.

Both Montour father and son, silent as breath, eased their bellies down onto the blanket rolls they carried across their shoulders and chests. Lazarus slid the top off the tin box, its metallic sound buffered by a thin layer of beeswax. Using parchment paper as a glove, he withdrew their offering: deer meat, huckleberries, nuts. No bear fat or pig fat. Oil from sunflower seeds as binder. Nourishment for a postpartum wolf mother and her pups.

He placed the small balls on the threshold to the den, then crept backward a respectful distance. The noise they made announced their withdrawal. No one should be surprised coming upon them at the den door.

She growled deep in her throat, waking her pups, who nursed greedily. Then she rose, tumbled them off her tits to the ground, nipped this one, swiped a paw at that one, licked and guided them. Three little brothers and one sister, her entire wealth, stood in an attentive clot, watched her every move, their adoration of her necessary to each one's survival.

Her mate lifted his head from his paws, looked her over. She was thin. Every rib showed clearly. He smelled the human offering, which had arrived just in time, as it had when he was a cub, and then when he was a bachelor, and now again that he had become a young father. He yawned and closed his eyes again. This was for her and their pups. He was hungry, yes, but he could eat later. He would eat when the cubs slept, after their First Food. She would hunt with him, fresh meat. She needed it. He had tasted her milk. It was rich, but thin and scant, like her. He grunted.

She heard him, told him she would be back. *Sleep. And then we will hunt, a dawn hunt, while the cubs sleep.*

He opened one yellow eye. *Yes*, he said. *A dawn hunt while the cubs sleep. Come back and tell me who left the offering.*

I will, she said and yipped at her pups. He watched as they left the den, her head and tail held high, ears pricked, the pups adopting her stance.

They were good, all of them, he thought. Holo perhaps a bit too adventurous for her own good, but she obeyed her mother and allowed herself to be governed. She would be a beauty. He sunk his muzzle back onto his paws. The den was perfectly quiet, free of all signals except his own. He would rather be out with her in the night, but he would rest instead. The dawn hunt would be his to lead. Her hunger was great, her strength played out to the cubs, but she would recover with his help. He knew exactly where they would go: to the doe whose twins came in a difficult birth, one lame, unable to thrive. It would be a morsel. He would let her eat the prime parts of the fawn; she would bring some home to disgorge for the pups. It was well before rutting time, and no stags would be about; he was as certain of this as he was of his own existence. He remembered how his uncle had been gutted by an angry stag. The light fading from the elder wolf's eyes as the pack looked on, helpless. The smell. His mother's keening for her brother. The revenge they took, his first hunt at not even a year old. He would go out in a while, smell for the presence of stags.

Outside, she stood alert. All her senses delivered one message: *The world quickens.* Her pups were good, close to her flanks on either side. They could smell the offering. Holo whimpered. Her mother nipped her, growled in her small ear so her brothers could hear the disapproval. A lenient mother might suffer four pups whimpering at once if she didn't maintain pack discipline. Some mothers never went out with a litter this big—four!—without another adult, but she had confidence in both herself and her pups. She was proud of them; they were hungry for their first solid meal, yes, but they knew how to wait. She would give the signal.

Ears pricked, she leaned her magnificence forward on her front legs, ruff distended, then lifted her nose to the sky and howled. The pups stirred beside her; they would not howl uninvited, though they wanted to.

From a distant ridge, another howl, her sister. *All is well here.*

The humans have been here with their offering. They will be on their way to you. She gave another howl for pure pleasure. *My white-ruffed son from the previous year is off courting.*

Her sister responded, confirmed her health and that of her pups, promised a reunion over fresh meat, blood on the jaws, the pleasure of a spring hunt come the full moon.

Lazarus and Thread thrilled to the sound of their wolf clanmothers howling at the night, and one wolf just a stone's throw away. The two men joined their breath, their heartbeats, their minds in a slow union, a way they had learned together as Thread grew through his boyhood and toward his young adulthood. They did not dare speak into the silence, even wordlessly in what the Women of the Silk called Dialog. They could not say if the wolves heard them communicate, and they wanted to keep the energy channels clear; they could not risk unintentional messages. If they were to sound like prey, they would certainly lose the respect of the wolves they served.

The sliver of the new moon had set long ago, when the sunset still stained the horizon; now Venus hung like a jewel in the predawn. The stars were lively, the sky full of activity. A high wind stirred the upper branches, signaled the return of warmer winds, the flow of sap, and, eventually, bud-break. No one in the tribe would starve this winter.

Both men found themselves where they wanted to be, in a state of alert mindfulness. Each emptied his mind and waited.

Darkness guide us, the matriarch wolf prayed. Did she smell fear? The stories were passed down from generation to generation. Only once had a suppliant who brought First Food been punished. She smelled closely: *No fear, not even from the young one*, she observed.

She stepped down off the mound that capped their den and leapt lightly on to the flat apron that surrounded their threshold, to the fragrant meal their human brothers had placed there. Earlier, she had introduced her pups to trees, to their slow motions, to the understory brothers and sisters, to the wind. She had brought elements of the world into their den. A bird. A mouse. She had shown them each of these kingdoms through single instances, a way of giving context to their First Food.

She pulled one ball into her mouth, growled with pleasure as her teeth ground the treat, hand-delivered only once a year by their human brothers, crawling on hands and knees out of respect. It was nothing she would deign to eat at any other time. One ball, then a second and a third. These humans had done a perfect job of keeping each of the elements separate, with no hint of their human handling. Her stomach growled. *Eh, good!*

Her pups lined up in front of her. Holo nipped her lip, opened her small mouth, and caught the hot stew her mother disgorged for her. *Now go sit down and enjoy your First Food*, her mother instructed with a switch of the tip of her tail and a descriptive cock of her ears and head. Holo trotted the distance of her mother's body and sat on her haunches, chewing the sweet, strange meal and watching as her brothers one by one took their portion and came to lie down or sit at the place Holo had chosen.

Their mother padded over to observe them. *Now stay!* she instructed with a low growl. *Do I need to tell you this is a test? Chew your food well. I will return.*

She turned back to the meal the humans had laid out.

The food is good; nothing like milk, the pups said to each other. *Strange.* Their mother had told them these things like a rhyme they were to remember, as it would be their lesson for the spring, when they would go out from the den in both daylight and starlight to discover their world. They rolled the tastes over their tongues, trying to sort out the different flavors. *Meat of a deer, meat of a nut tree, meat from a flower's fruit.* This was their first sensory contact with all three elements of the world. First there was deer, an animal like them. Then the meats from trees: nut and flower fruit. What did it mean? This was their first lesson in acquiring those answers. They had smelled their mother's breath when she had returned from feeding. She brought them things to smell, and they had noted the differences in the taste of her milk. Now, with their first solid food, they chewed and tasted and smelled even more carefully. And they tasted something else, something rich like milk, but more so.

Fat. Mother said it is fat. Holo spoke quietly.

Fat, her brothers said reflectively, each thinking they would like to have more of that fat.

When their mother returned, she chewed for a long time, then sighed, rolling on her back to scratched it, rubbing her fur into the roots of what would become new grass, the ground sweetening toward spring as the worms and bugs who lived there rose toward the surface, as the small animals—mice, moles, voles—woke from their own hibernations and gestations. She listened to them chirping beneath the surface and bade her pups listen, giving them another vision of what a meal could be.

Now, she instructed them.

They rose and walked together to the top of the hummock above their cave.

Now, she said, lifting her nose and indicating the four directions.

Here, she said and then swung her nose in the opposite direction and lifted it again. *And here.*

The pups emulated her movements. Yes, they smelled them, their bene-factors and brothers, the humans. The pups had been carefully schooled before they had left the den. But the specifics of who had brought their First Food were just being discovered: a father and a son. They smelled each human and distinguished between their similarities and their differences.

Father, their mother told them as they turned their small muzzles to one side, tasting the smell of that man. *And son,* she turned her head, cocked her senses toward the right. They followed her lead, tasting the smell of the son. *How different they are! Are our smells that different? Can we see them?* They had myriad questions, but they knew the terms of being in a pack, in the outside with their mother. She had trained them carefully; they would hold all their questions until they were back in the den, safe.

Now, their mother indicated. *Greet the world.* They heard the owl. Saw the possum. Smelled the men. Heard the creek. Saw the stars. *What are they?* they wondered.

And then their mother greeted the world. In their eyes, she was the equal of all creation, the source of their well-being.

Now, she said.

They each lifted their noses to the sky, their eyes to the stars, their ears to the noisy night world, and howled. Oh, how good it felt. *How much the universe loves me,* each thought.

And hark!—their aunt and cousins on a distant ridge howled back. They answered, greeting their aunt and their new cousins. A girl. A boy. One smaller girl had died not long after being born.

Father trotted out of the cave then and, mounting the rise, stood beside them with his thick body and howled his deep, eccentric male howl, har-monizing well with their mother, telling the world that it was spring, that their band had doubled and all was well.

Then, in the silence that followed, the human father howled, and now, beside him, the human son howled too. And they said this: *All is well.*

And they said something else, something the pups couldn't fully inter-pret. A warning. The pups were confident that their mother and father would understand what might be coming, would protect them.

Mother and Father thanked the humans, and then Mother nudged her pups back toward the den, and not a moment too soon for, having eaten their First Food, they were tired and wanted to sleep, curled nose to tail in a soft and fragrant bundle, three brothers and one sister, dreaming of the Three Meats—deer, nut, and fruit—and fat.

Lazarus nudged Thread, and the two men, father and son, backed away from the surround of the den, noting the coordinates of the related pack to the north, behind them where the other set of howls had come from. They would confirm the well-being of the two dens to their hosts and clanmembers back in Cattaraugus.

How long will the white population permit these last two wolf packs to exist, a half-day's trot from their settlements and flocks of sheep? Lazarus wondered and made a note to discuss this with the council so that he might have some context for the ridgeline he traveled between those two worlds. Lazarus was wanted for the murder of a white man who had come to assassinate the prophet Handsome Lake, years ago, a situation that necessitated his construction of a new life as He Who Hides, which in turn cultivated a hyperawareness of his surroundings in both worlds.

Lazarus glanced at his caramel-skinned, blue-eyed son, Threadneedle, whose hair was held back in long braids down his back, a colorful band framing his beloved face, his features in the process of molding into a man's face. *How will he do?* Lazarus wondered, thinking of the world that was becoming hostile to the commingling of European and native bloodlines, a prejudice that was rising not just from this newer wave of white settlers but also from his own People.

Lazarus, who was not accustomed to interrogating time, sank back into an awareness that had served him well, and led the way out of the woods, Thread following precisely in his footsteps. Both men held themselves completely in the here and now, without thought, thin as starlight.

When they reached their camp, happy from the hour of swinging along in the dark down a narrow path through the woods, like natural creatures, wolflike in their own pack, they collected the camp into the rucksacks they had swung high on a tree limb. They coiled the valuable length of silk and linen rope and stowed it carefully away from moisture in the waxed bag made for that purpose.

Thread prodded and coaxed the small fire to life and put water on to boil. They had a long, grueling trip back to Cattaraugus, where they would do their day's chores, report to their Wolf Clan how First Food had gone, and then welcome an early bedtime.

For now, they sat companionably side by side, ready to leave as soon as Lazarus indicated, but still treasuring their shared experience on behalf of their clan. Each sipped the tea that Thread had prepared for them and poured into cups. Serving his father first, Threadneedle waited to see whether Lazarus' first sip met his satisfaction. His father nodded, a minimal gesture that instructed his son to sit and enjoy his tea, to use the leisure to empty his mind, to digest his first feeding of the wolves in service to their clan.

Lazarus opened the tin he had kept close to him. Four pemmican balls remained inside. He offered the tin to his son. Thread knew better than to refuse his share and removed two balls with his slender fingers. Placing one in his mouth, he chewed slowly and waited for his father to speak.

If a young man were to experience fear, it would be now, Lazarus thought. *After*. It would be a bad sign if his son were not to experience fear at all, for fear was the driver that kept the hand steady. Fear kept a warrior safe.

Thread held out his cup in front of him, anticipating his father's concern. It shook. But a certain self-satisfied look grazed the young man's face, marking the lack of deeper humility that had concerned Kerioniakawida since his son had started crossing the threshold from boyhood to manhood. It was a look that said, *Don't I always hit the mark precisely?*

Lazarus heard Thread govern his breath, drive it down into his body, calm his thoughts, and become invisible in the morning twilight. Wasn't everything satisfactory but for that one flaw?

Lazarus wanted to allow himself the same privilege, reserved for warriors after battle, but before he sought a quiet mindfulness, he examined what he knew of the future. Having been in the warrior councils, he knew one thing to be true: war was coming. No one would escape notice. Everyone would be touched or maimed. This thing was larger than any of them, beyond any People's control. One could only prepare as the wave gathered to break.

And now it was Lazarus' turn to experience the metallic taste of fear. As morning began to appear, as birds started to stir in their nests and call out their location and condition, to greet the morning, Lazarus was still working with breath and heartbeat to master a fear that struggled to master him, two well-matched predators. And only one would be broken. His prayer continued, measured as breath. *Don't break my son.* In-breath. *I surrender to the will of the Creator.* Out-breath. Then: *What will I tell our clan?* As one who traveled the ridgeline between two cultures, all the evidence he collected pointed to the same thing: a mighty conflict approached. How did a People prepare to be broken again when so much had been taken already?

Their medicine men had been meditating on this question. They would fast, pray, travel out. For the past two hundred years the answers had been the same: the Wheel is turning. One day it will turn back.

PART ONE

1860

Chapter One

THE ADOPTION

The Quarter Holiday, May 1, 1860,
Cattaraugus Reservation, New York

After what seemed like an endless prelude, Kristiana was introduced to the Cattaraugus Haudenosaunee and adopted.

"She is my daughter in everything but name," Marguerite Montour had told the Council of Clanmothers. The evidence that they had made the right decision lay in the thunder that crashed around them the day of the adoption. *Wee-saw-say-hey-noo,* the Thunder People, spoke.

And then spoke again, a blessing on the day.

That morning, when they rose at the house Lazarus had been given, Grandmother Marguerite had advised Kristiana on her dress and how to style her hair while Delphine and Turtle Dawn watched. Three generations of Montour women brought the gravity of their lineage to the adoption, setting the tone: no corset, nothing white, no Regina Coeli labels on her clothing, even though Kristiana had started the successful company with her partner Turtle Dawn. Plain blue-and-white gingham and a clean sprigged pinafore. Muslin underclothes, undyed.

"The clanmothers and their daughters can't afford your dresses," Grandmother Marguerite said. "It will be better if we are modest and humble rather than dressed grandly, in our regalia."

"Our mothers and sisters in the tribe will be all the happier for the gifts we brought," Delphine said, reminding them archly that—both as Turtle Dawn's mother as well as the owner of the company that dyed all of Regina Coeli's fashions—she shared in the credit of giving the gross of Regina Coeli outfits, in different sizes and colors, each one marked with a specific name Grandmother Marguerite had provided for tagging.

Kristiana had scrubbed her face clean in a bucket of spring water and washed under her arms and breasts and between her legs before she pulled on her undergarments. Grandmother Marguerite and Delphine parted her hair in the middle, and—in a departure from tradition that both women agreed upon—styled Kristiana's hair in two braids and coiled each over her ears.

Now dressed, she was being inspected by the three generations of Montour women. Grandmother drew from her pocket a beaded necklace in neutral colors and put it around Kristiana's neck. "My gift to you, Kristiana: the Corn Maiden pattern." While Turtle Dawn, Delphine, and Grandmother Marguerite did not have on their full family regalia, each woman was wearing around her neck a significant piece of jewelry from the family collection.

Although Kristiana knew that the whole introduction and adoption ceremony was "of necessity" to ensure her son Threadneedle's lineage and inheritance in the Wolf Clan—and, if he were fortunate and found worthy, into further responsibilities—she was a little nervous. "There is no other door," Grandmother had assured her, and so she pressed on.

Kristiana was surprised to find that she was actually eager for the occasion. She knew little about the People she had married into, aside from their close relationship with the natural world, and the other things she had sucked in like air while she was being fostered in Grandmother's care. Turtle Dawn rarely brought her culture, or the fact that the Montours were Wolf Clan, into the household she shared with Kristiana. When she did, Kristiana did not recognize it as such. Kristiana had the impression that her mother-in-law Delphine's defection from the tribe had put a blank into Turtle Dawn's lineage, a blank solid as a wall. Because of this, Delphine's unexpected presence at the upcoming ceremony, despite her insistence that she not be "pegged and pigeonholed," made Kristiana feel the weight of her adoption all the more.

All seven of them—the four women plus Lazarus, Thread, and Delphine's husband Blaise—clustered together under an overhang so they didn't get wet while they waited outside the longhouse, where a council gathered for larger issues than this one. Men and women walked past and filed into the building.

A drum began from within, then the smell of tobacco drifted out. They heard a low grumbling like the thunder above as someone—a man—spoke.

A young woman with a baby waited outside as well. A sergeant-at-arms came to the door, gestured to the young mother, and escorted her in, letting the leather flap that covered the door fall back into place. After what seemed like a long time, during which murmurings were heard inside as different people spoke, she and the baby came out again, the mother's face transfixed with joy.

The sergeant-at-arms then beckoned to the group and they quietly passed in one by one.

Lazarus, Thread, and Blaise took seats on low benches in the circle of men on one side, while Turtle Dawn and Delphine found their places among the women on the other side. Grandmother Marguerite stood beside Kristiana, one hand on her back for comfort and to guide her.

A fire burned in the middle of the hearth. Two young men squatted in front, rearranging the wood so it didn't smoke. An older man sat by the pile of wood, supervising their moves. *Firekeepers*, Kristiana thought, reminding herself to take deep breaths, her earlier discipline as *maîtresse de la soie* for the Duladier family's silk venture, lending her strength and calm.

Grandmother Marguerite led her to a place near the hearth in front of the oldest group of men and women. The elders looked at her without commentary.

A woman with an abalone shell and a smoking brand of sage and cedar approached Grandmother Marguerite. With what looked like a grouse wing to Kristiana, the woman wafted the incense around Grandmother, from head to toe and—after Grandmother turned—up and down her back as well. Kristiana watched carefully as Grandmother used her hands to pull the smoke to her, a peaceful look on her face. When it was Kristiana's turn, she followed what her elder had done, turning around when the front of her was cleansed.

She saw no signal, but Turtle Dawn had told her that Grandmother Marguerite Montour would speak in Seneca, one of the languages of the Haudenosaunee, then repeat herself every so often in French, thanking the Council of Clanmothers and the Council of Chiefs—led by elders from the eight clans of the Seneca—for hearing her.

"I speak with my open heart," Marguerite said quietly, but loud enough for everyone in the longhouse to hear her. "This woman was fostered with me when her family came to this country, twenty years ago. She was still a girl. She and my granddaughter Turtle Dawn became like this," she held up two fingers joined. "We taught her everything about our world, the plants and insects, animals and trees—but not our ways. When she came of age, she chose Kerioniakawida to mate with." Marguerite had said a name Kristiana didn't recognize.

When Marguerite glanced over her shoulder, the look on Kristiana's face revealed that the younger woman had just heard Lazarus' true name for the first time. Then: "They called into being this young man you know as Katarioniecha."

Kristiana was surprised. *How have I never heard my son's true name until now?*

"You have known this young man since he was a boy," Grandmother continued, looking at Thread. "He has sought to be part of our People, to take up his place in the tribe with a full heart. He is worthy, as you know. He not only has his father—Kerioniakawida—but also his grandmother," she nodded at Delphine, "and my granddaughter," she nodded at Turtle Dawn, "among our people, but also all the people of the Wolf Clan. Only one thing stands in his way from taking his place among our people: his mother, whom we bring here before you. We have come to ask you to give her a name, to accept her as one of us."

Grandmother didn't need to nudge her forward. The simplicity of the ceremony, the faces before her, spoke to Kristiana. She realized she was asking something that had been building in her since she had arrived in New Jersey: to be accepted into the tribe of the Original People, this tribe. Her heart already open, she spoke her simple words in French. Many of these People had French bloodlines as well, testimony to a time when Europeans did not seek to conquer but simply to coexist, to learn how to make a good life here, a life in balance. Grandmother would translate Kristiana's words into Seneca, the native language she had in common with the People of Cattaraugus Reservation.

"I was born when I stepped onto these soils," she began, then paused, looking for the next true thing to say. "Perhaps I am here to take the place of one you have lost—a sister, a daughter. Grandmother Marguerite has prepared me. Everything I know—which is little—she has given to me generously." She looked at Marguerite and inclined her head. "I thank you, Grandmother. You are my mother on this continent."

Perhaps I should end it there, Kristiana thought. *Should I take it further?*

"This dress"—she fingered her calico—"is not buckskin. I come from a long lineage of mothers who know the secrets of unlocking thread from the silkworm and coaxing linen thread from the flax plant. I come to ask you for my true name. Delphine, Turtle Dawn, and I bring these gifts: linen clothing in the sizes and colors from the list you provided. Our son and his father, Lazarus, have brought silk bands for the men of the council to wear around their necks or foreheads in a design our son made to honor you. I humbly ask you to accept our gifts."

Delphine and Lazarus stepped forward with a sample of a dress and a silk band, presenting them to the leading clanmother, who bent to the main chief sitting beside her and placed the long silk band around his neck. He stroked it, admiringly, and turned to the other chiefs, nodding his approval.

A middle-aged woman near Grandmother reached out her arms, took the dress, and passed it back behind her. In perfect French, she said, "Daughter, it is true we have expected you. Marguerite has been telling us about you for many years. We give you your true name, which means 'rainbow' in your language. It is *O-nhyo-da* in ours." She turned again and someone in the back passed her a short cape made of ermine skins sewn together, the black tips of the tails hanging loose and a pattern of rainbow beads sewn on the shoulders as epaulettes.

The woman who had cleansed Grandmother Marguerite and Kristiana with cedar fastened the cape around Kristiana's shoulders. Petting it with her hand, Kristiana was struck speechless by its beauty. *No wonder the royalty of Europe all covet this fur!*

A breathy *ah!* swept through the gathering as everyone saw the rightness of the cape to mark Kristiana's true name.

"You are one of us now. Marguerite, Delphine, and Turtle Dawn—your Montour maternal line—will teach you how to observe our ways. When you come here, you are welcome to attend council meetings and perhaps, with time, you will be invited into the Women's Lodge. Marguerite will tell you about our sacred holidays and make sure you are invited."

A sudden murmuring of people in the audience commenting to each other told Kristiana that her adoption was over. Or seemed to be. While Kristiana exited the longhouse with the rest of the crowd, Thread, Lazarus, Turtle Dawn, and Delphine stayed behind. Presumably the Council of the Elders had some words for them.

They belong, Kristiana thought.

Grandmother Marguerite and Kristiana went out into the rain and back to Lazarus' house, where they took over the cooking of the feast that marked Kristiana's adoption. Corn, squash, beans—the Three Sisters—blended with venison in a savory soup. Tiny quail bodies quickly roasted over the bed of coals they had started before going to the council. The earliest mulberries had been sent up from Newtown and boiled with maple syrup. This compote would be served over a rich steamed corn pudding made two days earlier, dark with molasses and eggs, nuts and dried fruit.

Kristiana had been afraid that the adoption would be something *pro forma*, grudgingly given and insincere. *I have a lot to learn*, she reflected, glad that Marguerite and Turtle Dawn had brought a dozen dozen dresses to the tribe. Delphine had dyed them with a rainbow of natural hues drawn from the flowers and berries that grew here, and their pressers had steamed the wrinkles out of the garments, then carefully folded each creation into tissue, just as if they were shipping them to Albany. *I hope they appreciate the cost in both material and time that one gross of Regina Coeli outfits represents.* As soon as she had thought this, she erased it from the scrim of her mind as unworthy, a discipline she had practiced as a *maîtresse de la soie* many years ago, when Thread was a small boy.

Something had closed over and healed, a hole in her heart. She practiced saying her name in the Onondaga tongue. *O-nhyo-da.* The middle syllable closed the nose, making a nasal sound. She wasn't sure she liked the sound of it. But because it meant rainbow, she knew that it would sound different with time, as if she had grown up with it. Besides, the point was that she had cleared the way for Thread.

Thread had long anticipated this day, and it was he who had ordered the narrow striped silk bands in colors he knew his tribesmen would like—maroon and red, gold and green—from a mill in New England.

By the time the councilmembers and their families arrived for the feast, things became a blur for Kristiana. The sun broke through the clouds. Everyone aah-ed when a rainbow gave its blessing on her naming day. Kristiana's heart could not have been more full or her motives more pure as she and Turtle Dawn stood side by side, serving the food they had prepared for their guests.

The younger women of the reservation wasted no time in stepping into the back room of the house to try on their new dresses. Grandmother had been very careful. Names were affixed to the different colors and sizes. After some small confusion, every woman had her gift and had slipped it on to be sure it suited her. Others would be carried home to be delivered to those who could not attend.

The elder women, who had been served first, sat talking to each other, eying their new clanmember. They nodded, smiling.

"They like our food," Kristiana said to Turtle Dawn.

Turtle Dawn nodded.

"This changes everything," Kristiana said.

"I know," Turtle Dawn said, then smiled at Kristiana as if words would never be enough.

One of the clanmothers—the one from the Wolf Clan—called Kristiana and Turtle Dawn to stand before her. Grandmother Marguerite sat to the woman's left, and two other women, including the one who had given Kristiana her name, sat to her right. The Wolf Clan mother spoke first, addressing Kristiana. "I believe you know Blaise's aunt already, Matron Shenandoah," she said, gesturing to the woman on her right.

Kristiana realized she had met this clanmother before. *A woman whose smiles orchestrate all the wrinkles in her face, the sun breaking through her years to show her spirit*, Kristiana thought. She remembered her because her French was good, if a bit archaic. *Have I ever heard Blaise's maternal family name before? I wonder why Blaise chose to use his father's name, Lazar?*

"And to her right, Al Waterman's mother, Matron Audrey Waterman, here to speak for her son," the clanmother said to Turtle Dawn. Grandmother translated her words into French, and the woman sitting to the right of Matron Shenandoah nodded and smiled. Kristiana reminded herself that these musical family names—Waterman and Shenandoah—were something other than she was used to: these names had passed through their maternal lines for millennia.

Blaise's aunt, who held a close relationship to the Montours, then spoke to Turtle Dawn. "We have taken your son, Katarioniecha, your son with O-nhyo-da," she inclined her head to Kristiana, letting the sun of her smile break through, "into our tribe and into our hearts, Turtle Dawn, our little Gotga-hath-wih." The elders all laughed. Turtle Dawn did not. Kristiana presumed it was an inside joke and resolved to ask Turtle Dawn about it later. "We understand," Matron Shenandoah put her hand on her heart to show where this understanding dwelled, "you want a child of your own body. My nephew Blaise is already married into your lineage." She smiled at Delphine, who was hovering behind the two young women. Delphine nodded stiffly at this recognition of their formal familial relationship and stepped away, as if she were about some important errand she had forgotten.

"Auntie," Turtle Dawn said, stepping forward, speaking in a native tongue Kristiana thought could be either Seneca or Onondaga; Kristiana hadn't heard Haudenosaunee languages enough to distinguish between them. Grandmother's simultaneous French translation, Kristiana realized, was solely for her benefit. "I would like to have a child of my body, a sister or brother to Thread. I would like to ask if one of your sons or grandsons would mate with me, as Lazarus mated with Kristiana when she chose him."

Audrey Waterman, placing her hand next to her mouth, spoke into Matron Shenandoah's ear. Blaise's aunt, a clanmother of the Turtle Clan, nodded to the Wolf Clan mother to pick up the thread and continue. Grandmother began to translate again, from whatever native tongue the clanmother was speaking, into French.

The Wolf Clan mother spoke for both the women's council and for Audrey Waterman. "We don't think either of you are really two-spirit. You both like men, though you know very little of intimacy with them. You are still young. This"—she nodded first to Turtle Dawn, then to Kristiana— "has more to do with your destinies than with your being two-spirit."

Kristiana was not surprised to hear this; she had enjoyed her time conceiving Threadneedle with Lazarus. But Turtle Dawn? Her partner had never known a man. She had never even thought of Turtle Dawn as capable of loving a man.

Grandmother Marguerite resumed the narrative. "None of our elder women want their sons or grandsons to marry into your family, but not because they think you are two-spirit here or here," she pointed to Turtle Dawn's breasts and between her legs. "There is a deeper reason."

Turtle Dawn's heart sank.

The Wolf Clan spokeswoman took up the line of reasoning. The repetition in two languages fell over Turtle Dawn and Kristiana's disappointment like a waterfall, measured and inexorable. "Many of us are *métises*, mixed-blood women," she said, letting that sit for a long silence. "A man follows his wife into her home. We would be consigning one of our sons or grandsons to that forked life you lead, where spirits collide and quarrel. Like in the body of the son you call Threadneedle." Kristiana's face expressed surprise when Grandmother Marguerite translated what their clanmother had said. When she glanced at Turtle Dawn, she saw the impassivity her partner cultivated in times of trial.

I don't think Thread has a forked life! Kristiana thought.

"You have learned your son's name in our language, O-nhyo-da. He is named after Turtle Dawn's great-great-great-grandfather, Katarionie-cha. Your Grandmother Marguerite's great-grandfather. His name means 'He Who Breaks to Heal.' Grandmother seemed to be having a harder and harder time speaking the words of her friends and clanswomen back to them, as if she were swimming upstream. *Because they are hard words,* Kristiana realized.

"It may be that a new People are rising in this place, ones who may be proud and united, who take from each other and the land only what they give back. We call these people *métises*, mixed-bloods. But Katarioniecha? Do you see your son clearly? He is riven between the two. It gives him no peace."

Kristiana heard, as if for the first time, the beginning of her son's name in his native tongue: Katar. Her People, way back many centuries, had called themselves Cathar. Kristiana believed in the elemental power of sound. The Cathars had a hard destiny of persecution. Was this to be her son's fate— Duladier Cathars wedded to the hard history of the Montours?

Tears began to slide down Turtle Dawn's cheeks. The Wolf Clan mother took her hand. "We are not throwing you out of the tribe or the clan, daughter. You must know that what you are doing together will have no issue. Your line will stop." She said the word in such a way that Grandmother's choice of the archaic word in French, *rotundiare*, to round up, suggested its root meaning, to prune: her right hand echoed that meaning, making a circle and then an abrupt stop, a chopping down.

The clanmother's words echoed in Kristiana. '*You must know that what you are doing together will have no issue.*' *But what is it that we are doing? If loving each other is not the point of the clanmothers' refusal, what else could they mean?*

The Wolf Clan mother spoke again to Turtle Dawn.

I must learn her name, Kristiana realized.

"I am sorry," she was saying. "Not a woman has come forward to offer her son to you in marriage. And neither do we lend our men only to make children, as many of your people do—so it seems!" Grandmother's translation into French was a rebuke, gentle but clear.

Kristiana wondered how much, before Grandmother's translation, Turtle Dawn understood of what the Wolf Clan mother was saying. If Turtle Dawn knew the language, she had never spoken it in front of Kristiana before. And then Kristiana couldn't hold her tongue: "But what is it? Why do you refuse us?"

The six women were silent for a long time. Audrey Waterman spoke to Turtle Dawn, although it was Kristiana who had asked the question. "Does your maternal uncle Kerioniakawida knock on your door when he comes? Is it not his home also? Does his son not live there? You, his niece?" She turned to Kristiana then, to ask, "Could any of us come to your home and be admitted, O-nhyo-da?"

Kristiana wanted to bring out the tactful lie, but the answer was obvious: *It depends.*

The Wolf Clan mother turned to Turtle Dawn. "Whose house do you live in, child?"

Turtle Dawn's cheeks blazed with humiliation.

Kristiana became aware that Delphine had rejoined them at some point and was now standing beside Turtle Dawn. Her European clothing and her platinum hair, from a Dutch forefather, stood out like a second rebuke, putting a fine point on this clanmother's words.

Kristiana spoke again, though she hadn't made a conscious decision to speak. *"Ainsi soit-il."* So be it. The French phrase had a religious sound, echoing the "amen" used in English. With the phrase, Kristiana might have struck a gong of acceptance, but instead she said it with the sound of a closing door. Then: "We bring one final gift, Grandmothers." She looked at Turtle Dawn, who spoke:

"Every year we will bring you two percent of our profits from the linen so more needs can be met by the tribe: caring for the widow, the lone wolf, the cripple, the orphan."

Even as she spoke, however, Kristiana thought resentfully, *The gifts we have brought today are more than generous. And we have been turned down.*

She wanted to ask the clanmothers for something they could say yes to. "We have one more request. Will you send someone every year for ceremony, to bless our land and purify it?"

In response the Wolf Clan mother asked, "Do your iron plows open the soil? Do you plant one kind at a time, in rows?"

Both Kristiana and Turtle Dawn nodded, seeing what was coming. The native way was to plant the Three Sisters on mounds; these essential crops they had cultivated for centuries would then be supplemented by what they gathered.

The clanmother slowly shook her head. "On some things we will never see eye to eye." And then, to soften the blow, she added, "But that does not mean we will not bring both of you into ceremony and the sweat lodge with us. We will." She looked pointedly at Delphine, concluding, "If you want it, it is yours."

Delphine, who was nothing if not nervy, dared to ask in Dialog: *Who is being shut out here and who included?*

Now the response came from the vast repository of collective wisdom of all of the women and men who listened on both sides of the family lines, Huguenot and Haudenosaunee: *It depends. Who wants to be included?*

The gantlet had been thrown down. Delphine stormed out.

Fury swept through Kristiana. Even though it was clear their interview was over and the clanmothers were moving off, Kristiana still had a question, a hollow reed through which her rage could be fed to bring an ember to flame. "Grandmother," she said, prolonging their interview.

All four of the elders turned back, surprise in their eyes.

"Thread is already part of the Wolf Clan," Kristiana said. "What has he gained today with my adoption?"

"You ask a good question, daughter," the Wolf Clan mother answered. "He can elect to become part of the warrior society."

Kristiana felt angry tears start out of her eyes. "But I don't want him to go to war!"

"Daughter, the warrior society is an ancient part of our defense. They are bidden by the clanmothers. They are the Peacekeepers, chopping wood and repairing roofs for elders. Doing good." She leaned close to Kristiana and whispered, "And yet men must always be prepared to die to defend us."

"Why?" Kristiana pulled back. Others in the room looked at her and then looked quickly away. She knew she was making a scene but she couldn't help herself. Turtle Dawn touched her arm and she jerked away.

Then Matron Shenandoah spoke. "Clanmothers have often stepped in when a war party seemed frivolous, to forbid it, to deny it resources, to let it die."

When Kristiana heard these words, the hand gripping her heart eased up. "The clanmothers," she repeated, as if to confirm a safe refuge.

Grandmother Marguerite had the last word. "Yes. We govern the young men, the warrior society. If we feel that a raid is frivolous, we can cancel it. Where there is balance, there is strength."

The next afternoon, before they climbed into the wagon to head back home to Cottage, a half-day's travel in a cart, Grandmother said to Turtle Dawn and Kristiana, "Be very careful. When a mother gives up rearing her child to another—even a member of her family—at some point she will want the child back. And she may even resent the loss of those years and affection."

Kristiana thought Grandmother was speaking about Delphine and Turtle Dawn, as Delphine had not had the privilege and responsibility of raising her own daughter.

Turtle Dawn, however, knew Grandmother's words had introduced another level of meaning: she also meant Kristiana's resentment over the bringing up of Threadneedle. Turtle Dawn had largely raised Thread while Kristiana was busy with the family's silk and linen businesses. Grandmother was warning Turtle Dawn to expect the lash of Kristiana's hidden emotions, particularly if Turtle Dawn were to find a father to impregnate her. When would Kristiana get to be a mother, fully?

Delphine then got into the wagon, settled down across from Kristiana and Turtle Dawn, and said, "The next time you want to give away our products as gifts, I want to be consulted, before you make the decision."

When Turtle Dawn responded docilely, "Yes, Mother," Kristiana was grateful that Turtle Dawn understood all the subtleties at play here.

Now, together in the wagon, Kristiana felt she would not be intruding to ask the question she had held since the meeting with the clanmothers: "What does your name mean, Turtle Dawn, the one Matron Shenandoah called you?"

"It was my baby name, a joke."

Delphine leaned across to say, "It means 'She Who Stumbles.'"

Kristiana was always looking for information about how Turtle Dawn's top lip had been injured, the sweet knot that someone had sewn so perfectly that it had healed as a tiny rosebud. *Perhaps I know now*, she thought. *It must have been an accident.* But she had never seen Turtle Dawn being clumsy or awkward. What kind of stumbling had caused the women to give the child that name? Moreover, to tease her about it?

Later, as the wagon lurched Kristiana and Turtle Dawn along the trail to the house they shared, with the setting sun still staining the sky and the stars coming out above them, Kristiana asked, "Are you sad?"

Turtle Dawn was silent for so long that Kristiana thought perhaps she hadn't heard the question.

Then she spoke. "Yes. It's a lot to have forfeited in exchange for your love. I was—what?—thirteen when we first embraced. Fourteen when you chose Lazarus to father Thread. I had no idea what the consequences would be."

"And . . . ," Kristiana prompted.

"I have raised Thread while you built the business. Fourteen years as *maîtresse* of Duladier Soie. Then all the years with one foot in the silk in Newtown and the other in Cottage and linen."

"But now we are not straddling two places at once. We live in Cottage. We only have to attend to Regina Coeli. And Thread is twenty," Kristiana said. "He is a man."

"I'm tired, Kristiana. I need more."

Kristiana braced herself for what might be coming.

"I love being your partner," Turtle Dawn continued. "It has defined me. And I guess I wish that . . . my love had defined you more."

Kristiana bristled. "I just went through an adoption ceremony, Turtle Dawn. We brought gifts, pledged two percent of our profits. How has your love not penetrated me?"

"I just heard that my tribe will not offer me a father for my child. And why, Kristiana? Because that man would have to come into our house, the house of a white woman." She whispered the rest. "A white woman who acts like a white man. No woman wants that for her son. And—," Turtle Dawn's voice caught. "She said Thread's name means 'He Who Breaks to Heal.'" Turtle Dawn began to cry softly.

Kristiana reached up to her best friend's head and pulled it down into her lap. She patted Turtle Dawn's back and smoothed her hair until she fell asleep.

Then Kristiana wept alone, in the dark, where no one could see her. *Riven. She said Thread is riven. Why have I never seen it?*

Chapter Two

FOUNDERS MEETING

The Quarter Holiday, August 1, 1860,
Cottage, New York

"Isn't this the way it is? You know you're on the right path when everything goes smoothly," Kristiana remarked to her Uncle Philip as they stood together near a grassy area above town while they waited for the others to join them for a formal meeting of their business Regina Coeli.

Philip only laughed. "Now you're trying to provoke me, Kristiana. For what am I going to say to comfort you when things go wrong? It was meant to be?" He laughed but thought, *Nothing has ever gone wrong for Kristiana. It's as if the childhood bout with fever that left her slightly deaf was all that life would take from her.*

Philip Sechinger had come into the Duladier family just after *les Duladiers* had emigrated from Hesse, Germany, to Trenton, New Jersey. They had brought not only a treasure of gold and securities but also the accumulated storehouse of Huguenot knowledge about raising silk.

How had they fared since? Their hopes to establish the House of Duladier's reputation for producing fine silk in the New World had been realized. Philip, from a multigenerational merchant family, had married the young widow Catherine Duladier, the family's *maîtresse de la soie*, who had been leading the party on their first assignment. At the end of the first silk season, however, Catherine had been discredited and Kristiana, her fourteen-year-old niece and apprentice in the silk, had taken over the position. While that early failure had marked Catherine forever, Kristiana had made the family's subsequent success seem easy. But things had never gone smoothly for Catherine, neither before Philip met her nor since. *I can see no apparent reason*, Philip thought, *why one woman has enjoyed unbroken success while the other has been tried repeatedly and just as often found wanting.*

Different journeys of the soul, Philip concluded, although after many years of marriage and a meditation on his wife's fate, he also attributed it to the fact that Catherine habitually lied, first to herself and then to the rest of the world. It flawed her indelibly.

"We are markedly fortunate, Kristiana," he reminded his niece, "but you have also set up the conditions for Regina Coeli to enjoy success and to weather hardship without failing."

To ward off the bad luck that might follow such a provocative statement, Kristiana made a hex sign with her fingers hidden in the folds of her skirt. "It's more than *our* business, Philip," she chided him mildly. "All around us, communities like ours—devoted to industry, reimagining what a truly human society can be—are springing up like mushrooms and thriving."

Philip had to smile. This was part of Kristiana's set of speeches, detailing for others how their work at Cottage was part of a bigger movement that was happening, and perhaps inspiring them to become converts. Persuading others to join the struggle was part of what Kristiana imagined to be her responsibility. Well, he had to hand it to her: they had come from long lineages of people who struggled, who resisted. And who knew? This success might be the result of their ancestors smiling upon the venture.

She leaned in close to him: "Listen to me, Philip. We are at a watershed moment in history. What will win: The agrarian way of life that our ancestors perfected and gave to us and our communities? Or the soulless machine way-of-life that destroys communities, wasting the health of young and old alike, stealing our futures?" She grinned at him. "I know which one you are betting on, with all of your life, but will we win out?"

A month ago, they had stood in this place watching their fields of delicate blue flax flowers catch every vagrant breeze coming off Lakes Erie and

Ontario as they swept through to the fertile plains southwest of the thriving city of Buffalo, on the escarpment and plateau rolling off toward the Alleghenies. They lived on the frontier, really, even though the Erie Canal had opened up markets in cities along the Great Lakes, from Cleveland and Chicago to Duluth, in far-off Minnesota.

While Philadelphia and Trenton far to the south—cities the Duladiers had come through when they immigrated—had been civilized for nearly two centuries, Buffalo and Tonawanda, the terminus of the Erie Canal, were still rough and rude, with muddy and odorous streets, and no plumbing. Brokenhearted and drunken Indians, men and women alike ousted from their land, lay collapsed along the curbs, wearing bits of torn regalia alongside hand-me-downs from European households. Kristiana had asked once, "What has happened to the children of these poor derelicts?" and the way Turtle Dawn had bristled told her more about the circumstances of a child being raised by her grandmother than any history lesson could. Throughout the years since they had first met, the Montours kept educating the Duladiers in this subtle way. They had told their European family specifically about the Code of Handsome Lake, a generations-old call for the Haudenosaunee people to reclaim and preserve their traditional ways, which had been published a decade earlier by their ancestor. Kristiana could see for herself that the Prophet's prohibition against alcohol was beginning to have its restorative effect.

Now, as Kristiana and Philip waited for the other principals to arrive before the Founders Meeting could be called to order, talk of the year's crop carried on the air above the blankets the members had spread on the hillside in anticipation of both the meeting and the lunch Kristiana and Turtle Dawn had orchestrated to accompany it. While their flaxseed had not yet perfectly ripened in their fields, the strand of linen fiber hidden inside that supple stem had reached its zenith; it was this moment that would call the community to intensive action soon after the Founders Meeting. In anticipation of this necessity to process the tough flax stalk, they had been developing machinery that would improve their productivity—machinery that did not require inputs of energy aside from that produced by the human body. These mechanical devices saved the human body from being overworked and aging prematurely, while they also protected the streams from being polluted, the air from being fouled, and conserved the land from exhaustion.

The first task would be pulling the flax, to save the few inches of fiber that would be lost if they cut the stems with steel, and for this they had appropriated a pulling machine that looked like a medieval weapon to breach a wall. Wielded by two men, it represented a week's work on each ten acres of flax. The remaining workers then came behind, bundling the pulled flax into "stooks," or little haystacks.

In fortunate lowland fields, they could "dew rett" the stooks—letting the natural moisture of the ground soften fibers—but in most of their fields, which took advantage of superior drainage and high exposure to the sun, they were required to soak the stooks in ditches called "lint holes." When fermentation began, community workers then piled the stooks—soaking, stinking, and heavy with moisture—to the sides of the lint holes, where they were left to ferment the green portion away from the powerful fiber.

Regina Coeli had set aside a half acre of flax for seed that would be harvested in the standard cutting method and then put through a "ripple," a large toothed comb that Philip had carved and whittled for the purpose of removing the seeds from the stem. A portion of the seeds would be saved for planting next year's crops but the bulk would be taken to Montour Mill for pressing into linseed oil, a fine finish for furniture. The remaining nine acres of each plot would be pulled by this new machine, which performed the task that, without it, would otherwise have cut through leather gloves and bloodied hands.

"Multiply this by another ten, Uncle. We are building capacity, growing creek by creek, and yet only as much as the people can manage. Even the Shafers are growing for us," Kristiana said, speaking of her own paternal relatives.

She was being modest, Philip knew. She was building an empire, on her own terms. And all of the pieces were falling into place—*click*—just like that.

"Have you heard any grumblings about the scutching mills?" he asked more generally, and this attracted the attention of others who had come to the meeting.

Kristiana raised her eyebrows: "You mean the noise?" She glanced over at Tom Flusty, the leader of the Scots-Irish weavers and Philip's chief foreman, who was finishing a picnic lunch on the knoll with his wife, Maeve, and their two daughters. "Have you heard grumbling among the people that live near the mills?" The Scots-Irish who had stumbled upon Cottage were an irreplaceable part of the linen community; they had seen the Industrial Revolution in the British Isles and were firm in their convictions when it came to technology. Their resistance had been hardened on another continent into political parties, into actions. Into masks and torches in the night in the name of Ned Ludd.

Kristiana understood their limits: They would not be tempted into exploiting workers and setting up factory towns, with everyone under one roof, which would mean death for the craft village, the natural community of guildsmen. And she thought that the Scots-Irish workers understood this. But she asked. And waited for Tom Flusty's answer to be spoken aloud.

Philip himself wasn't always comfortable with modern advances—it seemed to him that everything he did now was measured out in wagon days, buggy days, canal boat days, or stagecoach days—and this newer sense of time rushing on, the machinery sounds in the background setting the pace, was a fresh experience, one he did not welcome. Take the railroad, for instance—the noise, the grime from the smokestack, the interruption of landscapes for continuous rails forking off in every direction like fish bones. Philip asked himself: Does speed make up for the noise and greasy smoke? Boats on a lake or ocean were faster, especially now with the steam engine, and yes, the canal was slow—but a good time! Did his views on the railroad make him an old fogey? He had fought in the War of 1812 as a young man. *Perhaps I am an old fogey.*

His grandfather, the *voyageur*, had bewailed the coming of the roads in his own time. For every change, his People—intruders—made up songs, a way to pass the emotional element of history down to the next generations, and in truth, the saddest song Kristiana knew was called "The Coming of the Road," which told about the end of a deeply rural way of life. Kristiana understood that wistfulness, but she did not consider herself a follower of the Luddites, whose nighttime posses threw wooden sabots into the gears of complex machinery in protest of technology. Ever learning, Kristiana queried Tom Flusty aloud. She knew Tom spoke for all the skilled workers who had moved to Cottage to make a success of Regina Coeli. "Do your people understand that the noise of the scutching mill is necessary and short-lived? Luddites aren't against everything mechanical, are they?"

But Tom, the leader of the weavers who had made it possible to create linen in commercial quantities for Cottage, pooh-poohed this caricature of their beliefs. "We h'aint agin everything," he had said. "Just the coal in the air, the lint going into the lungs of young maidens, twelve-hour days, children working . . ." Tom could go on like this indefinitely; he had made it clear to them all that this was an issue he would go down fighting for. "Our craft and our culture goes this far," Tom explained, speaking alternately with chops of his open hands and whirls of his fists. "It stops right here, where the machine run by wood and coal starts, all under one factory roof, the profits going into some land baron's pocket! Bloody thieves!"

The early talk of secession from the Union, led by New England textile barons, had also brought talk of war between the states. "We can't afford war," the captains of industry had concluded. "It's bad for profits." Kristiana's position was that their businesses were far enough from the border states to be safe.

A traveling farmer who had visited with his wife and children in a wagon last spring, but had chosen not to settle in Cottage, explained his own limits: "No one would ever begrudge using good farmland for fiber: linen, wool. But using good land to produce cotton clothing for people who live in cities, who thicken the air with coal smoke so you can't breathe, who dinna even grow their own food? By God, no!"

Kristiana had been glad when they moved on with their radical talk. *Let them head west until they find a peaceful place,* she thought. She couldn't help but be bitter about the fate of her adoptive People and added resentfully, *Let them take land that has belonged to a tribe of Indians for millennia. Let their children die one by one from disease and drowning.*

The other founders began gathering on the hillside. The usually laconic

Threadneedle, who had been relaxing nearby, talking with Turtle Dawn, now jumped to his feet to enter into the conversation. "The economics of King Cotton don't make sense. Cotton exhausts the land. You have to rotate the crop to turn it into products to deliver to markets, but the growers don't. And human slavery. Who could wear such fabric if they considered its cost?!"

"Thus, the factory town of Lowell was born on the backs of slaves." Regina, Philip's daughter, who had been helping Turtle Dawn arrange the picnic, could not sit silent in this kind of debate. Up on her knees, she leaned forward on her hands. "Lowell was built to be a 'new town' in the Industrial Revolution, with shorter hours, communal living and space for families, day care for babies, schools for children, lighting, good food . . ." Regina's lips went white from compression when she was on the soapbox. "That lasted as long as profits were being made. But as soon as the cotton embargo put a strain on the profits, all the evils of the industrial model came springing back. Why?" she asked rhetorically. "For profits!"

"Thread," Kristiana directed her son's rapt attention away from Regina. "Could you run to the upper village to fetch Kilian? We want to begin!" Thread's natural constitution—to make, to do, to move—sprang him into motion and he sprinted off.

Regina's strawberry blonde hair always tendrilled in the summer, Kristiana noticed, when the humidity loosened her corseting of hair and body and thought. Her lip curled whenever she contemplated what adulthood was bringing out in her young cousin. *In no way is she right for Thread!*

"These twin evils," Philip said, "cities and slavery, go hand in hand with war." *Our captain,* he glanced at his niece, *is steering a delicate balance between the traditional ways of producing linen by the season and the disruptive force of the mill towns, driving production, creating demand. And now cotton was again stimulating talk of secession. It is immoral,* Philip thought, stoking his well-honed Quaker outrage. As if on cue, Regina spoke up. He grinned, anticipating his daughter's timing so well.

"All well and good," she began, raising her voice to be heard by all involved in the conversation. "But isn't it even more immoral to keep half of the population—women—indentured to their male masters?!"

I wish Catherine were here, Philip thought, not for the first time. His wife stayed in Newtown with their older daughter, Lischen, to run the silk *magnanerie*. She couldn't stand to be around Kristiana, who had usurped her future. She couldn't be around this venture, had snapped after a few months with her emotions chafing at her. Now she stayed in Newtown except for brief visits every summer, after the *magnanerie* closed. She preferred to winter there, in southern Pennsylvania, where she could get out to Doylestown to lectures, to Trenton, to the homes of friends and family, the cities lively year-round.

The canal and Regina Coeli's markets along the lakes and rivers of the Northeast were a means to an end for Philip. Everything he counted dear could be reached by canal through the agency of Regina Coeli: Seneca Falls and his daughter, Regina. He had spent his adult life loving two Reginas—his daughter and her namesake, Regina the Elder—one openly, the other secretly. And Catherine. Their very business had been named for the elder Regina after she had died, twenty years earlier. *Isn't Regina Coeli, the empire they were building, tailor-made for my daughter's success?* But his Regina, his precious daughter who seemed to carry the flame of the elder, seemed stalled, diffused, letting her energy drain into too many rivulets.

He acutely wished she could find some way to secure a small role for herself within Regina Coeli, something she could do in Seneca Falls. She was already helping Delphine in her dyeing operation. So what if the silk doesn't speak to her? Then linen, perhaps. He would ask Kristiana about it.

Thread was coming down the hill toward them, using his hat to fan his face. He appeared to be talking to himself. And he was not returning with Kilian.

Philip admired Threadneedle, for his nephew was a prodigy with warping looms. Philip was in a good position to judge that, having apprenticed to a master weaver when he was a boy, younger than Thread, and earned his traveling papers, though he never practiced the trade.

"They say it takes two lifetimes to make a weaver," Philip had told his stepson, Kilian. "One sweating it out and the other under the charm of Grandmother Spider. Your cousin Thread is in his second lifetime." He and Catherine had contributed to the fund that would send Thread to Europe, to work and study in Krefeld, Hesse's fiber center.

"Just as well he'll be leaving soon," his wife had said. "I'd pay twice that to see him gone sooner." Catherine thought it was beneath their daughter Regina to marry someone with native blood, even though Thread was her own sister's grandchild. Philip couldn't bear to see the ugliness in her face when she said it, such disdain against that beautiful surface.

Catherine hoped that a year in apprenticeship across the ocean in Hesse would cool Thread down, lead him to channel it into his work and studies. Better yet, they hoped to buy time for the clanmothers to find Thread a mate from the tribe.

Even if Regina would consent to marry and have children, the clanmothers wanted Thread to marry a native woman, strengthening the Montour bloodlines rather than diluting them.

As Philip watched Threadneedle approach, his daughter made room for him on her blanket. Kristiana, he noticed, only had eyes for her son, a devotion that blinkered her from seeing the bigger picture where the boy was concerned.

Thread's blue-black hair was pushed back off his face by a bright red do-rag tied across his forehead to catch the sweat. His braids kept his hair from flying into the spinning and weaving equipment. His heart-shaped face was pure Duladier, blue eyes startling against his slightly caramelized skin tone. *It's good the lad has no idea how beautiful he is,* Philip thought.

Philip turned his attention to the crowd gathered for the Founders Meeting and then looked beyond them, to the workers and their families moving about the town during the lunch hour. The potato famine in Ireland and, earlier, the Farm Improvements and Lowland Clearances in Scotland had brought their enterprise a fine crop of weavers, hacklers, bleachers, and day laborers. *Without them,* Philip thought, as he often did, *we wouldn't have Regina Coeli.* To Philip that meant one thing: *We had better keep them happy.*

"Thread!" Kristiana held out her arm for a quick hug. "I thought you were going to fetch Kilian?"

"Mother. Uncle," the young man responded, stepping away from his mother's embrace. "He's busy. Said he'd be right along."

He picked up a dipper from a nearby water bucket, drank, then upended the bucket on his head, shaking himself like a dog. "Look!" he pointed to the sky. "It's the clouds of August." And surely they were: white flatiron clouds, dark at the bottom, sailing in an armada low across the land in a blue sky that darkened toward the horizon.

"They will carry us right through mid-October if we are lucky," Philip said.

"Are you hungry, Thread?" his mother asked.

"Is there enough for all of us?" he asked, grinning.

"There is," she said, pointing to two hampers on the rug spread beneath the chestnut tree that crowned the brow of the hill. Village church bells announced the noon hour. Kristiana and Philip watched with great satisfaction as work parties below broke up and found the shade of trees to unpack their hampers. Many of those who had gathered to hear the founders speak about their future, satisfied with the pre-meeting conversations, headed home where lunch and perhaps a nap awaited them.

"I can't feed them—not yet," Kristiana said. "We are not making enough of a profit to do that." Despite the fact that their opium business, which Kilian and Philip had started, ensured both silk and linen had enough money to operate, Kristiana insisted that Regina Coeli had to stand on its own and justify its expenses. Profits only came in from pieces sold.

"Do we really want to feed them lunch?" Philip asked, reaching into the hamper to pass sandwiches around. "Isn't that too much the philosophy of a benevolent mill town, Kristi? I say let them take care of themselves."

"Yes, Uncle." Kristiana sighed with pleasure. "And you are ever there to prick me when I stray from the right path. I am not to take over their lives," she recited as if from a catechism forgotten as soon as it was laid down.

"Uncle, do your joints ache?" Turtle Dawn's voice chimed in as she approached from the direction of the village, Blaise trailing after her, consulting his notebook.

"Blaise," Philip called out. "I hope you aren't going to spoil our digestion with sales figures while we are eating." Both men laughed.

Blaise and Philip were a similar age, born within a decade of each other and now in that long plateau the fortunate enjoy between fifty and sixty if age has not yet begun to bow the frame. While Philip was ever clean-shaven,

Blaise couldn't shave often enough to keep his beard off his face, and so he didn't bother with it, allowing it to grow and permitting Delphine to trim it for him now and then. His face was stamped with the features of the *métis*, the French *voyageurs* mixed with native bloodlines. He spoke French with the singsong up-country rhythms of the Québécois.

Turtle Dawn, dishing up their midday meal on tin plates they used to eat outside, called out the menu: "Tongue sandwiches with mustard. Does everyone have one? Three Sisters stew, huckleberry muffins, and tart sumac tea, sweetened with a bit of maple syrup. You'll have to pour it yourself." She ladled out the stew to the women first, from Delphine to the youngest, then the men, from Philip to Thread.

"Below," Thread jerked his head down toward the scutching mill, lint holes, and bleaching greens, "they're eating the eternal potato. Thank you, Tante TD, for our repast."

"For sparing us the potato, you mean," Blaise japed.

The women—Delphine, Kristiana, and Turtle Dawn, first to be served and first to finish—took no second helpings and so they stacked their tin plates, placed them back into the baskets they had arrived in, smoothed their aprons and smocks over their dresses, and fetched each other sumac tea. Nibbling muffins they passed around, they sat down closer together, partners who rarely had leisure time together in the high season. Turtle Dawn pulled charcoal and vellum out of one of the baskets and began to sketch.

"We got off the canal boat in Tonawanda," Delphine began, "and took the stagecoach. From Tonawanda to here? Overnight! And here by lunch."

She looked triumphant.

And well she should be, thought Philip. "How much did it cost?" Philip asked Blaise.

"The stagecoach cost twice as much as a wagon but was worth the time saved. Let's see . . . ," his eyes looked up as he figured it in his head, "we left Seneca Falls on Thursday, got to Tonawanda on Saturday."

"Did a bit of shopping in Buffalo, stayed with old friends," Delphine put in. When the Buffalo Creek Reservation had closed, many of her native friends found work in Buffalo in the mills and stayed in the city rather than move to the reservation on Cattaraugus Creek.

"Got on the stage yesterday," Blaise repeated for emphasis.

Philip whistled, impressed, then looked around and assessed the crowd now seated on the array of blankets. "It seems that we are all here . . . ," he announced, in charge of starting the meeting, ". . . but Kilian." He looked around as if his son might be hiding.

"He was writing. Said he'd be right down," Threadneedle repeated, looking a bit guilty for having failed his assignment.

They laughed. Philip and Catherine's son was notorious for having no sense of time when he was writing.

"Well, his stomach finally told him it was lunchtime," Thread said. "Here he comes."

Kilian was fingering his hair back, the balding at his temples setting off his high forehead, his pale eyes so recessed they seemed "like pale wells a young woman could drown herself in," his sister Regina had once teased him. But Kilian was star-crossed in love: his wife Eugenia—the couple had been promised to each other back in Newtown when they were children, their mothers sealing the pact—had died in childbirth a decade earlier and Kilian had not remarried.

Regina ran up to her brother. "You work too hard," she pouted. "You need a woman to take care of you," she whispered loud enough so everyone could hear.

"I'm waiting for you to bring me the right one," Kilian joked, chucking his sister under her chin. His ink-stained hands were long and sensitive, his palms and finger pads hard-callused. He both farmed and, in the judgment of the women of his family, thought too much. He had been trained by his Aunt Elisabeth back in Newtown when he was a boy to be the healer in his generation. He and Eugenia had started a small herbal medicine business they called Duladier Medicine. They had developed one product: a wallet of small vials of tinctures and powders, perfect for frontier practitioners. The family calculated that Duladier Medicine didn't require Kilian to work more than twelve hours a week, and the rest of the time he spent traveling with Philip on sales calls, reading books, and writing.

Kilian and Philip had developed the family's impressive business in opium, which would have supported their extended families alone if Regina

Coeli and Duladier Soie—linen and silk—hadn't managed to be as profitable as they were. They had plenty of capital to invest when they started developing Regina Coeli in Cottage, a deep treasury that they hadn't even begun to tap. And now that they had added the Montours' tobacco to the mix, a modest affluence marked the extended Duladier-Montour family.

"Most unusual," Philip said as Kilian tucked into his lunch. "Everyone who needs to be here *is* here."

"Regina," Thread put in, noisily sucking his fingers clean. "Come sit here beside me again. We can form a phalanx against the grown-ups."

Baby Regina, as they sometimes called her to distinguish her from the woman she had been named for, was in school near the Finger Lakes, studying to become . . . something. Her heart belonged to the so-called women's rights movement that had found its center in Seneca Falls, where the Women's Declaration of Sentiments had been drafted a dozen years earlier, having been based on the Declaration of Independence written some seventy-five years prior to that, and claiming the same moral high ground—equality—for half of the population: women.

The burden of business travel fell on the three men—Blaise, Philip, and Kilian—their sales work the source of Regina Coeli's success. That and Turtle Dawn's designs.

The scratch of Turtle Dawn's charcoal on vellum stopped for a moment as she held out her drawing at arms' length and squinted her eyes.

"Let us see," Blaise demanded.

She turned the vellum out toward them and everyone exclaimed.

"This is not what I expected at all!" Delphine said, peering over her daughter's shoulder.

"Here we thought you were drawing a bucolic landscape of our fields," Thread said and laughed.

"And instead you were drawing our luncheon party!" Kilian said, sitting up. "I," he leaned over to point his pen at the composition, "am leaning on my elbow . . . writing!" Kilian functioned also as secretary to the company.

"I'm going to use it this autumn as a study for a painting, when the linen goes to the scutching mill," Turtle Dawn said, her attention back to her page.

"Our newest hackler, a master from Ulster, will be arriving in Cottage this fall," put in Thread.

"When we begin our 'letting out' to spinners and seamstresses," Kristiana said, with considerable satisfaction, "we will keep our wagons busy hauling, full-time."

"And then won't the outskirts of Cottage"—for it was here the Flustys and their string of Scottish weavers had taken up residency, trailing from there down to the sloping flats, near the mill—"sound like a little mill town, with the continuous clack and clatter of looms," Turtle Dawn said.

"Hand looms," Kristiana added, making the important distinction. "Clacking away throughout the winter all the way to Tonawanda and the canal. The sound of our industry . . ."

"On our way down the canal, we saw the new fields you laid out," Delphine said.

Kristiana looked confused. "What do you mean? From Seneca Falls going west to Tonawanda? The fields we have there in the mucklands can't be seen from the canal."

Delphine's look changed from confusion to alarm.

There was a silence so profound Philip could hear his heart beating. "If they're not ours, then whose are they?" he said, speaking for all of them.

"We both saw them," Blaise explained. "Ten-acre pieces laid out just like ours, a patchwork quilt of them within sight of the canal at the top of the Finger Lakes. We thought maybe you had grown the operation faster than we could keep track." He started a laugh, but it died. Many a farmer grew flax, but in smaller plots that were still scutched by hand, whereas the family's larger fields sent crops to be processed at the company's nearby scutching mills, clustered around major local creeks that ran into Lake Erie. "We would have heard of another big flax production by now, wouldn't we?" Blaise finished lamely.

Kristiana sat musing. "Who else could be growing flax in that way, in those locations?"

Turtle Dawn suggested the obvious: "Someone who is copying us? Someone who plans to compete with us?"

"Thread," began Philip. "Send word to our scutching mill in Seneca Falls.

When someone they don't know brings in their stooks to process, ask if they would please let us know right away."

There was another uneasy silence.

"Philip?" Kristiana asked.

He shook his head. "I don't know, Kristiana. Not a clue."

"Philip . . . ?" Kristiana's tone was testy.

He bowed, with a bit of irony in his manner. "I will look into it, Kristiana."

Kristiana collected herself and continued with the meeting's business. "Now, I believe, a report from you, Delphine?"

"As you know, we have taken space in a mill on the south side of the canal in Seneca Falls. Regina lives with us and works in the dye pots when she isn't in school. The mill is brick, posing little danger from the fires under our dye pots. The owner of the building—an absentee landlord, at that!—put us on the top floor so that in case we do inadvertently start a fire—Mother help us!—only the roof will burn, not the whole building."

She laid out a fan of linen rectangles, each dyed a different color, their new palette for the next season, 1861: a rich red-brown, a pale lavender, a bright buttercup. "These are the colors Kristiana and Turtle Dawn like best," she said, suggesting that she wasn't wholly convinced. Delphine's features never could hide her finer emotions from her family. Her pale skin and tow-colored hair, both passed down from her Dutch forebears, contrasted with her dark eyebrows and eyes—a striking appearance that made strangers look twice. In her face now they could see the shadow of regret she had harbored since Kristiana's decision not to invest in an indigo plantation, which meant they could not develop their own indigo fermenting floor in Cottage. But that hadn't stopped Delphine; she made do with indigo others had grown. "And here are the swatches from our indigo pot," she offered, laying them out as if she were reading cards. "Linen. Silk. Wool. Hemp."

"Look at how differently each of the fibers takes the dye!" Turtle Dawn exclaimed. The women buzzed over the swatches, picking them up to feel the hand of each.

"As for sourcing our dye materials, with all of Buffalo Creek gone, our pickers are coming mainly from Tonawanda and Cattaraugus. But I've found an amazing new source for food-based dyes—beets and onion-skins—in the produce depots of Buffalo's port. And listen to this!" She leaned forward, eyes sparkling. "I've met a couple. She's an obeah from a long line of African healers, and they are starting an indigo plantation and fermentation shed near Albany."

Philip, having never seen Delphine this animated, mused, *She resembles nothing more than a magician pulling a white dove from under a red scarf.*

The family broke into disjointed conversations at this news, but Delphine was still holding back her trump card. Now she threw it out on the blanket. It was a square of bright-red linen that burned vivid in the sunshine. "Voila!" she said. "Our new red."

"How . . . ," Kristiana and Turtle Dawn both said at once and then grinned at each other.

"A small bag of cochineal, the new red from the cactus beetle the Mexicans raise in Oaxaca, came our way," Delphine explained. "Through our mysterious landlord. I was hoping for a dependable source. It's fabulously expensive. But so worth it, don't you think?" She dug in a bag she carried bandolier style over her shoulder and pulled out lengths of scarlet linen for everyone to sport as advertisements of this startling new color. She immediately tied one swatch into her hair, while Kilian experimented with winding one around his narrow waist like a cummerbund. "As you might guess, Grandmother loves it!" Delphine announced proudly.

The meeting erupted again in animated talk as everyone admired the new red dye.

Turtle Dawn was the only one not fingering the linen; instead, she was making long strokes on a fresh piece of vellum, which she would then fill in with crosshatching.

After the exclamations died down, Kristiana prompted, "Your turn, Thread."

"We've had our diggers going for a month, here and at the other plots within a day's journey of here, extending our lint holes for fermenting more stooks from our ten-acre plots. Ten times ten," Thread exalted in his quiet but intense way. "All the way from here to Gowanda. You've seen the fields," he said, "but you haven't seen the lint holes."

"And they are all disconnected from streams," Philip added for the others' benefit.

"Yes. We do not want to poison our neighbors' livestock," Thread confirmed.

"That leads us to another subject," Kristiana said. "I hope we agree that we have to move our bleaching greens to Seneca Falls, where Delphine can oversee them."

"And where there's room to lay them out all summer long," Thread interjected. "That's the main thing. Farmers here can't spare the land. They need their greens for pasture and other crops, while the banks of the canal between the villages are good for nothing but bleaching greens." Everyone knew that Thread was excited about moving the bleaching greens to Seneca Falls because he would be able to see Regina more often. He stopped to catch his breath. When he spoke again, he had tamped his voice back into a rhythmic tempo. "We'll have six mills scutching for us now, each local to the half-dozen fields we have growing near each mill. Believe me when I tell you that—," he paused and they watched him tamp down his excitement again, "—we will have 720 acres under cultivation soon, under contract, with another 1,500 acres fallowing in other crops, to give us the rotations we need. As of this year, we have all the lint hole capacity we need to have dried stooks processed in our scutching mills and ready for carting to our hacklers for finishing—," he gulped then, gaining control like a rider with a runaway horse, "—as well as scutching for local farmers still growing for their own needs."

Finally, he couldn't control his youthful enthusiasm and jumped to his feet, throwing his arms wide. "I am happy to report that we will be where we said we would be by next season." His audience laughed and lightly applauded, proud of their young prodigy. "And dispersed enough for us to let out the finished stricks to local spinners to make thread for our weavers." The trick had been to control the output of their mechanical production so as not to overextend the capacity of the households in each watershed to spin the resultant thread.

Kristiana then asked the leading question that brought Thread's presentation back home: "Are you saying, Thread, that our mills and hacklers and spinners will be close enough to each other and to Cottage to bring all that thread back here for Flusty and his string of weavers this winter?"

The look of pure joy on Thread's face gave them all pleasure in their group's accomplishments as he pronounced the single word, "Yes." It was going to be possible then, their dream of pulling it all together from such a large region. Thread cataloged what had changed: "With the train coming in to South Dayton? The canal boats faster with steam engines? Yes."

"What's Maeve going to do with the bleaching greens moving?" Kilian asked, looking at the couple, who were still sitting nearby.

Apparently he has been paying attention, Philip thought. Woolgathering was Kilian's worst character flaw, and Philip made no secret of trying to improve that aspect of the young man's makeup. They were partners in this venture, traveling out together on sales; Philip couldn't afford to have his son get a reputation for carelessness through inattention.

Kristiana was flushed from all the excitement. "Maeve's going to move there with her girls when the summer's sun is at its zenith . . . July, August, September. Come home when the bleaching season is done." She made a face and ducked her head. "I think you know what Tom thinks."

From where they sat they could see Maeve looking at her husband anxiously. He was passing a length of linen string—making cat's cradle figures—back and forth with his oldest daughter.

Thread said then, in perfect mimicry of Tom's usual bluster, "Sure, and it's the beginning of the end when a woman and her daughters go off to a mill town." Thread sighed, "Thomas, Thomas."

"You should listen to Thomas," Kilian said. "He's the voice of the guild. You are cruising perilously close to infecting our utopian idyll with the defects of the mill town."

Tom, hearing his name travel on the wind, looked up triumphantly at Kilian, his fingers laced with a string figure that his younger daughter's fingers now hovered over, as if to pounce.

Kilian's words put a damper on the group, who quieted and looked around at each other while Kilian blushed and pulled his mouth into a thin tightness.

"True," Kristiana said. "It's a fine balance. We are drawing the line at using steam engines to mechanize. Stopping short of putting all of our operation under one roof, making workers move out of their villages and into our *manufacture*," she added with a *soupçon* of heat and irony.

"It looks like you are already breaching some of these precepts," Kilian said, his eyes down to the paper on which he was taking minutes.

They all noted that Kilian was saying "you" rather than "we."

When no one rose to the bait, Kilian added, "What's the difference between a water-powered mill and a steam-powered one? They're both water. How is moving our dyeing operation and our bleaching operation to a Seneca Falls mill not exactly what Flusty says: a step toward the destruction of our guild?" They were all silent. Then, for drama, he added, "And, by-the-by, the destruction of our village!"

Kristiana spoke up then. "A steam engine requires more input than just flowing water, Kilian. We would also have to use coal or wood, and both send out soot that would defile our linen operation. *And*," she dragged out the word to indicate that she was going to address the second point, "more tellingly: the women of the silk go into the *magnanerie* for a month each spring to focus on the worms. Tom and his string of weavers will not be available all winter while they are weaving, just as Maeve and her girls will not be available during the high season of August's heat on the bleaching green. Whether they're here or there!" she added.

Kristiana's patience is a marvel, Philip thought.

"Philip? Kilian?" Kristiana prompted.

Philip glanced at Kilian as if warning him to be on his toes. "Sales are strong, as you know," he reassured his niece. "We have accounts in the cities all the way down the canal and westward to the cities building along the Great Lakes as far as Minnesota. Our earlier work from our Newtown *magnanerie* covered all the cities up the eastern seaboard." Philip nodded to Kilian, inviting him to pick up the next segment of their report.

"Our catalog is a great success, better than Godey's. We leave them wherever we stop: at haberdasheries, at dressmakers, dry goods stores, millineries. They get passed around. And then the letters with orders come pouring in." He smiled at Turtle Dawn, acknowledging her importance, but Turtle Dawn, whose hand was still moving across the pages of her vellum tablet, was not looking at Philip or Kilian. "As you know, our packing and shipping department benefits from all our experience in silk. Our success is owing in great measure to the designs that Turtle Dawn develops and then renders for our catalog."

The meeting broke out into various smaller conversations then, and after a time the church bells rang twice in Cottage.

"Two hours? How could it be?" Philip announced getting to his feet with a little groan, unfolding himself like a rusty pocketknife.

Kristiana glanced at her partner, whose hand and eyes were still focusing on her vellum, then shrugged and stood up, grabbing Regina's hand to run down the hill, as if she were as young a girl, carefree and lighthearted. "Philip!" she called over her shoulder, beckoning him to follow.

"Let's see it, Turtle Dawn," Kilian asked.

"No, not yet," she said.

Kilian squatted behind her to look over her shoulder. Turtle Dawn had done a portrait of her mother, capturing an animated Delphine looking like a blonde gypsy queen, hands expressive and gesturing, hair caught up in a combination of bands, practical rather than fussy, the red linen bandeau she had just added allowing a few curls to fall loose around the margins.

"It must be hard to capture pale hair with charcoal," he remarked. "Yes, I see. It needs the colored bands to define it." He reached over Turtle Dawn's shoulder to point at a detail in her drawing. He looked from the drawing to the subject, Delphine, letting his hand drop to Turtle Dawn's shoulder as if it were unintentional.

Delphine gathered her skirts and stood, then—without looking at her daughter's portrayal of her—stepped away, down the hill.

"She knows that too," he said, admiring Delphine's way of making artifice seem so natural. "Will you be coming over for dinner tonight?" he asked Turtle Dawn.

"Might be."

"Father says everyone is coming."

She glanced at him from under her brows, as if reminding him that where everyone else would gather was no concern of hers. "Will you be?"

"It depends." He began picking up empty bowls, filling the hampers. "I'll walk back with you," he said. "Help you carry these things. The others have gone down the hill to see the bleaching greens."

Philip called out: "Supper at six! Coming Turtle Dawn? Bring Delphine and Blaise of course! Kilian?"

"I'm walking back with TD, Father," he responded, avoiding the question.

With a start, Philip suddenly saw it all. He wasn't used to being a Seer. *Perhaps anyone would see it. And admit it, old man*, he told himself, *even you admire Turtle Dawn's unusual charms. From afar.*

Then he turned to catch up with the others heading down the hill to visit the bleaching greens, their enthusiasm for the progress of their enterprise carrying them quicker than Philip, and more quickly still until they were out of hallooing distance from him.

Philip wasn't the only one who noticed that Kilian and Turtle Dawn had left together, in the opposite direction from the others. Delphine was squatting just on the other side of the hill collecting red-orange Indian paintbrush, which she was bundling and stuffing into her bandolier bag. Philip drew up beside her and sat down in the grass. Plucking a young timothy from its sheath, he stuck it in his mouth. With the length of his body stretched out, his weight on his elbow, he sucked and chewed at the green stem, letting silence pool out between them. Plovers walked swiftly away from their nests, *peeting*, hoping to confuse both humans and any raptors who might be perched or hovering nearby.

"I have something to ask you," Delphine said without looking up.

"I thought so," Philip said. The two were within a decade of each other in age, and although each was happily married, they nursed the flame of a small natural attraction.

"Our people are different," she opened.

"That's an understatement," he said, and they both laughed lightly, relieved to hear truth spoken.

Delphine knew that Philip would give her all the time she needed to say the thing she needed to say. The only noise that broke the silence were the distant sounds of a calf bawling, the Flusty girls' Gaelic singing as they worked the bleaching greens, the plovers' anxious *peet*, and, closer still, the snap of stems as they went into the bunches Delphine collected. The day was gathering toward a thunderstorm after sunset; the cumulus that had begun building on the horizon earlier now reared up to challenge summer's perennial blue sky.

"We treat criminal behavior differently."

Uh-oh, Philip thought. *Where is this going?*

"What happened to your wife, Catherine, and to Regina the Elder would never be tolerated among our people who value women *first*." The implied words—*not last*—hung in the air.

"How do you know what happened to Catherine and Regina?" he asked, with more than a touch of temper for such an even-tempered man.

"That's the other thing: my people don't keep secrets—men from women, parents from children—the way your people do."

"Delphine." He was warning her that she was hying close to lines that might be unmarked but were nonetheless as jealously guarded as property boundaries. But then he remembered how natives felt about property boundaries, deeds, and fences.

"The thing is this, Philip: I'm not sure that I should be telling you."

He said nothing, as he knew when to keep quiet with this woman, just as he did with his wife and daughter. After a while, when it wasn't clear whether she would speak again, he asked cautiously, "Is this something you are sure I want to know?"

"Oh, yes!" she said, sitting back on her heels, the carnelian flowers of the Indian paintbrush adding color to her cheeks.

And then he smelled her femaleness, ripe as the apricots and peaches in their trees. He pulled up short. *Oh Lord, Philip,* he cautioned himself. *Be careful. She's Kristiana's mother-in-law.* He knew his wife would never forgive him an indiscretion with Delphine . . . even though it had been decades since he and Catherine had been intimate.

"If I tell you, you can't betray me. The others will find out soon enough. But knowing now . . . ," she seemed to think twice about what she was going to say, ". . . knowing now might give us some advantage when the time comes."

He groaned. "Oh, Delphine. Enough! Tell me, and I promise you I will keep your confidence."

"Wilhelm Shafer has returned. It's Kristiana's father who is growing linen. He gave me this small sample of cochineal to use in my dye pots. He is the single source for the dye on the continent. I'm trying to get an exclusive from him for our northeast waterways."

The day dimmed as the sun went behind a cloud, then brightened, then dimmed again, a reminder that the days were on their way to the winter side of the year, despite the current august conditions.

"Wilhelm Shafer," Philip said reflectively. "He was shunned twenty years ago." Then he seemed to realize something and lifted his head. "And you know why." It seemed to be as much a statement as a question.

"As I said, Philip, our people don't keep secrets. This man would have been not only shunned but tried—and perhaps sentenced to death—if it was determined that he was habitually violent against women."

Philip nodded. The extended silence between them was something her native branch had instilled in his European branch. Finally, Philip spoke. "This puts me in a very awkward position, Delphine," he said, rising and brushing off his pants. "And I thank you for trusting me with your confidence."

Delphine rose too, stuffing into her sack the last of the flowers she had picked; she had only picked a fraction of those growing on the hillside. The native way of gathering always was to leave some unharvested. "What are you going to do?"

"What would your people do?"

"They would have put him to death. Would have put him to death twenty years ago when he first revealed his violent treachery." One thought hung in the air: *Now he has returned with fresh treachery.* Delphine turned to Philip for a moment before they parted.

"He likes me. I can see that," she said simply. "Perhaps I can be useful."

In the distance, Turtle Dawn and Kilian headed across the field, shoulder to shoulder, the same height, she with a basket tucked under her outside arm, he carrying an armload of blankets and an empty kettle by its handle. Grasshoppers jumped up from the path in front of them with a whirr of their wings. August's cicadas put out a wall of buzz, stopping and starting on a timetable no one seemed to understand.

"I've been wondering something," Turtle Dawn said.

Hearing something in Turtle Dawn's voice, Kilian looked at her keenly. "Yes?"

"Could you like me?"

He flushed. "I'm not sure what you mean. I do like you."

"No, I mean . . . Am I attractive? Could a man like me?"

They walked side by side in silence, each caught in the webs of their own thoughts while the clouds threw shadows across the land briefly, one cloud eclipsing the sun momentarily and then another, a blinkered shadowing too brief to notice, one of the hallmarks of late summer in this latitude.

"Have you never had a man, Turtle Dawn?"

She smiled, a bit tremulously. "What do you think?" she asked.

"I've never thought of you that way, Turtle Dawn," he lied and then watched in dismay as her face clouded. "It's not because you're not beautiful! Turtle Dawn . . . ," he said, trailing off as if he wanted to say more.

And she was beautiful, right down to her smallest defect: the rosebud of her top lip that some frontier surgeon had repaired. He suddenly realized that only a woman surgeon—someone who embroidered with small colorful threads—could have made such a succulent bud out of a torn lip. And among his acquaintances, women surgeons were rare.

He wanted to take that bud into his mouth and suck gently. And that led him to wonder if that feature on her face might be repeated elsewhere on her anatomy. And then he was embarrassed, clutching the blankets he carried to the front of him, thinking about the Pythagorean theorem in hopes the evidence of his arousal would subside, and yet thinking about how the dynamics within a triangle was equivalent to hand friction on a fire-starting drill. He began conjugating Latin verbs: *amo, amas, amat* ... He blew out a great breath. They walked in silence to the place where their paths forked.

"So will you be going to Philip's tonight for dinner?" Turtle Dawn asked.

"Yes!" he blurted, although he had not been planning to go unless she would be there.

She collected his armload of blankets to take back to the home she shared with Kristiana and then wiggled the fingers of her left hand.

"What?" he asked, blushing furiously.

"My teakettle," she answered and grinned as he transferred the handle to her waiting fingers. "See you tonight."

Chapter Three

AN OLD ENEMY RETURNS

August 30, 1860, Cottage, New York

It is a fine day for haying, Kilian thought, shading his eyes against the sun. *Not a cloud on the horizon. Yet these days the simple pleasure of haying is a privilege that goes better with the help of two pairs of strong young arms from the neighbor boys.* He saluted his father, who was turning his team tightly at the end of the row, wagon dragging the high hayrick. While Philip and Kilian liked the traveling that came with their textile businesses, they also shared a common love for the actual farming that underpinned the whole edifice.

Just yesterday the line of scythers had sickled all the hay down, then raked it into rows. Today two young men from the village were working beside Philip and Kilian, pitching hay onto the hayrick. They kept some of the hay compressed in a common silo they all dipped into over the winter to feed their horses and cows. Most of the hay would be left in the field in haystacks until late autumn. In the row Philip was maneuvering his team beside, several experienced men worked to build haystacks in the Hessian manner.

"Cotton, hemp, wool, and linen," Philip had said to him just that morning. "Think on that, Killy. No need to worry about machines completely taking over. People can neither feed nor clothe themselves without cultivation, but can you imagine a machine that could produce a haystack as good as a team of men?"

While Kilian and Philip were harvesting, Threadneedle was doing his part: "running his lines," as the women of Regina Coeli styled his visit to the weavers in their cottages that lay from here to Tonawanda. On this trip, Thread was accompanying the women on the canal boat to Seneca Falls: Regina to return to school, Maeve Flusty to inspect the new bleaching greens, and Delphine to refresh her stock and ready her dye pots. From there, checking in with both his farmers and the mills, he would ride his horse, Bucephalus, named after Alexander the Great's steed, back to Cottage. "Thread's string," Philip called his nephew's continuous peregrinations over the distances of their fields and mill operations.

Both Philip and Kilian favored Cottage over Newtown and spent as little time to the south as care of the mulberry warranted. And yet they both missed the presence of Kilian's mother, Catherine. She had returned to Newtown as soon as Philip had come back from his and Kilian's trip to New York. Killian tried not to think on it, but he couldn't hold back the thought: *How is it possible that my mother sees no room for herself in our Cottage home?* Increasingly, Killy knew, she spent her idle summer days in the home Philip had built for her at their fish camp outside of Newtown, along Neshaminy Creek. The Pavilion, they called it.

What was happening to their old ways? When Kilian was growing up, running a farming household took the labor of several couples and growing children besides. Nowadays they hired folks who had no land themselves, in exchange for a share of the crop. He leaned on his hay rake, pulled his kerchief from his pocket, and mopped his brow and neck.

They were working to bring in the second haying—a late one—against the autumn rains coming. A few days past, a staggered line of men had worked their scythes down the field, leaving another line where the grass stood and where it fell, driving the meadowlarks up from their nests. Then, instead of everyone moving on to the neighboring field for more scything, only the hired men went on, leaving Thread and Philip behind to build their own haystacks with a team of workers. Thread couldn't decide which was the better system—all men helping from start to finish, or cutting the labor into separate jobs—but he noted that the latter resembled processing linen, where some had their own specializations while the rest were paid for general work. A linen operation of this size needed a powerful lot of unskilled labor, and it generated plenty of seasonal work for hired hands.

Kilian drank a ladleful of water from the buckets Philip had laid out for the hay rakers. Mindless work; in another half hour or so the bells would ring announcing the noon break. He picked up the hay rake again and gave himself over to the aimless roving of his mind that helped make the time pass. Most farm boys chewed tobacco to help pass the time, to numb them, but Kilian couldn't stand to take anything that dulled his senses; he was constitutionally against it. Except for the judicious application of alcohol, he congratulated himself that he had no vices.

His mother and his Aunt Elisabeth said that he thought too much. It's true he worried about certain things, including that ancient buried story about his mother, a story that nagged like a missing tooth whose space would not let the tongue be still. As the result of some crime, possibly against his mother, there had been a hearing, a sort of kangaroo court from what he could tell, but no one spoke of it any longer. He and Thread had put part of it together, however. The inquiry, held in Trenton like a real court, ended with the testimony of the banished Wilhelm Shafer, Kristiana's father and former head *cultivateur* for the silk venture, and in response the investors had voted "no confidence" in Catherine's continuing as *maîtresse de la soie.* They then confirmed the election of Kristiana to that position, despite her being only fourteen years old. Her grandmother, Hannah, the head *maîtresse* of the family's European operation, had come from Europe to back up the girl with both her considerable fortune and her unimpeachable knowledge as the head of the House of Duladier.

The two young men knew this much, plus more that Delphine had recently told them. Catherine, even if she regained her senses, the investors had said, would have no role in the future of the family business. Wasn't this a repeat of a costly mistake Catherine had made as a young woman when the Rothschilds had lost so much money in the perfume venture that went awry in Catherine's hands? What had her parents been thinking when they had sent her there as a consultant? This was the question the investors, all men, asked each other, with many innuendos. It seemed to the two young men, Thread and Kilian, that no one had come to Catherine's defense.

The church bells rang, signaling noon, and Kilian took off his hat and hallooed to his father on the far side of the hayfield; he was going home for lunch. When he got there, everything changed, as if a thunderbolt had come out of the blue summer sky without warning. After twenty-five years Kilian's Uncle Wilhelm was suddenly standing before him, both their hair-lines receding in the same family pattern. Kilian was flooded with affection for the man who had helped raise him. But while he felt and acknowledged this warmth to himself, he knew he had to be on guard until this man proved himself trustworthy. He had been shunned with reason, after all.

Settling Wilhelm in his kitchen, he ran straight to his cousin's house, thinking all the while about how to deal with the situation. He burst in the door, calling, "Kristiana!"

She came quietly from the storeroom, wiping her hands on a linen towel, brow quizzical. She peered at him over her smudged spectacles, hair falling in pieces from her bun, skirt hitched up, feet and ankles bare of shoes and stockings, careless of a man's glance on a fine, hot summer day like this one. Much later, he would remember the moment as the last time he would see this Kristiana.

"Uncle Wilhelm—your father!—is here."

"What? How do you know?"

"I found him on my doorstep. I came to get you immediately. He's waiting in my kitchen."

"Killy?" she asked in a tone that said she couldn't understand how Kilian's words could be true. "My . . . father?"

"It's him, all right," Kilian assured her. "He's been in Mexico for the past twenty years. He's balder. Hands freckled. Skin tanned dark."

Without another word, Kristiana flew down the road, walking then running, walking again, then slamming into Kilian's kitchen without knocking, without saying "hello," none of the pleasantries, just—after a moment of being struck dumb at the sight of the man sitting at the table thumbing the smooth sides of a cup—falling onto the bench beside him, into his arms, weeping. She eventually drew back to say, "Where have you been!"

and then fell against him again, wetting his chest. Sensing a disturbance, Turtle Dawn, who had been in a back room, came out and, seeing Wilhelm there, stayed, feeling a mixture of mild surprise and hesitant pleasure, for she knew the man, although she had been just a girl when he was shunned.

Later, eyes dried, the four of them sat over bowls of soup, tranches of bread between them. Wilhelm answered his daughter's and nephew's questions about how he had spent the last two decades.

"I went first to Mexico. Heard of a war for territory." Wilhelm barked a short humorless laugh. "Knew there was always money to be made wherever there's a war." He grinned as he shot his cuffs, showing off silver cufflinks with turquoise stones on each wrist. "Got me a new wife." He flashed that wolfish grin again. "Figured Elisabeth wasn't waiting for me." He ducked his head briefly, then looked up at Kristiana. "I kept track of you, even though you didn't know nada of me. Did anyone speak of me?"

Kilian could see Kristiana processing everything slowly. Was this man her father—the man she had loved like no other man, the man who had betrayed them to their investors, who had—or had not?—told those men, those bankers, about their ancient devotion to the Mother? Who had, moreover, at least according to Grandmother Marguerite, led two Frenchmen to Catherine who sought her across the ocean to settle some score? At her peril. Or something like that. Rumors …

Kristiana betrayed nothing visible to the eye, but neither Turtle Dawn nor Kilian could miss her slow contraction back into herself and away from this man. He had been shunned, twenty years ago. And now returned?

"You picked up an accent," she said, as it seemed a neutral enough statement to keep up an appearance of normalcy when things were threatening to get strange. Speak some Spanish."

He acknowledged her comments, as if inconsequential, with a lift of his brow. "And these," he was saying, drawing a small drawstring from his pocket, taking out a pinch of what looked like shriveled peppercorns. "These. My fortune. And yours if you want it."

"What are they?" she asked, drawing near again to look into the palm of his hand.

"Cochineal."

"Is that what it's supposed to look like?" she said almost to herself, peering at one between her fingers, pulverizing it in her palm, then spitting on it and stirring the mixture with her forefinger, a smile blooming on her face as a red stain spread across her hand.

He told them how this small beetle that lives on the nopal cactus is farmed by the highland people of Oaxaca, how he and his wife and children live among them, how the Oaxacan farmers had given him exclusive rights to distribute the dye in the eastern United States.

He'd been to Europe many times over the past decade, he said, his venture backed by their old financier's bank, their Rothschild now dead and his financial enterprise grown into something impersonal, nonjudgmental; no one cared about that old business thirty years ago. Ancient history.

The other three sitting at the table read him correctly: he seemed to be asking why he should still be shunned.

"I want you to have exclusive rights to the dye in this country," he told Kristiana. He knew all about Regina Coeli, rattling off statistics: sales, gross profits, his best guess at net profits. He scanned Kilian's house appraisingly, carefully overlooking Turtle Dawn.

He hired someone to spy on us, Kristiana realized.

Wilhelm pulled his neck out of his stiff shirt collar with a twist, a nervous tic he had picked up. "I tried to see Elisabeth and Catherine in Newtown. They cut me. Told my agent they wouldn't see me. Said I was dead to them." He hesitated, stopped, addressed his soup, head tucked.

Kristiana and Kilian exchanged glances that wondered, *Our mothers never said anything to us about Wilhelm Shafer trying to contact us?*

Wilhelm pushed back his bowl, took out a handkerchief, and mopped his brow, which was now expansive, moving up to a freckled bald pate, which he also blotted, though they were inside out of the sun. "I have a touch of malaria," he explained. "Not catchy. Never goes away." He pocketed his handkerchief, looked at Turtle Dawn and Kilian. "Could I speak to my daughter alone?"

"No," Kristiana said shortly as Turtle Dawn and Kilian stood to leave. "Kilian and Turtle Dawn are my partners. Speak in front of them or not at all."

He shrugged, then pushed his bowl away and brushed a space in front of him as if ready to lay out all his cards. "I've made a fortune. I didn't want to come back empty-handed. I've seen Lowell, the canals, bright and shiny factories. First millraces, now steam engines. Dormitories for young women. Three solid meals a day. Shifts for twenty-four hours of production. It's the future. I'm planning to set up a factory town on the Erie Canal. I want it to be for you, for Regina Coeli," he said in Kristiana's direction. His hands moved as if broad-brushing a world he had imagined. "Put the spinning, weaving, dyeing, cutting, sewing, and shipping all under one roof. You would have exclusive right to the dye, the most brilliant permanent red the world has ever known. Imagine it!" He hadn't looked directly at his daughter once during this entire speech.

Kilian and Turtle Dawn were thinking the same thing: *How could he not sense Kristiana moving away from him since her tears had stopped, since he had started talking?*

Just then, Philip walked in, the screen door slamming behind him. "I heard you were back."

Wilhelm looked up at Philip. "Catherine and Elisabeth sent out a rider?" He gave Philip a thin, wintery smile. "I know, Philip. You put the Pinkertons on me."

"Something like that." Philip sat at his son's table and accepted a cup of soup from Turtle Dawn. Then he looked at Wilhelm. "Do you still go by Wilhelm Shafer?"

"It's Guillermo in Mexico. Just Will here."

"Have you seen your people in South Dayton?"

"I'm staying with them. But this here's my people." He gestured at Kristiana, then more obliquely at Kilian, as if to say, *If you want to be included, I'm open to discussing it.* His broad shoulder and back shut Turtle Dawn out.

"They tell you what we're doing here?"

"The folks in South Dayton? Yeah, but I don't get it. Neither do they. You buy up this old town. Lay fifty miles of field drain tile in your acreage. Grow the most productive flax in the country. Buy more acreage." He looked up at them. "So far, so good, yes? You got a goldmine in Regina Coeli. All the young women in the civilized world here want one of your outfits. You plan to put in millraces, build more scutching mills." He looked at his hands on his knees, as if willing his fingers to be still. "And then what do you do?" His voice was rising. "You keep a string of old linen weavers going?" His voice was growing more incredulous. "You put out piecework?"

His voice lowered. He spoke then as if Philip didn't exist, barely included Turtle Dawn and Kilian, focusing his gaze entirely on his daughter. "Now, I married a señora myself. Three little brown children. I heard about your mistake after I left. A half-breed baby at fourteen." He swung his head like a weary pony. "Your boy is grown now, they tell me; helps you out with the warping. Threadneedle?" He managed to make three syllables out of the name, as if it were a word from an incomprehensible language. Another wan smile. "You made the best of it, raising him. He gone back to his own people?"

Kristiana was rising now, like a hot air balloon rises on its jet, smoothly, silkily, weightlessly. "Do you remember the last time I saw you?" she asked tonelessly.

"Regina's funeral. Yes."

"Did you not understand what happened that day? You were shunned."

Now, too late, he saw her anger. "Everything changes," he said, as if by way of explanation. He stood then, pulling the fob from his waistcoat, opening the watch, and clicking it shut. Another nervous habit, they all suspected. "Time passes." He shot his cuffs one more time, giving them another glimpse of his cufflinks. "Money talks." He hid his disappointment well, moving toward the door and dismissing them all before he could be dismissed, keeping what he would think of as the upper hand.

"Then you know that Regina Coeli doesn't need your money," Kristiana said. "I don't know who you are. Though I recognize you, all right. And I know this for sure: we don't want any of what you're selling."

Threadneedle walked in then, stowing his stick at the door and then looking up, from his mother's face to the man near the door to his Uncle Philip, Kilian, and Turtle Dawn. "I came as quickly as I could, Uncle."

Will was taking in Threadneedle. "My grandson." He breathed in. "Look at you," he said, exploding all that surprised breath. He glanced at Kilian and then back to Thread. "You might be Killy's brother, both of you throwbacks to our older stock—dark hair, blue eyes." He jabbed two fingers toward his own eyes. His hand gripped Thread's wrist. "Look at you." He threw his head back and laughed.

The others could see he had brought out charming Wilhelm. "If only my mother could have seen you!" he exclaimed. And then, as if it had just occurred to him: "What did Hannah think of you?"

Kristiana spoke, unable to stifle her maternal pride despite her better judgment. "Hannah said the family's breeding program had reached its perfection in Thread, that he should be fruitful and multiply, make more Duladiers to populate this continent."

"And so you shall, lad. So you shall. I was just leaving. We will see each other again." He placed his hands on Thread's shoulders, facing him. "My grandson." Now he spoke quietly, only to Thread. "I'm staying at South Dayton with the Shafers. They say they haven't seen you for a while. Ride over and see me. We have a lot to talk about."

His attention turned to Kristiana. "Kristi?" She flinched under the intimacy of the nickname. "Don't be overhasty. Think about what I've proposed. Think beyond yourself . . . to him." He jerked his head toward Thread. Kristiana was backing him out the door. He must have thought it afforded an opportunity for additional intimacy and continued, "You've made some mistakes, Kristi. They say you and that girl"—he jerked his head back toward the interior of the house—"are more than just friends. What happened to you? I'm your father. I have a right—a duty—to ask. Your reputation . . . "

Kilian, Turtle Dawn, and Philip were watching, amused and repelled. Thread's face showed nothing.

"My father betrayed us," Kristiana said to Wilhelm's face. "Left us. Not a word from him for twenty years." She pushed him, both hands against his chest. "Don't come back, Will. And don't wait for Thread to come calling."

"He's my grandson, Kristi. You can't keep him . . . keep me . . . "

"You were disowning him before you saw him," Kristiana responded, "before you saw who he is." She wiped her hands on her apron as if they were soiled. "I don't think we have anything to talk about. Your ideas?

That's not what we are doing here. Don't come back, Will," Kristiana repeated, stepping inside the door, holding it. "Mother and Aunt Catherine were right. You made a mistake coming here. Take your contagion somewhere else."

"You can't do—"

She closed the door and then leaned against it. The room was suddenly very quiet. When Kristiana turned from the door, they could see new lines and expression carved into her face, muscles gathering between her eyebrows. "Don't see him again, Thread."

"You don't tell me what to do, Mother," Thread said firmly. "I'll see him if I want."

"Killy." She turned to her cousin and partner. "Tell him! He's poison." She turned back to Thread. "He'll bite you before you see it coming. He is the enemy." She looked at both of them and then at Philip. Kilian was looking studiously away. Turtle Dawn's face was swollen with some emotion. "Philip—why are you looking at me like that? You know who he is!"

"He's still your father, Kristiana. And Thread's grandfather."

She felt as if all the wind had been knocked out of her. She reached her arm to the table as if to support herself, tried to speak and couldn't. Finally: "You all knew it was him coming for us." She sank to her knees on Kilian's kitchen floor. She looked at Turtle Dawn's shuttered face. "Did you know?" Turtle Dawn nodded, once. Kristiana looked at Kilian, searching, seeing nothing. "Did you know?" He lowered his eyes. When her gaze finally rested on Philip, she burst, like a dam held in check too long releases its waters. "How could you keep this from me?! We are supposed to be doing this together!"

"What difference has it made whether you knew or not?" Philip said, though they could all see the difference etched on her face. For once, Kristiana had been struck speechless. "We weren't sure," Philip continued. "I was waiting for more information."

They all shifted uncomfortably, feeling the full weight of keeping this information from Kristiana.

Philip spoke for the group: "The question remains . . . because sooner or later we will have to decide together: What do we do about this?"

"What do you do when the devil comes calling? Is one ever ready?" Kristiana raved, getting to her feet. "Have the children been warned not to look in his eyes? Do the women know to keep their blouses buttoned to the neck?"

"What did you tell him?" Thread was asking. "What did you tell him about me?"

Kristiana looked at her son. "What have we told you about this man?" she asked.

Avoiding looking at his mother, Thread focused on his Uncle Philip. "Why was he shunned? What did he actually do to harm us?"

Kristiana groaned. "You will tell me everything your spies have found out," she said to Philip.

He nodded tersely.

Kristiana turned sharply on Turtle Dawn. "What were you doing here? In Kilian's house?"

"Don't speak to me that way, Kristiana." Turtle Dawn's cheeks were blazing with high color and her dark eyes snapped. "Not if you know what is good for you. You don't own me! I can't even believe I am saying such a thing to any person . . . much less you!" Turtle Dawn picked up a sheaf of drawings she had been working on, held them to her breast. "The light is better here," she said defensively, looking pleadingly at Kilian as if to say, *Can't someone defend me from this woman?*

Kilian and Thread stole a glance at each other, clearly saying, *We will talk later.*

"Father," Kilian said. "Shall we get the hay cut and stacked before it rains? Thread, can you take a break, pitch in and help us, please?"

After the three men left the house together, Kristiana and Turtle Dawn behaved toward each other like metal filings whose poles had just been reversed: chaos, then a scattering in opposite directions, leaving the kitchen swept clean of inhabitants, the stove ticking for more fuel as it cooled. A western wind had come up, presaging rain, threatening the haying.

Chapter Four

BUTTERMILKING

September 21, 1860, Cottage, New York

"Today's the day, Kristiana!" Philip stuck his head into the room. "Long awaited."

She had left her door open to let in a breeze on the warm autumn day. She looked up from the letter she was writing to her father. Philip had convinced her that it was far better to keep their enemy near, so they could watch him. Letters flew back and forth, arguing their positions.

"I've got the prototype ready," Philip announced. "Six scutching stations. Come see." They didn't have to invite Regina, who stayed just behind her father's shoulder, determined to keep up with them.

Now at least here is one person moving at my speed, Kristiana thought as she strode along beside her uncle. *Someone who isn't always questioning my motives. A true partner: Philip.* The man had been trained as a master weaver and had the certificate to prove it. He had designed their first *magnanerie,* a more beautiful, small and perfect building to raise silkworms than you would ever find in this world. It lit up like a Japanese lantern at night. He was also a man who not only knew horses but could teach others his secrets. Raised in a merchant family to follow in their footsteps, he fulfilled his roles by tapping into his bloodlines, only revealing these secret selves as Regina Coeli developed and required them. And now, perhaps most trenchantly, he had shown himself to be a mechanic, someone who understood

Da Vinci, master of cogs and wheels, master of forces harnessing wind and water. *I should ask Philip to install the steam engine in the packing and shipping building,* she thought. *For heat this winter.*

"Regina!" she said, throwing out her arms and gesturing to the place where the newly renovated sawmill stood. "Now you are going to witness how mechanization increases production ten-fold."

The women grinned at each other. Today was the culmination of Kristiana's dreams. *How will I reduce it to words and numbers, to explain to our investors the importance of mills to our growth?* People were using daguerreotypes to make likenesses of themselves, and she wondered whether the technique could be used outside, to record a historic moment like this one?

Philip, Tom, and Kilian were fussing with a system of flags, moving everyone in their places, as if they were staging a theater piece. Regina wandered off, thrilled at being allowed backstage.

Kilian and Philip's response to Wilhelm's argument against village and guild was ever the same: "Here in Cottage, our workers have everything they need to sustain them." Wilhelm's replies also remained consistent: "Providing heat and light to one source rather than one hundred small cottages is more efficient. People will set up their communities again in collective buildings with individual apartments."

God knows Kristiana tried to show her father their vision, get him to listen. "Each under his own roof, human scale, small worksites. Everyone coming together for planting, weeding, pulling. Small groups breaking and scutching flax. Small groups bleaching and pegging. Guilds—the roots of community." She was tired of repeating it.

Wilhelm would snort at her reverence for community, show his contempt for her values. Yes, it stung. Philip had been right; he was her father after all. But . . . Kristiana was adamant; everyone in Cottage depended on her to hold the vision. *We have the solution. And here is the evidence,* she announced in Dialog triumphantly, sending the message out to all those who listened in.

But they didn't have all the answers. When they would be faced with production for wartime uniforms, for tents and haversacks, their means of production would simply not be up to snuff. Weaving was her stumbling block. In his factory, Wilhelm had machines clattering, turning out linen twenty-four hours a day. Yes, she had her own spies—mainly Delphine and Blaise, but others as well.

The dam they had built across the creek held a small reservoir behind it. Sluices filled from gates at the top, then flooded millraces and turned the great millwheel, like one on a paddleboat, which turned the cogs and wheels, Da Vinci's work on differentials translating into smoother, more accurate, more energy-conserving ways to drive small machinery.

Threadneedle was there, exuding pride as he spoke with Regina. Kilian, at their side, looked uncharacteristically skeptical. Kristiana turned to them. "Have you seen the millpond we built?" she asked Regina.

Regina laughed up at Thread, then turned to answer Kristiana, sassy. "I have been swimming in it all summer. Isn't that what we built it for?"

Kristiana had a momentary vision of her niece coming dripping out of the millpond, muslin bloomers and camisole clinging to her body.

Nearby, Tom Flusty gave orders to those who waited below, standing ready beside a large pile of retted and broken flax, while Philip was appearing and disappearing behind doors in the mill, checking on details, making sure everyone was at his or her proper station.

Now he signaled to Thread. "Open it up!"

Thread waved, then signaled above with a flag system Kilian had installed.

Kristiana could hear the sluices fill, the rattling of water in new pipe that sounded like chattering, like acorns racing down a chute, clanking and then hissing through the wood—machinery, yes, but not wood- or coal-fed machinery. Her blood raced. She ran inside the mill.

The millwright they had hired stood calmly beside Philip's scutching stations, six scutchers at the ready and six women ready to hand them fresh hanks. Six more women on the other end would take the scutched hanks to the hacklers in barrows, who would render the flax ready for the jennies to spin. Their Irish/Flemish wheels, run by a single man on each treadle, had been pushed to the side, unused but not discarded, just in case the modern technology failed and the old methods were needed once again. *Nostalgia?* Kristiana wondered. Her ancestors had valued this kind of duplication, never throwing all their eggs into one basket. She smiled as she thought how the old aphorism translated into the several languages those in Cottage spoke. *Rather than be victims of society's current definition of Progress, we—Regina Coeli's founders—bank on being slow and sure rather than headlong, flinging old ways aside. We must be careful not to overrun everything of value.*

The big wheel outside in the millrace was turning now. Philip had to decide when it was turning fast enough to drive the system of smaller cogs but still slowly enough to engage them. Philip and the millwright stood shoulder to shoulder, listening. They nodded at each other, then Philip threw the lever.

The circular motion of the wheel was converted into vertical gears, then another lever was thrown and the scutching wheels with their paddles began to turn. At the fulcrum point of all this mechanization, six millmen fed hanks of the dried and broken flax into the mouths of the scutching wheels, which each held eight curved wooden blades to beat the hank of flax until the millman judged it to be done. Apprentices and women who stood to either side took the scutched hanks, piled them on carts, then carted them toward an adjacent building where hacklers were already hard at work. Others formed a line of wheelbarrows in front to help the scutchers keep their hands full of broken flax, to feed it into the wheels to be pounded, each scutcher already a master at his art, pulling and pushing the flax through to be thoroughly pummeled by the wheels. Each man had a handbrake to slow or speed his own wheel. With the precision of a Swiss timepiece, where characters moved out of a door announcing each hour, the scene below, everyone moving in synchrony, was a fulfillment of their longheld dream.

A smile broke over Tom Flusty's face. Thread whooped. The noise of the machinery was monstrously, marvelously loud—the loudest sound in their world, as if one hundred scutchers worked at once.

Regina leaned in close to Thread's ear: "Remember that story we loved as children, from our German grandmothers, the Shafers? Rumpelstiltskin?"

"The evil imp and his dastardly bargain!" Thread hugged her close; it was that kind of day, anything goes.

Kristiana's arms fell onto Philip's neck, and he, mild Philip, turned and lifted her in exultation.

"We are going to have the harvest from one full acre scutched before nightfall," she said in triumph.

And then Kristiana—trust Kristiana to always be steps ahead!—was already on to the next challenge. The carts were being wheeled to the hacklers, and from there to the spinning jennies. People waited at their stations all over the village.

"But weaving, Philip," Kristiana yelled over the noise of the hackling. "If we are going to protect our linen production from Wilhelm ..."

He knew the rest: how they would mechanize their looms with water without killing village and guild, without decimating the forest and fouling the bleaching greens with coal dust. He allowed himself to dream. Maybe windmills, everything powered with gears and belts? The clean wind translated seamlessly to weaving machines, each one overseen by a master weaver. "We will figure it out," he yelled back.

In that moment, Regina was hovering near, worry lines between her eyebrows. "Have you seen Thread?" she asked. "He was right here."

"Why do you want to know?" Kristiana asked, peering closely at her cousin to suggest that the girl's thoughts should focus on what was at hand. "Threadneedle has his work. Would you like to continue our tour?"

Regina took the chiding and sauntered toward the next room, which was full of its own noise and packed with lined-up wheelbarrows waiting to be loaded before being pushed toward the next building. "And what is this?" Regina asked, tossing her words over her shoulder toward Kristiana, but not waiting for an answer. She walked into an anteroom, quieter by half, where a small group of older men worked, throwing switches of scutched flax over lengths of nails in graduated sizes that tore the remaining bits of vegetal matter from the thread.

Kristiana caught up with her. "These men are our hacklers." She touched one on the shoulder. He stopped for a moment to let Regina examine the appearance of the hank of flax he held. "They take great pride in their work."

Regina stroked the pale golden threads. "Yes, this is why they call my mother's hair flaxen."

"And Delphine's," Kristiana said, gesturing for the man to continue hackling again. "The beauty of linen belies its strength."

Here, at the end of the short production line, fine flaxen thread hanks hung on nails. "Like tails cut from palomino horses," Regina said. Her attention turned to a young woman standing at the end of the row of hacklers, twisting the tails. "Stricks!" Regina exclaimed. "This is how we used to get it, for spinning," she recalled, for what young girl did not help the women of her family spin linen thread to be woven into yard goods?

"This is where we save time and money by mechanizing, Regina. We have flying shuttles and spinning jennies to help increase production," Kristiana explained.

"Spinning jennies? Named for girls?" Regina laughed, then sobered. "Best that machines do that thankless job," she allowed, remembering her own Aunt Elizabeth tied to the spinning wheel whenever the women weren't *en magnanerie* in spring, or at the loom in winter, when the sounds of weaving rang through the bricks of the fireplace with Elisabeth's rhythmic pounding of heddles, whoosh of shuttles. Her own mother never spun. Deciding that things couldn't get any worse with her powerful cousin, Regina asked, "Are *maîtresses* prohibited from spinning, Kristiana? If anyone would know, you would."

Without pausing to acknowledge that Regina had spoken, Kristiana strode ahead to the long *manufacture*, where the sound of clacking looms struck the younger woman as seriously out of season. *When I was young,* Regina thought, *housewives in Newtown strung up their looms only in winter. Here in Cottage, the rhythmic sound of heddles and shuttles reverberates throughout the village all winter, punctuating the long nights. Here, men weave. And they have thread for their looms all year round.*

At one end, the *manufacture* was given over to spinning. Each of the spinning jennies was run by a woman, who dipped a hand into a gourd of water and then fed the fresh flax in and turned it to linen thread, an ancient alchemy. Regulating the speed of her machine with both hand and foot, each spinner took up a sliver of processed flax and twisted it to produce the finest thread. Girls wound it onto spools as it came off the spinning jenny almost faster than could be countenanced. From here the yarn was stretched onto the traditional click-wheel by young girls, who measured it into skeins. Beyond, another group of women wound the skeins onto pirns or bobbins, again with the help of a foot treadle. The loaded bobbins would then be fitted into the flying shuttles, which were stacked up for the weavers. A different gauge of thread could be made by twisting several threads together.

The vastness beyond the spinning area was filled with eight large floor looms, all of them working. Threadneedle "threw warp" for all these looms. "These are production looms," Kristiana told Regina above the noise. She pointed to a lever that hung above each loom, where a single pull of the weaver's arm shot the threaded shuttle back through alternating rows, harnesses directed by foot pedals. Regina was vague on the names and details of weaving, and these looms were moving so fast she was puzzled about the source of the energy.

"What is powering these looms?" she spoke close to Kristiana's ear. "Steam?"

Her cousin smiled triumphantly: "Only the weaver's arm and advanced mechanics." She never tired of watching it.

Regina waved to Colm, an apprentice weaver, who gave her a nod so as not to interrupt his rhythmic work at the loom. When he stopped to wind up the yardage, Kristiana stepped over for a word with him. Regina, trailing behind, ran her hand over the yard goods admiringly.

"Do they memorize passages to the rhythm of the loom the way our women do?" Regina asked Kristiana as Colm stepped away. "I have never heard eight looms operating together. It sounds like . . ."

"I don't know," Kristiana said shortly. "And you are never to speak of it, Regina."

"Oh," Regina said, "I'm such a dolt." She knew it was a secret that Duladier silk stewards memorized long passages from the Old Text and centuries-old prayers to La Madonna Noire as they wove, not just to guide the rhythm of the linen floor loom but also to be hauled out of their memory banks at significant moments: When the worms began their spinning. At births—her birth! And deaths.

Coming back to her cousin now, Kristiana gave a sharp warning: "Don't forget yourself, Regina. We keep our secrets with good reason. And if those men are memorizing something of their own ... why, that's their business. You may not work in the silk, but you are bound to keep the family's secrets, to abide by our rules."

Regina took this to heart, for—although the silk didn't speak to her—she was no Wilhelm and would not betray the family. She had never met the man—her own uncle!—who was shunned before her birth; she was a bit miffed that her cousin felt the need to scold her as if she were not only a child but a treacherous one as well.

Kristiana took Regina by the elbow—a gesture that only irritated Regina further—and led her out of the *manufacture*.

Turning to the young woman and changing gears, Kristiana softened the sting of her previous words with a smile. "And now," she said, "let's go to what you have been waiting impatiently to see, up close."

"The bleaching greens! It was always my favorite part at home."

They walked through a breeze rising from the passage of midday, toward the brook and the bleaching greens. Regina had not grown up with the Flustys' daughters and their friends who worked on the bleaching greens, and she wished she had. They were a lively bunch of girls, reminding Regina of Kristiana and Turtle Dawn and their friends when they had started Regina Coeli all those years ago, when Regina was a small child and the goings-on of the big girls filled her with longing to be part of their camaraderie.

They came over a small rise in the path overlooking the bleaching greens. Regina caught her breath. Below, on a meticulously kept green beside the flowing creek, lengths of linen were pegged out on the grass. An open-sided washhouse, made of local stone, and with a chimney and hearth in the middle and arched on all four sides in the old way, served as the locus of activity, much as a hive centralizes the comings and goings of a colony of bees.

Four girls pitched a flowing length of linen between them into the air, moving with the whole undulating cloth to the next space over, where the previous pegged length had just been folded up like parchment and hauled back to the washhouse. From one arch, heavy baskets of wet linen emerged, each carried between two women, while nearby another length was shaken, snapped in the air, and pegged down. The fresh linen rose and fell like the breasts of snowy geese, swelling and subsiding with each breath.

"What are they doing? Can we see up close?"

"Of course," Kristiana laughed.

Singing reached their ears in a tongue Regina didn't recognize. "Gaelic. Must be," she muttered as they pulled up short beside a group of young women whose singing and dancing bent them to their purpose. All were barefoot. One girl, younger than the others and still without breasts, poured a chalky, off-white liquid over the linen while four girls joined hands like skaters, their arms crossed over each other's midsections to make a chain. Their feet slid over the wet linen as the form blossomed, then came back together. Their feet moved in a curious dragging technique Regina had never seen before, as if they were lame dancers.

"It's buttermilking," Kristiana explained. "It is lovely, isn't it? The old way. The Scots-Irish brought it with them, along with the songs." She shook her head. "After this, the linen will be candled, smoothed with a marble rolling pin. All this culture we have lost along the way—restored." She threw her hand out to the dancers in an airy *voila!*

"Are you going to build another bleaching house in Seneca Falls?"

"Yes. You've been paying attention." Kristiana looked closely at Regina. "Silk may not call to you, but linen does? All right. Come on then and I'll introduce you to Dame Maeve Flusty."

A large, florid-faced woman Regina recognized stood just inside the washhouse on a platform where she was tending a large kettle with an oar.

"Maeve," Kristiana called, and the woman turned to answer her boss: "Ay?"

"Have you met my cousin Regina? Philip and Catherine's daughter."

"I've seen her." Maeve wiped her hands on the capacious apron spread between her hips. She threw a glance to the younger woman she was working with, indicating *I'm leaving you with this for a moment. You're up to it.*

"What do I call you, lass?" Maeve asked Regina with a close, squinty look.

Regina repeated her name.

"You want to work with me and the other girls, Regina, do you?"

"Yes," she blurted. "I want to work with you when you move to Seneca Falls. I work with Delphine and Blaise there in the dyeing works. I start school after the New Year. But I am free summers."

"Yes, well, we'll only work at this through October. Do you want to begin today?"

Regina nodded eagerly, looking at Kristiana for approval.

"You know I won't give you any favors just because you're the boss' cousin, eh?" Maeve said.

"And Philip's daughter," Kristiana grinned. They all knew she was giving Regina this tour as a favor to Philip, to see if the girl found any part of the family business that appealed to her.

"I don't want any favors. I want to learn this, that's all."

Maeve gestured to pegs and cupboards set in under the arches. "Take off your shoes. Fill a basin and scrub your feet. I'll put you with the lasses working in the buttermilk." She squinted at Regina again. "Can you sing and dance?"

She could. "What are you making over there?" she asked, nodding her head toward the large kettle Maeve had been stirring.

"Lye."

That accounted for the squint.

"Don't get mixed up and step onto cloth that's been lyed," Maeve warned. "You'll burn the skin off your feet. Just follow my lasses."

"Are you all right here then?" Kristiana asked once Regina had scrubbed her feet and was headed over to join the buttermilking girls. "I can count on you?"

"Yes. This is where I want to be."

A young woman reached out from the form and dragged Regina across, linking arms with her, showing her the steps, which, from what Kristiana could see, didn't differ in any substantial way from a traditional *schottische*.

On her own now, Kristiana stood a moment in the sunshine, tapping her feet. "I suppose they call it a jig," she muttered to herself, happy to be free of the obligation of showing Regina around. Then she laughed to herself: *Does Maeve have any idea what she's taking on? Regina will have her girls painting up placards, marching for women's votes before winter!*

She had tried repeatedly picturing Regina for her son. *My daughter-in-law*, she tested. *No . . . already his cousin. She's all wrong for Thread. She has Regina's fire; it would kill my son to be wed to such a woman. Talk about riven!* "Shall I feed the baby or draft this pamphlet?" Thread's Krefeld apprenticeship would break it up, she was certain. *At their age, absence does not make the heart grow fonder.*

Chapter Five

BURYING THE HATCHET

October 1, 1860, Cottage, New York

Kristiana had something serious to deal with. Thread was spending all his free time practicing the drills on horseback that the warrior society prescribed for their initiates. She wasn't fooled by their disguising it as a kind of polo; she heard their yips and cries, saw the colors and feathers, heard the lead young man uttering moves to maneuvers that the rest of them all followed. Neither Kilian nor any of Thread's other white friends from Cottage were invited to play.

These are war games, Kristiana acknowledged to herself, furious that they thought she wouldn't recognize it, furious that she had let herself be led to believe the clanmother's assurances that the warrior society was a helpful group of young men controlled by the council of elder women.

Well, I know how to make war too, she thought with grim assurance. *No one is taking my son from me. I brought him into this world. "Riven" indeed.*

She would give him one chance to show he understood his Quaker upbringing as well as the native way. One chance to choose the right path, the path of moderation. And if he failed, she would choose it for him. Her deafness had molded her, made her more focused than others: being flawed was a gift from the gods.

She finished packing her saddlebag and slung it toward the door, where it would be ready to go when she set out with Thread the next day.

If he failed tomorrow's test, she would open the way for him to perfect his spirit in the furnace, the same way pottery is hardened by fire. It would either finish and strengthen him or—like a clay pot with air bubbles concealed in its structure—he would burst apart in the heat. *I am willing to take that risk to save my son,* she reassured herself. *I will be an example to other mothers. The clanmothers will be proud of me. My Quaker sisters will be proud of me. Even Regina will be proud of me.* Her cousin was the family's firebrand, passionate about the Quakers' triumvirate of core values—pacifism, manumission of slaves, and equality for women—and because of this Kristiana unwittingly sought her approval, although the girl was a generation younger.

Kristiana couldn't, however, allow herself to contemplate what Turtle Dawn and Lazarus might think. When Turtle Dawn had seen Kristiana filling the saddlebag and asked what she was packing for, Kristiana had answered simply, "A walk out with Thread. We both need some time off."

How else will we put an end to the millennial sport we call war? Nothing has worked so far! In Dialog, Kristiana made the argument that Grecian women, Aristophanes wrote, had withheld sex to put an end to the Peloponnesian War. Even as she said these things, she was imagining the Dialog chatter that would take place after she acted. Kristiana convinced herself that her family would be impressed with her taking leadership on this issue. They would at least respect her right to keep her son from becoming a warrior.

In the small, quiet place inside her, she honestly prayed that Thread would not fail her test. She could imagine it: him falling to his knees, struck by the necessity to shrive himself of this urge to make war, to rid himself of what was rising up in him as he became a young man. She, acting as a queen, would knight him as he knelt. Then, *Rise, Threadneedle of Cottage, Peacekeeper.*

"It is good to walk out with you unburdened," Thread said to his mother when they set out the next day.

She said not a word, but set out in front of him as if she had not heard—a trick of hers—letting him trail along, presuming he always would follow this youthful mother of his, in part so he should judge how like a native she moved through the woods. She had insisted on bringing their donkey Modestine, but today the little beast was balky, and finally Kristiana lost her patience with the donkey's stop-and-start pace.

"And yet, we are not in a hurry, are we?" Thread asked his mother's retreating back. "This is our time to relax."

The sweet donkey, who never dug in her hooves when Thread asked her to help, carried their food and water, some small tools, and their bedrolls, "in case we need to set camp," she had said. When Thread took Modestine's lead away from his mother, the small beast of burden calmed.

Thread followed Kristiana, his moccasins stepping into the prints hers vacated, her steps links in the chain of the Long Walk she had intuited even before adolescing, when her family had just arrived in the New World, bringing their ancestral knowledge of silkworm and mulberry to these shores.

Thus had his Montour people walked from the Susquehanna to Canada after their villages were destroyed eighty years ago. And just a century earlier, his Huguenot forebears had walked silently from the fastness of the Cévennes mountains to the border, fleeing persecution.

Thread was not fooled for a moment. He knew his mother had brought him out into the wilderness to have a serious talk with him. She had brought everything they needed to camp out. Tonight, sitting around their campfire, she would talk to him.

Well, I have something I want to speak with her about as well, Thread thought to himself, noting how the eerie silence of midday had started earlier than normal, with a strange haze from the north. *Storm coming? Pay attention!* His training as an initiate clicked in. Behind him, Modestine stepped on a loud branch with a crack that sounded like a pistol shot. *Noise is the disadvantage of bringing a donkey to carry your things,* Thread noted. No jays, no crows sounded. Was that a Cooper's hawk working the woods in front of them? All around, the yellowing leaves of the black cherry drifted down in what appeared to be an empty wood.

Why won't she tell me where we are heading? It was beginning to grate on Thread that his mother expected him to follow, to ask no questions. He picked up his pace, intending to surprise her by drawing alongside her, breaking their pattern.

She saw him every day, among the cutting tables and the shears, among the rows of treadle machines. She was his guardian spirit when he worked with the weavers. *But does she see me?* Deep in his heart another question echoed: *Does she love me?* He would never question Turtle Dawn's love for him. Although Kristiana had borne him, Turtle Dawn had kissed his skinned knees, comforted him after nightmares.

Although he had intended to pick up his pace, his thoughts were slowing him down, as if he were carrying them in a burden basket. His training with his tribe reminded him that he could not let himself woolgather, as that was when enemies were most likely to attack. Out of the thick false silence of calm came ambush. He opened his senses, and they flowered out from him, gathering impressions.

And yet he allowed himself then to feel the painful question that had only just welled up for answering: *Why doesn't she love me as I am?*

That he walked a dangerous path was clear even to him at his age. But he believed if he walked with honor, as a whole man, blameless and true-hearted, his integrity would be his shield. And isn't this the first fallacy a young man falls prey to? How else would old generals and flag-blinkered mothers lead young men into being warriors if they did not feel their state of grace protected them?

His mother's form was retreating in front of him. She never looked back to see how he and Modestine were coming along. Her partial deafness sealed her in a single-mindedness that he was beginning to find oppressive. His skin prickled with unease as the silence that had spread throughout the woods continued to deepen, the sky becoming pale with a haze that suggested a storm.

And with this observation he allowed his mind to quiet. Autumn rains brought a bounty of mushrooms. In beds of perfect moss, the dew of the day still trapped on each floret, the smallest mushrooms already proliferated.

A light breeze brought the sound and feeling of nearby water. Falling water. Trees rubbed against each other, groaning beneath the load of their harvest, their job done. Fruit and nuts ripening in the branches were attracting their natural partners, while on the ground he saw the feathers that told him turkeys had been here, fattening themselves for winter. Thread could see where bears had abandoned unwanted hairs in the bark of their scratching trees, along with leaving behind scent messages about their current well-being, the journey behind them, the one anticipated before them. Just as in spring, skunks were restless now, having released their tiny progeny earlier in the year to find their own burrows, to establish their own households, to mark off their own kitchens and middens. Blackbirds would be gathering to migrate south together, but first they would perform their annual Dionysian rites in the high, swinging branches of the black cherry groves as the fruit ripened and fermented, calling more of their kind to the raucous bacchanal.

But where is everybody? he wondered. The unnatural hush must be due to some factor that he could not pinpoint no matter how far he threw his sensory net.

His rumbling stomach alerted him to the fact they had been walking half a day. He reached into his pouch, drew out a handful of pemmican, and kept it in his mouth to soak up his saliva before he began the slow, delicious mastication. As he looked around, he started to see where she was leading him. *But why?* Heading due south and west, they would intersect Cattaraugus Creek upstream of the Cattaraugus Reservation—one of his homes—where his father, Lazarus, lived and where Grandmother Marguerite spent most of her time. A large, ancient fault had created a deep rift here, where virgin trees dominated the landscape. Thread noted the quaking aspen turning gold that announced the change in altitude, the threshold of larch and spruce woods. Now he could hear small creatures scuttling in the leaf duff gathering acorns. Not a breath of wind but still the oppressive approach of a gathering storm.

He stripped off his shirt. Surely she would hear that he had stopped, but no. Kristiana disappeared around a bend. Now that he knew where he was, he didn't need her to lead their entry to one of the most powerful places in his People's world.

When he got there, he found she had already settled in, backpack on the ground, a small fire snapping in a stone circle. Was that her tomahawk he saw, its head heating in the flames, its handle anchored by a stone?

The clearing on the side of the hill was marked by three cairns, each larger than a tall man and bigger around than four barrels.

When he released Modestine, the donkey found a patch of clover, and settled in to snuffle and chomp in place. And yet the expected release of their arrival did not occur; instead, the tension he had felt throughout their walk increased. He took a pinch of tobacco out of his waist pouch and, with a prayer to the powers in that sacred spot, put it into the fire. He looked around for fallen wood to gather, as the day was past zenith and they would need to prepare if they were spending the night. But no, his mother shook her head impatiently and gestured for him to join her.

His unease blossomed into dread. He considered what the effect might be if he broke the silence with words. She had unbound her hair, a brown so pale as to appear colorless; it stood out from her head, long and slightly waving. He knew what her smell would be: the harsh tang of tobacco, the bitter breath of coffee. Her yellowed fingertips and dirty nails, stained with all the textile elements she evaluated continuously. The rosemary oil she massaged into her scalp. He knew her well, and yet he had never really seen this woman, with her snapping eyes that did not see. He had heard rumors but had dismissed them. Didn't he know his mother better than anyone, save Turtle Dawn? She was powerful—yet didn't every boy think that of his mother? But she was no witch! Now with more rigor, he honestly asked himself if she had shielded him from her true identity: a practitioner of the dark arts. She picked up her tomahawk from the fire, doused its heat in the nearby stream, and tucked it into her belt, all without a word or glance.

Kristiana stepped up to one cairn, lined it up with the second cairn along the blade of her hand and, with outstretched arm and extended index finger, indicated a direction that went off invisibly to the east, through the woods to the Mohawk River and the Erie Canal.

Ley lines, he knew. He repeated it in Dialog, *Ley lines*. These cairns marked both ancestral bones and the magnetic lines of power that ran underneath the earth. Sometimes it seemed to Thread that his mother didn't know anything about his People's ancient ways until the answer came in Dialog: *Ley lines demarcate the earth's magnetic pattern, pole to pole, everywhere. People mark them with stone cairns, power spots.*

He knew what she was saying by indicating the eastern direction, along the Mohawk River. His Montour lineage had begun generations back with the adoption of a Mohawk princess by the French viceroy of Québec, and also, if the Duladiers' suppositions were correct, by the introduction of that remote patrilineal ancestor, the original Montour, who had crossed his Huguenot bloodline with the Haudenosaunee bloodline when he had married that Mohawk princess, establishing a unique lineage, one marked by his name. *Mon tour. My tower.* A symbol of imprisonment, of suffering. Threadneedle's Haudenosaunee ancestors had taken that man's name for their own—unheard of in a matrilineal culture. Thread himself was six generations down from that time.

He had heard how the ancient Haudenosaunee, before the time of the Peacemaker, had admired the man who could endure torture without revealing his pain. Thread knew the stories of the suffering his own Montour family had experience during the retreat, their crops and homes burned just as winter was coming on, the Long March to Canadian safety. And this trial had come three generations after the Revocation of the Edict of Nantes had criminalized the Duladier people—his other family—in France, forcing them to flee.

Thread's life had been marked by the successes of Regina Coeli and Duladier Soie, his family's opium and tobacco domination, their affluence. The accomplishments of his European ancestors had made him impatient. *How can I make my own indelible mark if I am coddled?*

This resentment of his lot brought him back with a start into the present moment, into the clearing, this sacred ground, with his mother. *How could I be taken by surprise*, he wondered. *How did she ambush me into coming with her on this unspecified journey?*

It took all his strength not to bolt and run deeper into the woods. He thought about what he had been told about women's power during part of his initiation in the sweat lodge. Kristiana was fairly crackling with energy. A great weight was bearing down on his chest.

She was lining up the third cairn with the second along the blade of her hand, one eye closed to focus better, indicating a perpendicular direction, from northeast to southwest. The double watersheds of the Allegheny and Genesee Rivers and their Seneca family, he guessed. A powerful wind had risen; leaves were flying in whirlwinds and eddies as if swept by a giant broom.

I have no idea what she is doing, what she wants from me, he virtually screamed in Dialog.

A response came quickly back: *Where are you?*

At the cairns. Near Cattaraugus Creek.

Kristiana gave him a black look for speaking in Dialog when she meant to command his undiluted presence. A murder of crows cawed overhead, whirling with the leaves, the wind, the approaching night.

"What do you mean by indicating the Seneca Western Door, Mother?" He spoke, increasing the tension.

She raised her eyebrows and marked the line again for him with the blade of her hand, her legs spread into a V, her body leaning back from her sightline.

No amount of swallowing would lessen the lump in his throat. *This is fear,* he said to himself. His warrior chiefs had warned the initiates of moments like these: "You will feel fear. And you must be able to go on, with the fear, and do what needs to be done." Thread breathed deeply, once, twice, and felt his mind begin to clear. *I am a warrior,* he told himself. *No witchcraft can turn me. I will hold my ground.*

Kristiana strode over to Modestine and, lifting off the saddlebag, put her hand into the pocket and drew out a jar, which she uncorked and held out to Thread to see and smell.

He knew it—a tarlike drawing ointment that came from the ground, one the women use to make their medicines. The earth shifted under him as if he were on the deck of a boat. He planted his feet. *She will not throw me off balance!*

She dipped her first two fingers in and her thumb, rubbing the dark, greasy ointment into the ham of her hand, and then lifted her hand to him. He flinched. In Dialog, the secret language of the Duladier Women of the Silk, shared by the Montours, and perfected over millennia, she sent him an image, the gift Marguerite Montour had recognized when she had first met Kristiana as a girl.

Threadneedle let his mind pool out, proving he was a better receiver than sender—a trait he and his mothers, Turtle Dawn and Kristiana, had discovered at an early age. *A dark, oily seepage.* She was the Seer, he an imperfect instrument. *What do you want me to see?*

She made a circle of her index and thumb, then pushed the greasy index finger of her right hand through it in the universal symbol of *baiser*, to fuck. The crude gesture didn't bother him; his Montour family were famously earthy and candid about sex. *But what are you saying and why are you saying it to me?!* Thread took a deep breath. He needed to gather himself for whatever was coming.

A wind shook the tops of the trees. A distant thunder. Their name came to Thread with their voice: *Wee-saw-say-hay-noo.* The Thunder People spoke to him from within the fog of Dialog: *Is she putting herself in the place of the Prophet?*

Thread's mind raced. *A lubricant. A superior lubricant. In the Seneca lands, by the Western Door, one finds a superior lubricant. Ah. But what can she mean?* Living with a mother who was a Seer required that he stand back, decide what he thought for himself, keep a piece of himself intact and inviolable. He ran a check over his whole body, calming it with his breath.

Using her hands to indicate throwing a shuttle through the bed of threads on a loom, she sent him another image, one of a weaving machine, mechanized, coming to a grinding halt with a shriek of metal on metal. His teeth hurt. As a thrower of warp, a prodigy, they said, at setting up a loom pattern, nothing haunted his nightmares worse than this image of a loom tangling.

And then he saw something she didn't see. Beyond the grove that defined the cairns, a horizontal sliding. The wolves. They were watching. *They are protecting me,* he thought. He could smell them. He tried to open himself to them, to hear what they were saying. But if they were speaking to him, they only reinforced the one message he was getting without them: *Danger.*

He thought quickly, *Do they know my mother?* He was certain they did not. After a girlhood spent in the woods near Newtown, where she had learned everything she wanted to know about this new continent, this grown Kristiana never, as far as he knew, went into the woods around Cottage or Cattaraugus.

And now, her body drawn like a bow, her garments flapping against her as if they were wings, she indicated the final coordinate, directly north/south, lined up with her toes, her narrow body, and finally the blade of her hand. *North.* She closed one eye, as if just before sighting along an arrow. *South.*

He summoned his courage and waited in that state he knew made him most receptive to her sending. Then, without warning, he was knocked to the ground as a flash of gunpowder blasted around him and simultaneously, in his mind's eye, he heard the screaming of horses and of men. It was over as quickly as it began. He felt sick, nauseated from the smell of gunpowder. The lingering smoke rose into the trees, drawn there by the wind. *War. The reality. Is it really going to be like that? Am I going to be ready . . . for that?*

She levered him to his feet. Placing her hands on each of his shoulders, facing him squarely, she spoke for the first time since they had arrived in the clearing. "You will not go. Do you understand? You are a warrior, but you will not go to this bloody war. It's—not—our—war."

How will you keep me from going? he asked in Dialog. All who listened there heard him.

Her voice, the rising volume of it, the argumentation, was a violation of the sanctity of the place: "Our clanmother told me that the women are the ones who decide if and when young men go to war."

"We are going. It is decided," he said.

A red rage came over her. "You don't have the right to throw your life away for this!" she shouted.

What do the wolves see? Will they attack her? "Mother," he said, stepping forward so his face was one hand's length away from her face. He would not shout; he would not argue. But she must hear him. "You gave me life. And for that I thank you. But this is men's business—war—and you have no say over whether I go or not."

She screamed, a war cry. *You will obey us!* she declared in Dialog. She seized the handle of her tomahawk from her belt and lifted it high in the air. The blade flashed down in a long, slow arc as she buried it in his foot, the arc's image hanging in the air for several seconds.

He grunted, then screamed. The sound flew before him, and a thunder of jays and crows startled up from the trees, a grouse from its brushy cover.

She is going to kill me! He kicked out to run, but his leg would not respond. He fell, his foot gushing blood over a thick layer of pine needles.

His mother was not continuing her attack but was standing with one hand clasping her chest as if she were having a heart attack, her eyes rolled back in her head, the bloody hatchet still in the hand at her side. "I . . . I . . . ," she stammered.

"Help me," he said through clenched teeth. "Mother!" The pain, the reality, the consequence was ringing down around him. *You will not faint!*

Then Kristiana, as if coming awake with a start, stumbled to Modestine, who was stamping nervously around the clearing, sensing the wolves, smelling blood. Hands fumbling, Kristiana untied a case from the donkey's load. She was beside Thread on the ground now, opening the case, her hands trembling.

Not good in an emergency, he saw. Her hands were covered with blood. He grunted and raised himself to sitting. *Someone has to do this,* he told himself as he unwrapped the band that had held his hair back and tightened it around his foot for a tourniquet, then inserted a stick—miraculously at hand—for loosening and tightening. The bleeding slowed, then stopped.

"What?!" he stuttered. "What were you *thinking?!*" He shrieked the last word. *Do you mean to kill me, Mother?* he asked coldly in Dialog. Then, calmly, he said out loud, "I have to know what you plan to do with me." All across their world, family members stopped what they were doing and listened.

"No!" she exploded. "Kill you? No! Just . . . maim you. But . . ." She was unrolling bandages from her kit, swiping the tarry ointment over his foot, to draw out the metal contaminant, he supposed. She was weeping now, at the edge of hysteria.

As part of his preparation for initiation into the tribe, they had practiced this kind of frontier medicine. He knew he had a brief time before the real pain set in. "Did you bring opium?" he asked.

"Yes," she breathed. "Yes! I thought of everything!" she screamed to the sky. "Except this." She lifted her hands, covered with blood, and paled as it dripped off her elbows. "Something's there," she said, pointing into the woods, where the wolves were clustered, interpreting the human scene.

I have no time for her hysteria! he thought. "Give me the medicine kit. Now." He got to his feet while he still could. "If you are not going to kill me, then I need to get home. Help me . . . get home!" He took the ampule of opium she extracted from one of Kilian's frontier medicine kits and, fumbling, handed it to him.

He let his pants drop and shoved it in his anus, waiting to feel the relief while his mother made lunges at the woods, at the wolves hidden there. But he knew they would not let her see them. *Was she in danger from them?* he asked himself rhetorically, part of his mind cool and observant, as if from above. *Damn her!* He couldn't waste an iota of his strength worrying about *her.* His pants still dropped around his ankles, he found he was bleeding again, a red tide welling up out of the bandage and soaking his clothes.

Kristiana pulled his pants up and tied them, then maneuvered herself under Thread's arm and half dragged him, jumping on one foot, to Modestine. The animal stood still, seeming to understand that she was now center stage. Letting Thread lean against the animal, Kristiana brought over a small rock to use as a footstool.

He stepped on it with his good foot and swung his injured foot over the small donkey, gasping with the pain. He had been assured that often after a man has been injured he can carry on for a short time, even when it seems impossible. He felt that surge of power. He reached down to his ankle and gave the stick that controlled the tourniquet a turn, loose for two heartbeats and then forward again, tightened. He would make it back before night rang down, leaving her behind this time.

He was in the hands of the Mother. With luck, his family could save his foot, if they all came together.

He sent out a message in Dialog: *I am coming home. Aide-moi!* With the cool part of his brain, he noted that in crisis he reverted to the Duladiers' native tongue, French.

The opium kicked in. All the world gathered him up in its velvet blanket. He tied himself to Modestine's broad neck with his belt, laying his head on the sweet, soft fur where her shoulder met her neck. *She will get me home.* He slapped her side, a signal of his trust in her, and the small animal set off at a clip he knew she could sustain.

As Modestine jogged along and Thread drifted in and out of consciousness, the combination of the drug and the injury sent him into another state of mind. His will had already gathered itself to face this new reality: he resolved that he would be a match for his mother from then on. *It is my life to live,* he said in Dialog for all to hear. *Never again will I let myself be unguarded, not from you. Or anyone else.* It shocked him to realize it, but he had to face it: his mother had become his enemy.

Back at the cairns, the smell of fresh blood in the air, with only the wolves bearing witness, the woman fell on all fours and howled.

What she said was this: *I am sorry. I didn't know.*

Chapter Six

KNITTING FLESH

October 2–December 21, 1860, Cottage, New York

Having heard the epic battle between Threadneedle and Kristiana in Dialog, the whole family gathered from every corner—setting out from Newtown on the fastest stagecoaches; from Seneca Falls on the train to Buffalo; east from Cattaraugus, a couple of hours' hard ride on a good horse; and no expense spared in a private coach from the terminus at Tonawanda. The extravagance of Kristiana's premeditated move, the irrevocability of it—chopping into her son's foot!—drew them all to Cottage.

When Kristiana returned half a day behind a delirious Thread, most of the villagers witnessed the aftermath of the violent scene. Thread, who had arrived the evening before, was taken directly to Kilian's, where lamp oil burned throughout the night. Weak as Thread had been from loss of blood and shock when Philip and Kilian had first encountered him, he had asked to be taken to his cousin's, bypassing even Turtle Dawn's home as the safest refuge.

Kristiana arrived in town the next morning, which, presaged by the unnatural stillness of the day before, had dawned with a gray pallor. A stiff wind had banged loose shutters in the night and was still throwing leaves to the ground. She had not even washed the blood from her arms and hands or changed her gory clothing. Her unbound hair was tangled with burrs and dead leaves.

Now, in the early morning, neighbors couldn't help but gather. Years after, this would be referred to as the most dramatic and lawless event Cottage had ever seen. Lazarus held Kristiana firmly by the upper arm while she stood outside her own home and wailed through the door that Turtle Dawn had barred, shrieking about how it had been her right to maim Thread.

Tall and imposing, Turtle Dawn at last opened the door. "Go away from my house, Kristiana," she said. "Or I will call others who will make you stay away."

Kristiana was nearly speechless. She wanted to say, *It's my house too*, but instead said only, "Where will I go?" quietly, as if to herself.

"You should have asked yourself that before you took it upon yourself to break our family, to maim our son," Turtle Dawn said. "My son!"

"And my son," Lazarus echoed. "You have made your own bed now, Kristiana," he told her as he released her and then jumped on his horse, leaving her furious and bereft still, although no longer pounding on the door. She began sifting through her things, which Turtle Dawn, having listened in on the Dialog messages from the day before, had moved into the street prior to Kristiana's return.

"Will no one take my part?" Kristiana asked plaintively, facing the direction of the dust stirred up by Lazarus' departing horse. Then, noticing the neighbors who had gathered, she began screaming again. "Why are you standing here, gawking?!" she shrieked, waving her hands and moving forward in a crouch, as if scattering chickens, or vultures. The collection of adults and children who watched with both horror and fascination began to disperse by twos and threes. "Don't you have anything else to do? I'm paying you to work, Donald! Matilda!" she challenged, now standing straight, arms akimbo.

Kristiana turned back to the house. Not only had Turtle Dawn moved all of her things into the street and barred her from entering her own home, but likely Turtle Dawn would now turn her back when they met on the street. In the Haudenosaunee way-of-life—and indeed the way-of-life of *any* matrilineal society, as Kristiana understood it—when a woman divorced a man, he came home to find his things outside the door. "You cannot divorce me!" Kristiana yelled. "Between two women? We own too much in common. Can you chop our cookstove down the middle?"

But Kristiana had gotten the message: she had been behaving like a white man in their relationship. Once a Haudenosaunee woman put her husband's shoes outside the door, that was that: they were divorced.

And now what? Kristiana thought. *How can this be happening? To me! How can they be such moral cowards?*

Later that day, she stood outside the Quaker Meeting Hall, where the congregation had gathered to pray for Threadneedle's life, and yelled, "You say you are against war! But can't you see it? Your hypocrisy!" She had had no idea she was so universally disliked, so easy to despise.

After church, Kilian and Philip had wordlessly brought their horse and cart to help Kristiana move to the cabin in back of Kilian's, where he kept his supplies for Duladier Medicine. After Philip and Kilian moved Kristiana's things, Lazarus was seen sprinkling cornmeal in a circle around Kilian's house, his lips moving in prayer.

Except for the wounding glances thrown her way, Kristiana felt as though she were a phantom. Neighbors brushed past her to greet each other, and her own family members conferred in whispers in corners and by the cupboard as they were drawing out ingredients or bandages in the fight to save Thread's foot. Turtle Dawn, Philip, Regina, Kilian . . . all strangers now, their faces masks. They were impervious to her explanations. Worse, she could see why they were not interested in her rationale for having committed such an atrocity. It began to creep over her slowly that this act, this immutable act, had placed her beyond the pale of her closest family members. "But I did it to save him from further damage, from *war!*" she cried out. Like a hideous skin growing over her identity, she began to experience what shunning might have felt like to her father. *They wouldn't do that to me!* she thought to herself, alarmed.

Sundays now she stood in Cottage's town green outside of church and screamed as the members filed into their carriages or walked in family groups back to their homes. "You cannot shun me! I own this town!" she declared, while simultaneously wondering if she were going too far. *I am not going far enough,* she answered herself. "Will no one take my part? Does no one see why I did this? The courage?" She might as well have been invisible. Her words died on her heels, fell to the ground as if unheard.

Regina had booked a first-class seat on the train from Seneca Falls to South Dayton as soon as the messages she received in Dialog made it clear what had happened to Thread. Aside from requiring care for his physical injury, she knew he would need comfort in other ways. His departure for the apprenticeship in Krefeld would be postponed at least until spring, if not indefinitely. *If he lives,* Regina reminded herself.

I detest Kristiana, she thought, grinding her teeth. *Detest her! She wastes all her power, her considerable power, on this useless, destructive gesture. She cares only for herself. And Thread. But look how she deals with her son, the only one she truly loves!*

By the time Regina arrived in town, Kilian had organized his house to serve those working day and night to save Thread. Kilian gave the orders, and foremost among them was that Kristiana was not allowed near Thread's sickroom. Instead, she held vigil from the settle outside the front door, which was where she was when Regina arrived from Seneca Falls.

"Regina," Kristiana plucked at her cousin's sleeve. "Regina, what would *you* do to secure women's rights?" When Regina turned to face her, stopping to actually engage, Kristiana, thinking that this was her chance, said, "Surely, of all of us, you must see why I did what I did."

"I would not harm one of your hairs, Kristiana. You cannot make a right with violence," Regina said, then she turned and walked through kitchen door, letting it slam behind her.

"If you believe that, your passions for change are baseless!" Kristiana called after her, to no apparent effect. Then, calling into the kitchen, Kristiana said, "Will someone please listen to me, please?" She was rewarded only with another rapier-like diagonal glance, this time from Kilian as he came out of the house to throw a basin of used water to a mountain laurel bush nearby.

"We have no time to listen to you, Kristiana," Kilian said coldly when she tried to enter through the open door. He brushed past her on his way into the inner room, which had been converted from a pantry and hired man's bedroom into Thread's sickroom. "I suggest you stay out of the way. You have your own room. We give you food. Isn't that enough?" He closed the door pointedly, shutting her out.

Kristiana had taken from Thread his future as a warrior of the Wolf Clan, and she had done so without hesitation, claiming her right as his mother to maim him in order to save him, an original move she declared to be hers immutably. She had actually planned it, her detractors claimed, for a time when their mutual business with Regina Coeli allowed them leisure to travel for personal reasons.

Grandmother Montour moved from her house at Cattaraugus into Turtle Dawn's house to be close to Thread and to Kilian's supply of raw materials for medicines and equipment for preparing remedies. When she arrived in the middle of the night from the reservation, before stepping into the house she paused to reassure Kristiana, who was in her place on the settle outside the door. Placing her cool hand along Kristiana's cheek, Marguerite said, "My child, you have become confused. You have been working too hard . . . for years now. Your judgment has suffered." She pressed her index finger to Kristiana's mouth as it opened to object. "Hush," Grandmother said. "I am going to send Turtle Dawn out to you tonight with a sleeping draught. And know this: Nothing Kilian nor I can do to prevent infection will be left undone."

Later, Marguerite returned and placed a bowl of stew and a hunk of bread on the bench beside Kristiana. The elder woman sat and took the younger woman's hand in hers. "You were mistaken, Kristiana. This was not well done." She used the German word for "well done": *wohlgetan*. The word carried more meaning in that language, since it was nearly always used to describe God's perfection. God's actions were *wohlgetan*. Being aligned with God, no matter how hard, was *wohlgetan*.

Grandmother was neither subtle nor oblique, perhaps telling of her French bloodline. "What you did was not aligned with God's purposes, not *wohlgetan*. And who are you to take on the role that is reserved for the Creator? I am afraid for you, Kristiana."

Grandmother's judgment was echoed in Dialog for all who listened there: *Violence begets violence.*

They want to see violence, I'll show them violence, thought Kristiana. *I'll take the whole company with me, lock, stock, and barrel. They will have nothing. Nothing! My name is on all the papers.* Then, abruptly, a reversal: "It was my right!" she wailed out loud. "I did it to protect him!"

Inside the house, the others listened in to the conversation, whispering to each other at the stove as they waited for water to boil. They agreed: Kristiana had overstepped, presumed to act as God. The clanmothers, it was said, were debating her action before passing judgment.

In the days that followed, Kristiana continued in her attempt to rally at least one member of her family to side with her, but she was consistently taken aback by everyone's unanimous censure. In all of her thirty-three years, she had never experienced such failure. Gone was the supportive praise she had come to rely on from the community she had built. Her family continued to isolate her, speaking to her only when necessary, not allowing her to be part of the remedy. United against her, all seemed to agree that now was not the time to reason with her. Kristiana was slowly going mad as the social repercussions of what she had done finally came into focus. She blamed the men: *They will always hang together to wage war,* she raved to herself. But deep down, she blamed the clanmothers most: *They lied to me. They have no authority over chiefs and their need to send younger men out to exhaust themselves and all of our wealth in war.* Especially Regina should have understood why Kristiana had risked her reputation to make this point on behalf of all mothers.

But Regina wouldn't even sit down with Kristiana so she could explain! She made a rude cutting gesture when Kristiana offered a cup of hot broth she had kept warm specifically for Regina when she passed, a broth she had made over a tiny fire in the yard outside the shack she occupied on Kilian's homestead.

She had but one choice. Barred from Thread's sickroom and her own house with Turtle Dawn, Kristiana eventually gave up her spot on the settle and threw herself into her work, spending all of her time down below, where Tom and Maeve Flusty wordlessly accepted her leadership in their common linen enterprise, exchanging looks when Kristiana sat up with a lantern over accounting books whose numbers seemed to dance on the page. They continued to bring her portions of lamb stew, even knowing it would congeal in its own grease as night wore on toward dawn.

Perhaps worst of all, Kristiana could not admit that she had been wrong, but persisted in justifying her action to anyone who would listen, making herself into a pacifist hero, the mother who would maim her son rather than let him go to war.

"I have no regrets," she said during those hours she kept vigil outside of Kilian's house while those inside sat beside Threadneedle's bed in shifts, swabbing his taut young body as if it were the embattled deck of a ship. She cared, she told herself, yet not a single detail of his progress, os his suffering, drew a tear from her eye, his mother, product of millennial training as a *maîtresse* of the silk.

"She is Hannah's granddaughter, through and through," Catherine had once famously said of her niece, and now she said it again upon her arrival in Cottage. She didn't have to spell it out, as they all knew what she meant: Hard. Unbending. Remorseless. Catherine usually came north to live with Philip in the winter, as the silk didn't require her presence, but this year she had come up early from Newtown as soon as she had heard Thread cry out in Dialog. Her daughter Lischen, the House of Duladier's current *maîtresse de la soie* and mother to a brood of children, could make do without the help of their matron. If need be, Lischen could hire someone in Newtown to help her finish putting up their harvest. Truth be told, Lischen did not appear to be much of a Duladier, and instead followed her husband to his family's gatherings. More tellingly, she had taken his name, Weaver.

Catherine spent extra money on a faster stagecoach to Cottage. She hadn't fully realized how fond she was of her nephew Threadneedle, how much she missed her daughter Regina. Besides, Catherine was happy to see Kristiana get a bit of comeuppance; twenty-some years later, she was still bitter about how Kristiana had usurped her place as *maîtresse de la soie*. Ancient history, true, but still it smarted in the cave of her bruised heart.

Three generations of Montour women had taken over the cottage that used to be Kristiana and Turtle Dawn's. Marguerite wanted to be close to Thread's sickbed and Kilian's store of medicines, but what had called Delphine to join this family group? The typically close-mouthed Delphine gave them no clues, but they were grateful to have her help at Thread's bedside and to keep the fires going at the other cabin. Lazarus crossed back and forth between the reservation and Cottage, as if he didn't know where he belonged. The Duladiers presumed he was running messages and doing errands for Marguerite and the tribe, knitting them to what was transpiring with Thread.

After a few weeks had passed, the clanmothers at last sent a message with Lazarus, asking Kristiana to come to their council. She ignored it, worked odd hours down below, her face and body increasingly stiff and pale. The clanmothers didn't ask again. Many wondered if the business would survive this breach between the partners. Winter was not the time to make a move, but many families began to think about where they would go next should Regina Coeli fail.

Meanwhile, Montours and Huguenots, all members of the family except Kristiana, attended Thread in shifts, watching his wound carefully for suppuration, for the small threads of red and purple traveling up the leg from the wound that would signal the need for amputation. During Thread's critical care, they learned much from each other. His Haudenosaunee relations did not find the Huguenots' whispered prayers to the Madonna strange, for they themselves honored a female deity in Mother Earth. The Three Sisters. Being a matrilineal People themselves, it would never occur to them that most other Europeans saw the face of the divine as bearded.

With this single unnatural act of Kristiana's, the entire family had moved from secrecy to disclosure and from strict definition of roles by gender to a common purpose: one arm, one eye, one ear, one wisdom, all pulling together—Quaker, German Lutheran, French, Haudenosaunee, Lenape, man, woman, and child—to bring Threadneedle, Thread of the violet eyes, through this ordeal. It took longer than they had imagined to reknit his flesh, though the cut was clean. He burned with fever even though there was no evidence of infection.

"It is a wound from steel," they said. "Harder for the flesh to heal."

"He who is riven," the Montours whispered to each other. *Katarioniecha. He Who Breaks to Heal.* Now they all heard it—Montour and Duladier—the beginning of Thread's native name: *Katar, like Cathar.* The name summoned their common forefathers and -mothers, the Cathars who had died by the sword, been burned on pyres, or jumped from tall cliffs rather than submit their faith to the corrupt Christians who sought it by violence. Who wanted their land.

No wonder then that, centuries later, their descendants, the people called Huguenots by outsiders, people whose legitimate right to practice their faith had again been criminalized by the majority Catholics in France, would spend their days carving *"resistez, resistez,"* over and over, with fingernails and pebbles into the walls of the Tower of Constance, overlooking the Mediterranean, where the women were imprisoned for life. Now all, Native and European, saw that the Montour name united them in one bloodline. *Mon tour.* My tower. Not a person in the family disputed the evidence: if you followed the lineage back far enough, they were of the same blood. Evenings, they sat around Kilian's kitchen, Duladier and Montour, and discussed the finer points of their ethical similarities and differences as two peoples.

Winter came early. Soup stock, beeswax for candles, and a kettle of hot water always sat ready at the back of the woodstove. Kilian and Philip kept a supply of wood split in just the right fractions. Someone was always shoving in several splits and pulling the kettle to the front of the stove to set water to boil for medicine for Thread.

The wind was howling like a train right outside, occasionally throwing sleet and hail at the windows with a staccato rattle as the year devolved toward solstice.

Catherine had her hand around a cup of mint tea, the cup glazed with a slip that Kilian favored—celadon green sliding over the native red clay. "The question is this," she began, speaking to all of them. "Will this act of Kristiana's shrive Thread down to the bottom of his soul, freeing him of the necessity to go to war, as Kristiana has gambled?"

"No!" Kilian shouted this at his mother. "Are you tone deaf?"

Catherine sighed. "I was playing devil's advocate, just for this: to have people express their opinions, Kilian. You are overwrought."

Overwrought. Would she now pass her hand over his forehead, check him for fever, then send him to his room? Kilian's chair scraped on the floor as he pushed it back. He was visibly clamping his tongue to keep from being disrespectful to his mother, but his eyes were wild, as if he wanted to dash out into the storm. Instead, when Turtle Dawn turned from the stove and laid her hand on his shoulder, he calmed. He stood and went to stand beside her.

Turtle Dawn brought the soup pot to the front, opened the door to the woodbox, which squeaked its protest, and threw in a three-quarter chunk of wood. They were burning ash and apple now. Oak and maple were in the woodshed, but their native family used maple for ceremonial fires, and the oak was being saved for their fireplaces in the depth of winter. Turtle Dawn made no move to return to her seat but stood with her hand on her hip, sighing. "Mother Catherine . . . I mean no disrespect. But do you *know* my son Threadneedle?"

Two red spots appeared high on Catherine's cheeks.

Kilian, calmer now after his outburst, took down several stoneware bowls from his shelves and set them out, with a ladle for the soup and spoons for those who found the necessity to eat. At the table, his mother, sister, father, Grandmother Marguerite, and Delphine sat with their faces lit by the single oil lamp in the middle of the table. In the corner of the room, a pewter candelabra with five candles shivered and danced in the vagrant drafts. Without being asked, Regina rose, ladled out soup in four bowls, and placed them in front of her elders: Catherine, Philip, Delphine, and Grandmother.

With the flames of defiance flaring in his eyes, Kilian drew out a bottle of his green walnut digestive from the cupboard, along with two pewter cups, which he set down hard in the middle of the table, as if anticipating a challenge to his right to drink hard liquor in his own house.

He poured two portions of the medicine, passed one cup to his father, took a sip from his own, and let out a long, explosive breath. He stood across the table from Turtle Dawn, who was still at the stove. He looked at her before saying, "Threadneedle is a warrior from the top of his head to the bottoms of his feet." He threw challenging looks at each person sitting at the table.

"Don't look at me that way, Kilian Sechinger," Delphine challenged. "I'm the one who is manufacturing uniforms for the Zouave companies. And you? Aren't you preparing our country to go to war as well, seeking contracts for making uniforms?" She made a face expressing her disgust with hypocrisy of all kinds.

Grandmother nodded her head slowly, her eyes never lifting from the dogbane she had been twisting into twine.

They could each call up their own image of Thread, as he emerged from a pack of boys on horses, swung a mallet down on the ball of leather they had designated as the head of their enemy, urged his team members on as they swirled to his shouted exhortations: "To me! To me!" or "Go out for it!" When Thread sat at a table to speak to Tom Flusty's string of weavers on their lunch break, his word was taken as authority among them, despite their superior age.

"But what does it mean?" Philip asked, directing his question to Turtle Dawn and Grandmother, gesturing toward them with his spoon. "What does it mean to your people to be a warrior?" He placed his hand over Catherine's, as if to give her comfort, perhaps even to remind her to think before she spoke.

Catherine did not take his hand as a warning but spoke immediately. Perhaps because she spent the bulk of her time in Newtown, the influence of their native family was less profound on her than on the others, who had become used to letting a long digestive silence pass between responses. "You know that this notion of pacifism is new to our family, having lived for a century and a half in among the Hessians, who—I don't need to remind you—are famed mercenaries who were given out to hire to King George in his war against the colonies." Catherine withdrew her hand from underneath Philip's and took up her handwork, letting her hook fly as she made a kind of pioneer lace from linen thread that went round and round in scallops, a fashionable collar to grace a woman's neckline. While the women of the silk, like Catherine and her sister, would wear such things when they visited Trenton, these lacy collars were out of place in Cottage.

She took a sip of her tea and looked up. "And before that, in 1685, when our families felt the necessity of fleeing from the bloody enthusiasms of the Catholics in France against our people." They had all heard it *ad infinitum*, but it still held a sort of fascination, to reflect on the bloodlines these two families shared through their Huguenot heritage. "Those years *au desert*, for those who didn't make it to the borders before they closed—our family!—found a steel trap sprung on them. Condemning them to more than a century of flight, pursuit, and punishment, trapped in France." Her hook flew again, without her having to look at her hands working, as if they had a mind of their own. She glanced across the table at Regina, saying, "Do you see why you are the only one of us who can go to them, to redeem the Old Text and bring a copy back to us?"

Catherine seemed to have no notion that her lifelong burning desire to have their Old Text restored to them, to guide their way when shut up in a silk *magnanerie* spinning out of balance, seemed thin and purposeless to the younger generation of Duladiers, much less to the earthier Montours.

"And are you talking about silk?" Delphine laughed bitterly. "Silk?" She threw out one hand as if warding off an absurdity. "Please. What use is it?"

Catherine visibly bristled at this unexpected challenge to her life's work.

Grandmother Marguerite lifted another dogbane stick from the bundle beside her and handed it to Turtle Dawn, who sat down and selected another one for herself. They all knew Grandmother's story of her own mother, who as a girl of twelve had fled before General Sullivan's armed men as winter was coming, her People's homes burned behind them, their ancient fruit orchards cut down, corn trampled under marching feet. Frightened children on a forced march. This, one hundred years after the Huguenots had fled France.

Grandmother looked at Turtle Dawn, and some understanding seemed to pass between them. Then she seemed to be speaking directly to Delphine.

"What none of you know is that my mother, just a girl then, was raped by a white soldier. He released her after he had impregnated her. The oldest form of colonial warfare—rape—was used against our People by those who don't hesitate to rape women, a crime that would get a man from our own community killed. That kind of violence and disrespect toward a woman was—and still is—unimaginably rare among us."

Regina gasped and put her head down on the table, arms wrapped around herself for comfort, cradling her ribs in her hands. After a moment, during which only the snapping of the stove broke the silence, she lifted her head to look at each of them, her natural family members, and the members of the native family who had become her own, her cheeks wet with tears. "I'm sorry, but I am beginning to feel like Thread! Finding it harder and harder to consider Europeans my rootstock. Finding the native People expressing a humanity that only makes sense." She looked at her mother and father for guidance. "How did we go so wrong? Aren't there signs that we were matrilineal people at one time in the distant past?" As Catherine and Philip glanced at each other, having no immediate answer, Regina's chair scraped back. "Why don't you feel the insult of it all, as I do!" she cried. "Don't you see? European men have been making war on women in the most heinous ways for millennia!" And when they still didn't answer, she threw her hands up and announced, "I'm going in to Thread," and then rushed from the room.

"You ask what being a warrior means to our people," Grandmother began, looking at Philip and Catherine. "It means being prepared to defend your family and your tribe." She looked around the table. "Are any of you not prepared to defend yourselves from attack?"

As if in answer, Delphine put her hand at the sheath she carried at her waist and drew out her knife, laying it on the table.

Kilian groaned. "I am not prepared to take up arms to defend my family," he said. "I cannot shoot—or stab—another human being; it is against my nature. I might as well shoot a family member or kill myself. That's how much harm it would do me to take another life." He looked at Grandmother Marguerite. "I have been raised since I was a boy to be against war. Now, in my mid-thirties, am I to force myself to change? Do you have any idea how hard this is for me? To countenance that someone I know would plan ahead to take up a hatchet and plunge it into her son's foot? Her son, my blood brother, my cousin? For pacifism!"

Turtle Dawn moved from the stove to touch Kilian's arm. "We know this is hard for you."

Philip put his quiet oar in: "But these things—violence—can come out of nowhere. All of a sudden."

Kilian shifted his weight from one leg to another, considering. "Would I know if someone were coming to harm us?" he ventured, his words subtly asking his father if—for any reason—he were guarding secrets.

Philip sighed. "Is there anyone who doesn't know this?" He looked at his wife resolutely and told her forthrightly what they all knew. "We know who is planting flax over near Seneca Falls. Wilhelm Shafer. He wants us to go into business with him. Or—he threatens to become our competitor."

Catherine stood, glaring down at Philip.

"I only wanted to protect you," he said lamely. "Catherine, sit down. How could I protect you unless I knew how serious the threat was going to be?"

But his wife was not going to sit down. She spoke with a great deal of control, yet each word had a sharp edge. "Now everything is clear to me. I have no place here, no role, nothing to do of any consequence. As soon as travel becomes possible again, I will return to Newtown. Where I belong." She gathered her coat and shawl and mittens, revealing a firmness they hadn't seen in Catherine before. She shot her hand out toward Philip, who had half risen in his chair, his eyes pleading. "No!" she spat at him. "Don't follow me. I need to be alone. To think."

"Let her go," Kilian said to his father.

When Delphine spoke again, she spoke directly to Philip. "Your niece," her gaze broadened to include Kilian, "took my grandson out into the woods to test him. She maimed him. She might have killed him. What punishment are we contemplating for her? For surely she must be punished."

Regina called out from the sickroom, and Grandmother rose quickly and left the room. A moment later her head poked through the curtain that separated the hallway to the pantry from the kitchen. "Philip. We need to turn him." Philip rose and Grandmother Marguerite took her seat at the table again.

Turtle Dawn spoke. "Are you telling me, Kilian, that you wouldn't have stopped Kristiana if you had been there?"

Kilian gripped the back of the chair he was standing behind with both hands, as if he held a railing over a precipice, looked down into a swirling void.

Turtle Dawn spoke again. "What would you do if a man was attempting to rape me, Kilian? In plain English, would you come to my defense?"

"Of course I would," Kilian said stoutly.

Turtle Dawn's voice slipped into a whisper. "We were children when Regina the Elder was raped. When Wilhelm led those men to Catherine, trussed her up like a turkey. Were going to *cut* her."

Kilian made a shushing sound with his lips, his eyes and head indicating to the room beyond, where Regina and Philip were tending Thread.

Delphine's voice was bitter, her laugh razor sharp. "What, Kilian? Are you saying 'the children' shouldn't know?"

Grandmother Marguerite's hands stopped processing the dogbane, twisting the twine.

Delphine hissed like a snake, like a whole knot of snakes. "Our bloodline has been polluted with these two, father and daughter, Wilhelm and Kristiana. I don't know what disease they carry. But there my grandson lies!"

Regina parted the curtain and entered the room, carrying a bowl and cloths. They all looked at her. "His fever has broken," she announced. The silence was peppered with a burst of thanks: *"Grâce de Dieu!" "Madonne!" "Gott sei Dank!"*

Regina looked around. "What did I miss?"

Kilian, who had earlier insisted that Regina be included in these serious discussions, hesitated now. Was talk of rape going too far? "We are discussing the conflicts between our Quaker pacifism and the need to defend one's family. We are also discussing what punishment should be meted out to Kristiana."

Regina nodded her head as she took a seat, her eyes alight with joy at finally being old enough to weigh in on such serious subjects.

"If you and Thread went to war and enemies were coming for Thread," Turtle Dawn asked Kilian quietly but insistently, "would you kill them if you could?"

Kilian shook his head with a dogged look, as if a plague of flies were besetting a tired-out but angry ox.

Apparently Turtle Dawn felt she hadn't salted the pot enough, for she added, "Thread would shoot someone coming to kill you. Or me. That is being a warrior."

Still Kilian didn't speak but only shook his head slowly, his eyes focused on something far away.

"Then I am sorry for your family," Grandmother Marguerite said. "Perhaps you have gotten confused by these Quaker beliefs that molded you when you were young."

Tongue-tied, Regina and Kilian looked at each other. No one had ever challenged their Quaker pacifism like this. The manumission of slaves, the liberation of women—those were easy beliefs for them both to espouse, certain that this was the moral high ground.

"Kilian," Grandmother Marguerite said, covering his hand with hers. "I don't believe you. You are stuck in your head, between ideas you have been raised with and your basic instincts to protect your family. Wait until you have a woman and child you love. Then see." She rose, pulling her cloak around her shoulders. "As for Kristiana, don't you think that this banishment she has been suffering under is punishment enough?"

Kilian answered as if he had no doubts. "When she shows remorse, that she is regretful and sees the error of her ways, then and only then should she be forgiven."

Regina added hotly, "Do any of us believe that Kristiana would ever do that or even apologize?"

Turtle Dawn rose now as well, gathering herself to accompany Grandmother home, after they first checked on Threadneedle and conferred with Kilian and Regina on his care throughout the night. "I don't believe you either, Kilian," she said. "I know you would defend me." She gave him a smile of incomparable sweetness before following Grandmother back to Thread's sickroom to see if anything else was immediately needed.

This discussion between family members had a larger stage elsewhere. Pacifism and abolition of slavery were going up against each other as hostilities brewed between the northern and southern states. In this battle of values, members of the local Quaker leadership had supported John Brown's cause, but the federal government, the Quaker hierarchy in Switzerland and New England, and the textile barons would not abide sectional violence outside of the federal government's sole right to declare war. "War is still bad for business," articles in the newspapers declared, "but anarchy will bring us all down."

Southern slaveowners had stepped up their efforts to chase and recover runaway slaves, and heavy fines were being imposed on those who aided runaways. The Shafer family in South Dayton—related to the Duladiers through Wilhelm's lineage—said that local militia were forming, beginning to muster and train.

"We will all have to wait for the ice in the canal to break to see it sorted out," Philip said, both in response to the matter of Kristiana and to the world's larger problems.

"Why?" Regina demanded. "We are the ones who will set a punishment for Kristiana."

Now Turtle Dawn stepped back into the warm kitchen, ushering Grandmother in.

"We have to work with her," Turtle Dawn spoke the obvious. "She is still one of the major shareholders in Regina Coeli."

A collective sigh filled the room, matching the snapping sounds coming from the stove, the hiss of the teakettle.

Grandmother had the last word. "What if her heart softens?" she suggested. "Yes, and she experiences remorse. Then what? Will we forgive her?"

∞

Deep winter had fallen, snow winnowing down continuously. A vast silence that seemed to emanate from Cattaraugus spread across the land. No one moved between the reservation—where the Seneca had entrenched after losing Buffalo Creek, where both Marguerite and Lazarus kept their adjacent homes—and Cottage, a half-day's ride away, where the Duladier family had their linen operation. Both Cattaraugus and Cottage lay just south of Lake Erie, off the plain, on the escarpment that ran south to the Allegheny Mountains. Winter brought a bounty of fine powder snow sifting down from the watershed that lay between two watersheds, both the creeks that flowed north into Lake Erie and those that drained south into the Ohio and eventually into the Mississippi.

The principals of Regina Coeli could not move to visit their accounts until the canal unfroze. The railroad was often laid up and could not be counted on when snows were deep, and the days of coaches and roadhouses were largely past. Unless a sleigh arrived to retrieve her for an important ceremony, Grandmother was marooned in Cottage. The combined families accepted being snowbound together as more evidence that they should band together to pull Threadneedle out of this threat to his leg, to his life.

Grandmother Marguerite moved between Turtle Dawn's house, Thread's sickbed at Kilian's house, and Kristiana's little shack out back, where she had taken shelter from winter's storms, expressing an evenhanded compassion that shocked everyone mobilized to save Thread. Perhaps, Grandmother signaled, Kristiana also needed saving.

Chapter Seven

WATER MAIDEN

Winter Solstice 1860, Cottage, New York

In three months, Regina only left Thread's side to sleep or have a little food.

"Baby," Thread moaned. "I need water."

Regina had brought two buckets of icy spring water, one for his body and one for drinking. She gently sponged his face and neck, his collarbone, and each of his arms, letting his hands drift through a bowl of water. She let him suck on a clean linen rag that she soaked repeatedly in the water reserved for drinking. She sponged his belly, clinical as a nurse, and, keeping his modesty intact, left his privates covered. She sponged down his legs to his good foot, and then in a gesture of mercy and compassion that was something the Duladiers had never seen, she kissed his injured foot, sucking at the air around it, then spitting to the side, sucking, spitting, until the foot's throbbing was cooled and the foul green aura around it had been driven back.

"Where did you learn that?" Kilian asked her after he first observed this healing technique. It had not been part of his Aunt Elisabeth's repertoire.

"I have been studying with an Onondaga healer I met in Seneca Falls," she told him.

She rinsed her own mouth repeatedly in the clean water, though she had taken in no substance from him during her procedure, and then she rose to swab the floor on the side of the bed.

Having pulled all of the dis-ease out of Threadneedle that she was capable of, Regina sent him her love and her vision of his wholeness as she tucked the covers up over him, her precious brother-boy. "Hush, little baby, don't you cry, Mama's gonna sing you a lullaby," she sang while he drifted off to sleep, the sounds of the adults talking in the next room drifting over them like the wild, withered black cherries, which were even now being pelted to the ground by a shrill wind from Canada. "Hush, little baby, don't say a word, Mama's gonna buy you a mockingbird." Regina's sweet voice wafted throughout the family compound that Kilian's house had become. "And if that mockingbird don't sing, Mama's gonna buy you a diamond ring . . ."

Grandmother Marguerite knocked on the door of the shack that stood adjacent to Kilian's house. Its original use was as a summer kitchen, but it had been Kristiana's home now for months.

"Who is it?" Kristiana's voice sounded rusty, as if it had been left out in the rain.

"It's me. Grandmother. Please open the door. I have soup."

Kristiana did not have energy to spare for manners. She opened the door but turned away immediately, leaving Grandmother to let herself in and close the door against the gusting wind that was pelting sleet at a diagonal slant. The small woodstove that was used during sugaring season sent heat to the cot piled with furs, which Kristiana now crawled back into, but the corners of the room were as cold as the outside.

Grandmother set the small pot she had brought in on top of the stove. She then pulled a wooden chair from the corner to Kristiana's side, checking to see if the legs were sound, but not bothering to dust off the seat. Before sitting down, she took a bowl and spoon out of her cloak and carefully dipped a small amount of soup from the pot into the bowl.

"Kristiana?"

No answer.

"Can you sit up?"

No answer. Kristiana had a paroxysm of coughing that rattled at the end rather than bringing up phlegm.

"Kristiana," Grandmother spoke a third time.

Kristiana looked over her shoulder at Grandmother. "Please leave me alone, Grandmother. I want to die."

Now Grandmother was firm. "Perhaps I will leave you to die. I haven't decided yet." She thought but didn't say, "It would make the others happy," in part because it wasn't quite true.

The empty burlap feed sacks that covered the walls for insulation bellied in and sucked out with the wind, leaving Grandmother Marguerite feeling dizzy, as if she had entered a nether-realm. "Listen to me, Kristiana!"

Kristiana groaned, but she turned from her side, away from the stove, to lay on her back, her head propped by a feed sack stuffed with batting. Her lips were dry and cracked. Grandmother set the bowl on the floor and from her cloak produced a little round tin, which she opened. She dipped in a finger and patted a small amount of her legendary salve on Kristiana's lips. She then drew a flask from her cloak and pulled the cloak tighter around herself, shivering. She put her hand on Kristiana's head, stroking it. She was hot with fever. Kristiana began to cry weakly, like a kitten.

"Are those tears of contrition?" Grandmother asked gently.

"No!" Kristiana spat. "They are the tears of a mother whose son has turned his back on her. Whose wife has thrown her out of her house in the deep of winter. They are the tears of someone who has been betrayed by her whole family!"

"Nothing is so repulsive as the combination of self-pity, lack of insight, and arrogance, Kristiana," Grandmother said. She gathered her cloak about her again and rose. "I am going to leave you to die."

Now Kristiana sat bolt upright. Her eyes wild and her hair in knots, she raved, "I regret the day I chose Lazarus! That's where all the trouble started. *With you!*"

Marguerite flinched; she could see that Kristiana meant not just her but the entire Montour family.

"Yes, you!" Kristiana continued, her voice falling like a hammer. "You have no respect for our values. We are trying to do something here, to create a new society, for all men and women. War—is—wrong! Women have tried many things over the centuries: withholding sex, food, money, children. Nothing has worked." Kristiana panted. "Your own prophet, the Peacemaker? You love him because he put an end to warring against each other, because he made a group of tribesmen who had centuries of wrongs to tally up, centuries of reasons to justify their despising each other . . . he made them indivisible, helped them to come together as one!"

She grabbed the bowl from the floor and tasted the soup. Then she swigged it down, gulp after gulp, as if she were catching her breath, mounting her energy to rave some more. "How did that begin? With a radical act of insight that at first seemed wrong to everyone. It's because I'm a woman, isn't it? I shared with Thread everything I have seen in the visions—the importance of that black sticky stuff that boils up from your springs near Cuba. I showed him the primacy of the east-west waters, how all transportation will follow that meridian." She was out of breath again, huffing like a long-distance runner. But she would not stop her marathon of truthtelling. "He came along. Came along with me. Until I showed him war. He stood up to me then, when I said he would not go. That it was not our war. He! Said I was powerless over him. Had already been decided." Kristiana's voice, which had been mounting in pitch, now fell flat as she dropped back on her sacking. "The clanmothers promised me. You! *You*—stole my son from me!" Now Kristiana wept different tears, not the tears of rage but the tears of sorrow and despair.

"Hush!" Grandmother Marguerite stroked Kristiana's head, refilled the bowl from the pot, and held it out to Kristiana, who took a sip and swallowed.

"Bone marrow broth," the younger woman sighed, unable to ward off deep satisfaction any longer. She closed her eyes. She sat up and put her hands around the bowl, draining it sip by sip. She lay back again on her cot, head on the feed sack. Her hands folded over her sternum and her ankles crossed under the furs. She stared at the ceiling as if it held a bleak future.

"You were seen," Grandmother said. "Never mind by who. Someone checking their traplines. They saw the flash powder you used, like a cheap magician. They saw how ill-prepared you were for the consequences of your actions, after you chopped into Katarioniecha's foot. They saw our wolf pack stalk you, marking you for their female yearlings, a meal of a big mammal to prepare them for whelping next spring. You were deranged, covered with blood, a perfect victim. That person, who could have stopped you or offered you up, beat the deer into the path of the wolves just as the wolves had begun to stalk you. You had injured a man they have a clan relationship with. Did that never occur to you? Did you think this was all coincidence being played out on the stage of your overweening ambition? Nature mimicking human theater?"

I did think that, Kristiana admitted to herself, and flushed. *I thought it was all being staged for my benefit.*

"It was I who made a mistake," Grandmother continued, "way back then, when you had not begun to bleed. I saw the Seer in you. I wanted that. I wanted that."

Kristiana stirred. Was Grandmother Marguerite making an act of contrition?

"I fostered you—a snake!—thinking I could turn your fate. Thinking I could make you my creature. I sent Turtle Dawn into the woods with you. I put Lazarus in your path. I arranged for your adoption. Now I see I was deluded. You are a snake, Kristiana, and nothing, *nothing* has altered your basic character. You have perverted my granddaughter Turtle Dawn, allowing her to think that it is acceptable that you play the white man in our lives, imagining that the home you shared with her was your domain, imagining that the company we have all built together is yours to run. Or ruin! You even imagine that you know how things should turn out, that your good fortune so far is the mark of your abilities. You have turned your light into darkness. You have become an agent of darkness. And now we all see it."

Kristiana burned with an emotion she could not name. *Could it be shame?* she asked herself in a deep voice that seemed to come from within—a voice she rarely listened to.

Grandmother poked in the corners until she found a fur that had been stored in a box. She draped it over her chair and pulled it around her.

"Go!" Kristiana croaked. "Go! I don't want you here."

"Sit up, Kristiana," Grandmother commanded with all of her authority, holding in front of her now a small ceramic flask she had extracted from her capacious pockets.

"No!"

"Do you want me to bring two men in here to force you?"

Kristiana sat up, knowing that every man in her family despised her.

Grandmother Marguerite put the flask to Kristiana's lips and watched as the weakened woman took a sip, then turned her head and spat. "It's bitter!"

"It's medicine."

"What is it?"

"I don't have a white man's name for it. In French: *mescaline*. Spirit medicine from the deserts, something to capture your wayward spirits and bring them home."

Kristiana took the bottle but hesitated.

"I will stay here with you until dawn. And beyond. I will be here with you," Grandmother reassured her.

Kristiana drank deeply, retched, and lay back down.

Marguerite put two more quarters of wood into the stove.

Night became full of the sound of wings, water birds swooping around each other, taking up all the flight space in the room with grace, vast wings, snowy breasts. Slow, dip dip dip, beat, and slow. As Kristiana stared at the roof, it peeled back and revealed the heavens. The constellations, Milky Way, and nameless stars pulsed with intelligent communication. A light snow drifted down, glorious crystals of water. The tree limbs danced, never so glorious as in winter, their naked branches shifting around each other, molting old bark, stimulating their roots, their common ground. Time passed like water.

Marguerite pulled a drum from the shadows and began to tap out a light rhythm, like the heartbeat of the planet.

Someone came into the shed. Someone in white. "The Water Maiden," Grandmother said simply.

Kristiana recognized the figure as Turtle Dawn, standing there with a pitcher and a basin. Kristiana looked at her in awe. How had she never seen this woman as she truly was?

Kristiana drank deeply from the basin, then washed her hands and face in the water. She let Turtle Dawn towel her dry.

When Kristiana spoke, she sounded different. "I am so ashamed," she said. She took one of Turtle Dawn's hands in hers. "I ask for your forgiveness. I have been . . . so wrongheaded. I see now . . . I see you now. I see that trying to make things happen my way is . . ." She blubbered briefly, then regained control and continued. "Oh, Grandmother," she said, turning her head toward her elder. "I see that violence against my son, my own flesh, is the violence that keeps war going. I force my ideas on people!" She hiccupped, then whispered, "I am so humiliated."

Turtle Dawn backed toward the door of the shed.

"Wait! Don't go," Kristiana pleaded.

"Get better," Turtle Dawn said, "and I will return." She stepped out and shut the door behind her.

Kristiana could see the light of false dawn in the sky.

"Grandmother," she said. "Tell me what I can do. To make things right again."

"I can't tell you, daughter. Much has gone wrong."

"Turtle Dawn!"

"You can woo her again, perhaps. You can try. You can show her your awakened heart, how you have changed. And maybe . . . maybe you are not meant for each other. And if this is so, you must accept it. Do you see now? You are not the one who decides how things will turn out."

"Thread?" Kristiana asked with a quivering voice.

Grandmother sighed, then said, "I don't see the way there."

A long silence fell over them. A couple of morning birds spoke to the day.

"You must all work together in the business. But he has closed his heart to you. You have placed a deep scar on his body, a scar that is engraved on his heart—a line that you can never cross again. Yes, his fever has broken. It seems that he will live. That he will keep his foot, his leg."

Now Kristiana wept a third kind of tears: tears of joy, of absolution.

"I can't imagine he will take you back into his heart. He is orphaned now, he feels, by his true mother. He followed the path you led him on. And it wound up badly for him. So 'No more!' he says. He says he has no mother but Turtle Dawn."

Kristiana drew her first breath in this new reality and cried out in anguish. "What can I do?"

"There is nothing you can *do*. Work on your character. Leave Thread alone. Do not meddle in his life. Ever again. Let him live out his own destiny. Can you do that?"

Grandmother Marguerite did not have to say the words. *If not, I will leave you here to die. You have done too much harm.* She got up to leave.

Kristiana's vision of a universe that included her, that connected her to everything else, cracked open. A door . . . "I will try," she said. "I will try. But . . ."

"Trying . . . ," Grandmother said as she went out the door and then closed it hard behind her, " . . . is not enough." These last words came to Kristiana through the heavy wood.

Don't try. Become it. Let the world be, rang in Dialog.

Chapter Eight

A WOMAN'S PLACE

New Year's Eve Day 1860, Cottage, New York

Regina and the older women she worked with in the movement were putting all their progress at risk to make their point, even if they had to change their tone from wheedling to harsh and uncompromising.

"Women's rights and the abolition of slavery have to go hand in hand!" Regina told her family. "It is unconscionable that the Quaker leadership would vote to keep women from speaking on the floor of our international conferences." She looked at her brother and father across Kilian's table while those on shift moved about between the stove and inventory of herbal supplies to Thread's bedroom. "Which part of 'all men are created equal' do my brothers and cousins not understand? Are we women not included in mankind?"

Like Kristiana, Regina was also going mad, but slowly. In an attempt to ground herself again in the world, nightly she found the place between her legs and assaulted herself, crying out in a frustration that would still not be assuaged by the release. *They have all lied to me.* Her father Philip, her brother Kilian. *They are not moved to action by the humiliation of their wives and daughters. No wonder my mother went mad after they burned the silk. No one stood by her! Our men were not good for their word then; they will not be good for their word now!* How could it be, she marveled, that the men in their community—fine men, principled men, Quaker men—did not speak out for her mother? *Why don't our men use their power to help secure our rights and the rights of all women? Are we not deserving of their respect? Do they doubt their own power so much that they are loathe to share it, even with the women in their lives?*

Regina asked herself what else she could do. Some action was necessary. Women were finding many bizarre ways to protest the lack of their men's support—acts that embarrassed their husbands and sons. One popular way women were expressing outrage was by chaining themselves to trees. But this didn't speak to Regina. And she wanted to be sure her protest would have the desired outcome. Kristiana's action against war had gone horribly wrong, and Regina certainly didn't want to harm anyone like Kristiana had. *How could she do that to her son?!* she thought for the thousandth time. But now her deeper thoughts betrayed her: *Will I ever have a son? A son in the image of Threadneedle?*

Turtle Dawn's signal of her divorce from Kristiana—putting her belongings out in the yard and barring the door—shook all of the women in Cottage. The difference between those of the Haudenosaunee nation and those of European extraction who counted their lineage through the male line was a sharp stick in the eye of every white woman in Cottage.

In response to the injury Kristiana had inflicted on Threadneedle, Regina's beloved cradlemate, the girl looked for some action that would express her outrage. At the same time, while it may not have been clear to many of her sisters in the movement for universal suffrage, Regina saw that they needed men to support their cause.

After turning over many alternatives during sleepless hours, she began to settle on one action: the forfeiture of her natural right to a sexual relationship with a man, along with her estate as a potential mother. Regina would choose chastity. "Until European women enjoy the same rights as Haudenosaunee women," Regina declared to the women in her native family, the Montour women, "I will not allow a man to bed me."

Her brother and father were men of good conscience, with all the right attitudes, but that wasn't enough. "Why don't they see how their inaction stings me?" she would cry out to Grandmother and Turtle Dawn. "They have power! With every breath of every day their inaction flays me. Surely they see that!" On good days, she had to believe that they turned over in their hearts what actions they could undertake that might make a difference. The alternative—that they didn't want to or didn't care—wounded her too deeply. That was the knife in Regina's heart every time she placed a platter of food in front of those two fine, considerate, and principled gentlemen.

Once, only once, she said to herself in the dark, quiet recesses of her self-examination, *Is it possible that Kristiana has asked herself the same question, about war, and that this act—maiming Thread—was her response? How could Kristiana conclude that this was the only way to protest against war?* This was a conundrum she couldn't even contemplate in her own case.

Regina's days were so focused on the struggle between the necessity of freeing the slaves and the imperative to give half the population their rights that she couldn't even think about the third leg of Quaker moral principles: pacifism. She herself waged a war night and day for women's rights within the larger society, but oh! the silent battle with the men of her own family struck deeper. "Do they think that my words, written and spoken, are not for them but for other men? Do they think that by starting Cottage, supporting Regina Coeli, and dealing equitably with the women in our family that they have done enough?" She asked these questions whenever she had a chance to sit down with Turtle Dawn or Grandmother, who could do nothing but commiserate.

"Kilian has the power of his pen! Father the ear of our investors! They both have the vote in our country and the power to speak up in the Quaker council. And have they used it to lobby for my right to vote? For Delphine's right to speak in the International Congress coming up? For my right to inherit and own some of our family property here in Cottage?"

Grandmother reached out and touched her knee, a small action that reverberated through Regina's body. "Forgive me for presuming, daughter," Grandmother said. "But are you also afraid of bearing a baby?"

Both Turtle Dawn and Grandmother could see the truth as Regina digested her response to the question.

Turtle Dawn said, "I see." Taking Regina by the hand, she led her to the pantry, where Kilian's storehouse of herbs was kept. And there she showed Regina the importance of dosage: "This dosage will prevent conception. Take this much," Turtle Dawn said as she piled the herb in the middle of her palm, "and steep it in a cup of boiling water each morning when you are fertile." Turtle Dawn told Regina how to count forward from the first day she bled each month. "Pay attention, Regina. You will feel it on alternating sides of your lower abdomen in alternating months. Count . . . and then listen to your body. But be careful! In a slightly larger dose, it could abort a baby you might be carrying. And in a larger dose?—I am not going to show you that or give you the recipe, Regina. It will sterilize you."

Regina shuddered involuntarily.

Turtle Dawn studied her and then said, "Would you consider my son, if you were not given over to your women's rights?"

Regina was so grateful to speak about her conundrum that she blurted it out: "Yes!" Then: "Who else?"

Turtle Dawn packaged enough of the herb to last through several months and then instructed Regina to store it in an airtight container. "Do you have one?"

Regina nodded miserably. *What am I doing?*

Turtle Dawn patted her shoulder and tears fell down Regina's cheeks.

"Just in case you change your mind, Regina," Turtle Dawn said softly. "You will know if you are ready to change your mind."

Grandmother and Turtle Dawn never had to raise their voices. They were born with their rights, coming to them from their mothers' mothers' mothers, uncounted centuries, from their culture founded on the principles of matrilineality. Regina had learned from close observation, from asking questions, that matrilineality did not mean the women were in charge; *au contraire*, it was the condition of patrilineality that led one to such assumptions. No, it meant that that men and women were equal, had parity. Even though they performed different functions in the tribe—the men as chiefs representing the tribe in the outer world, the women's council voting to elect the chiefs—it was the women's council who took a chief down if he did not uphold the principles he had been elected to serve.

Hadn't the legacy of silk shaped her family into something very similar to the matrilineal structure of the Haudenosaunee? Women were the inner power of the Duladier family as well; women raised the silk thread, nurtured the worms, and men marketed it, cultivated the mulberry. And perhaps this thread passed through the centuries of Christian domination in Europe, passed through from their Druid ancestors. Perhaps there was an even older legacy, one that came through the silk and from no other roots than that, the warp thread that defined how women and men in her family worked together and knew their places, so much like these tribes of the eastern states of the Americas.

But Kristiana! She took it upon herself to act as a chief, to take the role of the man in her family, to market their Regina Coeli line by traveling out with the men, and to—she had heard whispers of this—take sex when and where she wanted. And now this! She was unnatural, a Medea, a monster not a woman.

As for Regina, she teetered in her commitment to remain chaste. Thread was so much better, and she now had a means of preventing pregnancy, which had lifted the dread of childbirth. Also, she and the other women were still lobbying to have her invited to attend the Quaker International Congress in Europe that spring, to represent the women's movement and its roots here on this continent. With this knowledge that she was on the verge of leaving Thread after so many months of helping him to heal, she began to reconsider her form of protest. Still, she faced another barrier: loving a man was evidently a risky business. Giving her heart to another? Yes, she had given her heart to Thread long ago, when they were children. But giving her heart into the hands of Thread the man? Oh, and he was a man! She had seen his manhood uncoiling in the fork above his legs and it both frightened and fascinated her. *What did it look like fully unsprung?* she wondered.

And hadn't love been the source of Kristiana's curse? Consumed by her passion for their business, by her mission in life, Kristiana didn't have room to truly love anyone . . . except Thread, her Achilles' heel, her child. *She had to love him! Who wouldn't?* Regina didn't know how she could love anyone else.

Thus does a young person with no knowledge of love outside filial devotion obsess about the state as she stands on the threshold on which she is held captive, like a fly in amber, but alive.

For Regina knew nothing of love. She spoke as a child, with a child's voice.

She was twenty years old, and while she knew much about the way the world worked, she knew nothing about love and how it could make a person violate what she holds to be her own precious beliefs.

Kilian knew this would be a great honor for his sister, to be asked to represent the interests and be one of the voices of the women's movement within the Society of Friends, but whether those in charge of the program at their International Congress in Switzerland would change their policy to admit women in to the proceedings, to invite them to speak—ah! that was another matter. And the question of inviting Delphine, a woman and a native, to present the way Haudenosaunee's matrilineal system had functioned for centuries, perhaps for millennia, was beyond the pale, wasn't it?

"When is it?" he asked as they stood at the cupboard that held Thread's medicines.

"Spring," she said. "Before the hurricane season."

"Will you go?" he asked.

"If The Three say so, I will," she answered. "The Three" was code for their three elders: Grandmother Marguerite; their mother, Catherine; and their Aunt Elisabeth. "But Mother shouldn't have a say," Regina pouted.

"Of course she has a say," Kilian laughed. "Why shouldn't she have a say?"

"Father will let me go. He already said so."

"You'd better be sweet with Grandmother Marguerite then . . . if you are going to be sour about Mother." He handed her the tea and a spoon for giving the medicine to Thread. "Are you sure you want to go?" he asked.

"Why do you ask?" she said, whirling on him.

"I wonder if Mother will ask you to go to the Cévennes," he replied mildly, raising his hands, palms out, defensively.

"It's a long trip from Switzerland into the Cévennes mountains of

France," Regina said reflectively. "Though I hear a train line has opened from Paris to both Dijon and Lyon."

He blushed. "I don't want you traveling alone."

"Delphine and Blaise might also like to visit the Cévennes with me. Or at least Lyon."

"If Mother gives you the key . . ."

The key had first been entrusted to that long-ago ancestor who had fled early for the border after the Revocation of the Edict of Nantes took away the rights of the sect that had been styled "heretical" in the south of France. Like many subjugated people, they were given the name Huguenot by outsiders who did not know what these people—these people who had died by sword and fire in the tens of thousands—called themselves. That's why Regina always referred to the native people in her family as Haudenosaunee, instead of Iroquois, a name given to them by foreigners. It was simply respectful. But Regina had no idea what her People had called themselves. Huguenots, Shadow People, stuck to them. The key, which had passed from mother to daughter in the Duladier family over the last 175 years, was the sign that the bearer had the right to copy the secrets from their original Old Text to bring to their home *magnanerie,* the place where silk was raised each spring.

"She would give me the key of course," Regina told Kilian. "Who else is in a position to go? I can't pass up the opportunity."

"If you are nice to Mother she will give you the key, you mean!" Kilian observed hotly.

A year ago, word had come by post in a letter on the thinnest onionskin paper—which they had passed around until it was worn even thinner—from their distant relations in the Cévennes, the stronghold of the Huguenots who had been trapped in France when the borders were closed. The Duladier family there had a copy of the Old Text, a volume of ancient collective wisdom on silk production, and, they said, if the descendants of the House of Duladier in the New World would come and present their key, they might be allowed to copy the revered text.

"What do you think they want from us?" Kilian asked.

"Maybe just to meet us." Regina pursed her lips. "Maybe money?" She observed her brother keenly for a moment. "Why don't you come with me?" she offered brightly. "You could report on it for the paper."

"You know I can't."

She did know, though neither of them said why: too many people depended on him.

"You would be more likely to meet a suitable wife there than here," she observed, lilting away lightly, as if he might swat at her for her foolishness. *I know about you, Kilian,* she said in Dialog, wondering if she was violating the tone of that channel to play with her brother like this. No one had referred to her brother's relationship with Turtle Dawn in her hearing yet.

"I don't need you to find me a wife. We should have more of a care for *your* reputation," he groused. Then: *You know* what *about me?* he asked in Dialog.

They had never spoken to each other in Dialog before.

"I'll be chaperoned by Delphine and Blaise. We're taking a steamship."

Then: *Have a care,* came the response in Dialog.

"Aren't you afraid of becoming an old stick-in-the-mud?" Regina said, even though what she wanted to say was *Why don't you live with Turtle Dawn?* Someday she would say it aloud. For now, it was too delicate to come down on.

He groaned, then set his hands to another task, putting together field wallets of medicines for his customers. He drew down a wooden box from the shelf, then sat at the table, all his ingredients arrayed before him.

"Is there something I can do to help you, Kilian?" Regina asked, hoping it might jar her brother into turning that question around, so that Regina would not have to ask him to give her what he should see she needed from him.

"Would you ink labels, Regina? You have such a fine hand."

He took down an inkpot, a quill, and a small pile of carefully cut papers for his sister. The two sat companionably working together, the only sound the soft murmur of Threadneedle and Turtle Dawn in the next room, the soughing sound of the wind making fresh drifts of snow. The stand of pines to the side of the house played the wind's silky tune. The occasional rattle of hail gusted against the luxury of their glass windowpanes, compliments of their opium profits.

"I am afraid," he admitted, "that we might have a war here, soon. A civil war between North and South. War might trap you and Delphine and Blaise in Europe." *So her plans are already made,* Kilian thought. *Did she tell me that the Quaker hierarchy here had asked her, merely to preserve the conventions of older brother and younger sister? Or does she want something from me, something she won't articulate?* Then a fresh thought still: "Will they let you speak?"

"Do you mean the men? Will they let me speak?" she asked. Then after a pause she said, "That's why we have insisted that Delphine and Blaise attend me—so they can testify for their own People about the matrilineal ways native to this eastern seaboard. Oh!" she exclaimed, in obvious distress.

"What?"

"Oh, nothing. I made an ink blot on that one. It's just that . . . How can I make them understand that Delphine is the representative of the clan-mothers, that she brings their word? How can I make them see that Blaise is just a mouthpiece to the outer world, merely acting on the joint policy of the clanmothers and the chiefs? They'll think he is a chief!" She sighed. "Our ways are so different from their ways." She shifted in her seat as if she were truly uncomfortable, as if these thoughts were prods and pricks that never let her rest. "What if they refuse to let Delphine speak?"

Kilian thought for a moment, then said, "Would you like me to write something to them, introducing you and Delphine and Blaise, giving them a grounding in Haudenosaunee ways? I could get Philip to sign it too."

She smiled brilliantly.

A lump arose in his throat. He had this continuing feeling that he wasn't doing enough for his younger sister, and in that moment he asked himself if there was something he was not seeing.

"Would you, Kilian?" She smiled again, this time sweetly, illuminating all the space around her, her fountain of light falling on him like golden dew. Then she added, "Maybe a gentle reminder that this equality, this balance, is something that Quakers have advocated since our earliest formative years."

Now it was Kilian's turn to smile. His sister was off and running.

Her eyes were slitted as she looked inside. "Why don't they understand that the three legs of Quaker principles—abolition of slavery, women's rights, and pacifism—depend on each other, absolutely?" She slumped. "It's greed that's got to them, Kilian. They want to hold their power to themselves . . . ," she glanced at him quickly, ". . . like all men," she concluded.

"Not all men," he corrected. "We have also learned a great deal from our Montour family," he said, wondering what Turtle Dawn thought of him as a man.

"No, not all men," she acknowledged, thinking of Threadneedle, who lay just there, in the next room, needing her attendance on him. Just as quickly, she shifted her thoughts away from him to thinking about the International Congress and whether a letter from the Duladier men would persuade the Quaker elders in Zurich to allow Delphine—and perhaps even herself—to speak, if only to introduce Delphine. "Oh, drat!" she exclaimed. "Look! I have written 'Threadneedle' on all of them instead of 'feverfew.'" She blushed. And then she baffled her brother. She put her face in her hands and wept, as though the cost of ink and paper were so dear they could never be replaced.

PART TWO

1861

Chapter Nine

CLAN COMPATIBILITY

February 1, 1861, Cottage, New York

"Maybe it's because Eugenia and I knew each other all our lives," Killian told Turtle Dawn, carefully looking at the ceiling. "There was no . . . ," he let his hand hover above her pubic hair as if dowsing for water, ". . . no electricity. There." He breathed in her gasp as he let his hand fall. "We were comfortable as a pair of old slippers. No bites, no scratches . . ." Now he was mounting her as his words and her sigh went straight to his groin and hers, inflaming them, his throat engorged as if he had her in his mouth like another tongue.

After, in the after, he continued as if he had not been interrupted by their passion. "Do you know what I am saying? I felt like Eugenia was my sister."

"It's the clan," Turtle Dawn said.

"What do you mean?" he asked, up on his elbow now, looking down at her face, at the length of her, like a bolt of silk satin against the linen sheets.

"Well," she began slowly, her deliberation bringing blood to him, her every gesture, word, and breath exciting his member as if a silk ribbon were being pulled taut against it like reins, slip and tighten. Slip, tighten.

She laughed at his obvious reaction and, swiveling lightly out of bed, walked away to throw two small split logs into the middle of the cavernous fireplace they maintained both for cooking and heat. "Isn't it funny?" she said. "When Kristi and I separated households, I took our stove over to

Cattaraugus. Now I'm back to cooking on the hearth again." She pulled on the hook that carried the heavy teakettle, moving it to the front, just over the quickening flame.

"You're getting a stove," he said.

Her eyes widened. "See what I mean? Kristi simply orders a stove without asking me what I want."

"She didn't order it; I ordered the stove." He watched Turtle Dawn's eyes widen, and it occurred to him then that he had done the same thing Kristiana would have: assumed he would know what she wanted, without asking her. His realization struck them both with force. He stepped into the lacuna. "You have to tell me what you want me to do. I can't guess. Don't you like surprises?"

She smiled at his open invitation, and he jumped out of bed and rushed at her, but she was more than his match. He never saw her move, and yet, when he reached the spot where she had been standing, she was at the ladder that led to the loft and now swung from the second rung, taunting him with her angles: bum, elbow, jaw, heel.

He moved up behind her. "Let me," he murmured. She made a sound, feigning a faint, hanging limply from the rung so that the weight of her on the palm of his hand was heavy and delicious like a ripe peach on a tree. He split her open with one hand, while with his other hand he guided himself to that opening, putting just the head into her heat. They flowered together.

She was muscular and she was long; he marveled that it was as if she were a bird with hollow bones for flying. He lifted her from the ladder and carried her back to bed, joined to him at the hips, her head limp on his shoulder, her hair scented silk. He pulled the linen sheet over them. She convulsed back, her breasts arching toward the ceiling, and he came. He couldn't get enough of her. Ever. Then, nestling into her side, he fell asleep.

When he woke, Turtle Dawn was ladling stew into two bowls.

They sat across from each other on the bed, ravenous, dipping chunks of bread into the stew, feeding each other, laughing about nothing.

As the sun was setting outside the window in the afterglow of their lovemaking, with the logs blazing up that Turtle Dawn had thrown on the fire, while they waited for desire to rise again he asked her, "What do you mean by the clan?"

Now it was she who spoke to the ceiling as if unwilling to meet his eyes. "Even though Europeans walked away from clans when Christianity took over the old religions, the fact is that—somewhere beneath the surface— the clans still function as they did for millennia. What? It's less than two millennia since the clans and the old religions prevailed in Ireland, France, Germany. *Gallia est omnis divisa in partes tres*. First the Romans chopped down the sacred groves and then polluted the bloodlines."

She didn't have to say it; he measured in his own memory what they had lost fleeing from France to Germany. *Your mothers chose to stay with the old ways*, he said to her lazily, in Dialog, still fearful—though also filled with a sense of power—at being able to speak, and listen to women speak, in Dialog, a form of communication that had been forbidden to the men of his silk guild in the Old World. They had been forbidden even to listen in.

She rose up on her elbow and looked down at him. "The Frenchman, Montour, he married into the family," she said.

"Why did your family take his name?" He wanted to ask her, *What name did you give up?* but didn't. One thing at a time.

She sucked on a tooth, as if deciding whether to speak or stay silent.

"He was a lost man. Like your family. A Huguenot. A ghost. My great-grandmother said her grandmother said that making him give up his name was too profound a sacrifice to ask of that man."

Her confiding one of the great secrets of her maternal line felt like she had wrapped him in the finest Merino wool. He searched his memory to find something of equal value to offer her in exchange.

"Do you know that my Uncle Wilhelm has given us an offer to buy us out?" He had been struck by a sudden certainty that Wilhelm, who had been shunned for his treachery a generation ago, had himself both listened in and perhaps spoken in this secret channel that had, among his people, once been reserved for women only.

Turtle Dawn hissed. "Does Kristiana know?"

"Did *you* know?" he asked curiously.

"My mother told me but swore me to secrecy. And then Kristi . . ."

Yes, they both knew that Kristiana had put herself beyond the pale, but still . . .

"She told me that my father said he had something to show her in Seneca Falls, so perhaps . . ." He shrugged. Changing the subject back to what he found more interesting, he asked, "Are you saying that Eugenia and I were probably the same clan and therefore felt a natural neutrality, or antipathy, toward mating with each other?"

"How do you feel with me?" she asked suggestively.

"If you're Wolf clan, I must be—Turtle? Or Bear?"

"Turkey!" she threw at him, and laughter led to tussling until Kilian had her bent backward over the edge of the couch, his hands holding her wrists over her head so that her high breasts were lifted nearly to her throat. "Oh God," he said deep in his throat. And then she rolled, flipping him over onto his back, and lifted a leg as if she were mounting a horse, and he moaned again, bucking his hips up to meet her riding down.

With no one from the family around, and it being midwinter, night and day melded for the couple. They ate and slept when they would, a rhythm broken only by copulating in new ways, each time expanding their repertoire. And bringing in wood to keep their fire going.

He licked his lips, smelled the ham of his hand. Turtle Dawn's peppery nutmeg smell and taste were imprinted all over him. He was about to say, "I love you, Turtle Dawn; I want to spend my life with you," when she interrupted his train of thought, saying, "I have something hard to discuss with you, Kilian."

He sat up, the skins wound around his hips, his taut abdomen contracted from the sharp warring sensations of the heat from the fireplace and the cold wind whistling through the cracks in the walls, creating drafts like chilly currents from underground springs in a pond whose surface is heated by the summer's sun.

"The women in our female line, the Montours, have a tradition. After that first man, the Montour, whose name we took for our own, we have never named the fathers of our children."

"What?" This information sent him reeling, as if he had been struck by a wet sandbag swinging freely from a rope attached to a barn hook. Blindsided. He bent in half, pulled his hair at the temples straight up, clenched his teeth, then sat up and grabbed her by both shoulders. "Didn't you owe it to me to tell me this before I stepped across your threshold?"

He wanted to get dressed and walk out into the bracing cold, return to his own home, curl in a ball, and sleep a dreamless sleep until spring. But he was too sick with this new knowledge to move.

Turtle Dawn spoke softly as her hands moved soothingly over his shoulder and back. "The women in our family have chosen both European men and native men from different tribes to father their children. By not naming the father, the child is mine and only mine, as it should be. If I choose a European father, thinning our bloodline, the tribe can never argue with me about it as long as they don't know. And no Europeans can call my child 'half-breed' if they can't trace his paternity. Look at how the clanmothers pressured Thread about Regina. They wanted him to choose a native woman to give birth to his children. I cannot allow our elders to pressure me in that way. You see the wisdom in it? If no one knows . . . for sure . . ."

He thought it through. Delphine was partnered with Blaise after Turtle Dawn was a small child; Delphine would not name Turtle Dawn's father. Turtle Dawn's grandfather was rumored to be Handsome Lake, but Marguerite would not say for sure. "And Marguerite's father?" he asked.

She flushed. "Marguerite's mother was raped by a white soldier when she was still a girl," she said, her eyes lowered. "Were you out of the room when she told us all, outside of Thread's sickroom, last month?"

"No, I was there. I forgot. And so when Kristi named Lazarus as Thread's father . . ."

"It was a great honor for Lazarus," she finished. "And the door to Thread's acceptance into the tribe. Lazarus is a Montour man, very important to the lineage."

"Lord help us!" he implored the ceiling. Could it be possible he wasn't going to be allowed that recognition if he and Turtle Dawn should have a child? He wasn't Lazarus or Handsome Lake. He had no standing with the tribe. "Who will raise our child?" he asked rhetorically, then burrowed into the covers as if he were hibernating.

She left him there, walked across the room, then returned, touched him, put a cup of water into his hands, which he drained. He opened his eyes and looked at her. He felt as though his face had changed. An older man looked out from his eyes. "Who is your father, Turtle Dawn?"

"I do not know," she answered. "Delphine has never told me. There are some rumors but ..."

"Do you care?" he asked.

She rested her cheek on her fist, looking to see if she cared, to give him an honest answer if she found one. She glanced down shyly. "I like to think that Handsome Lake might be my grandfather," she said. "And that is enough for me."

"Who was he?" Kilian asked

"Ask Delphine or Lazarus about him some time. He was a great prophet. Cornplanter's brother. Lazarus is He Who Hides because he killed a white man who tried to assassinate Handsome Lake." She smiled at him tremulously. "Yes, I like to think about Handsome Lake and the rumor that he could be my grandfather."

He was aware that she had given him another of the secrets of her maternal line. *Is this how these Montour women reel in their men,* he thought, *by revealing their secrets?*

Now he moved carefully, his newfound love for this woman he had known most of his life making him tread lightly, so he almost whispered.

"Where did Delphine get that platinum hair?"

"Grandmother will never say. And yet Dutch blood in my maternal line is emblazoned on Delphine with her unseemly appearance. It might have been the rapist of Grandmother's mother, an underage female in flight from Sullivan's army." She colored deeply. "We are not loose women, Kilian. But, like the women in your family—and that is unusual for European families, yes? It comes through the silk?—we women choose our mates carefully. Often a man of your race finds a mate for his daughter and imposes him on her, for dynastic reasons, even if she would choose someone else."

"I must admit I was surprised to hear Grandmother tell us that her mother had been raped by a white soldier. She was part of Queen Esther Montour's people fleeing with her sister's band back to Canada, before the onslaught of soldiers who pillaged and burned, an early scorched-earth policy," Kilian said. Grandmother had told him it was done "to make the Susquehanna safe for English settlers who couldn't consider living in harmony. It served them to style us 'savages.'"

"That was a great mark of favor from Grandmother to you and your family," Turtle Dawn said, "to reveal that her father was an unknown white man who conceived her with an act of violence. And on an immature female, too. Can you imagine how much Grandmother has had to grow since she first found out about her father?"

"Perhaps it would have been better if she had never known."

"It has made her who she is, to find out that she is part white. It has given her great compassion for your people."

"You chose me!" he said accusingly, and then he was in Turtle Dawn's arms, crying out: "How can I find myself in this situation where no one will know for sure that I am my child's father?"

Later, when Turtle Dawn had lit the lamps and they were settling down to another bowl of lamb stew, he asked, "And Kristiana? What will she be to our child?" He couldn't help himself; he growled it.

"She will have no rights. She acts like a white man and doesn't know how to behave." Then, realizing she had just insulted her lover, she touched his arm and said, "Sorry."

"Turtle Dawn," he said, aware that now he would put on his heavy winter clothes and go back to his own home. "You told me that the women of your line choose the fathers of their children carefully. Thank you. You chose me, sometime before that day last summer when we carried up the lunch baskets together."

She nodded and smiled, her eyes downcast.

She's flirting with me! he realized, and then spoke from his heart so she would be sure to understand his serious tone. "Both of our families know that Kristiana chose Lazarus to father Threadneedle. Lazarus has some status as Thread's father. I need that from you, with our child. And so I will not ask you again . . . but I am telling you this is what I want. This is what I need! I will not be estranged from our child. We are going to have to moderate our two People's customs to work for us and our child. I promise you: I will never act the white man with you or our child. Ever." *But I will act the white man with my cousin Kristiana, if I choose,* he thought.

Turtle Dawn had one more thing to say as she handed him out the door into the thaw of the late February evening. "You *are* a white man. Ask yourself: Can I behave differently?"

Chapter Ten

BIOLOGY WILL HAVE
ITS DAY

March 21, 1861, Newtown, Pennsylvania

Now Kilian had business to conduct. Serious business. Regina had left Seneca Falls for Europe before deep winter set in, and Thread would soon be leaving too, for his apprenticeship in Krefeld, if he hadn't already. And then it would be too late. *Dawn will be showing by the time Thread hears of it! And by letter! No.* He had to get down to Newtown before that happened, had to tell Thread what was going on. *I am the father of Turtle Dawn's child.* He owed it to Thread to tell him that before he left.

It would take a week by regular coach, and so he dipped into his Duladier Medicine funds to pay for a faster stage, on the pretext of calling on the Patterson Thread Factory, carrying messages in a flurry of importance from the Cottage branch to the Newtown branch. The women in Newtown were preparing to go *en magnanerie* and he needed to make it before then.

"Now *why* are you here?" his mother Catherine had asked when he appeared at his childhood home, having come directly from the stagecoach and wanting some straight answers from her.

"To see Thread before he leaves."

"You can see Thread is here in Newtown; he is going nowhere." She shrugged. "You'll go back together. You can help him face Kristiana when he tells her it was Grandmother's decision that he stay." Catherine laughed ruefully.

"Mother," he said, planting himself squarely in front of her, "Thread will not face Kristiana to tell her that Grandmother has decided. It is no business of Kristiana's that he will not go to his apprenticeship in Krefeld because Grandmother Marguerite and her clanmothers decided it."

"Oh?" Catherine said. "She is still his mother."

She still doesn't understand how it works, Kilian thought. He sat down, hard, in a chair. "There's more. I came down because I wanted you to know that we have voted to work with Uncle Wilhelm." He had to unburden himself from this web of secrets his family kept.

"Yes," she said, "I know." She sat now too, hands folded in her lap, resigned, as if giving in to something much bigger than herself, withdrawing into her own cocoon where nothing could touch her, her face paler than he had ever seen it.

"Mother," he said, putting his hand on her shoulder. He wanted to say, *What did that man do to you?* But he didn't.

Instead he said the harder thing. "I need to know, Mother. Who is my father?"

Now it appeared that his mother had learned a thing or two about long bouts of silence from the Montours. The clock in the corner counted out the seconds and the minutes. He was about to say, "I have to know, Mother," when she sighed and spoke so softly he had to lean in to hear her and read her lips.

"I don't know which one." She was twisting and retwisting a linen handkerchief she had edged with lace, her knuckles as pale as the edges of her lips.

He wanted to comfort her. He couldn't. He turned away. He told himself it was because he needed to see Thread.

Kilian learned that Grandmother had arrived in Newtown just before Threadneedle had set out for Trenton to board the ship for Krefeld. She had told the young man that he would not be going anywhere. Krefeld was off. Thread would stay on these shores. Grandmother would handle Kristiana.

"We are letting you pursue Regina freely," Grandmother had told her great-grandson confidentially. "Your path has been interfered with enough. Now you must choose where you should be. And who you should court."

"But the terms are the same?" Thread had asked. "Regina must choose me?"

She nodded. "That is the way of our People. If we think that the Duladier once were matrilineal people like us, the Montours, then yes, that is the way the world works for all of us. Even silkmoths."

With Regina already overseas, Thread had decided he would stay south for the spring anyway and then meet Regina when she got off the boat from Europe later in the spring. As far as he was concerned, his mother would have nothing to say anymore about the choices he made.

And now Kilian had come south. Thread asked himself why. He thought he knew. The two young men wasted no time in riding off for an evening away from the settlement. Around a campfire, away from the family members who pruned and defined their lives, they could talk freely.

"Where is Regina now? Do you know?" Kilian asked, trying to be casual as he fed quarter-sized logs into the fire that was snapping with small chunks of seasoned wood.

Thread pretended to think. "Geneva, Switzerland," he said. "She changed her speech to the convention. She told the International Society of Friends about the clanmothers' contribution to the women's movement. Delphine spoke. The entire body was deeply moved, Regina said. She should be home—in Newtown—" he clarified, "one month from tonight." He caught his breath. "She wired me. She's not staying as long as she thought. She wants to come home. Delphine and Blaise also want to be home, in time for Turtle Dawn's baby."

Kilian almost snorted. "You thug!" Kilian had his cousin in a neckhold. "You know to the second when she's leaving, when she's arriving. Don't even *try* to pull the wool over my eyes." He drew back to take a closer look at Thread. *He knows about our baby?* Kilian wondered, then just as quickly answered himself: *Wake up,* dummkopf! *The entire Montour family must know about the baby. But does he know that I am the father?*

Thread looked directly at Kilian then and spoke in Dialog, asking, *And you? Have you been trying to pull the wool over my eyes?*

Kilian was shocked silent. He had just begun to try out the secret channel of his family women on Turtle Dawn, but he had never conversed there with another man except his father. He felt as though Thread, with whom he shared many secrets, was gazing at his nakedness with an objective regard. "When . . . ?" he ventured.

"My father's People," Thread said. "Do you still not know how it works?"

"Of course I know," Kilian blubbered. "I just thought . . ."

"You thought it was secret."

"You told me Dialog was secret," Kilian said. "Though we have never spoken there, I knew that's what it was . . ."

"Who have you spoken with in Dialog?" The two men knew it was forbidden to use Dialog for argumentation or even interrogation, so Thread spoke aloud.

"My father. Philip. He taught me when the prohibition against men using Dialog was lifted."

"Have you ever spoken there with the women?" Thread asked, looking at Kilian out from under his eyebrows as he bent to put a small chunk of wood under the larger logs.

There—it was out. Kilian could omit information, and yet he could not tell a lie when he was directly questioned. The silence stretched out. "I came here to tell you," he began.

Thread leaned forward to unstring the quail from the spit. "I already know," he grunted.

Kilian didn't know whether Thread would punch him or embrace him. *What would I do if the tables were turned and he and Regina . . . ,* Kilian thought.

"So I am to be uncle to your child," Thread said, coming up with a smile on his face. Then asked: "Do you have any idea what that means to my People?"

Kilian winced. "It means you are more important to my child than I, with my errant seed. Correct?"

And now the younger man appeared to have made up his mind to confide in his blood brother, for the two had exchanged blood when they were boys, then again as adults. They were cousins through their female line. Thus they were bound to each other under the supervision of both the Duladier and Montour families. "Listen, Killy. If there is a war, I am going to enlist. I am twice as strong on a horse as I was when mother injured me. I have more than made up the deficit."

"Cavalry?" Kilian asked, his heart sinking.

"Yes." Thread waited.

"I am coming with you," Kilian said.

"You'll have to fight."

"Maybe not. I hear they're using cavalry for sentries and orderlies. They'll need someone to take care of the horses. I can stitch up wounds, administer medicines," Kilan added, ever hopeful. Then: "What will your mother do?"

"Nothing. It's too late for her to do anything," Thread said. "And your mother?"

Bitterly Kilian responded, "What could she do? She's a broken woman." And now he decided to come fully clean: "And Regina? How is she going to feel about your going to fight?"

Thread thought for a long time. "I'm done with letting women rule me. My mother killed that. I love Regina. I want to marry her, Killy." He put up his hands to stop his cousin from saying what he thought he might say. "The clanmothers? I am going to marry the person I love," he said. "Grandmother said they would stop trying to influence me, leave me to determine my own path. That's why I am going home after Regina returns, instead of to Krefeld."

"About time," Kilian growled.

"I hope I have your agreement," Thread added, as an afterthought.

"As if that would make a difference," Kilian said, then threw his arms around this young man whom he would give his life for. A moment later, though, he pulled back. Something Turtle Dawn had told him sprung to mind and brought him up short. "Won't the clanmothers insist that Regina ask you, and not the other way around?"

Thread's mouth tightened in an uncharacteristic look. "She will ask me. Without my forcing her hand, she will ask me."

"But Regina?" Kilian asked. "I know my sister; she doesn't want to have children." The answer they both knew hung the air between the two men. *But she wants Thread more.* Kilian realized this, his own lesson with desire stirring his blood. *Desire trumps fear,* he thought. *Biology will have its day.*

Chapter Eleven

BINDING SPELL

May 1, 1861, Newtown, Pennsylvania

Regina found him there, by their old fishing hole on Neshaminy Creek, where it left Newtown to flow into the Delaware. Everything was happening earlier this far south of Cottage. On May Day, not only had the lilacs just finished blooming but the wild roses and brambles were budding. Dandelions spread their message everywhere, and the intoxicating smell of wild strawberry flowers filled the air. Dressed in calico gingham that she had shortened against the prohibition of their times, a ruffle of bloomers giving her freedom of movement, Regina, holding her lace-up shoes in one hand, stepped across the stones on the riffle that led across the creek to where Threadneedle sat on the bank.

Thread was smitten; no words can describe the feeling of ecstasy that rose up in him in her presence. As he looked at her now, his throat threatened to close with suppressed emotion. He was barefooted for fishing, for getting his feet primed for summer calluses. His indigo-dyed linen pants were turned up to his knees, and a red do-rag kept his hair from his face. He was tending two poles; he expected her.

Reaching him, she silently took up one pole, reeled it in, put more bait on the line; he hadn't been watching and it had been nibbled away. She cast it in, and then stood there, beside him, facing the creek.

Both the day and the season were young. A small breeze, full of spring's fragrances, rustled her skirts, teased her petticoats. Freckles were beginning to stand out on the bridge of her nose, summer's spice. Her eyes changed color with the season, the day, what she was wearing. One glance and he could see that today they were the color of bottle glass, of water.

How will we breach the distance created by her being away in Europe for four months? She looked different to him; she had changed. *She has become a woman. Has she found someone else?* His heart seized at the thought. *Am I too late?*

Any stranger could see what there was in her that Threadneedle adored: the way her hair tendrilled out in a slight breeze, while around her face and neck shorter curls almost clung to her skin. Backlit as she was in the afternoon sun, her hair was a glory that even Titian had failed to capture. She was an archangel. It was not the first time Thread had drawn that comparison, but still, every time he saw her, he was struck anew. Her strength! Her golden-rosy beauty! And, yes, her armor. Her armor of ideas and principles. What did he have that would gently pierce that steel corset of her warrior-being?

Nothing, he admitted. *Nothing but my adoration of her.* He could not even imagine that what he felt for Regina—had felt since they were babies, then toddlers and young children being brought up together—was not reciprocated by her. Before their mothers separated them, with Regina being parceled off to become a woman and Thread released into his boyhood, she had been a hoyden. They had fished, climbed trees, built forts, shot arrows. She was as good at all these things as he was. But for that armor, he could not imagine that she did not share his feelings.

She has no idea what I'm planning, does she? How I am plotting to marry her soon? Will she ever ask me to marry her? The terms his Montour grandmother had placed on him seemed preposterous to Threadneedle as he sat now at Regina's feet for the first time after their long absence. He had so many things he wanted to ask her. He knew she hoped not to marry; everyone knew. They had never touched, never kissed. They had not declared themselves to each other, had not been promised to each other in childhood. And yet Threadneedle could not imagine his life without her.

And now they sat beside each other, she dawdling her bare feet alternately, left, right, the feet whose soles he longed to caress. She tended her pole, seemed happy to be home. He sighed deep into the pleasure of the day, of being in her company. *Can't I just be satisfied with this much?* he chided himself, and relaxed, letting his anxiety flow out.

"Do your parents want you to marry, Regina?" he blurted.

"Of course. I suppose they do. But they are not pressing me. With Lischen married and *maîtresse* of the *magnanerie*, and her two babies, Mother and Father have much to occupy them." Her forehead crinkled, two lines between her brows; she was puzzling something through. "It has to do with Regina the Elder. Here's what I think, really, Thread: Regina paid the bill for me. Her early death . . ." Regina stopped and bit her lower lip. "You see?"

He did. He also longed to take her lower lip gently between his teeth.

Her eyes squeezed shut. "And thus I have been given a free ticket. Like your mother, Aunt Kristiana, I am free to go anywhere I need to. An unusual position for a woman of our times. Why would I marry, Thread? It would tie me down and maybe kill me. You know the dangers of having a baby. And what man would put up with a wife who travels as much as I do? No, Thread, I think I shall have to be a spinster."

His heart gave a sickening lurch, but he thrust the feeling aside, confident that he and Regina were fated for each other. *How difficult will it be?* he interrogated himself. But the Creator was silent. *It is up to me*, he thought. *To allow it to happen. To find my way in. To see the clues.*

She had a nibble. He watched as she jerked up sharply, setting the hook; then—with the pole bowing over—she reeled it in, the muscles in her arms taut, the whiplike length of her body in counterpart to the arching pole. A brook trout broke the water, thrashing on the end of the line to be free. She removed the fish from the hook, then strung it through its gills and placed it in the water, anchored by an overhanging branch while they caught more. She rebaited her hook. He hadn't had a nibble.

"You haven't been paying attention, Threadneedle. Two bits your bait has all been eaten away," she teased. "You are preoccupied. Here." She held her hand out, "Give it here." She took his pole, threaded a worm around the empty hook, and handed it back.

"Lunch?" she asked absentmindedly, sitting back down beside him, but not before glancing at the sack she had brought. Then, "What are you doing out here fishing, Thread? I knew exactly where I'd find you. Working something out? One of those conversations with Grandmother Marguerite?"

He grunted. That meant he would get to Grandmother Marguerite in his own time. "You seem changed, Regina," he said. "You got a bellyful there in Europe, didn't you?" Nothing escaped his notice; she felt always held in his regard.

"Is it that obvious, Thread?" she said with an uncharacteristic twist to her mouth. *How will I be when he is gone to war?* she wondered. *Will that invisible connection remain strung taut and responsive?* She couldn't bear to think about it. "I'm heading back, Thread . . . back to Cottage and Seneca Falls." She looked at him obliquely. "Back to my life. The Three gave me the key before I left," she said, calling their Duladier elders—Catherine, Elisabeth, and Grandmother Marguerite—by their code name. "Delphine and Blaise came to the Cévennes with me. Met our family there."

He looked at her sharply. "I heard. Did you bring back a copy of the Old Text?" Knowing that others also noticed Regina's extraordinary traits strengthened his regard for her. "But don't rush me along, Regina. I want to hear it all. I heard you spoke at the Congress. That they listened to you, and to Delphine when she spoke."

"Yes," she replied.

They grinned at each other.

"That was a triumph," he said. "And the Cévennes? Tell me. I . . . may never see that homeland," he said, as if realizing it for the first time.

She glanced at him. Were there tears in his voice? "I had to stay there for six weeks to make a copy. I liked it there." She looked at him significantly. "Our cousins are fierce people, honed by their century *au désert.*" She could see he wanted more and so she warmed to her subject. It occurred to her that no one else had asked her for details of her trip! The elders had been interested only in the Old Text.

"The Cévennes are so different from the south of France. Provence is warm and vibrant and open to the sun and sea." Her hand stretched out from the pole as she accented her words. "But the Cévennes are a fastness: Protestant, severe, houses built high on rocky cliffs. Caves, Thread. Caves where ancient people have painted their spirit animals on the walls, in red and black." She knew about spirit animals, the clans . . . Many of the things that her People had lost in their battles over Christian beliefs had been restored to her through Thread and his connections with his People, native to this continent. Now that she had been to the Cévennes and seen her European ancestors' pagan roots, she felt closer to what her Haudenosaunee family here felt for their traditions.

"Yes," he said, warming. He loved her voice, missed it when she was absent. "Did you meet someone there?" he asked, bracing himself for her response.

"I met many *someones*," she laughed and began drawing on her boots before hooking the buttons that closed them.

And then he had a bite. He reeled in another brookie, a big one, eight inches, unhooked it, slipped it onto their line, rebaited his hook, began whistling, and, after casting out, sat down beside her.

"Who chaperoned you there?"

She knew he was fishing, trying to find out if she had had a romance there, among their relations. She raised an eyebrow. "Does a lady need a chaperone among family?" She longed to say, *Why, did you miss me?* but didn't want to bait him. She was not going to set the hook for Thread. As close as they were, he frightened her with his intensity. *And I have my vows,* she thought to herself fiercely. *With good reason.* "Delphine and Blaise brought back huge orders from Europe. They had shipped samples of their cochineal ahead of them, as well as catalogs of Regina Coeli's spring and summer lines. Didn't you know?"

He raised his eyebrows. "I knew Mother was shipping out ten gross of Regina Coeli outfits every month, on average, but . . . I can't keep track of everything. Not even you could!" He gave Regina the fish eye and a jab in her ribs.

She laughed, sprang to her feet, and took flight, giggling, then looked back and saw he had gotten to his feet but wasn't following. She circled back. "I'm sorry, Thread. I forgot. Forgive me." She knelt on the ground in front of him, put her hands on either side of the moccasin made especially for his injured foot and, bending close, whispered, "I'm sorry, foot. I forgot you can't chase me anymore."

"Can't chase you, can't plant a field without a mule, can't work out with my cohort." He was furious now. "Like an old man. Only good to watch the children, keep the crows from the corn."

She burst into tears. "Thread . . . Thread . . . why?" she finally managed. She put her arms around his legs. "Why did she do it?"

He squeezed her upper arm, as if chastising her for being on the ground in front of him, and she took his hand as he levered her to her feet. He stood passively, his arms loose at his sides until she gained control of herself, then he handed her his handkerchief. *Why? Why can't you lift an arm to draw her into an embrace!* he challenged himself. *Are you a horse or a mule? It was your foot that was cut, not your balls!*

They sat down again on the bank, leaving their poles wedged in the rocks. They had lost their appetite for catching lunch.

Regina had control of both breath and voice, and yet tears kept plopping down on the moss. "How could a mother do that to her own child?" she said wonderingly. "I know I couldn't."

"She says she didn't want me to go to war. And I, Wolf Clan!" He paused to let her ponder on the significance of that. "Grandmother says it shows that Mother can't understand what it means to be an initiate in a warrior society. That it just goes to show that adoption into the clan and into the tribe misses important steps of transferring a lot of the inner tradition."

"Same with the silk," Regina said. Then: "Did she have to learn a lot to be adopted?"

"She brought a lot from the silk," he said. "But yes, she had to learn our customs, promise to raise me by my People's ways." He was aware that he was reciting for Regina the terms of her marriage to him, set by the clanmothers. *You will raise our children by the way of the tribe.* The world shimmered when he imagined his future with Regina.

She had to ask: "I have often wondered how your mother chose Lazarus."

"She never told me. I think it's something that women know." Silence fell.

"I still don't understand why your trip to Krefeld was canceled," Regina asked casually.

Just then, a fish tugged hard at Thread's pole, refusing to be ignored; he jumped to the distraction. When he had reeled in another brookie of the same size as his last one and put it on the stringer, he answered her question.

"Grandmother Marguerite lifted the terms of my engagement to a girl from the tribe," he said quietly.

He let her digest this for a while, feeling that he was leading her to draw the conclusions he hoped she would draw: his clanmothers were giving him permission to pursue her for a mate. She looked thoughtful, but he began to worry that their silence was becoming too long. Perhaps it was time for a gift—the gift of a secret. He wanted it to appear offhanded yet openhanded: "Kilian and I spoke in Dialog for the first time right here in Newtown last month."

"Everyone in the Montour family speaks and hears in Dialog?" Regina asked quietly.

"Yes," he said. "And everyone prays to the Mother."

"Then the two families are more alike than is apparent."

"Yes. And you, Regina? Do you have the silk in your blood?" His voice was husky.

How does he dare to ask such an intimate question? It's all through me when I make love to myself, she thought. *Is it so for all women?* She had no one to ask. She couldn't ask Thread; he was as much a virgin as she was. She'd know if he'd done it, wouldn't she? Instead she said, "The silk doesn't call me. I seem to draw on another tradition, a straight transmission from Regina the Elder: Loudmouth." She laughed.

"Before, you said . . . ," he ventured. "You wondered how my mother knew what? That Lazarus was the one?"

She didn't have to say yes. Her bent head, the flush on her cheeks, her dark lashes brushing down on them told him that, despite her shyness, this is what she had wanted to ask.

He would be gentle. This was the path the Mother was opening for him. He took a deep breath and entered. "Our families are more alike than we first realized. Among the Duladier, among the Montour, and just like the female silkmoth, the female chooses the male with whom she will mate."

"Has someone chosen you, Thread?" Her whispery voice sounded as though she were having trouble catching her breath.

She understands the terms Grandmother placed on me.

Thread noticed a stillness in the day. Had the day gone into stasis—no birds singing, no dragonflies whirring past, no crickets thrumming time— or were their ears and eyes simply buffered by the profound silence in their hearts? Everything waited.

A catfish broke the surface, struggling at the end of Regina's line, a bottom feeder. And yet Grandmother Marguerite savored her catfish. Regina reeled it in and put it with the others on the stringer.

He couldn't say why he dodged now, why he skirted the moment, let it pass. He cursed himself. *Am I a coward?* he asked in Dialog.

Then she started babbling, equally nervous, equally disarmed. "Do you know about Regina the Elder, Thread? I know almost nothing. Who was she really? I don't even have a miniature of her. Mother's described her. Father has told me about her. Killy will talk about her, if he's in the mood." When she reached the end of her inquiry, wild thoughts filling the space that had opened between them, the silence of the day and the place again took hold of them with a powerful grip.

They relaxed together into that silence for a long time, Regina thinking about how a family closes in around the loss of one of their young family members, in adults usually through childbirth or a mishap with machinery. In children, death came mostly through diseases.

Thread's heart grew heavier as he thought through why he could not seem to act in Regina's presence, even when the Mother had opened up a doorway. Perhaps he had only one path: to be a warrior, to lead men.

"And war . . . ," Regina was chattering on, her nerves firing. "War is certainly coming our way. In Europe everyone was talking about it. Here, the same."

There were a lot of things he might say to match her, but he found he couldn't. He was facing his own moment of truth.

"Mother says," Regina lowered her eyes, "that Kilian has been keeping company with Turtle Dawn."

"Did he tell her that?" Thread was startled. He didn't think his Duladier family indulged in that much candor.

"No. She said Grandmother Marguerite told her. Came over for tea with her and Father."

"Do you think they could be happy?" Thread asked, eyes firmly on the middle ground. "Kilian and Turtle Dawn?"

"How would I know?" she concluded.

"I thought you might have feelings of your own," he said, meaning more. He found he was breathing hard even though he hadn't moved. He and Regina had always made a fetish out of telling the truth, and yet this was the first time they were old enough to talk about his two mothers and their way of loving each other, against all norms.

She shied away. They were quiet again for a long time.

They are lovers, Thread thought, *as we must be lovers,* and burst out, "She is pregnant with Kilian's child."

Regina looked surprised. "How do you know that, Thread?"

"Kilian told me. And she is my mother; she raised me after Kristiana gave me life." *I know her smell. I know her body. That's how I know.* Then he said, "Why are adults so complicated! When life is so simple?"

Regina was looking at him, head cocked, curious.

"We work," he said. "We love." He shot a glance at her, her rosy cheek, her eyes so full of—what? "We die," he finished.

She leaned across the small space separating them then and pressed her lips to his cheek.

He felt her breath. *Regina.* He took up her hand, opening her palm to his gaze, and planted a kiss squarely in the middle of it, where he imagined an eye, the center of her feelings, resided. When he looked up, her eyes were slits and she was breathing through her mouth.

"Don't, Thread," she said huskily.

He knew enough about girls to know when that meant: "Yes—but only so far." He refused to forfeit her hand and—looking at her face—bent and kissed the pulse at her wrist.

A moan escaped her parted lips.

"Please, Regina. Please . . . let me . . . take down your hair. Let me see you . . ."

She seemed in a trance. He lifted out the pins he knew instinctively held the architecture of her hairstyle aloft, defying gravity, and, with a tumble and a cataract, her hair fell across her shoulders and down her back to the ground, curling around her heels and buttocks.

Thread sat back on his heels, studying her. Now he knew what he had been seeing in her eyes. He knew it because he could feel it in his eyes. Now he was certain of this one thing, with all of his young being: he could not rush this original spirit, his cradlemate, or she would flee. He recognized her as a colt of wild parentage, one who would never be tamed and yet one who could come to trust him. Him. *One man only. One woman only.* He was flooded with a jolt, with the chemistry of certainty. *Will she take me? Will she see it—our inevitability?* Would she, as his grandmother had put it succinctly, choose him for a mate? Because now he could clearly see the wisdom of his People's insistence that the women must choose. His entire body urged him to press, to force her to see. *Everything I am—the sum of my life—is at stake!* And as this wisdom deepened, another spiral of the shell flowed into place before it hardened around him. *This is how it has always been*, he assured himself, taming the spring freshet of his sexuality. *The female of the species sets the terms, the pace, the impulse.*

He would bind her. He saw that now. He would have to put a binding spell on her, to ensure that she would appreciate fully that he, and only he, was her timeless and eternal mate. He would begin with her feet, as she had begun with his, nine months ago when he was healing. He began unhooking the buttons on her boots with the spare tool he used to string fish through their gills.

Her eyes opened, alarmed. "What are you doing?"

"Hitch up your skirts and come wading with me, Regina. This may be the last chance we have to be kids again." She glanced at him sharply. "War is coming, Regina." He looked fully and deeply into her eyes. "That is another reason that Grandmother released me from the trip to Krefeld." He lowered his voice. "We are running out of time."

Regina's heart lurched to hear these words. *What if I don't see what is plain right in front of me? What if it is only later that I see what there is to see?* "Yes," her voice dragged as she pulled herself back from Thread's thought that they could be running out of time. *Time to do what?* "Yes, the war is all they talked about at the International Congress. The natural conflict between freeing slaves and pacifism, the inevitability of violence. Yet with half of the European world held in bondage, not much thought was given to women's rights! It did me such good to see those complacent men hear about your world, through Delphine. She set them on their ears!"

Through the minutes while she confessed her pleasure in this, the only pleasure she would admit to, he held her right foot, held the arch in his hand, the toes relaxed—wiggling!—in his palm. He stroked the ball of her foot like a prayer. Intoned the way he had been taught: through his body like a sounding board, silently, carefully, through his arm and into her foot. All this in an instant.

And then he released her. It's all the time he had. *Did it take?* he wondered, studying her closely, her flushed cheeks, the heat from her to him, her thudding heart, his.

"Yes!" she said, hitching her skirts up into her waistband, her eyes lit with the prospect of wading like kids again, like the kids they still were, looking for crayfish, splashing each other and laughing until one of them said "uncle." Picking blackberries in July, their lips and tongues and hands stained. Coming home with a string of fish for each household after frying one up in cornmeal, right here on the creek bank.

Who will I be when you come home from war? Who will you be? she asked in Dialog.

The familiar intimacy of Dialog made him ask himself if he could remember when the two of them had begun speaking in Dialog to each other. *Was there ever a beginning?* Or was this way of thinking thoughts aloud innate in them both, there even as they swung side by side in their cradleboards on a bough while their mothers worked nearby?

He leaned over and touched his lips to hers, briefly, breathing her breath into his, breathing it back into her mouth. *We will be who we are now,* he said in Dialog, drawing back, having staked his claim. Leaving her wanting more.

Now that she understood that he would not take any liberties without her permission, he knew he could set the pace. Let that kiss spread its wildfire over the next months, he intended, as the realization slowly dawns on her that her brother Kilian has impregnated Turtle Dawn. As the lessons of Europe bring home to her the refuge she will find in his matrilineal tribe, where women hold equal sway with men, where women are respected and honored. If he were careful and able to very slowly bind her to him, he realized he would only hear "yes" from her from now on. Let the creek, the fish, the wind spread his message to her while she was in Seneca Falls at the bleaching greens and in school, while he was working in Cottage. He would wait patiently for her to come to him, to ask.

Chapter Twelve

EATING SEED CORN

Summer Solstice 1861, Seneca Falls, New York

The girl was lithe as a dancer. As she lifted the length of saffron-colored linen, backlit by the afternoon sun, her hair—which was braided and also wet, as if she had just climbed out of the canal, an *ondine*—appeared to be the same color as the linen she was rinsing before pegging it out on the bleaching greens.

The braid swung over her shoulder, just as the length of linen swung in the air from her hand, her body bowing in counterpart to the force and smack of the wet linen. *An archer, angular. One of those warrior women from the Greek days,* he thought. The girl dipped the length of linen repeatedly in the cold bath, a formal stone structure with four arched sides that was still under construction. The muscles in her arms, her sleeves pushed up to work, her skin tawny from sun spoke to him. Between the swinging braid and the dripping length of linen, her blouse was wet in front, clinging to her breasts. He felt a stirring in his loins from the beauty of this tableau being staged for his solitary delectation.

And wasn't there something in her profile like a crescent moon, chin jutting, nose strong. There! In the crease between nostrils and cheek. Suddenly he was certain. It came upon him all at once. This girl had to be his blood relation. What was she doing here, in Delphine's dye works? He racked his brain: who could she be? Suddenly, this girl who had struck him

as desirable was worth twice as much as an easy conquest. If she proved to
be in his lineage? A treasure!

He walked quickly back across the bridge over the river to the factory,
leaving the bleaching greens behind.

He looked down in the river where the lengths of linens were pegged
down, snapping and pulling in the slight current as their colors cured. *They
are all beautiful,* he thought, giving them the names Blaise and Delphine
had given them: straw, squash, mulberry, indigo, rue. And then scarlet. He
beamed down at *his* creation, compliments of the cochineal beetle, the cloth
as intensely red as a sunset staining the river, king of colors. Fire in water.

With war on the horizon, orders were pouring in for the Zouave uniforms that had captured the imagination of the nation's youth: the fez that
made the wearer several inches taller, the red baggy pants and vest with
contrasting *passementerie* that harkened back to the time when the Zouaves
were a legendary force in North Africa, when "warrior" meant something.
He had heard them drilling; their calls of *"Zou! Zou! Zou! Zou!"* were
frightening. Delphine had jumped on this bandwagon, one of the first to
see the potential, and now, with war imminent, they couldn't keep up with
the orders and had fallen three months behind. *Unacceptable!* he thought,
even as he grudgingly admired what this woman's ability to anticipate the
future would mean in terms of sheer profits.

With Turtle Dawn's help, Delphine had designed a costume for women,
the *vivandières,* she called them, with a turban for the head, pants so wide
as to appear to be a skirt, and bandoliers rigged to carry skins of water
and wine, and maybe also drums. "This is from a tradition," she said in her
printed material, "where women were welcome warriors, and where the
defense and honor of a native People included women. After all, our backs
are strong from digging and gathering, carrying water to our crops on this
continent, the Three Sisters of corn, beans, and squash. This is from a tradition where women bring spirit to their men at all times, whether they are
victorious, bored stupid on watch, or wounded and dying."

"It is a woman's job to do these things," Delphine's text had concluded
stubbornly. "Who else will be there for men? When have they ever been

without us?" When Wilhelm finished reading these words, he was incredulous.

Delphine had published this pamphlet to be sent out with orders for Zouave uniforms, and soon enough, requests for *vivandière* costumes came in, first as a trickle, then a flood. Turtle Dawn's designs were a marvel, a concoction from pure fantasy. At the bottom of the brochure was their slogan: *A real woman belongs on the battlefield beside her man.*

Is it any wonder I prefer younger women to their elders? Wilhelm thought, turning over a comparison between Delphine and this girlish sprite he had seen on the bleaching grounds. "Who is she?" Wilhelm demanded, walking up to Blaise on the *manufacture* floor.

"Who?" Blaise put down his pen and notations.

"That girl!" Wilhelm said. "The one who looks like a Duladier."

Blaise looked around for Delphine and, catching her eye, motioned to her, jerking his head in the direction of their office.

She climbed down from the vat she was stirring, handed her paddle to the woman who worked with her, wiped her hands on her apron, and rewrapped her headscarf as she walked toward them.

God, she is a handsome woman! Wilhelm thought not for the first time. *I would have her if it weren't for the fact of our relatedness. And how,* he asked himself, *had a woman become his colleague in his* manufacture?

Wilhelm had few illusions about his age and attractiveness, and yet a few traits sustained him, at least in his own eyes. For one, his wealth gave him access to women who would have been beyond him at one time, as when he first came to this country as the Duladier *cultivateur* and Elisabeth Duladier's mate. For another, he satisfied women in a way that he could scarcely believe was as rare a trait among men as women gave him to believe. Once his wealth had endowed him with the boldness and access to approach any woman he desired, he found that she wanted him because of what he had in his fingers. Wilhelm put it this way: *I feel what is alive, and it rises to my hands.* He was muscular and had a member that never failed him. These things also helped mediate his age as he approached sixty.

Wilhelm had always had a divining rod for a woman's heat, a woman's smell. Wherever a woman blossomed with heat and that animal scent, he went. And where he went, she opened to him. Breathing into a woman's ears or touching the nape of her neck released a woman's stays surer than a kiss on the lips or fumbling at her breasts, both actions that were more likely to get you slapped and reproved. "Tongue in the ear every time," he told his cronies when they asked about his successes. "Tongue in the ear, butter in your hands."

Just that one failure: Catherine, his sister-in-law and former *maîtresse de la soie.* He didn't like to dwell on it—his grand and defining passion, frustrated. He often found himself going to it, like a tongue continually seeks out the space in the jaw where a rotten tooth had been pulled. She would be old now, more than fifty. How had she aged? He couldn't help but wonder.

This one would fight me, he thought as Delphine approached, moving like an animal, all the color in her face. *Rosy brown nipples,* he guessed, admiring her bronze skin, even with that flaxen hair. *Knees to drive a man wild,* he thought as she thrust out her hand, *à la mode* for businessmen, and said, "Wilhelm Shafer. Good to see you again."

She glanced around, at packing crates being wrenched open with crowbars, at heavy machinery emerging, apparently seeing them for the first time. What were they doing here? It all seemed to have arrived with Wilhelm. "May I ask? What is all this?" She indicated the floor that was slowly filling with crates in various stages of disassembly.

Strange . . . She did not call me "Herr Shafer." Familiar. Brazen, even. Wilhelm followed Blaise and Delphine and stepped into the office of the dye works, but not before he caught the look that passed between Blaise and his woman. *Still just affianced, even though they have several children together,* he thought. He remembered the children who had run in a pack at Marguerite's, several of them towheaded. Turtle Dawn had been Delphine's first child, born to her before she met Blaise, by a father she never named.

Do not forget who she is, he reminded himself. "These women, if it can be believed," he had told his cronies, "have the effrontery to claim their children as their own. And more! It's always *their* houses, *their* entitlements, *their* clan. Their name!" He was still, more than twenty years later, nonplussed by the matrilineal system of "these natives."

That had not been the way of things down south in Mexico, where he had fled the wrath of his family. "None of that nonsense," he had told his cronies, "with the woman I married deep in Mexico." In the years after he'd left Newtown, he'd learned that beating a woman—he'd never dared lay a hand on Elisabeth—kept her pliant, obedient, willing even. "Shows her who's boss," he'd said, often miming his dominance for his drunken companions by pulling up his pants, putting his braces back on his shoulders, tucking in his cock. It always got a laugh.

When the door closed, Wilhelm didn't take the chair Blaise offered. "Let's not play games, Lazar. Who is she?"

The glance Blaise and Delphine exchanged told him Delphine would handle it.

"Who?" she asked.

Don't even try to bully this woman, instinct told him.

"Delphine, there's a Duladier woman working your bleaching greens." *Blood calls to blood.* He used Dialog, loving how their eyes widened when he did it.

"It's Regina, Catherine's daughter, conceived the day you left Newtown."

Now it was Wilhelm's turn to be surprised. "From the Spinning?" he asked.

Delphine shrugged her shoulders. She had never had anything to do with the silk.

"From Catherine and Philip?"

"Who else?" Delphine said.

"They named her after that troublemaker," he said as if to himself.

"Regina Miller died of cholera. Just before the first *volte* of worms began to spin. You know that," Blaise said.

"Died. Yes, I was there for the funeral." Wilhelm digested this fact. *So*

Catherine named her daughter after Regina, that redheaded bitch she'd cuck-
olded Philip with.

"Regina's in school nearby," Delphine picked up the story. She comes
down to help out. She doesn't want to go home. It's too far, she says. She
and her mother—well . . ."

"Introduce us."

Delphine hesitated, flicked her eyes to Blaise, who had placed himself
behind Wilhelm's right shoulder. He shrugged as if to say, What can we do?

"I am her uncle!" Wilhelm asserted.

"All right," Blaise said. "When the lunch whistle blows."

Blaise took over now, walking into Wilhelm's line of vision, sitting down,
gesturing him to a chair. He himself took one of the chairs at the desk while
Delphine continued to pace. "With the cotton embargo, linen's going to
keep coming on strong. Tell us where the stoppages are in your system.
We're—," his eyes cut to his papers, "—six weeks behind schedule, shipping." He checked something off on his top page. "Give me something to tell
our customers. We're bringing our bleaching greens here, beside the canal.
But that goes to *next* summer's line. Delphine and Turtle Dawn have crafted
a canny blend in their *vivandière* costume: wool underclothes for winter,
wool waistcoat over all. Wool stockings for winter and linen for summer:
check. Linen skirt and blouse, linen waistcoat for summer." Check, check,
check. He gestured at the window where a wan but fierce autumn sun
slanted sideways onto the boards of the dyeing office floor. "This season."
Check. He looked up. "Give me something to tell them. Where is the linen
we need to dye, and that you need to cut and sew?"

Wilhelm gestured to the floor, down to the *manufacture*—his *manufacture* as of that morning, although Blaise and Delphine didn't know that
yet. "I've got it in hand," he said. "Uncrating it now. It's the newest thing:
a dobby loom. It will allow us to crank up production to meet and exceed
your demand."

"How long will it take to set up the warp?"

Wilhelm grinned, a nasty grin. "It could be as much as a month."

Delphine sucked in her breath.

"But . . ." He was drawing it out, enjoying their discomfort. "Look," he said, clasping his hands on his lap, then throwing them open. "I am no longer a tenant like you. I bought this building this morning. I am installing a coal-gas lighting system as well, to give us light twenty-four hours a day if we want it. I am ready to put another dozen seamstresses to work on their treadles. You'll have all the yardage you want in a fortnight. Just give me Threadneedle to throw warp—my grandson—," he added pointedly, "and we will be on schedule again."

Blaise and Delphine glanced at each other and then she spoke. "That will be fine. Blaise will let our customers know. And we will see what we can do about Threadneedle."

They didn't dare speak in Dialog, as it seemed to them that Wilhelm might hear them there. But they had been a couple long enough to know what the other was thinking: *Did the man know that Thread's trip to Krefeld had been canceled?*

Wilhelm walked to the window and looked out, his back to them. "Linen won't last," he said. "We need to get Turtle Dawn to design these Zouave costumes differently, eliminating the linen."

"What makes you think linen won't last?" Delphine asked.

"Cotton is easy to work. A guaranteed crop. You don't have this damnable seven-year rotation. It's cheap. And the cloth is easy to print." He shrugged, anticipating what he saw would be their next point: "Cotton doesn't hold up as long, true. All that means is folks will buy it more often." They were shaking their heads in disbelief; he changed his tack. "It takes too long to produce linen: two seasons from flaxseed to harvest, to processing, spinning, weaving, and bleaching, cutting and sewing yard goods. Besides, back at the beginning of this century, when Jefferson threatened a cotton embargo, England got their cotton from Egypt and India. The price of cotton stabilized. That's happening again now . . . if to a lesser extent. Natives restless in Egypt and India." He slowly rolled up the cuffs of his handmade shirt, surely shipped from the capital of one of those far-off countries. He pocketed his expensive cufflinks as if they were nothing.

"All right," said Blaise, after a long digestive pause. "Let's say this linen boom won't last. As soon as the war and the cotton embargo are over—phut! Back to specialty uses, a smaller share of the total yard-goods market." His implication was clear: *What's wrong with that?*

"Right," Wilhelm picked up the thread of Blaise's argument. "So I say let's hit it hard while the cotton embargo's on."

"How?" Delphine asked.

"Don't rotate. Use the cotton model—Lowell—with everything under one roof."

"But—"

"The soil will become impoverished? It'll recover, with time. Let's make hay while the sun shines, eh? I've bought up whole stretches of mucklands. Laying tiles like Kristi did. There by the Montezuma swamp. We're already building our first scutching mill. I've been letting out piecework to process the flax I've been growing. No more of that, I say! Bring it all under one roof. Mechanize. Steam engines. We'll get a half-dozen years out of those fields before they're exhausted. No rotation. All flax."

Blaise and Delphine considered him.

Delphine said, "Eating our seed corn."

Wilhelm stood. "Who cares? There's more where that came from. They're wastelands now. Lay tile, take our profit from them, leave them wastelands again. Sell them cheap . . . to farmers who don't mind the slow and steady. We'll walk away rich."

"My mother won't like it," Delphine put in.

"Marguerite? She's two days away at best. F'r crissake, she's older than me. Has she ever been up here?"

"She comes up to Onondaga," she said, then folded her arms across her chest. She wouldn't tell him that Marguerite was a highly respected and influential clanmother. This man wouldn't care. An elder woman was an old woman in his pantheon, at the bottom of the pile of valuable things, washed up, useless. Delphine knew; she had heard everything this man believed, many times over.

Blaise took the lead. "We'll dye all the linen goods you produce. But you're on your own raising muckland flax without rotation."

"They are saying the same thing with my coal gasification plant. Straight from London. I'll work three shifts with gaslight in my *manufacture*."

"You'll work young women blind," Delphine murmured.

"Keep them out of trouble," he asserted.

He would have liked to step up to her, take her muscled upper arm in his hand, feel the soft side of her breast pressing, and say, *I'll fuck you blind*.

He put up his hands, palms out. "All right. I'll do it myself. We will get your Zouave orders filled. And you'll get all the dyeing work. So make sure you have the quantities of raw material you'll need. You'll buy all your cochineal from me." They were to learn that this was a Wilhelm joke: he controlled all the cochineal trade from Mexico, both east and west of the Mississippi.

They heard a light step across the *manufacture* floor, a tap at the door.

"Come in."

The girl peeked around the door.

Glorious. She is glorious, he exulted to himself. Pale reddish-blonde hair just like her namesake. Like some rare metal from another planet. Probably freckled from head to toe.

"Sorry—you have company," Regina said, polite but obviously curious.

"No, we were just going to break for lunch and come and get you to join us," Blaise said.

"Herr Shafer has been subcontracting our linen and wool production on the floor below. May I tell her?" Delphine asked Wilhelm, who nodded. "He has just bought this building and thus is also our landlord. Regina, may I present Wilhelm Shafer, your uncle."

Chapter Thirteen

A FOUNTAIN
OF RADIANT LIGHT

August 1, 1861, Seneca Falls, New York

He tried every way he could think of to corrupt her without tipping his hand. She didn't need money; didn't care for it. She had apparently—through soul transference or simple aping—sucked in her namesake's values, even though the eponymous Regina had been dead nine months when this child was born.

Some things are beyond explaining.

She let this man—her uncle—know right away that she knew who he was, why the family had thrust him out. A traitor.

He knew better than to argue, thought that the girl's differences with her mother would lead her to question what had really happened, maybe enough to let him in. After all, Catherine had lost her position as *maîtresse* in a judgment brought down on her from outsiders, their investor group in Trenton.

"Perhaps I was only speaking the truth when I criticized your mother's choices," he suggested softly when the moment presented itself, opening his hands to suggest that the jury was still out. "They removed her from her position. Oh, but—all this? Before you were born. Ancient history." He waved his hands. He could see she had decided to make up her own mind about her uncle.

He also soon discovered that Regina had a special feeling for his grandson

Threadneedle. He thought perhaps he might get to Thread through this girl, who was blasting away her youth, her beauty, her sexual fire on this haranguing need for some women to occupy the positions that were traditionally reserved for men, who were accustomed to doing as they pleased.

He knew better than to say anything, instead attempting to influence her by his actions. He put her coach and canal fares on his bill, which she took graciously as her due. Then he deposited a small monthly allowance directly in her account, which she alluded to obliquely rather than thanking him directly, asking him how he thought she had earned this allowance. *Ah, she is too refined to mention money*, he thought.

"You are my niece," he said, with a Gallic shrug that implied that it was nothing. "And I am proud of the work that you do here in Seneca Falls, both for Delphine and for your fair sex." He bowed his head; she took the hook.

Soon enough, this trap he had baited for Thread was ready to spring. The day came when Thread appeared on the *manufacture* floor, looking around with astonishment: one hundred sewing machines, bales of half-completed clothing, scores of pressers, folders, shippers. And one floor down, the latest dobby looms, two—working on steam—twenty-four hours a day. A coal gasification plant provided light during the night shift. A steam engine provided heat all winter long. One floor up, Thread's aunt and uncle's dyeing operation worked at full capacity.

"Does Mother know about this?" Thread asked, unable to hide how impressed he was with his grandfather's grasp of the future.

"Kristiana? You tell me . . . Does she know?" Wilhelm treated Thread to one of his wolfish smiles. "No, why should she? She turned my business proposal down.

"Mother won't like it."

"Won't she? This is reality." He put his arm around the younger man's shoulder loosely. "Where did you get that limp, lad?"

Thread didn't answer. If his grandfather didn't know, he wasn't going to tell him. He didn't need this man's sympathy.

"Have you ever thrown warp on a dobby loom?" Wilhelm asked. "No? Would you like to see it?"

Looking out the expansive windows as they passed from the office into the production room, Thread could see fields of blue flowers, a crazy quilt of blue out to the horizon. Coming up the canal, the same—blue fields of flax everywhere. "How are you doing it?"

"Chemistry. Lime, phosphate, potash. Then urea, ammonia. Nitrates."

"Mother—," he covered up his gaffe with a cough, "—Kristiana knows you are competing with us. Philip says you have made a formal merger offer." He ducked his head, not knowing how much this man, his grandfather, knew about what had occurred between him and his mother. "Do you talk to Kristiana?"

"We write back and forth," Wilhelm said. "Mostly argue. Why? Do you talk to her?" Wilhelm studied his grandson's uneasy laugh, the way he threw out his hands as if to say, "Of course we do!" *Something's not right there.* "Way down deep, Kristiana knows how big I am. I told her what I am doing. This is the future. I'll just keeping it growing and working until she arrives. ¿*Comprende?*"

Thread thought he was successful in hiding his feelings, one benefit of his training with the tribe.

Wilhelm felt his heart swell with pride. Threadneedle was the son he'd never had, come to him when he was old enough to be a grandfather to this adult man. He bit his lip to keep from saying the trite phrases that came to mind: *All this could be yours, lad . . . Just say the word.* No, he had to be far subtler than that. "Let's go find Regina. She's been in meetings all morning. I've reserved us a table for lunch at the City Club."

"I'm not hungry," Thread said. "Although I would like to see Regina."

"She's expecting us," Wilhelm said firmly. "If you're not hungry, don't eat. Sit with us." *Now if the rat would please step this way . . .*

It was the oldest trick in the book. Wilhelm had not only been supporting Regina but had been earmarking funds—significant funds—for the women's movement. They wanted a series of meetings with the Haudenosaunee clan mothers? Regina would arrange it through Delphine, and Wilhelm would finance it, surreptitiously, through his charities, which were fronted by his brethren in the Quaker church. It was all done anonymously and was therefore beyond reproach. Yet he was letting Regina bring in the funds, and everyone in her organization knew who was behind the largesse.

And now she owes me, he told himself with satisfaction. He only needed to see her face when he walked through the door with Thread. He wanted to feel Thread beside him, feel the vernal rush of him toward her. And through them, he could recall a time when . . .

Pulling himself together, he took a menu from the waiter, thrilled to be across from these two young people, to revel in the feelings passing around the table, hardening him beneath his napkin. They didn't care, these two. They only wanted to sit within the penumbra of each other. He was free to give in to his erotic memories while going through the motions of being a good host.

He had financed and started this exclusive club; the staff knew what he wanted before he had to ask, and as they served him he let his sensations wander into the magnetic force of these two young people's attraction to each other, let it bring his own erotic memories to the surface, like carp go to the surface to feed around the water lilies that bloom there.

Staying present in the company of these two young people who yearned for each other would warm his old bones many years from now, when he was in a rocker on a porch.

I've always said this about myself: I made a great cultivateur *because I could feel life stir, and make it respond.*

Now with their food in front of them, he asked himself, *Do they know the other knows? Are they playing around with each other, still pretending they don't want each other? Because they sure as hell aren't doing it.* What they had was a different kind of fever, dry versus wet.

He wanted to talk to his grandson alone. "Can we walk you somewhere after lunch, Regina?" he asked, although not surprised when she said she'd stay, thank you, if it was all right with both men. Thread had asked her to; he could see that.

"When are you two going to get hitched?" he asked bluntly.

"We aren't," Regina said. "I have my work. It's more important to me than having children."

He saw it in a flash: she was afraid. Afraid of dying in childbirth. *Funny*, he said to himself. *I can remember her father Philip suffering from the same fear before Lischen was born. Live or die? Cast of the dice. But then I'm not a woman.*

"You'll forgive me speaking bluntly. I'm your uncle," he said to Regina, "and your grandfather, Thread. If I can't speak, who can? I'm on your maternal side, after all." *I can use the clan stuff as well as any redskin*, he thought.

"Speak," she said.

"You don't need to stay celibate because you don't want children. Ask any of his native relations: Delphine, Turtle Dawn. Heck, ask Marguerite. They'll give you one of the preparations they use to prevent conception. Each of those women chooses when they're going to have a baby. Haven't you noticed, Regina?"

She looked at him directly. "I don't want to be rude, Uncle Wilhelm. But this is none of your business."

Thread looked startled, and Wilhelm noticed. *So this is news to him? And she's already protecting herself.* Even so, he was still sure they had not yet taken each other as mates.

"Do you want each other?" he directed this question to Thread.

Thread looked at Regina. He took a deep breath. "Do you want me, Regina? Among our people, you have to choose me. I've been waiting for you to speak." He modestly dropped his eyes, though his shoulders were lifted against the potential rebuff.

"Thread," she said—only his name and a golden shower fell over all three of them, a fountain of radiant light.

Falling on me as well, Wilhelm thought with amazement. *An unworthy recipient, a base fornicator. On me as well. It's the real article: love.*

"You have to say the words," Thread whispered, Wilhelm as unlikely witness to this intimate exchange.

I midwifed this, Wilhelm thought, ablaze with gratitude.

"I choose you, Thread." She looked up, face transfigured.

Thread looked up now too, eyes leaping to hers. Their hands met across the damask tablecloth.

Madonne Noire, Wilhelm breathed and wished he could disappear.

"Who else would I choose?" she laughed, spilling her tears, then licking at them through her smile.

There was only one thing Wilhelm could do. He walked to the kitchen door and opened it. "Champagne!" he called. It stood ready and chilling in a bucket, poised for a different celebration, the one Thread might have thought Wilhelm was engineering: stealing Thread from Kristi, taking her only son to run his looms, both personal reward and comeuppance for his daughter after all those chilly rebuffs to his overtures.

His thoughts drifted back to all the ways he had been wronged. He had been shunned for decades. He had lost his family and everything he owned. Kristi refused to modernize and mechanize, and why else but to spite him? He broke out in a spontaneous malarial sweat when he remembered how she had backed him out of her house! The pack of them in that idiot village of theirs, imagining they could stand in the face of the onslaught of progress, of modernity. *The guilds?* he liked to say. *They're history!*

Instead of acting as the agent of his daughter's ruin, he told himself, he was merely acting as an agent of destiny. And here that same destiny—one he thought had booted him out—he was now including him in a nuptial mystery he knew he didn't deserve.

His training didn't desert him now. He spoke in Dialog, for everyone to note. Hannah was dead, and he still had his balls! *Thank you, Madonne Noire,* he said, and noted how Thread's eyes widened in surprise, while Regina didn't seem to notice, two isolated yet fascinating facts. *He speaks there; she doesn't? Is it possible this girl has none of the silk in her?*

He arranged for a small, private Quaker ceremony after the banns had been published. He witnessed their marriage, along with Delphine and Philip. He put them up at Seneca Falls' best and most discreet hotel.

Later that week, they lay together under the canopy of the bridal suite.

"Are you sure you are safe?" Threadneedle asked.

"Delphine assured me—it's what they do, what they've done for millennia. Please, please, please, please . . . ," Regina winced away from too much sensation, "don't touch me there." He pulled away and she grabbed his hand. "Oh, do, do, do, do! Oh my darling. Touch me there. But softly." She laughed and cried and it caused the muscles in her vagina to tighten where Thread had his finger.

He eased her open. She had already given it to him, there, a tidal wave that she surrendered herself to, and it had not been easy for her to let go, no, but finally she had been swept away in a tsunami of ecstasy. He watched her face every moment, felt the great convulsions grab his finger. He wanted to feel that convulsing on his member again. He rose up until his body was above hers.

"My grandfather and his wife," he said, "your Aunt Elisabeth . . ."

"Yes, yes," she gasped.

The head of his penis was just inside her inner lips.

"They practiced a special ritual, only once a month." He was speaking now to delay, to control what was inevitable. "But I'm too hard for that, my queen." He hesitated. "I don't want to hurt you."

She grabbed his hips and plunged him home.

Chapter Fourteen

COMPLACENCY
A TREACHERY

September 22, 1861, Cottage, New York

"When are you leaving?" Philip asked his son.

Kilian was rummaging through his things, organizing as he packed, a separate duffel for his frontier medicine kits.

"Can you sit for a minute?" Philip asked.

Kilian might as well have been alone for all the attention he was paying. "Hmmm?" His eyebrows raised in an expression of irritation at the interruption. "What is it, Papa?" He noted Philip's insistent look and wondered if this was the moment for a little father-son speech. Instead, Philip surprised him.

"Is there anything you would like me to take care of while you are gone?" He let a moment pass and then suggested, "Perhaps Nesting Swan?"

Kilian flushed, now openly irritated with the interruption of the packing that took all of his concentration. "Father, I presume you will look after Swan's interests. Do I have to ask?" He heaved the duffel with the medicine wallets in it from the table onto the floor near the door. "Actually, if I don't return," he waved away his father's objections, "I do need to ask you this: If I don't return, everything of mine goes to Turtle Dawn—my shares of Regina Coeli, this house, the Duladier Medicine business." Without waiting for an answer, he turned to continue packing.

"There's something more," came Philip's response.

"What?" Kilian turned.

"Can't you sit, son?"

"Why do I have to sit, Papa? Can't you talk while I work? I only have a week to settle everything, and I can't say how long I will be gone."

"It's about your Uncle Wilhelm."

"What about him? He's been our competitor, and now we are subcontracting to him. Can we trust him? No."

"There's more. Twenty years ago . . ."

"He betrayed mother to the investors. He was shunned. I know this. Surely you aren't bringing this up again, against Wilhelm. It doesn't matter anymore, Father!"

"I need you to tell this story to Thread. If you will listen. Please."

"What?" The intimation that this was a story Kilian had never heard, that his father was counting on him to transmit it to Thread, frightened and sobered Kilian. "What happened?"

Philip had thought many times over the intervening years about how this story could be told to the family's sons and grandsons. "Regina—Regina the Elder—was violated by two men who came looking for your mother. Men from your mother's past in France. Men who wanted to hurt her." He looked down. "Regina died. And her daughter, your cousin, as well."

I know this already, Kilian thought. *Why is he telling me this?*

A silence stretched. The fire snapped in the hearth. Kilian knew that if he went outside he would see Aldebaran in Taurus rising. "What are you trying to say, Father?"

"Wilhelm led the men to your mother. He was in the room as one of them prepared to violate her. She was tied to the bed when Marguerite and Lazarus rescued her. They subdued the man and surprised Wilhelm, who was nearby and tried to deny his complicity. I'm sorry, son. You have to know who this man is who has shown up here twenty years later. You have to know the treachery he is capable of."

"Why didn't you tell me this before?"

"We thought it enough that you knew he had betrayed us to our investors. Enough to know he was shunned." Philip heard how weak his defense sounded and hung his head.

"You know the Montours would never do this! Keep essential information like this from their male children!" Kilian banged his hand on the table and stood.

"Your mother didn't want you to know."

"Didn't want me to know?! Know what, *Father?*" He let his emphasis hang in the air, but he didn't have the guts to reveal to Philip what Catherine had told him about his parentage. "And now you want me to tell Thread?!" Something collapsed inside him. "We are not the Montours. You have the nerve to tell me now—two decades later—that Wilhelm was involved in the attempted rape of my mother and the death of Regina the Elder? And where are these men? Are they still alive?" Now he was seeing how a person could kill another to protect his family. He was taken aback by his first taste of vengeance.

"The one who raped her carried cholera. He died."

Kilian put his face in his hands. *Was this one my father?* "Do you hear what you are saying?!" His voice was rising. "It's wrong, Philip." Philip was shocked to hear his son call him by his first name outside of a business setting. "It's wrong that the women keep these secrets of their abuse from their sons. Among the Montours, a violent crime against a woman is punishable by death."

"The Montours took their vengeance on the man who tied up your mother."

"How?"

"They . . ." Philip couldn't say it. Their relationship had never been so candid. "They cut him."

"Cut him?"

"So he will never have children."

"Oh. They gelded him?" *Perhaps this was the man who was my father,* he thought. *What contagion am I carrying? Could anything rise up from me, unbidden?*

"Yes. And now the Pinkertons are after Lazarus for the death of this man."

"You are telling me that we allowed the Montours to exact punishment on this man who killed Regina and were going to rape my mother? Your wife?" Kilian's voice dripped with irony. "And now the state seeks to punish Lazarus for exacting justice against the man who would have raped my mother?"

Philip rose, his face stiff. "I'm sorry, Kilian. In fact, I'm ashamed. You can't imagine how many times I have thought it through. We should have told you before now, but your mother . . ." He tried again. "It was our first season; she had only been in this country a couple of years. We were just getting to know the Montours. Shunning . . . was the worst thing we could imagine to punish the man you call uncle." Then he seemed to be speaking to himself. ". . . as for ourselves?" He shook his head.

"And this is why Mother is such a wasted person," Kilian said, as if to himself. "If only I could have known the whole story . . ."

"What would have been different?" Philip asked. "Ask yourself, as I have asked myself many times: What would you have changed if you had known?"

"How can I say, Papa?" Kilian spread the fingers wide on each of his hands, which had been hanging at his side, a sudden expression of frustration that was not lost on Philip. "Certainly I would never have welcomed this man back. How could you tolerate seeing him in my home that first time he visited? He was party to a nefarious plot that killed Regina and might as well have killed Mother." He finished lamely, in an affectless tone, facing down Philip's incredulous stare: "She might as well be dead for all the interest she shows in her grandchild. In me. In you." *When did her soul become lost?* he wondered. *How can a young person's life be ruined at eighteen?*

"Well, prepare yourself, son, because your mother is on her way up here to try to convince you not to enlist."

"I'm only going to enlist if I can get myself out of here in time! Thread and all his Wolf brothers from Cattaraugus are leaving in a week. With any luck, Mother and I will pass on the road, unseen and unnoticed by the other."

"I'll miss you, son. You and Thread are irreplaceable here." They clasped each other close. Philip's eyes were wet. "Come home safe and bring Thread home too."

Kilian's voice was thick. He had to know, and he might never have another opportunity. "These men from my mother's past . . . Do you know? One of them was my father." He seemed to have trouble swallowing. "My actual father. Please don't tell me again that fiction that my father was her first husband."

Philip cleared his throat. "I don't know. You would have to ask your mother."

"I did ask her. And it never occurred to *you* to ask her?" He just couldn't tell Philip, this man who had been everything any boy would want for a father, that his mother had told him she "didn't know which one."

"What happened there in Grasse?" he ventured.

"There were rumors."

"What rumors? She was eighteen years old!" Then: "I have a right to know who my father is!" *I hope when my time comes, I prove to be more of a man than you,* Kilian said in Dialog, stunning this man who had been his father since he was nine, and also his business partner and friend. And then his thoughts redounded on him: My time has come. I am a father. And I am as helpless as Philip to be recognized properly.

Philip thought, *Dialog is never to be used in anger or to reprove. Is it possible that when Duladier men had been taught to communicate in Dialog they hadn't been told the codes of conduct?* Philip felt a jolt of guilt as he realized in that moment that it might have been *his* responsibility to teach his stepson.

Kilian snorted with disgust and, turning away, made a great show of stuffing clothes willy-nilly into his rucksack.

"You have to understand the interruption that was caused by whole families emigrating from their homelands. I didn't experience it because my family has been here for generations, but I saw it happen with others.

Word trickled through the Trenton community that Catherine . . . your mother . . ." He groped for time to think what to say, what not to say. "They said she had tricked her first husband into thinking that . . . you . . ." He trailed off. Neither stepson nor stepfather had the balls to say what had to be said.

Kilian put his head in his hands again. His shoulders shook. Philip approached his back, stretched out his hand to touch his son, but then withdrew that hand as Kilian shook his head violently. "Don't touch me. Don't speak to me. Please leave, now."

Philip slipped out the door, closing it quietly behind him, devastated at how time had brought this revelation before them, had duped the men of their family into complacency, amounting to a kind of treachery, what must have seemed like a small thing decades earlier, when this was all women's business.

He heard Kilian roar behind him in the empty house: "How could you have pretended all this wasn't happening?" Then Philip heard the young man almost croon: "How could you have let it go on for so long?"

Chapter Fifteen

WHOSE PEOPLE?

October 31, 1861, Cottage, New York

"May I come in?"

"The baby is sleeping."

"I'll be quiet."

"She sleeps through anything. We can speak normally."

"Dawn."

"Kilian."

"I've missed you."

"You've seen me."

"That's not what I mean." He looked around like he might take his cue from the wings. "I like the way you've fixed your cottage. Do you like your stove?" He was circling, circling. He riffled through piles of papers on the table, as if he were in his own home.

"What are these? Oh! You've been designing a new line."

"Yes."

"With the war, do you think they'll be made?"

"Kristiana has promised me a percent of this year's linen."

"Really? I thought we had subcontracted with Wilhelm for all our linen. For the war effort . . ."

"Wilhelm will not notice. Maeve will make sure."

"Do you mind if I look at them?"

The first page showed a woman's outfit with a military air, based loosely on the *vivandière* costume they had made so popular. Turtle Dawn had sketched two hats, one a jaunty kepi with a saucy thrust of feathers on the side, the other a fez with a tassel. The jacket had some shoulder detailing with epaulettes.

"Is this buckskin?" Kilian asked, pointing to the bandolier bag.

"Yes."

Kilian's slow smile spread. "And a pleated skirt?" he noticed.

"For riding a horse," she explained. "Based on Argentinian gauchos." She loved this Kilian, equal parts surprise and delight on his face, the discovery unfolding in his eyebrows, the corners of his mouth.

He put the first page aside to see the second. He was learning the language, and indeed he'd had to, for the buyers. He had learned things like how to refer to the "hand" of the cloth. On this second page the "fashion detailing" was all *métis*: buckskin leggings, felted boots, silver conchos, a blanket skirt, a sash, a head wrap *à la* Delphine. "You're robbing your mother for ideas?"

She made an expression that set off that roguish grin of hers. "When a daughter adopts her mother's style, it isn't called 'robbing.'" She reached across the table for his fingers, caressed them. She never took her eyes from his.

With the same deliberation, she then took his index finger in her mouth and he moved around the table to slowly lift her skirt to her knees. Reclaiming his lubricated finger, he placed it where he knew he could do the most harm to her detachment from him since Swan's birth.

She groaned, the sound wrenched from the shifting plates deep inside her. She squeezed and released his finger, an invitation.

His throat was dry, and his heart pounded like it held a caged wild creature. It wan an invitation to an hour's pleasure on an October afternoon. "Come," he said.

And she did—first on his finger, then on his mouth, and finally around the whole of him, embedded in her, hips to hips, belly to belly, her breasts arching away from him toward the ceiling. He ran his hands over her as if she were a manuscript of rolled vellum. She was in control, pinning him to his chair, dancing on him with a beat that only she could hear, that only he could feel, temple drums, restrained—convulse, relax, convulse, relax.

Only much later, when they heard Swan whimper and then call out, did they come to consciousness and realize they were still joined, sticky between them, and could have started again if the baby were not awake. They smiled at each other. At least they were saying goodbye at a time when they could not get enough of each other.

Kilian was the first to get up, striding to Swan, swinging her in the air to make her shriek with delight. "How's my girl?" he said to her, then clasped her close. "How's Daddy's baby?" he crooned, moving in a dance step.

Dawn was looking at him through slit eyes, arms behind her head. "Bring her here," she said and threw the covers open for both of them. "Here, Baby," she said, giving Swan her nipple.

Kilian moved in behind, spooning his lover, pulling faces over her shoulder at the baby to make her laugh, but Swan was focused, down to business, letting her father know after the first milk-bubbly smile that she was about the serious task of nursing her mother's breasts dry.

From the back, Kilian opened Turtle Dawn with the fingers of one hand, and she arched toward him as he guided the top of his glans in. And then he stayed there, not moving, both of them throbbing until he could hold back no more and she surrendered to the ecstasy of both nursing and penetration.

"Dawn?"

"Ummm?"

"If I don't come back . . ."

"Shush." The baby was sleeping again.

She rolled over to face him, put her finger on his lips. "Don't, Kilian, please."

"Dawn. We have to talk. I've given a letter to my father, and if I don't come back to you, it leaves everything that's mine—my share of Regina Coeli, my house and grounds, Duladier Medicine—to you and Swan."

She was laughing and crying at the same time. "Thank you, Kilian. And what if you come back and don't want us anymore? If you marry a white woman while you're away?" she teased.

"Turtle Dawn," he said reprovingly. "I know you don't need anyone to take care of you. But if you did, I would want it to be me. Dead or alive, know this: We are joined for the rest of our lives. We are joined."

She nodded solemnly. "We are joined."

"Would you marry me?"

She smiled. Shook her head. *No.* "But thank you for asking." She hastened to add, "If I married anyone, it would be you." She didn't have to say the words he knew she was thinking: *But what would I gain?* As one of the two founders of Regina Coeli, her share of the business was already greater than his. She had her own house.

"Swan would have a father," he said.

"She has a father."

"You don't care what people say?"

"Whose People?"

Part Three

1862

Chapter Sixteen

UNRAVELING

April 1, 1862, Somewhere outside of Richmond, Virginia

Delphine sat down with a cup of real coffee and a stack of newspapers and letters that Blaise had brought back from his latest trip to resupply their sutler tent. First, the coffee. It had been so long since she had tasted and smelled the real thing! For months they had had nothing but brewed chicory, which they had dug last fall, back home, where it bloomed magnificently in July, its bright flowers echoing the rare blue of the flax. They had boiled and reboiled their original stash of coffee with some chicory mixed in, but eventually there was nothing left to taste or smell but the bitter chicory. With Blaise's return to camp, she now had newspapers and real coffee again. He had ridden in on horseback and made the delivery of personal comforts along with bags of cornmeal packed into his saddlebags and loaded onto their donkey.

He kissed her and felt her buttocks, making the heat rise in her. He told her their wagon had a broken wheel. It was being fixed twenty miles out, still loaded with supplies, and he would have to return on horseback to bring it back in. But first . . . Delphine had moaned as he bit her neck. Retiring to their tent, they had wrestled on the floor like two men, the sound of the army marching out for maneuvers enough to muffle her growls and cries. Delphine had tapped into a deeper eroticism now that she was nearly past her monthly bleeding, and Blaise responded powerfully to this new sexuality.

Now Blaise was preparing to ride out again. "Back before night," he said, still puttering around.

She sighed and flipped open the oldest issue of the *Bucks County Intelligencer*. There it was! Kilian's byline. *They are publishing his reports.* But the more she read, the more puzzled she became. The headline said it all: "In War, Silence Is Not Golden; Water Scarce."

Silence drifted down on us, silvered every feature, the absence of sound more startling than the sounds of cannons, the shrieks of men downed by minié balls and scrap, the mounted officers on horseback above the heads and shoulders of the boys and their unshod fathers, ordering them to march forward.

And this is war, they say. Prolonged intervals of apparent normalcy, moving your bowels twice a day, like a normal man would do, little spats in the neighborhood, resentments sizzling in winter camp and summer but for one difference: water.

Water: to give the horses, to wash or boil the lice out of seams, to put one's whole body beneath, pale limbs wavy and gleaming. Summer's long ennui, no matter how hot our woolen uniforms, I find vastly preferable to winter's hoarse, hacking cough, the moan of those losing their water to dysentery, the stench of our tentmates. Silence may be silver or leaden as the case may be, but water, the universal solvent, is golden.

My native neighbors from back home, those in our company, seem to move in an idyll, stepping lightly out of camp to return with a brace of ducks or a furry chain of rabbits and squirrels to put some heft and savor into the dinner pot. My native neighbors and friends never stink because they don't have the same superstitious aversion to immersion in water that many of the white country boys seem to feel.

And the few women who have been given roles on the battlefield—vivandières, nurses, call them what you will—how far from camp do these women need to ride (for they always ride, just in case) to get out of

*the circle of influence of this man's world we call war? How can these few
women be here in this place, bringing their civilizing instincts to us savages, organized to murder each other?*

Riveted by Kilian's account, Delphine mused aloud that Kilian was more
observant than she had imagined.

Blaise, passing through their little backyard, protected from the universal
prying eyes of soldiers by bedspreads hung on lines, heard her exclamation.
"What?" he asked, distracted.

"Have you read Kilian's dispatches, Blaise?"

"I was hoping you would read me out the parts that are worth hearing,
Delphine." Now he gave her his full attention.

"Listen to this," and she read:

*We are not venting a short, murderous rage, taking scalps, counting coup
and collecting hostages to raise in the place of others we have lost, like the
Native people make war.*

*No, we are here, day after day, on a long campaign to dehumanize
ourselves and our enemy . . . who are just like ourselves.*

Blaise said nothing, so Delphine just shook her head and continued to read.

*And for what? To free those our enemy has enslaved. Negroes, as we call
them, brought generations ago from their native Africa. Somehow we have
more compassion for these benighted souls than we do for the women who
bring us solace and partnership every day of our lives: our mothers, our
sisters, our daughters. Half the world . . . with no rights of their own . . .
though they give us freely the blessed water of their compassion, the water
that becomes the milk of their body they feed us as infants, the water that
washes away our sins, the water that becomes the soup that nourishes us.*

"What?!" Delphine exclaimed aloud, throwing down the newspaper, laughing. "This is sedition! You have to read it yourself, Blaise."

"Why?" Blaise asked idly, preoccupied with packing saddlebags for what
promised to be a short trip out and a short return, although in war one

could never really be certain of such things. Anyone leaving the lines had
to be prepared for contingencies.

"I had no idea Kilian was such a champion of women's rights," she said,
flatly amazed, then buried her nose in the text again. "Listen to this," she
said and read the preceding paragraph out loud.

Blaise just shook his head with a mix of disgust and amazement. She
knew what that gesture meant: *White men.* White men are men who realize
the value of women but exert no power to change their beknighted estate.
Happy with the status quo. And why not?

"'Why?'" she continued to read to Blaise. "'So we can work another day,
yes. We are physically stronger than they, who transform water into wine
to lighten our way.'"

"Ha!" Delphine pitched her voice to reach Blaise, who was saddling up
just beyond the curtains, which rose and fell with the spring wind, April's
occasional heat meeting the defrosting earth.

"'Then how did we invent this time away from women—this prolonged
campaign to dehumanize ourselves—that we call war? We tell ourselves
we are bivouacked here in order to kill and maim each other to defend
women from this enemy *who is ourselves.* Both armies will burn and kill,
break the very codes of warfare, to take up a more savage war against the
women and children and elders of those we deem the Other: slaves, natives,
women.'" Delphine jumped to her feet, energized by reading these printed
words, written by a man—a man she knew!—saying so explicitly what
she knew to be true but had never heard a white man say, much less write
for publication!

"Do you believe this?" Delphine asked Blaise, who was preparing to
mount.

"I didn't know Kilian had it in him," he said, putting his foot into the
stirrup.

Delphine sent Blaise off with her full attention, but she returned to her
reading and coffee before his hoofbeats had receded into the distance. After
a few moments, Threadneedle drifted through, hungry, always hungry. *Still
a growing boy,* she realized, and then the shock of this small observation

caused her to examine her grandson carefully for what felt like the first time in a long while.

"You look like shit, Threadneedle Montour! What have you been doing?" She shook out the newspaper, then folded it to keep her place.

Thread had picked up a pot from the edge of the smoldering fire, beans caked and singed at the bottom. He was digging into the mess and shoveling beans into his mouth. "Why do you care, *Gran'mère?*" he said.

"I have a whole company of men to care about!" she retorted.

He snorted.

"When did you become such a cynic?" she asked.

"What's that?" he asked.

"It means 'What happened to the sweet boy I used to know?'" she said.

He gave her a level gaze, threw down the pot, and strode out. *As if you don't know*, he said in Dialog.

She tried to return to her reading, tried to restore a sense of detachment through controlled breathing. Killian's column continued:

> *Here, on the battlefield, water has become a stand-in for mother. Whether at rest or in battle, I feel most keenly for those who are gutshot and cry piteously for a drink of water as the life slowly and majestically empties away from them. When their screams and hoarse shouts peter away, that is when silence becomes an essential ingredient of survival. Any one of us would happily crawl out onto the battlefield in the role of Angel of Death to bring release for those boys, if only it didn't also mean we might catch a minié ball in performing such an act of mercy.*
>
> *The silence of Death having arrived to release your child, the one who had no notion of what he was signing up for, is a silence that allows each man to curl up in his blanket on the ground, cold or warm, the air flickering with fireflies or snowflakes, and let himself fall into the arms of Morpheus, as if he were simply drifting off to sleep.*
>
> *This peaceful silence is not at all the silence that murders sleep, on those nights when no amount of drugs or alcohol can arrest the continuous images of horror and loss playing on the inside of your eyelids. The*

*men of two armies, tens of thousands of them, all lying awake staring into
the middle distance, suppressing the scream that threatens to arise when
one finds oneself in a world gone out of time, spun into one of the circles
of Dante's Inferno, no escape except through death on the battlefield or
through being hung for desertion.*

Yes, that is the way it is, Delphine thought. Kilian had taken it upon
himself to seduce the entire Quaker population of Bucks County into
imagining what it might be like for their brothers, fathers, sons who had
gone to war.

And then:

*Older men must dream these engagements up, because young men do
not have the capacity to imagine them. Titans, God, and the Devil pitted
against each other in the wrestling arena, perfectly matched. And what
about the Mother, the one who brings rain when it's needed, who attends
the woman pushing overlong in labor, who minds the time of bud-break?
I ask you: Where is She in all this? She hides Her head in Her arms,
heartbroken at the slaughter of Her sons, by Her sons.*

*Is it possible that Her deeper grief—the subjugation of women by
men—keeps Her from halting this slaughter?*

Each time Delphine read the word "mother" in Kilian's column, she
stumbled over it, her mind wanting her to stop. But she refused its prompt-
ing. *The mind is a cagey devil, always trying to seduce you into going in another
direction,* she reminded herself.

Kilian himself then wandered into their yard, looking around dreamily
for something, anything, that would relieve the tedium of war.

"Left column, front page! Impressive. Bravo!" Delphine cried, throwing
the folded paper in his direction, an invitation to sit down, to read and
celebrate the publication of his column.

"They published one of my dispatches?" he asked, shoving his hair back
from his forehead, the baldness at his temples deepening in such a way that
Delphine could plainly see there would eventually be nothing but a monk's

fringe of a hairline left on top. *How old is Kilian?* She did the figuring. He was eleven or twelve when her daughter Turtle Dawn and his cousin Kristiana were thirteen, fourteen. He would be in his mid-thirties now.

Kilian grabbed up the paper and plopped onto the ground, peering down nearsightedly at the print.

Kilian's words being published made Delphine feel anxious about her own meager accomplishments in this war. Yes, she had made a tidy sum in Zouave uniforms for the companies that styled themselves after the fierce North African warriors. She congratulated herself for her prescience on that move. More, the Zouave uniforms had been her ticket onto the battlefield; she couldn't imagine being left at home with the other women. Her sales literature called the *viviandière* costume "a model of form and function, with elements for winter and summer comfort." And they featured plenty of red, the color that gave Delphine her power. Clothed in this uniform, she felt more like herself than any other *persona* she had donned. The *pièce de résistance* was the cross of bandoliers that accented her breasts, still high at fifty plus, each strap studded with loops that held at hand all the elements of comfort on the battlefield: brandy, smelling salts, compression bandages, a sewing kit containing silk thread, a needle, scissors, and a hemostat, and of course Kilian's vials of frontier medicine, including opium.

Woman to a whole company of men, most of them young enough to be her sons, a voice within her had once asked, *And where are your sons, Delphine? Do you even know?* She had shaken her head like a horse bedeviled by flies, attempting to shoo away such unproductive thoughts. Delphine reassured herself: sons or not, she had an important role here as Blaise's partner in the sutler tent. And now, with Blaise gone on the broken-wheel errand, she would turn her attention to the bags of cornmeal, repackaging essentials like salt, which they sold to the soldiers who would swarm their tent as soon as they returned from their drills. Blaise would return with the loaded wagon and the bulk of the supplies and then together they would work far into the night. *Yes*, Delphine reassured herself, *I have success on my own terms, something few white women can claim. And I can have more—if I want it.* She was still not certain she wanted to lead Regina Coeli, nor that she even had what it would take to head the company. *Perhaps,* she told herself. *Perhaps.*

Kilian riffled through the stack of newspapers Blaise had left. "There! Here's another of my pieces! But where are the other papers? Didn't they arrive?" Kilian had come to feel that his very existence depended on his ability to have his expressions of the realities of war sent out to a public who he knew had no idea what war was like, what their sons and brothers and husbands were suffering. He wiped his brow with the back of his hand and marvelled as he read.

He threw the paper to Delphine to read, and she sat on it both to keep her bottom from the dampness of the ground and to keep the paper from being blown by the wind.

"Why didn't you march out with the rest of the army?" Delphine asked.

"Because I am wanted in the surgery tent," he answered. "Where is Threadneedle?"

"He looked terrible when I saw him earlier. Cranky too," Delphine replied.

"You saw him? They left him behind on a picket to protect the camp. They know he is one of our best sharpshooters." He lowered his voice. "He goes out on sniping raids at night. I worry about him." Kilian studied the morning's sun. "Let's see. He was relieved about an hour ago. He'll want to eat before he sleeps."

"I told you; I already saw him," Delphine repeated. "He is probably sleeping."

"What did he say?" Kilian asked. "Did he get anything to eat?"

"He ate the rest of those beans." Delphine scoured her brain. *What did he actually say?* she thought, trying to flesh out the bones of the testy scene with Thread. *Anything I remember, to convey to Kilian?* "I think he misses his mothers," she said.

Kilian cocked his head and looked at her with curiosity. "He probably misses my sister."

"Someone to cook for him," Delphine said dryly, picking up the neatly folded paper on which she had been sitting, procrastinating going into the tent to repackage supplies. She rattled the paper. "He's still growing!" she said. Then, as if answering herself: "I didn't come here to be a cook."

Why are *you here?* they both heard in Dialog.

Kilian looked at her. "Did you hear that?" he asked, still new to this nonverbal language that once allowed only women to communicate with each other. As if talking to himself, he said, "I don't know why I am here. I ask myself that every minute of every day."

Delphine stood and threw down the paper, not caring whether it scattered. If Kilian wanted to save it from being blown away by an errant wind, he would have to do it himself. "I don't have to justify my existence here to anyone," she said and stomped off to the tent.

Chapter Seventeen

WE ARE ALL GOING MAD

Late October 1862, After Antietam

One arm flung over his eyes, Kilian lay boneless in the hammock Wilhelm had sent, a colorful Mexican string design woven by a tribe he called the Lacandones.

Delphine puttered in their stores, reassigning priority space to the massive amount of inventory their sutler tent would have to hold once Blaise returned that day or the next with another wagonload of vital supplies and fresh news from home. *He's been gone a long time, this time,* she thought, lonely and out of sorts with herself and all of existence.

Thread's horse, Bucephalus, hitched to an aspen tree nearby, noisily finished his bucket of oats, upending it with his nose to tell the world with a clatter what he thought of his meager rations.

Delphine hauled several sacks of cornmeal into the tent, tied its flaps shut, hung the "Closed" sign out front, and then hovered over Kilian's supine form. She made it clear with her movements that she was done inside and would now occupy their yard, which they had enclosed with clothesline strung on three sides, from which hung several colorful spreads that sucked and sighed in the fickle winds of this warm October day. "Indian summer" they called it. Here in their yard, Blaise and Delphine maintained their kitchen, dining room, bath, and laundry in good weather, no matter which battlefield they were camping on or near. They were here, anticipating their first winter in a war camp, selling provisions from their sutler tent that the Army of the Potomac did not see necessary to provide their own soldiers.

"I am going to make some lunch, Kilian," Delphine said. "Would you like to join me?"

Kilian came out of the hammock in articulated pieces, as if someone were pulling his strings. He threw two hunks of wood on the fire and picked up the blue-and-white spatterware coffeepot, which he could feel was almost empty. He lifted the lid off the pot, grunted, and carried it to the large leather *bota* they kept slung in a tree. He yawned as he opened the pip and let water fill the pot. He walked slowly back to the fire, stretching his legs, and placed the pot on a strategic spot above the fire, which was now popping and crackling around the greenish wood. It was not a guest's place to suggest that more coffee grounds be added to a pot; he knew his host would provide them on her own schedule.

He reached into his side pocket and drew out a pad of paper and a graphite pencil, which he carefully sharpened. He asked, "Do you mind if I work, Delphine?" Then as an afterthought: "Do you need help?"

"I made some campfire muffins this morning, Killy. They're a little scorched on the edges. I'm going to fry some potatoes, put in a couple eggs, and open a can of corned beef. Nothing to it." She inserted the tip of a bayonet into the lid of the can and twisted several times. "Voila!" she said, pointing the can toward him so he could see the pink meat within. "A feast."

"I'm ravenous. I can't think of the last time I had a meal that didn't completely come from our own campfire. Canned corned beef—what will they think of next? Is there enough for us to save a portion for Thread?" he asked. "He'll be hungry when he wakes."

"That boy is always hungry," Delphine growled. "Save him half of yours. And I will save Blaise half of mine."

Kilian nodded distractedly. "Can I read you my latest dispatch to the *Intelligencer*, Delphine?" he asked, shuffling his papers. "I think I finally figured out what happened here at Antietam. Then maybe once Blaise brings the other papers I can factor in what Washington and the editors are saying. It's a strange form of triangulating into a story. But who won this battle?" He lifted his head, looking at her slicing potatoes into a skillet. "The Union side is saying we won, and the Confederates are saying they won."

"Maybe it's both," Delphine murmured. *And maybe both sides lost,* she thought.

A week after the battle, the death count had finally come in: 23,000 dead in one day, their worse casualties to date, and on Union soil. Finally, all of their dead, horses and men, had been put into the ground by the usual battalions of men working with shovels and picks. The surgery tents bulged with the blasted and dying. It was astonishing to Kilian how quickly a human being turned to a repulsive pile of meat.

"It starts with a poem." Kilian rustled open his pad of paper.

I was meant to be someone else.
Long black hair and one frozen eye.
Flocks of starlings rose above the vacant fields and blotted out the sun.
A crow welcomed me home.
The shade deepened slowly in pools.
One image has slowed me to a crawl,
away from the mazurka of madness.

Kilian flipped the paper to its other side and Delphine could see it was covered in marks—crossouts and ink blots. He tossed his hair, which always needed trimming, and continued, but not before glancing at Delphine to see if she was listening.

A man, curling himself around a tree, holds its trunk in an obscene embrace, his clothes stripped from him by the enemy at night, when we do not dare walk out on the battlefield. Anyone left behind will not be alive in the morning. This man—robbed of clothing and boots, weapons, and personal memorabilia—crawled to this tree thinking of kinship. His last partner twists darkly on its spine, all of his blood spilled into its roots. I taste through my natural revulsion the bond of living things everywhere. "This then," I think to myself, "is a death worth envying. This man's life had earned him a good death and, despite everything, he found it."
I collapsed to my knees, buried my forehead in a small clump of grass

protected by a hummock, and smelled it, tasted it, rubbed my face and cheeks into it, watered it with grateful tears, and knew I was safe on the breast of my beloved, my Mother, my home.

A small ant crawled up a blade of grass past my cheek. Snot dripped from my nose. I was deliriously happy. I did not feel small or humbled. I felt one with it all. I am one with it all.

Know this, good citizens of Bucks County, Quaker brethren: We are in hell here. Comfort is found in small ways I would never have imagined before I jumped into this war with my brothers, your sons.

Delphine straightened from the fire, a hand on her lower back. "Kilian," she said weakly, but whether to reprove or comfort wasn't clear. "Will they print this?"

All of his pieces, without exception, were gory and, well, too realistic for a civilian audience worried about their sons and husbands. *This was a report on Antietam? Why not? All the battles had become like all the other battles, hadn't they?* The only thing that distinguished one from another, here on the ground, were fresh details: "Man embraces tree."

The aftermath of each battle was becoming routine: shoveling up body parts, the sound of picks and shovels slamming into earth, digging pits for disposal of the dead—men and horses, blasted and bloated—and for latrines as well. The shrieks of men and horses during battle merely turned to screams from the surgery tents, where Kilian had just spent the past week with little food or sleep.

"Frankly, Kilian, I am full of admiration that you can write at all," Delphine said, squatting by the fire.

"I hope to God Blaise found some chloroform. More opium," he said.

"He will. I know he will." Neither of them needed to say that with their family having been deeply engaged in opium trading before the war, they shouldn't have a problem supplying both Washington and their own sutler tent with a range of substances to numb the senses.

Delphine studied the sky. Pale ribs of clouds stretching into wings marched from southeast to northwest. "Weather's coming," she announced.

"I don't know how to read this weather," Kilian groused. "A half-a-day crow's flight from the Pennsylvania line, but it might as well be China for all the similarity to home." He blew out a lungful of air, laced his fingers in front of him, stretched his arms, shoulders, back.

Delphine beat four precious eggs in a bowl, then carefully added them to the potatoes she had sliced into the skillet. She pinched salt from a bag and covered the whole lot to steam, drawing the pan slightly away from the fire.

"I hope Uncle Wilhelm can see his way to sending fresh supplies here rather than to the depot in Washington. We need tents."

"And Wilhelm needs his invoices stamped for the exchequer to pay ...," Delphine said, saying what they both knew. "Like all of us."

Kilian began to cry, angry tears, frustrated. He swiped at his nose with the back of his hand, accidentally smudging charcoal across his face. He hung his head and noticed he still had gore drying on his jersey from his stint in the operating tent. He pulled a do-rag from his britches pocket and blew his nose. "Damn it all to hell!"

Delphine handed him a tin plate and fork, then settled herself gracefully on the grass nearby and began to eat, bending over her plate, which she had placed on a slice of log. "All the amenities of home, Kilian, see," she said, indicating her improvised table. "Eat, Kilian!" she urged. "Don't forget: When there's food ... !"

His laugh was well meant, but it aggravated her nervousness, putting them both on edge. Even in their enclosure built of clothesline and bedspreads, they could not completely ignore the outside world. In brief moments, it helped to be inside this coffer, their sightlines protected while they cooked their food, ate, did their wash, relaxed. In fostering the illusion of elsewhere, it protected their eyes, however fleetingly, from the blasted landscape, the work details going about the grisly business of war. But no amount of curtaining could block the noxious fumes of decomposition that provoked their gag reflexes even when they ate. Delphine jealously guarded the pile of dried cedar she kept by her campfire, and now she threw a small handful of chips onto the fire, the smoke that arose miraculously cleansing the air.

Kilian stuffed his notes back into his field jacket. Picking up a muffin, he began to nibble the edges. Then, as if an alarm rang in his head, warning him that woolgathering in war will get you killed, his eyes focused on the potatoes, eggs, beans, and generous helping of corned beef on his plate.

"I didn't dare fry the tinned beef," she said.

He knew what she meant. It would attract too much attention in the vast encampment, where one expected the same smells to come from every campfire. Even the eggs were a provocation. He indicated them with a raised brow and his fork.

"I went out at dawn," she said modestly.

"I don't want to know," he said, tucking back into the food on his plate with sighs and groans of satisfaction as his taste buds sparked a wealth of happy memories, bringing solace to his poor, shriveled heart. Delphine could see him calculating the half of his plate to be saved for Thread. He was practically counting the beans.

Then, after a moment of focused eating, he waved his fork in the air and said, "I . . . don't even know you, Delphine." He rushed forward into his unplanned disclosure, even if he couldn't see where he was going. "And I know your daughter and your mother well; Turtle Dawn and Marguerite were staples in my life growing up in Newtown. But you were never around. How . . ." He gestured again with his fork, this time looking around. "How do you wind up being here?" Implicit in his question was *Why you, when the other women—all the other women—are back there?*

She laughed, deep in her throat.

"How did I get to be so different from the others? Is that what you mean? How did I grow up racing horses and sparring with sticks rather than tending the home fires?"

"Just so," he said, licking his fork of the remains of breakfast.

"My mother recognized my breed." She raised her head, but he showed no sign of knowing what she meant. "My people allow a lot of room for differences. I am not two-spirited—a man in a woman's body or a woman in a man's—but Mother saw my unique nature from the start. 'A wolf tree: alone in a field made by fire,' she used to say. An open field allows a tree to spread in every direction following its true nature. That is who I am."

Kilian reflected, repeating her words. "'Alone in a field made by fire.' You are a warrior. And a woman." He jumped to his feet. "And you must know how it is that you got this way."

Delphine, who had never felt the urge to reveal herself to people, asked herself, *What is it about war that allows people to assume a certain intimacy, to ask questions that are so close to the bone?* No matter how long she had known a person, Delphine always felt he or she remained a stranger.

She nodded, then chortled. "I am past fifty. The true age of power for a woman. After childrearing. But I will not be defined by my womanness. And I will not be defined by being Lenape or Huron or French. I am a *citoyenne du monde*, a citizen of the world."

"At what point in your life did you aspire to be a *citoyenne du monde?*"

Delphine masterfully deflected his direct question, controlling this interview herself. "You are a true journalist, Kilian." She was protective of herself, but also flattered. Flattered that he cared enough to ask. "We call ourselves cosmopolitans. Not bound by country or flag. Not pigeonholed by tribe or gender."

"You are not like any other woman I know," Kilian said. "Did you even do any childrearing? Did you raise Turtle Dawn when Buffalo Creek was still in your People's hands?"

"Yes!" she said with a finality that indicated the end of that conversation.

Kilian pulled back and poured them each a cup of coffee from the pot. He sniffed his. It smelled strong enough, with just a hint of chicory adding strength to the treasured coffee grounds. He looked around, then stage whispered, "Sugar?"

She stood in one swift motion, took his coffee cup, ducked low under the flaps into the tent. She emerged, spoon in his cup, stirring it. "Honey," she said.

"Isn't that what you call Blaise, in private, out of earshot?" he said mildly—so mildly she couldn't mistake it for anything but a harmless jape. *Could she?*

"Surely you aren't flirting with me, Kilian?"

Kilian, who always paid close attention to women and what they looked like, how they dressed, noted now how Delphine always wore her flaxen hair under a turban, keeping up her role as *vivandière* even during her private hours. A woman with such a striking combination of pale hair and dark features—dark eyes, dark eyebrows and lashes, richly colored skin—was a rarity, even in this land of mixed blood; perhaps she didn't want to draw attention to herself. He studied her clothes: She wore boots like a man's, which disappeared up into a calf-length skirt, cut like a kilt, with pleats that knifed out with every step. Under that were what had been called bloomers a decade earlier. He had read in the Zouave literature that the bloomers were made of wool, leather, or linen depending on the weather, and that they made it easier for a woman to ride a horse. Delphine kept her own horse, a spotted paint, and she had, early on, made it clear to the authorities who sanctioned her presence in the warzone that her horse, Brushfire, could never be requisitioned.

Right now, Brushfire and Bucephalus were nickering to each other as they nosed the autumn fringe of weeds and grasses that edged the aspen grove where they were loosely tethered. The leaves, golden this far into the autumn, still had not fallen and were quaking in the slight breeze against a sky that would reveal its cloudless blue as the day wore on. A bunch of goldenrod and purple aster Delphine had picked graced their makeshift dining room in a graceless bucket.

Yes, I would like to flirt with you, he said in Dialog, the first time he had spoken there to a woman outside of his family. He sipped his coffee reflectively, wondering if she had heard him. Perhaps Delphine, who rejected both sides of her heritage, couldn't speak in Dialog. He took a wicked joy in wondering who else in the family had heard him speak there.

She stepped away, then turned and squatted, her back against the pivotal tree that held the hammock, the water *bota*, and the clotheslines supporting the soft walls that enclosed them. She had deliberately picked a spot that placed her on a line with Kilian, side by side, army body language that said, *Now we are going to speak intimately, but without eye contact.* The code also dictated that their words be spoken in a monotone, without inflection.

She unbuckled her knife sheath, awkward in a squat, and placed it to her right side, at hand. One couldn't be a *vivandière* in a war that had lasted this long and not be wary, even of family. She had vowed that she would never be raped, and she was prepared to defend herself with moves she practiced every day with Blaise, sharpening her skills with knife and stick.

"You are a child, Kilian. Thirty-five to my fifty . . . but your men seem to mature so late, not marrying until they have an education, a position. Our men begin to earn their own way early."

She is taunting me, Kilian told himself. *If this is flirting, then the game is on!* "You forget perhaps that I have been married, I own a couple of businesses . . . ," he said mildly, turning his cup in his hands, as if critiquing its round, its glaze. As if he could crack it with his hands if he chose. "I have a child. One of your grandchildren," he added, cuttingly.

"Yes," she drawled. "A child. With my daughter." She shifted and her thigh brushed against her plate on the ground, her knife clattering against it, a tinpan tattoo signaling the rattled state of her nerves. "And what will be Kristiana's role in raising this child?" she asked provocatively. "What will be your role?"

"I am Eliza's father," he said. "I'm just waiting to find out what that means to you." He had used the child's European name to provoke his mother-in-law.

"That means you bring home the bacon," she said. "But here you are instead. Doing what?"

Stay calm, he instructed himself. *She won't provoke me.* "And what are you doing here, Delphine? Playing dress-up? Thread is also your grandchild. What have you ever done for him?"

Delphine was not used to this kind of talk. He could feel her beside him preparing a counterattack and braced himself.

"Your women—white women, your mother Catherine, your cousin Kristiana, your sister Regina—whine about not having a vote." She stopped, giving him time to absorb her criticism of Regina and the others in his family who pressed for their rights even as the Quaker majority insisted on the abolition of slavery first, considering it their primary moral imperative.

How it must sting Regina, he thought. He was glad that he had written to the Quaker hierarchy to urge them to let Delphine speak at their international convention. *If we had chosen to focus on ending the subjugation*

of women before freeing the slaves, would that have resulted in a bloody war? I
don't think the women would have allowed it! And yet the same kinds of issues
are at stake, although here half of the population is in bondage rather than one
fifth. These economics affect every household. The moral turpitude of it! He
began to imagine writing a dispatch on the subject.

"My granddaughter Nesting Swan will have a vote when she comes of
age. The women in my family have always had a vote."

Her words slammed him back into his body, heart cowering. Though
shriveled—and maybe vestigial—his heart could still feel, ache. Didn't he
walk into that surgery tent every day after a battle and have to take in the
devastation of men and their bodies, fathers and sons side by side? Boys
who had gone to school with Thread. *Delphine will not provoke me, or . . .*

He reminded himself that he could not lose his temper with this woman.
She is Turtle Dawn's mother, f'r crissake!

She reached forward and grabbed two buckets, one empty, the other full
of dried corn still on the cob. She clamped the empty bucket tight between
her knees and took a cob in her hands. Her kilt fell away to either side of
her thighs.

Her long thigh bone thrust up from her hip, and Kilian could see the
muscles stand out as she tensed around the bucket.

He was instantly hard.

She slipped a ring onto her finger that assisted in shelling the corn. The
sound of dried kernels dropping into the bucket punctuated her words.

He longed to run his hand down her flanks. *How would she respond?*

"To be considered the property of another is unimaginable to me. What
happened to your mother when the investors—all men—decided to take
her down would never happen among my people. The Council of Clanmothers would have taken it to the Grand Council. To allow men like
Wilhelm—or even Philip!—to have the last word would humiliate us both
as individuals. And humiliate our families. Humiliate our tribe."

He longed to say it, but he had too much compassion for this woman:
What do you know of your tribe? She was his mother-in-law, he kept reminding himself, but here she sat, bare calves clamped around this bucket.

She picked up another ear of corn and began running her tool down the length, sending up a tintinabulation of sound. "Your women . . . ," she began, then stopped, adjusting the tool on her finger.

His entire body throbbed.

"They imagined they came to this continent to enjoy new freedoms. Just like you men. But for the most part—and I am not indicting your family personally, Kilian—but for the most part, European women live in servitude."

Now her words were coming in a torrent, like the corn kernels cascading into the bucket, down the side of the bucket. He recognized it as a milking bucket that had been in their barn back in Pennsylvania. The sound stopped as she reached for another cob.

He couldn't help it. He imagined her hand running down his penis. With the men out on maneuvers, his tent would be empty but for a sleeping Thread. Kilian knew he would have to relieve himself when he returned to their small tent.

"We also work beside our husbands and sisters, raise children, make homes, heal sickness, help bring life into and out of this world. We weave, tan, and decorate clothing. Weed and cultivate crops. We do all the things a woman does for her family, with one difference: Your women work for their husband's benefit, as individuals with no rights of their own, which takes all the sweetness from their labor. The land you men break with your iron ploughs, the land women and children tend, is tended in their husband's name: Shafer, Sechinger. See?"

He did, and with a clarity he had never seen before, despite a lifetime of living with the women of his family, all of whom, to one degree or another, were vocal advocates of universal suffrage. And how—now, in this moment—could he reconcile his fine feelings for women and still suffer the unbearable hard-on he felt for this woman, this family member, if only through marriage? *Perhaps I will never figure out how to live with such irreconcilable feelings,* he allowed.

"Even your children are branded with their fathers' names. Your women have no right to the children who come out of their own bodies. If man and wife separate, if he dies, his family takes the child from the mother."

"And what is Eliza's surname?" he asked archly, making his point. "Duladier."

"I told you that I didn't mean you and your family specifically, Kilian. What do you say when I tell you that your daughter's name is Nesting Swan Montour?"

They were speaking about identity, a quality that had felt tenuous in Kilian lately, as the war hammered on his spirit daily. He wished Turtle Dawn were there with him, right now. She steadied him, his North Star.

"My daughter, my mother, and I—and your daughter Swan—," Delphine continued, "have never known disrespect, abuse, rape and beatings from our men. A man who did this would be censured and punished by the tribe and certainly divorced by his wife. If it didn't stop, he would be sent from the tribe or even put to death. These insults all of the women in your family have tasted."

He startled, felt he had to look directly at her now. "What do you know that I don't?" he asked. Aside from his mother's having been put aside as *maîtresse* a generation earlier, he knew nothing of what Delphine was describing—beatings, abuse, insults, rape—in his family. He thought guiltily about his mother's imperishable answer to his question about his true father. He couldn't countenance her answer. Under what circumstances would a woman of her breeding not be able to name his father from two apparent candidates? He simply was not able to walk that through to any conclusions. Was it violence against her? Why did her parents August and Hannah do nothing about it?

"Yes," she said, "your women keep their secrets from you. Like slaves do from their masters. They keep you weak by withholding important information about the family, to keep you on that side of the wall you have built, and then they send you off to war to be broken without their succor." Kilian lifted his head. "It's the small revenge of the slave on the master," she added, as if to herself.

Her voice was getting lower and lower as she spoke these hard things he had never heard. "I am here, where a woman without children can be, to give you my strength when you flag. To help you learn what it is worth to care for yourselves and each other. Wash your own clothes, cook your own food, build your own fire, put up your own tents. That's why men love war! Because, for the first time, without a woman doing it for him, he learns how to care for himself and his brothers." She shook her head, then stood, hand at the small of her back again. "Why war doesn't make men wake to the unfortunate servitude of their wives and sisters . . ."

She picked up her full bucket of dried corn kernels, which he knew she would make into hominy, to be mixed with horsemeat and green chilis. "What do you imagine they are doing back home?" she asked rhetorically. "Their work . . . and *your* work!" *All this while you are here, doing—what?* she thought, certain that she didn't need to say the words for Kilian to understand.

Stung, Kilian rose, gathered up the cobs and the dried cornhusks abandoned nearby, and put them into the fire. He knew she could wrap tamales in the husks, but he burned them anyway, as a sacrifice. To whom? Maybe to the god she prayed to, if she prayed, because he knew instinctively that this proud, cold woman was going to get her comeuppance.

As he poured hot water from the kettle into the washbasin, he looked around at the morning's dishes and asked, "Did you save Blaise's portion?" Delphine made an impatient gesture that did not answer his question, and he turned away to scrub the eggs and grease off the plates and forks and rinse out the cups, upending them on the drain board. He threw the basin of water to a clump of lilacs near the foundation of a shed that had been burned down long since.

"Can I do a small wash?" he asked. His longjohns were lousy after the week of battle and the week since, spent in surgery.

She gestured. "Help yourself. Where are your dirty clothes?"

He looked down at himself, gesturing at the gore dried on his shirt, his pants.

"I'll leave you to yourself, then. You can undress here. Do you have clothes to wear while these dry?"

He nodded, turned on his heel, and went to Bucephalus, where he fished around in his saddlebags slung next to Thread's.

Delphine poured hot water from one kettle over the corn in the bucket and then, using a short-handled shovel set beside the firepit, shoveled ash into the bucket. She refilled the kettle from the *bota* slung in the tree, and, weighing the bottom of the bladder with the palm of her hand, said, "We need more water."

He grunted to let her know he had heard. "Consider it done, Delphine. And many thanks for a fine meal. And the medicine of your company," he added to her retreating back. *Bitter medicine,* he said to himself, wondering if Delphine had ever had to comfort someone who was dying.

He filled both kettles to the top with water from the bladder, added three sticks of split wood to the fire, and watched to see them catch. Hands on the small of his back, he stretched backward, then forward, bending to touch his knees with his nose but coming too close to his offending trousers, which were covered in stinking surgical bits and pieces. He carelessly slipped his suspenders off his shoulders and began unbuttoning his fly, conscious that Delphine was still in the yard. He pulled his shirt up over his head, slowly. He was growing hard again and perversely, he wanted her to see his cock, a kind of revenge for her hard words. How long had Blaise been gone? He wondered if Blaise had other women when he traveled out. *God knows I need a woman!* It wasn't the same, yanking on yourself in the company of men bedded down in close proximity, making their own beds shudder. He pulled on his clean clothes, slightly less stinking than those he had removed.

When he saw that Delphine had disappeared, he attached the *bota* to Bucephalus' saddle and rode off, to splash his body in the chilly Antietam Creek, soap under his arms and his crotch, making an attempt to freeze the lice out of his hair before his own scalp froze first. Then he returned to the camp, where he filled kettles and set them boiling to wash his other change of clothes.

Thread was there, poking around the campfire. He had found his portion of food near the fire and was nibbling at the beans, eying the canned meat. "What is this?" he asked, gesturing. He smiled at Kilian. "It's sure not horsemeat!"

"Corned beef," Kilian replied, raising his eyebrows to signal shared delight.

Thread sighed with pleasure: "Eggs!"

"Yes, Delphine went out this morning to get them." *You are being cared for, Thread,* he meant. "Where did you go last night, Thread?" Kilian asked.

Thread's face went blank. "Just out. Couldn't sleep."

"I hate it when you lie to me." Kilian flung his hands out, fingers splayed, a gesture that was coming to define him. "How am I going to watch over you if I don't know where you are?"

Thread laughed. "You watch over me, Kilian?" They both laughed, Kilian a bit uneasily.

"I promised our family," Kilian continued stubbornly. "What if my sister did come here, to the battlefield? What would I tell her? Yes, I watch over you!"

"Regina has no idea what it is like here. And I don't ever want her to know! We don't have to explain anything to anyone. What is true, and what they can't understand, is that I can't protect you and you can't protect me."

"You could be a bit more careful," Kilian said. "That last battle, you were head and shoulders above the rest of the company, a perfect target."

"I've discovered my natural talent for leadership," Thread said. "What are you saying, Kilian? Do you want to come out with us? I wouldn't have you. You are untrained, unskilled in the art of stalking. You are a poor shot. You have scruples about killing."

"What are you becoming, Thread?" Kilian asked. Now the two were a meter from each other, looking directly into each other's eyes. They spoke softly.

"I want this war over, Killy. Just as much as you do. This is the only way I know how to contribute what I have to the war effort." He said these last words with such bitter irony that Kilian reached out his hand to his cousin's shoulder and squeezed.

At that touch, the tension in Thread collapsed out of him and he sat on the ground. "The bastards!" he cried. "They think that because they are country boys and from the South they are the best—and only!—sharp-shooters. One shot and they finish a man. They pick us off like sitting ducks. I can't sit by and let it happen, Killy! They have to taste the fear of knowing that someone may be coming for them in the dark." Now he had control of himself again. "We all feel that way, Kilian." Thread looked up at his cousin and then jackknifed to his feet. Tension once again in his body, he paced like a big cat, saying, "I couldn't do what you do, couldn't walk into a tent and see a shattered boy lying next to his blinded father and begin to see what I could suture, cauterize, and wrap. You are a man of extraordinary courage."

For Kilian, these words were benediction. He was not a coward. His cousin, the bravest man Kilian had ever known, had said so. His work here mattered as much as Thread's.

"I've put the wash water up to boil," he said. Silence fell between them then as they remembered that the entire army was out on maneuvers. Kilian sat on the ground, leaning against a tree, legs stretched out before him. "My god," he mused. "You could hear a calf bawl in this silence."

Minutes later, Kilian, nodding off from exhaustion, half-heard Bucephalus gallop away, Thread on him.

Kilian called out to Delphine, his voice carrying through the afternoon light pungent with woodsmoke from all the campfires. He heard her moving inside the tent and offered, "I'll read my dispatch to you before I send it out."

Something fell, clanging against other objects before it landed, and he heard her swear softly. She sang out, "I can't help you, Kilian. I have my own things to take care of."

No, Thread said to himself, *you can't help any of us.* Afraid to hurt her, he didn't want to say it aloud, but he couldn't help the cynicism that war had developed, in both Kilian and himself. *None of us can be rescued. Because we are already lost.*

After the laundry had been done and hung up to dry, Kilian returned to the surgery tent for the finer work that was possible in the languorous weeks following a battle. Thread reported to the picket that guarded their perimeter, and Delphine stayed behind to pick up the cups that were left scattered about. Finding real coffee in several of them, she sat down in the late afternoon light to read the paper. Noticing that her stomach was upset, indeed gripping, she spat out her mouthful of coffee and threw the rest into the fire, enjoying its sputtering hiss.

Another of Kilian's stories was printed in the most recent paper. She flipped it open, pretending that it was still early morning, with a fresh day in front of her. She sighed as she read the first sentence. *I can't believe they are publishing this. A fly!*

A single fly rose up, circled, and fell back down again. Then, as my horse and I went by, a host of flies rose up buzzing from their morsel of rotting meat. Where had birdsong fled? Were the birds in the trees but stifled by war? The tranquility of the everyday contains every sound but this: the sound of war. Certainly the everyday, the diurnal, the quotidien, can include the sound of a child wailing or a calf bawling in the distance. But it does not apply to the host of suffering creatures who cry aloud here. Here, the morning's hardtack cried, crows and vultures cried, broken men cried, many without a wound on them to show where they had been broken.

We all remember a time when the morning used to hold a cup of peace, the prospect of a smile, a lazy whistle for a slumbering dog. In time, all these blasted fields will swallow up these shattered boys' bodies, swallow up the pools of blood, even the smell of carrion. But like some ghastly container, my being will always hold this smell, these sounds, this shattered cup that no amount of plaster can repair.

Up to a point, the horror of war opens the poor flayed heart, and compassion blooms in the average eye. Witness the soldier who goes out at night with canteens of water to bring a drink to those boys who are dying, needing just that one thing. For water reminds us of home. Each drop of the precious substance stands in for the lake where I draw a fish for supper, the river where I immerse my wavering limbs, the pitcher whose gurgling sound heals the wounded, the single tear whose salt reprises birth.

Delphine let the paper drop in her lap. *He repeats and repeats himself. Water. Silence.* Then, a fresh realization, an old one made new: *We are all going mad.* Compelled, she read on.

And yet, as the year grinds to a close, our hearts no longer open or contract, systole/diastole, for they have died of the overdose no human should bear: the deep knowledge that not only is there not a god worth beseeching, a

Mother who will listen, but only this brutal species bent on tearing human-
ity from any breast that harbors it, a species not worth the attention of any
deity, Mother or Father.

"Oh," she cried, exasperated. "On and on he goes: mother, mother, mother, mother! Doesn't he have an editor who cares about this repetition? He's going to snap." She made a crude noise, then scanned the ending.

My horse stops at our tent, its nervous hooves saying, "We are here." And
yet every time we travel back to this place, we have passed through a fresh
ring of hell to arrive home. He—my horse!—breaks my heart. Doesn't
this loyal animal, with his courageous heart, deserve the certainty of the
journey to match the welcome of arrival? He came all the way from Bucks
County, left his barn, friends, and family, to come with me to this place,
this unconscionable theater.

We all came from Bucks County with him, and he thinks only of his horse!
Something was nagging at Delphine, something that hurt, that she hadn't looked at. A wound that she refused to see, a pain she kept hidden from herself. She suddenly became acutely aware of the bottle of laudanum she kept hidden in her trunk. It began calling to her need, saying, "I am here, antidote to your suffering." She calculated. *How long had Blaise been gone?* Now she faced it: *Too long. He could be dead.* She jerked herself away from these thoughts that could drown a person, thoughts of dying, of sudden death. She turned away from the sweet relief of the dark, sticky drug waiting for her.

Delphine rose with the weariness of an aged crone and set to her next task: to put up a tent for Marie Tepe. Blaise had asked the commander of their unit if the other *viviandière*'s tent could be pitched in the lee of their sutler tent. *Another woman,* Delphine thought as she turned the corner around the tent and saw the smile break over Marie's face. *Thank you, Mother. Another woman.*

Chapter Eighteen

SCISSORS AND ASHES

November 1862, Fredericksburg, Virginia

Marie Tepe carried both a small-caliber pistol and a curving knife thrust through her belt. The unit commander figured that these two women on the battlefield—Marie and Delphine, so good for the men's morale—should be able to defend themselves, and he had given permission for Delphine to carry both knife and pistol on her person as well.

The women went out every morning with Blaise for target practice and to engage in friendly hand-to-hand combat as a way of enhancing their skills. Blaise showed them how to use the energy and forward momentum of an attacker to bring the aggressor on his back or to his knees. A woman with a handheld weapon would be no match for a rifle, but nonetheless . . .

In the weeks since Marie's arrival, they had become a threesome and had developed a routine that brought its own assurances. All three were *metises*; Blaise and Delphine were an amalgam of racial types—mostly Lenape, Seneca, French, and Dutch—and Marie was Mohawk and French. Thus, certain customs and preferences from their cultures could be taken for granted: their reverence for the natural world, their ability to eke out food from nature, their physical and spiritual strength. But war is a great leveler. What matters is not your accent, your profession, or even your skin color; what matters is that you have your fellows' backs.

This afternoon, Blaise took up his usual place on their practice ground, behind the sutler tent, standing with knees bent, ready for action. "Marie, come on," he instructed, a puff of air from his mouth visible in the chilly morning air.

Marie moved forward, soft on her feet, elbows bent, arms poised at belt level, relaxed.

Blaise moved in quickly and grabbed her arm, and as soon as Marie felt him, she touched the arm that sought to hold her, pivoted, and quickly brought Blaise to one knee. "Good!" he praised. "Again. And this time place both hands on my hand after I grab your arm. Put your hand on mine and look at me sweetly, as if you want me." Marie looked puzzled. "Delphine!" he called, addressing the two of them as their drill sergeant. "This is your defense, the two of you: you are women. You don't have superior strength, so you must have something else." He twisted Marie's arm and she went to one knee, grimacing. "Use your wiles!" He grabbed her again. This time she started her countermove as a caress, stepping into him with a smile, then continuing the move aggressively, soon subduing Blaise. "Good, Marie!" he said.

"Now Delphine. Come." He gestured with one hand. Marie moved up behind her, one arm around her neck to bring her down. Delphine seemed to collapse, but then in an instant Marie was on her back on the ground, the breath knocked out of her.

"Oh!" she gasped. "Delphine. That was good!" She jumped to her feet, bent over double, hands on her knees, catching her breath, and then, "Let me do it to you."

After combat practice, the three sat by the fire they kept going all day. Even though their unit had fallen back to Virginia again, by the Rappahannock, familiar territory to them by now, the calendar had turned to a chilly November, and the days sometimes felt as cold as the nights. Marie told them she had joined the war because she saw the opportunity for adventure, away from her family. She had seen a much-fingered brochure of Delphine's Zouave uniforms and moved across the Canadian border to sign up. Blaise and Delphine privately speculated that the young woman was running away from something.

They had often discussed their situation, sometimes with Kilian or Thread there, but more often just the three of them who camped together. The mood of the war after Antietam had shifted. Where once honor and glory were uppermost, now lack of morale had eroded the civilities, and one could no longer count on another's goodwill. As winter began to set in, bringing disease and subtracting those creature comforts that helped make civility possible, the rough world of men and their survival called into question the wisdom of the women's role on the battlefield.

"Everything's changing . . . ," Delphine said, then paused, collecting her thoughts. "For one thing—and you know this is hard for me to admit—the Zouave spirit is dead. The sharpshooters have an easier time picking out the red turbaned head. Our men are wearing kepis now, like any other company."

"And the cummerbund is at the bottom of their packs or in the surgical tent, to tie off hemorrhages," Marie said.

"Our shirts, while linen and sturdy," Blaise added, "are gray from mud and constant wearing. The cold demands soldiers wear a woolen coat, but ours do not button tightly enough." Blaise hated to be critical of Turtle Dawn's designs for the Zouve units, but it seemed they needed to face the truth, just as the Zouave units themselves had.

"In the winter, the vest goes and only the baggy pants remain," Marie said.

"You can't blame them," Blaise murmured.

The three of them were quiet for several long minutes as they contemplated the death of the Zouave spirit that had given the two women their *raison d'être* on the battlefield.

"Has the commander said anything yet about this?"

"He follows his men's lead, his chief virtue."

"And so . . . where does that leave the two of you?" Blaise asked.

Delphine and Marie glanced at each other.

"Someone is going to ask you this, and soon," Blaise said. "What are you two doing here?" The words *Where you don't belong*, though not spoken, were strongly implied. "Couldn't you do more for the Union somewhere else, somewhere safe? I'm playing devil's advocate, but someone is going to say it, and you'd better have an honest answer."

"They're already saying it," Delphine admitted. "In every anonymous jibe, every stolen article of clothing, every whistle."

"The war has changed, become more brutal . . . ," Blaise said.

Marie ducked her head, her hair twisted into a dark bun at the nape of her neck, then raised her hand as if to ward off some evil. "Please don't embarrass me by protesting," she began, shaking her head, "but I am not that attractive a woman. And yet the men's eyes follow me everywhere. I keep a chamberpot in my tent, as do you, but everything—even washing, hanging my clothes on a line outside, dumping my wash water from my basin into a ditch to the side . . . All of these ordinary activities are bringing a coarseness out of our own men I have not experienced . . . until now."

"The men are weary of war," Blaise said. "They're becoming animals. Worse: terrified animals."

Blaise put fresh tobacco in his pipe, lit it, and then passed his pouch to Marie, who took a pipe out of the kit she kept slung across her chest. After she filled her pipe, she lifted a burning stick from the fire and lit up, puffing to get a coal going. And then Delphine followed suit, until they were all enjoying a smoke, savoring what would come next: a cup of the camp tea they kept brewing on the fire, adding ingredients as the day wore on—licorice, mint, oregano, clippings from weeds they found around their campsite.

"I don't dare use our own coffee," Blaise said as he poured the hot liquid into three cups. "It's so rare that even the smell of it might breed resentment." He didn't need to finish his thought, for he had voiced it many times: *And resentment might breed insurrection. Then anarchy.* Their sutler tent had never been overrun, but they had heard of it happening to others. A delicate balance kept them safe, but everything conspired to throw that balance off. In his tent, Blaise had two women, tobacco, coffee, honey, maple syrup, and opium . . . all the things that money could buy—or force could gain—to make life in camp easier for a man who hadn't been paid in months, whose grub was reduced to horsemeat, rancid lard, and weevily flour. A man who slept in the rain and cold most nights, with predatory death all around. And worse: disease and disfigurement. Death from a slow infection in a minor wound.

"This General Burnside," Delphine groused, "is devoted to an austerity that is unseemly with winter coming on." She said it even though their kinship with the company commander meant their unit got good cornmeal, salt, and honey as part of their rations, while other companies gnawed on hardtack, smoked pork, and salt cod to keep a briny mass going on their campfires they could call stew. Horsemeat was welcome and common in the aftermath of battle, though all the butchers seemed to be working in the surgery tents, every one of their saws and cleavers spoken for.

A man could subsist on potatoes and buttermilk, like one Irish brigade did, but now even potatoes were in short supply. Marie had asked once, "But when it's only potatoes, no salt, no buttermilk, how is a man supposed to keep fever, ague, *la grippe* at bay?"

The three sat puffing companionably, puzzling at the riddle they had posed: Should the women remain in camp? If they left, could they get out of the warzone safely?

Blaise concluded with more certainty than he had mustered before: "Both of you ought to go home while you still can. If we thought McClellan was slow to make a decision, Burnside is worse. He's added poor rations and no pay to the mix."

"Our conversations always come to this," Delphine said. "Blaise, you never tell me what it's like out there. The last time, when you were gone so long, I kept thinking, 'He could be dead and I would never know it.'" She unfolded herself in one smooth motion. "Could you eat a bowl of mush, Marie?"

Marie nodded, sunk in thought from within the blue haze of her tobacco smoke and the tight wrap of the blanket she had pulled up around her shoulders and neck.

When Delphine returned, both Blaise and Marie were deep in thought. They startled when she asked, "Blaise? What are you seeing out there? In the real world."

He grunted. It said, *Leave me in peace, woman.*

"Do you want some mush?" She emphasized each word, as if she needed to drill her way into the haze he had surrounded himself with.

He stood, suddenly angry. She had rarely seen him angry, in all their years together. "What am I seeing out there, Delphine?"

Suddenly she didn't want to know. She wished Marie Tepe would disappear, not be there to witness this breakdown in their usual demeanor.

"Do you remember those two lads you gave birth to? That your mother and the tribe raised? Remember when we saw them last? Their manhood ceremonies. They were boys. I had to go to their company, miles away from here, build a box, and put Simon's blasted and rotting body in the box while his brother, Lance Corporal Malachi Montour, wept until the snot came out of his nose." Blaise collapsed. "And that's just one of the things that I am seeing out there, Delphine," he whispered.

A sound came from Marie Tepe like a squeezebox concertina with a rip in its bellows. "You have sons?" she asked Blaise.

Delphine strode to the tent and opened the cupboard with the laudanum. Blaise ran in after her and swiped at her hand so that the bottle fell. It didn't break, and she lunged for it as it rolled across the tent floor.

"I will not allow you to numb yourself to this, Delphine," he said quietly.

You will not cry, she told herself.

"I want you to feel it, Delphine," he said.

"Why?" she said.

"Because feelings make us human."

She simply observed him for a long minute.

"Please come out here and serve us the mush you offered."

As Delphine dished out the hot and salted cornmeal with a plug of oil at the center and a generous dollop of maple syrup on top, they each looked forward to the homey clatter of bowls and spoons which would allow them to hide behind the act of eating.

"Blaise," Delphine said, after handing each a full bowl from the stewpot, "you have more gray in your beard this year." Blaise was one of the men who let his beard grow thick as autumn wore on into winter, then marked spring and summer partially shaven. Delphine insisted on barbering him in all seasons because, she said, he needed to keep up appearances as a trader working many sides: soldiers and suppliers, bureaucrats in Washington and black marketers. His thick beard and lantern jaw spoke of his French *voyageur* heritage while Thread, with similar bloodlines but a higher percentage of native blood, despaired of ever growing even a mustache.

Marie said simply for them all, "Mother, we thank you for this meal. And pray that you bring mercy to those who suffer. And an end to this war."

"Amen!" Blaise said.

They would not waste this bowl of food talking about the war when they might only have this meal today, and—with luck—maybe another after dark, a stew of meat and root vegetables. Only by attending closely to every spoonful did their bellies and minds feel satisfaction from a hot meal. Only by fussing over food preparation and then eating together did they ease their pain; food was a flimsy substitute for opium.

The morning's mist was burning off. A thin sun flickered around, warming the air. Delphine set aside her bowl of food and let her blanket slip off her shoulders and pool around her hips. She unbound her hair from the braids she and Marie maintained for each other, a tactic that kept their hair easy to bind inside a turban and safe from being grabbed by someone from behind. Her hands moved together from the end of each long braid to unravel the hair. She worked her way up, loosening, combing with her fingers until her hair stood out around her head and shoulders like a ripe milkweed pod just breaking open to seduce its seedlings to fly off. A mild wind lifted the web of unbound tangles in a gentle bid for her attention.

Delphine tried to concentrate on her food, but her mind drew her back to thoughts of her sons, and a darkness built within her. Delphine's bloodlines dictated an antidote for this, a sorrow her heart was not accustomed to bearing. She could find comfort taking scissors in hand and cutting her hair off, in the way of the Old People. She could roll in ashes, hire professional wailers to make the sounds of mourning, sounds that might midwife her into feeling the loss more deeply. And would that be good? Or was burying those feelings better? She and Blaise hadn't laid eyes on Simon or Malachi in perhaps five years, during a Lenape ceremony they had attended on Marguerite's insistence, there at their old home on the Delaware. She had never seen them again after they had become men. They were her sons, and she knew nothing about them. Until now.

Marie, following Delphine's lead, also let her blanket slip, unwound her turban, and uncoiled her braids. She scratched at her scalp. "I don't think I've washed my hair in two months," she said. "And I can feel the lice working their way through it like a forest, mating, laying their nits, dying." She was trying for humor and falling short. "Do you want me to work on yours?" she asked Delphine.

"Would you?"

Marie rose and, kneeling behind Delphine, began to part her pale hair, picking out the lice as she found them, crushing them between thumb and forefinger, flicking them away while she talked. "Delphine," she said, I didn't know you had sons here in the war." She paused to consider what one said in these situations, and then, finding it, said with feeling, "I am so sorry for your loss." She looked at Blaise too. Had Delphine made a small noise, or was that the sound of a log snapping? "There's not one of us who has to stay," Marie changed her conversational tack as she continued to sift through Delphine's hair. "Blaise, you're here as your own independent merchant. You could sell off your merchandise and not resupply."

"I have a contract," Blaise said.

"You could break your contract, Blaise!" Delphine said, as if this was not the first time they had had this exact conversation, as if Blaise were being willfully dense or purposefully not hearing her.

"But then none of us would be able to do business with the federal government again," he replied mildly.

"We could, under my name," Delphine replied.

"But the Lazar name would be muddied," Blaise reminded her, implying that the honor of several generations of Lazar traders, not just his own, would be forfeited.

"At least we didn't follow the army to the wilderness," Marie said. The two women had cited their health as reason not to accompany the army on their sortie west in an exercise to keep the bored and sick-to-death men on their feet. Blaise's imperative to provide necessary supplies had also excused him from following the men, where the threat of unseen snipers held power over the troops' psyche. Everyone knew the next battle would be fought right here, on the Rappahannock, at Fredericksburg.

"I'm not leaving you, Blaise!" Delphine said then, with more emotion than the other two had heard from her during this whole campaign. She immediately sought to cover up this gaffe, this slip of her tough persona, this accidental revelation of a wounded and vulnerable Delphine. "I'd go crazy wondering if everything was going to pieces. At least when you're here I know what is happening."

"I'm all right!" Blaise pulled the blanket up to his ears as the sun went behind a cloud. "I'll be all right! When the men come back, I'll be busy. I won't even notice if you are here or gone," he lied. "And I'm not on the front lines." *And let that be an end to it!* his manner suggested. "Delphine," he said, stating the obvious. "There's not a man here who has his wife with him."

"I'd feel guilty too," Marie said, jumping to Delphine's defense. "None of these men can leave. They'd be shot by their own commander. No deserters! I can't walk away from this just because I'm a woman. I'd lose the self-respect I've gained with this position. Back home, after the war, I'd have to face the men who stayed here to confront death. I have no one waiting for me, husband or children. Time was, the women of my lineage were war chiefs, carrying fearsome cudgels, weapons that were legendary skull-breakers, were named." Blaise and Delphine nodded. They had heard the stories; there had been a time before the Peacemaker when women went into battle with their men. "Oh no!" Marie shook her head vigorously. "The women of our tribe would be shamed if I came home because I lacked their comforts." She delivered this with a wicked grin and a great spoonful of irony.

Delphine jumped up, craving action, anything to exorcize her demons. "Come on, Marie. Let me put up all our kettles on the fire to heat. We'll drag the washtubs into the tent and have ourselves a last bath before the winter sets in. After we bathe and wash our hair, I'll work on your head. Today's a great day to spend right here in our yard, drying our hair and combing out nits. We'll wash our small clothes. You too, Blaise."

"I have Marguerite's remedy against catarrh," Blaise offered.

Delphine had helped brew it. "Rosehips," she sang out. "Elderberry.

Sassafras." Liquor could be almost as good as laudanum to chase away what plagued her.

While she sang the ingredients, Blaise rummaged in the tent and reemerged with a bottle. "And all suspended in the best alcohol." He grinned at the two women, gesturing with the bottle while they pretended to ignore him, busy filling every pot with water, building up the fire.

"I'll go to the river and refill our *botas*," he offered.

"I'll bring in a stack of wood for the fire," Marie said, reaching for the burden basket.

"And I'll make room in the tent for our ablutions," said Delphine. "River wash over me," she sang, "cleanse and make me new."

The day was growing toward noon. An unseasonable warmth suffused the air and invigorated them. Brought in by that western wind, it would have filled the sails were they nearer the ocean.

Blaise picked up the spirit of the song with his baritone: "Oh, the river is deep and the river is wide . . ." He grabbed the *botas* and headed out to his horse.

Marie, dragging a dead branch that had fortuitously come down nearby during the night, responded to his lyric with her contralto, "Take me over to the other side."

"You go in first, Marie," Delphine instructed, the tattoo of Brushfire's hooves as Blaise rode away punctuating her resolve. "When Blaise returns from the river, he and I can bathe together."

In the tent, they filled their biggest washtub full of the water they had heated in the kettles. Being the first into the bath was a privilege; filling a deep tub was too labor intensive to allow for changing the water between each bather. Afterward, they would wash their underclothes in the same bathwater all three of them had bathed in.

"Here's some soaproot. Call me when you're ready to rinse, and I'll bring in a clean bucket of warm water scented with lavender, to rinse your head." Delphine rummaged around in Blaise's tools until she found a pair of shears.

"Maybe I'll feel like a woman again when I am clean, my hair unbound and drying in the sun," Marie mused.

Neither of them had to say it, because they both felt it: their senses expanded and they felt palpable relief without the press of the men's camp around them. Marie stripped off her clothes and lowered herself into the steaming water with a blissful look on her face as she splashed her breasts.

Delphine went back out to build up the fire, using her foot to snap the branch Marie had dragged in. *Am I going to do this?* she asked herself. *Yes, yes you are.* She shoveled ashes into a bucket. *They will serve.*

Marie immersed herself and began to scrub, singing a French song Delphine recognized. *"Arma, arma, armata. Soussoukine, soussoukine, atamra."* Delphine joined in, making it a round. Marguerite had sung it to her when she was a child. When they finished, Marie launched into *"Le coq est mort."*

When Blaise returned, Delphine helped him carry in the *botas*, full of chilly river water, and together they hoisted them up into the trees. "Are you all right?" he asked her, touching her elbow. She knew her smile was not reassuring, but she turned away from him to refill the kettles and stoke the fire once more.

Marie called out, "Delphine! I'm ready. Quick! I have soap in my eyes."

"Don't spill water on our floor," Blaise reminded her in a low voice, then he grabbed her wrists. "Do you remember when our boys would get soap in their eyes when we bathed them?" he asked.

"I try not to," she said, meaning much more. She unshuttered her heart for a split second to show Blaise her coffered misery, then closed it down just as quickly.

Delphine rolled up her sleeves and picked up the bucket of warm water she had prepared with a generous splash of lavender water. She took up the other bucket of ashes in her free hand, eluding Blaise.

"I laid down canvas," she said and ducked into the tent.

Marie was wrong about herself. She was an attractive woman. Now she stood, like a Grecian statue, small-breasted, lean-hipped, her V generous with dark, curly hair, her stomach taut, arms and legs muscled.

"Stand still, Marie," Delphine said. "I am going to stand on this camp stool and pour water over your head. Use your hands to lift your hair so the soap sluices down into the tub. All right, here we go." She slowly poured the warm water in a continuous stream while Marie lifted and wrung her long, straight dark hair over one shoulder. Marie gasped, opened her eyes.

During the spring and summer and well into the fall, the two women had bathed in the closest creek or river. It had been difficult to find a time and place where they could have privacy, and they always needed Blaise to stand guard. While they hadn't had leisure time to soak and play, they had at least managed to keep themselves clean. Winter was going to bring a fresh challenge.

The inside of the tent was warm and steamy from the bath. Delphine had laid the bucket of ashes and the scissors on the far side of the tub. "Your body is firm and young. You *are* attractive, Marie Tepe!" Delphine scolded her friend. She handed Marie a length of Turkish toweling, one of the real luxuries they afforded themselves that the fighting men around them did not have.

"I haven't ever worn a corset," Marie allowed.

Delphine stepped out of her skirt, unbuttoned her blouse, unlaced her corset, dropped her pantaloons, and removed her small clothes and stockings. She ran a hand reflexively down her stomach. "Sometimes I think my corset keeps me girded against harm, pulled up and fortified. Other times I can feel myself sagging against it."

"Why do you wear it?" asked Marie, toweling her hair.

"Even when I am sagging," Delphine allowed, with a little smile playing at the corners of her lips, "inside my corset I still feel girded. For battle. Or whatever comes."

"A tightly wrapped cummerbund works just as well for me," Marie said. "I have to breathe," she added. "Have to feel my heart beat." Then Marie dared to go further: "I want a child. And you have had three. I don't see how you can bear it."

Delphine couldn't allow herself to take in Marie's words. Keeping the upper hand, she directed, "Marie, don't you dare get back into those dirty, lousy clothes." The twenty-year difference between the two women allowed Delphine certain privileges as elder. "I've laid out two sets of a fresh *viviandière* uniform, over there on my trunk. One for each of us, new from our stores. We can wash our old ones and hang them up outside today to dry."

Marie raised her eyebrows but, following Delphine's instructions, took the pile of fresh clothes and drew them on. Delphine began to lower herself into the tub.

"Delphine, I'm bringing in a kettle of hot water for that tub," Marie said. "Don't sit down in it yet."

When Marie returned, she poured an entire kettle of hot water into the tub. Delphine sighed and sat down into it gingerly. The older woman executed something like a shoulder stand to wet her head, tucking her legs back under her, hair streaming water over her face and shoulders.

"Neatly done, Delphine. Here's the soaproot."

"Send Blaise in when I holler."

As soon as Marie turned her back, Delphine reached for the scissors. With wet hair, it was easy. Four, five snips. She stepped out of the tub quickly. *Now the ashes.* She rubbed them onto her face, breasts, stomach, buttocks, and then lay doubled up on the wet canvas, indulging in the luxury of allowing herself to feel the loss of her sons.

Blaise called as he stepped into the tent: "Are you ready for me?" Then, seeing her, "Delphine."

She shook off his hand on her head, like a wet dog.

He helped her back into the tub, gently. He poured a pitcher of water over her head, sudsed up his hands and removed the charcoal from her breasts, buttocks, stomach, humming a lullaby they had sung to their children when they were infants.

He took her to bed.

"I wasn't there for you, Blaise," she said. "You weren't meant to face burying Simon alone."

After, Delphine wrapped her head in a fresh Zouave turban and dressed while Blaise took his turn in the lukewarm bathwater. Like all of the native men, he kept his hair long, and Delphine helped wash his head in the tub.

When he was done, he draped the Turkish towel on his head and chased the women around the yard, delighted to hear them shriek when he lunged at one of them. The absence of the army allowed them to play. Something had been exorcised. They all felt it.

They gathered their blankets and flannels from their bedrolls, hung them on the lines, and—watching them carefully so they didn't burn—turned them with long sticks, smoking the lice out of their bedding. The fresh breeze that had risen up in the morning continued into the early afternoon, and the sun had come out fully; Blaise was in shirtsleeves, the women in their layers of underclothing.

Blaise bent his neck to have Delphine inspect his head. While she picked, pinched, and flicked, he resumed their earlier conversation: "Thread could get you out of camp under cover of night."

Nearby, Marie worked on their evening's stew, adding onion, carrot, and potato as well as the herbs and spices the sutler tent afforded to their stewpot: black pepper, *fines herbes*, a bay leaf. She lifted her head as if Blaise's words were a whiff of smoke warning her of an enemy encampment in the woods ahead.

Blaise took another nip from the bottle of lung medicine Marguerite had sent along, a whole caseful for their personal consumption. He handed it off to Delphine, who took a break from Blaise's hair to sit and sip.

"Delphine," he said, "you woke again in the night screaming."

Delphine looked as if she were about to argue.

"I heard you in my tent," Marie confirmed as she dumped a board full of rough-cut carrots and cabbage into the pot.

"I certainly wouldn't be the first in this camp to scream in the night," Delphine observed dryly.

Blaise pondered, reaching for his pipe, clearing the channel, then filling, tamping, and lighting it. He passed it to Delphine, who passed the bottle to Marie before taking the pipe.

Marie squatted beside the couple, forming a triangle just off to the side of the fire. "I think my hair's dry enough to braid, Delphine. Would you?"

Delphine stood behind Marie with a large-toothed comb, parted the hair, lifted it to dry, let it drop. She worked for a while with the comb, picking out any remaining nits, and then she made a neat part down the back of Marie's head, divided her hair into two falls, each one going over Marie's shoulders and then down onto her knees. "Marie," she said, "it's going to tangle unless you stand."

When the two women stood, Delphine opened a bottle of oil, poured a bit into her palms, and oiled one long fall of Marie's hair. Then, drawing the hair out to the side, above Marie's ears, she divided that hank into three and began to braid, holding the tension in each strand until the braid took hold and she could continue on down the length of the hair. When she let it fall, the braid came down to Marie's hip. Delphine went around in front of her friend, checked the lay of the braid she had just finished, and, pouring oil into her palms again, took the other section of hair in hand.

"They didn't cut your hair when you were small," she murmured to Marie.

"Every once in a while," Marie said. "My mother would cut off the ends at the new moon. To stimulate growth, she said."

"Blaise," Delphine said, firmness in her voice as she picked up their earlier thread of conversation. "I also have no one to go home to. Oh, there's Mother. And the aunts in Newtown. But if I had to guess, they have gone north, to Cottage, out of harm's way. If I were to go all the way to Cottage, and then to Seneca Falls, I could be useful, perhaps. But let's face it, with our Zouave business finished, I would be at loose ends. Turtle Dawn and I are not close; she would not welcome me into her house. And she is busy keeping the business going with Philip. Wilhelm has found someone to run our dyeing business; they are dyeing for both Regina Coeli and his own operation."

Blaise looked startled. "How do you know all this?"

"Kilian gets posts," she said. "And I don't always remember to tell you the details."

All of the earlier steam had gone out of her, after the bath. She rested near the fire, sipping from the bottle, lifting her hair to dry before Marie French-braided what was left of it close to her head. "The one who should go home is Kilian," she said. They all knew Kilian was close to breaking down. "This is not what he signed up for. But," she sighed, "as he is the first to say, he is here for Thread." Although what he might be doing for Thread, no one could say.

"Blaise," she said, suddenly tired. "I am going to nap. My hair is almost dry. And"—she fingered the pants of her uniform on the line—"the clothes will be dry before the sun starts to go down in—what?—another couple of hours? Then we can eat our stew in the tent, by candlelight."

"I will come with you," Blaise said, reaching for the line to pull off their flannels and quilts.

"I will watch the fire and stir the stew," Marie said. "Perhaps I'll make some fresh johnnycake."

They all knew Blaise and Delphine were going to the tent to couple, only afterward to nap. Marie was conflicted; she didn't know whether she liked men or women. No one had ever asked her to couple, nor had she ever felt the urge to have someone other than herself touch her ... there. Until then, she would be the one keeping the fire. She heard them talking in low voices in the tent and wished with all her heart for what they had—whatever it was, whatever she was capable of. "Mother, hear me," she prayed aloud.

Blaise looked down at Delphine, her short braids undone, her hair spread across her pillow like dandelion fluff. "Delphine," he said, gently. "I was with you in Buffalo Creek. I saw you lock up your heart when the tribe lost your home." He sighed deeply. "I stood beside you when your mother took both Turtle Dawn and the two small boys. Simon and Malachi."

A lump had risen in his throat. They had never grieved the loss of their children, together. They had risen from their bed of grief after the children were gone, the Ogden Land Company at their door with the wrecking crew, with one mind, one heart: to live life fully to make up for their losses, to die with no regrets, having filled their cup to brimming.

Delphine had her back to him. He gently tugged on her right shoulder so that she had to turn toward him. Tears ran down her cheeks. He knew she was crying because she barely remembered their sons. They had packed them away in cotton batting to always remain boys. She knew nothing about them as men. Blaise held her and together they fell asleep, letting their grief wash through them, at last.

Chapter Nineteen

UNDER THE
AURORA BOREALIS

December 11–15, 1862, Fredericksburg, Virginia

A fortnight later, the army began to arrive back at camp from the wilderness, the usual straggling procession of footsore soldiers. Wagons that had left with provisions returned with the maimed and wounded. Groaning resumed at their camp, and, as the surgery tent opened up for business, screaming. Kilian and Thread checked in, had supper, and, exhausted, gave their reports. Both men gratefully accepted packages of creature comforts Blaise and Delphine had given them to share with their company, and promised to return the next night, when they were rested.

Blaise and Delphine were ready for the onslaught of customers and anticipated their extra needs now that the days and nights were unremittingly cold, November having given way to December. General Burnside didn't seem to have coaxed Washington into sending enough of the rations they needed desperately, nor had the men received chits to represent their back pay. The last of a soldier's meager treasures were now presented for currency at the sutler tent.

As for Kilian, he only wanted one thing: to have his dispatches read; he asked Blaise to take them out on his next supply run. Blaise and Delphine privately wondered if any more had been printed beyond the two they had seen in the *Bucks County Intelligencer*. The one Blaise had read to her? They had no way of knowing if subsequent dispatches were well met in the

Quaker community, as Blaise didn't ask about them on his infrequent trips out to resupply. Neither Blaise nor Delphine were Quakers or part of that community, although they had lived most of their lives close to Newtown, where the Society of Friends were the majority, as they were throughout Bucks County and Philadelphia.

In camp, Burnside kept his engineers busy, telegraphing his intentions to the opposition by building pontoon bridges across the Rappahannock in those places he intended to concentrate his troops. The parts had arrived late from Washington, and now the work parties were beset by snipers, making the building of the pontoons the opening salvo of the Battle of Fredericksburg.

When the pontoon bridges were completed early in December, Union companies poured across and—infuriated by the losses they'd suffered under cover of the Fredericksburg homes—sacked, looted, and plundered the town like the basest of any army in history. The inhabitants had long since fled, but the behavior of the Union soldiers—parading around drunkenly in ladies' undergarments, building fires of heirloom furniture, indiscriminately smashing chandeliers and family portraits—was a mighty show of rage against the accumulated culture of the South, where everyone seemed wealthier and more cultivated than the soldiers from the North. The conspicuous differences and provocations inflamed the Union soldiers, true enough, but Burnside accepted no excuses; his letters to Washington backed up his assertion that he was appalled by the behavior of his countrymen.

Confederate soldiers who witnessed the mayhem from afar were "loaded for bear" the next day, when the battle commenced. General Lee compared the Union soldiers to Vandals. Burnside made a point of sending those companies who looted, and who were then deeply hung over, into battle first.

The assault of Marye's Heights began at first light. The Confederates were protected by stone walls lining the sunken road and barricades constructed above the plains. From behind those shelters, they sent a brutal fusillade against the locked-shoulder formations of the Union companies, battalion by battalion, row after endless row of men, a living wall of farm boys shoulder to shoulder with their fathers, set up like dominos.

Marie and Delphine saw it with their own eyes from a nearby copse where they had taken shelter. By noon, men who had been shot earlier in the morning were plucking at the legs of their comrades, pleading with them to not go forward into certain death and dismemberment.

The two women were turned to stone by the spectacle. They held each other in a lock, afraid to look but unwilling not to, as the endless columns of men and boys marched in step, having to lift their legs over the growing pile of bodies. Eight hours later, by nightfall, the dead and wounded had become an effective shield. Although they were ordered to march upright, the Union soldiers defied orders by lying flat on their bellies to fire and reload, their rifles propped against this half-living wall. The Confederate sharpshooters, crouched behind the impermeable stone wall that lay at the foot of Marye's Heights along the Sunken Road, continued to pour lead into the soft bodies of the fallen.

Blaise crawled out to the copse under cover of twilight and guided the two women, paralyzed by fear and horror, away from the battlefield and back to the sutler tent, where he comforted them as best he could with what little they had. He unearthed a small flask of brandy, half full, and a packet of sweet biscuits, so stale they had to dunk them in the brandy to make them chewable. He was afraid to drug the women; in their state, they might not waken. He had to save their personal reserve of opium for an emergency. He had spent the day loading his supply wagon in case they needed to make a hasty retreat, which seemed likely. He had a small packet of Kilian's dispatches tucked into his belt pouch.

The shooting did not stop as it traditionally did after a day's slaughter, to give the survivors a chance to pull the dead and wounded off the battlefield. Burnside, they said, was throwing everything he had into this battle, but-tressing Lincoln's Emancipation Proclamation. The Union needed a clear victory, especially after the loss at Antietam.

Marie sat in the sutler tent, shaking uncontrollably, salty tears pouring in runnels down her cheeks. Delphine, still as a statue, only her eyes betray-ing her altered state, sharpened her knife against a grindstone in a circular dragging motion whose sound was beginning to get on Blaise's nerves. The night air sang with minié balls thudding into and winging off anything solid: horses, wagons, tins, bodies. They were in that place again: lost to time. Hell on earth was becoming familiar home ground.

"We've got to bring our horses in, Blaise," Marie announced suddenly and was through the flaps of the tent before either of them could react.

She had not gone ten steps from the tent when she cried out.

Delphine snapped out of her paralysis and ran out to find Marie hunched over her leg.

"My ankle," she gasped. "I've taken a minié ball."

Blaise and Delphine helped her into the tent, suddenly conscious that bullets were whizzing through the air all around them, a swarm of stinging insects seeking the flesh of solid victims.

They eased Marie onto a cot and took off her bloody boot.

Blaise reached for an opium suppository while Delphine examined the ragged wound.

"Marie," Delphine said, lifting her skirt. The younger woman, in shock, nodded her head. Delphine slipped her fingers between Marie's pantaloons, found her anus, and shoved the suppository up as far as her index finger would go, then eased Marie's knees back down. "Give her some water," she instructed Blaise, in part to help distract their patient while Delphine prepared to remove the projectile.

First she doused the wound with alcohol, which made Marie screech, although her sound became lost in the field of what had become thousands of wounded and dying soldiers screaming, roaring, calling for their mothers in the abyss of the freezing night.

When Marie began to tremble violently, Blaise piled blankets on her. Delphine probed the ankle with her thinnest calipers, following the entry wound, and when she felt them touch metal, she opened them cautiously, which she could see caused Marie, her friend and sister-in-arms, searing pain. When Marie bucked up, Blaise put his body over hers to hold her down. Blaise and Delphine were operating in the theater of war as if they were a well-rehearsed team.

Calipers spread, Delphine thrust them in farther until she felt the leaden mass inside the two tines. She clamped the caliper closed and slowly pulled the bullet from the massive hole, bringing with it chunks of bone and muscle. The bullet clanked when she dropped it into a white enameled bowl.

Delphine poured alcohol on the wound again, but by now the opium had dulled Marie's nerves and she bore the sting better. Delphine applied a poultice of yarrow, angelica, and goldenseal and wrapped fresh gauze and then clean linen strips around Marie's ankle. She had already fallen into a stupor, snoring like a drunk, mouth open, arms and legs slack.

Blaise and Delphine looked at each other and crawled into their furs. There was nothing more they could do that night except try to get some rest. As they lay together in the dark, they noticed a change in the timbre of the groans and shrieks from the battlefield, and then they realized the side of the tent was being illuminated from outside by a strange light.

"What is it?" Blaise whispered.

They rose and went out.

The sky was dancing. The night was lit with shafts and curtains of light—rose, aqua, gold—as tens of thousands of souls rose from the freezing ground, their devastated bodies left below. It looked as if creative mercy were lifting these sufferers away from their pitiable existence with a palette designed to delight those remaining behind.

The sounds of the dying had turned into the sounds celebrants made during incendiary displays on patriotic holidays, their ahs, ohs, and gasps interspersed with the calls of those begging to go along, afraid to stay, beseeching the Mother to accept their shattered and tortured flesh back into the womb of life, to put Her hand on their brow. The shooting had stopped as both sides contemplated their common universe. God was speaking to man once more, soundlessly, in a play of light, in dance.

"This must be what they call angels," they heard a man say.

Another responded, "They call it aurora borealis, but I've never heard of it this far south."

A wind came up. Now Delphine heard a symphony. Everyone was listening. She could feel their silence, part of the music and the dance.

Kilian galloped up and, seeing the departing spirits made visible in the colorful light, he raised both arms to the sky. He had come from the surgery tent and was covered in the blood and stringy flesh of his fellow man. "I have decided to desert," he said, sliding down off his horse. "I have come to say goodbye." All three looked up at the sky, whose splendors continued, then ducked their heads to go into the tent.

Delphine and Blaise indicated with a whisper that he must be careful of Marie, who lay unconscious on the cot. Kilian fell onto his knees at her side, and even after they assured him that she had only taken a minié ball in her ankle, he continued to pour out his grief on her body, as if she were an altar and he the priest.

As Delphine watched him, she found something unsettling in Kilian's behavior, and she was even more grateful for Blaise's presence.

After a while, Kilian stood and removed a brooch from his pocket. "Here," he said, putting it on the table. "I will not make it out of here alive. Kilian, the man you have known, is gone from this place. He cannot stay here." Then his mood changed suddenly, a garish grin taking over his features.

Delphine walked up to him, touched his arm. "We know, Kilian. We know and we are sorry." She put her arm around his shoulder, which stiffened.

"What do you want us to do with the brooch, Kilian?" Blaise asked.

"It was Eugenia's," he said. "I can't carry it anymore. Right now, I need opium," Kilian said. "How much can you give me?"

"Who is it for, Kilian?" Blaise asked.

"You have no right to ask, Blaise," Kilian said. "I built that business. I'm telling you I need as much as you can give me."

"That is not the way to desert, Kilian," Blaise said quietly, stepping in close.

Kilian groaned. "Don't do this to me, Blaise! It's the sweetest way to desert! Those lights—," he tossed his head to indicate the lights that continued to flicker outside the tent. "I can go with all of them, a procession. I don't want to be just another body to dump into the ditch and cover up with sweet, dark, heavy soil."

"You'll have to take the opium from me by force, Kilian." Blaise assumed a fighting position. "I'm not going to put the rope around your neck, damn it!"

Delphine stepped in. "Stop it, both of you." Then she turned to Kilian.

"How would I explain this to my daughter?" She lifted his chin so he had to look straight at her. "Tell me that. Are you a man? Or a coward?"

"A man would do this to escape this hell," Kilian answered, but they could see his resolve collapsing at the mention of Turtle Dawn.

Blaise uncorked another bottle of the catarrh medicine and soon the three of them were sitting and passing the bottle around while Kilian relayed details about the conditions outside. The surgery tents were practically empty, as no one could go onto the battlefield to bring back the wounded, an unheard-of precedent. From the cold light of dawn until the last light fled from the sky, Burnside had marched company after company against the well-protected defenders of Marye's Heights, who slaughtered an estimated one thousand men per hour, not counting the wounded, who could not be rescued from their agony without more men risking bullets in their own flesh.

Delphine turned slowly and, with that deadly calm of a soldier going out on a suicide mission, moved toward the flap of the tent and slipped outside. Blaise threw the bottle to the ground and ran after her, calling, "Delphine! Where are you going?!"

He couldn't hold her. She tore away, jumped onto Bucephalus, and rode off into the night toward the direction she knew General Burnside's tent to be. After settling Kilian, checking Marie's vital signs, and saddling up, Blaise followed on Brushfire, but not soon enough.

What happened then became history. Blaise heard the details from Delphine herself, but after Fredericksburg, while two women and a whole campful of men bandaged their wounds and laid low, he had to tell someone else what he knew. He rode out to resupply—at least that was the thin excuse he gave Delphine, who didn't seem to care—but he was really off to relate the story to Lazarus, his spiritual guide, who came down to Newtown to meet Blaise at his summons. The invention of the telegraph had revolutionized communications; Lazarus set out on the train and was able to meet Blaise within a week of his telegram.

The two men sat around a campfire on the brow of the hill above Newtown, a place that had gained significance to the family over the generations. When Blaise was ready, he began.

"As far as I can gather, Lazarus, your niece, my wife, rode up to Burnside's tent and pulled her horse to a stop, sliding off him all in one motion and girding herself for her ill-formed attempt to break through the general's elite guard. I don't know what she had in mind: assassination? The sky was still bleeding color, the night loud with the cacophony of the wounded chorus who suffered alone, or in a pile where they had fallen. Burnside's elite guard were looking up at the sky in a trance.

"She said that when she sidled up to slip into the general's tent they noticed her. They interpreted her as a gift from the gods, an epiphany equal to the display of the aurora borealis, a magical being appearing for their delight. A Valkyrie. She responded to their caresses with moans and tosses of her fragrant chopped hair, her breasts coming unbound.

"They took her out, four of them, away from the tent in the dark and, holding her mouth closed, gently made love to her, one after another, buckles coming undone, pants sliding down, taking hold of their aching flesh, whispering endearments, their adoration of her parts, opening her, holding each other back from violence, from using her as a vessel for violence. That's what she told me. They held her like a precious icon, worshipping her in the only way they knew, pleasuring her as she gave them her gift: pleasuring them. These are the words she used."

Blaise lifted his head from his chest, where he held his temples in his hands, and continued.

"Eventually her cries of ecstasy, the men's gasps of pleasure, the unintentional shouts of such acute sensations, long-deprived, finally attracted the great man himself, who came tearing at his own belt buckle. He was ready to rape her, any woman, his reward for a day of blood and slaughter, he must have figured."

Blaise breathed a great sigh and released it, ruffling his beard with one hand, composing himself.

"I rode up in the darkness, slid off Brushfire, and coldcocked Burnside while his officers, his elite guard, Delphine's lovers, gathered her up, arranged her clothing, her hair, all the while murmuring their devotion and prayers.

"I . . . I was beside myself," he told Lazarus. "I drew my steel saber, throwing sparks into the darkness. The four men, weaponless, backed up in a clot, afraid to die. I whistled to the horses, then lifted Delphine onto Brushfire and jumped up behind her, her body boneless and . . . yes, silky from ecstasy. A feeling of her flesh I am very familiar with," he said quietly, as if to himself. Then: "Uncertain which way to go, and with Bucephalus tethered behind us, confused and stuttering around in a circle, I prayed, *Darkness, protect me!*"

Silence fell and the two men listened to the night. Lazarus rose and put one log, then another on the fire, sparks flying up into the night.

Blaise spoke again, the story unravelling itself like a spool of ribbon rolling down a hill. "I know you have spent your life in hiding after an act such as this one, Lazarus, and so you know: I couldn't do anything else, damn the consequences! Holding my pistol aloft, I fired it, once, twice, three times, four, into the ground, one shot for each of the men now standing around the inert body of their general, the colors still dripping from the sky, spilling over them like one of Turtle Dawn's paintings. And then I fired once again, hoping to hit Burnside's body, butcher, rapist, intending to send a message: This man should die.

"But here's the part that gets me: Later, Delphine insisted it hadn't been like that. 'They didn't rape me, Blaise. They loved me; I loved them.' She told me, 'It was a ritual act. Not a rape, but perfection, a piece of the whole.'"

"'Disgusting whore,' I thought." I couldn't help myself from thinking it, although I never betrayed that feeling to her. I haven't touched her since," he said contemplatively. Then he lifted his head to look at Lazarus. "I am glad she decided to keep the details of that night between the two of us. But I had to tell someone." He stood up and paced around the fire, unseeing of the night, the stars, his companion. "Do you believe that, Lazarus? Not a rape." He shook his head like a bull that has been teased and pricked by the picadors in a bullfight and has one last charge in him. "Four men."

Lazarus asked if the men had come after Blaise, if his identity had been discovered.

Blaise laughed, a rueful laugh that made Lazarus wonder how long the damage from this incident would last, how severe the blow would be to his nephew's spirits.

"The next day," he said, "information came from the surgery tent that Burnside's balls had been scorched by a bullet, a warning from a man whose identity would remain hidden. If anyone knew how it had happened, not a person existed who would step forward to explain it."

Before they parted the next morning, one to head south and the other north, Lazarus asked Blaise if there was anything he could do.

Blaise blew a lot of air from his lungs before answering. Their horses stood ready, warm air coming from their nostrils in great jets like locomotive steam on a frosty morning such as this. They stomped their feet and tossed their manes. "Fredericksburg will go down in history as the day and the night of no reason," Blaise said. "No excuses, and no defense. I'll be sending Delphine out, to return to the tribe, a safer place for her to unravel than down there on the battlefield."

Lazarus had the last word: "Can you forgive her?"

Blaise threw his leg over the saddle and saluted his mentor. "Watch out for her, Kerioniakawida."

Chapter Twenty

WITHOUT WORDS, WHAT?

Mid-December 1862, Fredericksburg, Virginia

Blaise sent Delphine home alone.

"I can't leave until my supplies are lower," he explained. "But I've secured safe passage through the warzone for you. There's a large sutler wagon convoy going out with the wounded; they have agreed to see you safely to the Pennsylvania border. I'll give you bullion. You can get a fast stagecoach or train into South Dayton from there."

"And Marie?" Delphine asked. Her fellow *viviandière* had been hobbling around camp on improvised crutches; there was now a surplus of crutches, so many of the wounded having died.

"We will move her tent back to her company." Both of them knew it would not be proper for Marie to stay in Blaise's camp, not with Delphine gone. "She is not yet ready to travel."

Alone together later that morning, Delphine spoke with Marie. "You will be all right?"

Marie fussed with the bandages around her ankle, an image Delphine returned to again and again in the months to come, obsessively. She should have *seen*. "I will move my tent back tonight. Kilian has agreed to help me. Until I can get off these crutches . . ."

Delphine noticed the way Marie talked about Kilian. *Does she have her eye on him?* She wondered, but she was under too much pressure to be concerned about such things.

"You did a professional job on me, removing the minié ball, Delphine. I don't know what I was thinking, dashing out of the tent like that." She lowered her lashes to her cheeks as if embarrassed. Or apologizing.

She doesn't know about me, about what happened, Delphine realized. "None of us were thinking." Then: "What will you do, Marie?"

"I guess I'll go back home to my family, up in Québec," Marie said. She lay on the cot watching Delphine pack.

Delphine closed her worn saddlebag with a tug on the straps that cinched it tight. "You'll leave information on how we can reach you?"

She knew they wouldn't see each other again—the distances were too great—and since Marie could neither read nor write, there was little hope that letters would produce an enduring intimacy. The two women had been through an unusual experience together, one that would mark them, but each would have to carry those scars by herself.

No one in camp questioned Delphine's leaving. She wondered if her commander had heard about the vision of a woman at Burnside's tent and suspected either her or Marie. Her usual response to those who asked was, "No, Fredericksburg has bested me." And she considered it her new mission: to return home. Return to her family, her mother Marguerite, her daughter Turtle Dawn, and now her granddaughter, Nesting Swan. But more, she would return to herself—to her tribe, to her history, to her tradition.

She would not forget what had happened during her time in the war. She had never felt closer to Blaise, but now—after three decades of operating as one unit—there had to be a time apart. Blaise would hold down the business, survive this war, and return to their life together. Something had changed between them, but she could not query it, not yet.

Delphine gave Marie the small misshapen ball of lead she had dug out of her friend's ankle, putting it in a small doeskin bag with a lump of angelica root, sacred to Delphine's people and perhaps to Marie's. At the last minute, feeling she owed Marie more, she decided to sacrifice a chunk of native ginseng. Along with careful instructions for using it to make a tea for the man Marie would choose to father her child, she explained, "This will strengthen a man's seed and help you conceive. Is this still what you want?"

In turn, Marie bested Delphine in the gift exchange, insisting that the beautifully tooled leather saddlebag her grandfather had made for her did not put Delphine in Marie's debt but quite the opposite. Later, Delphine realized Marie had been accurate: *She thought she could buy my complicity.*

Delphine's honor guard—Blaise, Kilian, and Thread—accompanied her out of the camp to a safe perimeter, where they camped for the night one last time. Kilian and Thread sent word back to their company that they would return and should not be counted as deserters.

That evening, Kilian, happy for this rare chance at solitude, had built his own campfire apart from the small family threesome, then sharpened his lead so that he could write until the light faded, until his tin-can candle guttered. The others had gone to bed. The full moon was so bright it threw long shadows. In the midst of a serious internal conversation with himself about stealing into the woods, being well away by morning, he was jolted by the sounds of an approaching horse, then its reining in and a single pair of booted feet hitting the ground.

"Sir."

Kilian sighed, aware that this was the consequence that came from having given a fellow soldier details about where they would be camped. He rose reluctantly, leaving that small moment of sanity, that fleeting freedom to choose between desertion or writing another column, that infinitesimal measure of rightness, of commanding his own skin. He greeted the messenger, his gun drawn, wondering if he was going to have to kill him. He looked into the eyes of a man who brought very bad news indeed. "Yes?"

This boy didn't even shave yet. The rigors of upholding his military bearing in the face of reporting bad news to such a seasoned soldier as Kilian had put a stain on his cheeks. The boy cleared his throat. "I have spent part of the night looking for you, sir."

"And now you have found me," Kilian said sharply.

"My superior officer says you must stop sending out your dispatches, sir!" The stain spread from his cheeks to his ears and down to his collar.

Then the meaning of the words the boy had said slowly crept into Kilian, and he grew hot with a fury he had never felt. Rage arose in him, perfectly formed, too big for his veins to carry, erupting into his overtaxed liver, sending an unspeakable need to throttle someone, anyone, with his hands. *No, not this boy*, he thought, *this catamite of the captain's. He is not worthy of being my first coldblooded murder.*

He considered his options: *I can jump on my horse, ride hard back to the encampment, tear into the captain's tent, ask him what the hell? I can go over his head, talk to the regimental commander, remind him of my connections with the press. I can continue sending out my dispatches in protest against this strutting martinet of a man, my captain.* Then: "Tell the captain . . ."

The messenger boy stammered: "Sir, these orders don't come from the captain."

"Curiouser and curiouser . . ."

"They come from the general, sir." The boy reached into his pocket and withdrew a brooch. "He said to give this token to you, which was found outside his tent, engraved on the back with your name and a woman's. He said you would know what it meant."

Kilian was puzzled. How had this brooch, which he had traded to Blaise for opium on that fateful night, been dropped by Burnside's tent? He felt it was nothing less than a sign, another omen. *Do Burnside's singed balls have something to do with me?* he asked himself, trying to puzzle it out.

The boy cleared his throat. "The general said to tell you this: His picket came across your man, sir. Emptied his pouch, found your dispatches, then shot him for a traitor."

"Killed for my words? My courier? He was just a boy . . ." Kilian looked up into the night sky, as if to interrogate the indifferent face of this god who had left such omens in his path. There had been a casualty—the Quaker boy who had come into this war hoping to be a simple courier, hoping to avoid violence—and his death was Kilian's fault. The boy had considered it a noble mission to carry Killian's dispatches to the *Bucks County*

Intelligencer, to a Quaker audience. *And now he has given his life, that boy,* Kilian thought. Just another boy among thousands. His parents would never hear how it had happened; they would always wonder.

Kilian's thoughts began to spiral. *Without my words interpreting this world for those who stayed behind, without this tenuous thread, woven to represent this outlandish, nightmarish, taboo world . . . to that world of denial, of conjecture, of procrastination and making decisions based on absolutely no information at all . . . Without my words, what will I be doing here? Sewing up lads and their fathers? Thinking of murder?*

Kilian's fury confounded his tongue. *I cannot live without a more honorable role to play.* "Tell your captain to tell his commander to tell his general to take me out and shoot me for a traitor," he said with resolve. "I cannot—will not—stop sending out my dispatches!"

"Sir, I suggest you tell him yourself." The words hung in the air as the boy rode off to find his death at another's hands perhaps, although not tonight.

Kilian recognized defeat when he heard it: the sound of doors closing far away, then closer and closer, doors closing until, finally, the sound was that of the lid falling on his coffin. How long could he fight it, this feeling that he could not survive another hour as the privations of this war ground at his sanity? Now he saw how ridiculous he had been. His mission had not been to save Thread. He couldn't even save himself! His mission was not to use the newspaper to inform that other world, that fantasy world of breakfast and Eugenia's bright-pink scarf, and all by the agency of their daily newspaper. Preposterous.

No, his mission—the mission of all of them!—was to be wheat broken under the flail, a necessary sacrifice so that they might be transformed into the bread of life. *Threshing,* he said to himself, and then risked saying more in Dialog: *We are all being threshed.*

Blaise, Thread, and Delphine sat around their snapping fire after eating the dinner that was meant to be celebratory. "*Gran'mère,*" Thread said, holding out his hand, upon which rested a small pouch with a braided cord. "I made this for you. To put your most precious things into." He blushed as she dug into the soft doeskin and withdrew a small tooth. "Mother gave this to me before I left. One of my baby teeth she kept."

How like Turtle Dawn to be the sentimental one, the one who kept locks of hair, dried umbilical cord, baby teeth, Delphine thought. To relieve his embarrassment at the naked emotion of this gift, she saw her way to thank him. Through this fully grown man from her bloodline, she also thanked Simon, her son, now dead, whom she would never be able to thank in person. "I will need this bag to keep my precious things when I return to our People. An amulet bag. Thank you."

He nodded, relieved that she understood.

"Thread," she said, as if she were speaking to Simon as he began his journey, to Malachi as he made his way through this endless war alone. "You are not abandoned here. All of our ancestors are here with you, to protect you, to guide you." She almost believed it herself. She tugged on the amulet bag and said, "I will keep this safe for you."

Later, much later, just as her eyes were closing in the last moment before falling into a deep sleep, Blaise touched her shoulder. "I have to get back, Delphine. I am leaving at first light, perhaps before you wake. I have something to put in that amulet bag." She was fully awake then and sat up, holding the hand that touched her so she could judge where he was in the absolute darkness. "I took this off Simon's body," he said, putting a small object into her hand.

"How did you know where to find our boys?" Delphine knew this moment with Blaise, in the dark, was the last moment she would have to ask this question.

"Our tribesmen let me know. You remember when I was late returning from getting supplies? I went by and found both of them, Malachi grieving, kiyi-ing, putting ashes on his face. He was glad to see me. He's a man now, Delphine. I was there for both of them, to send Simon off to our ancestors, to see his flesh into the earth."

She ran her hand over the small thing, so much like a baby tooth, but all curves. It was one of the two shells they had given each of their sons when they had reached the age of being accepted as initiates into their Lenape Wolf Clan. Their whorled surfaces had been drilled so they could be strung on a small whipcord.

She took his hand in the dark, pressed her lips like a seal on the rough ham of his palm, beneath the thumb. "Stay safe," she said. "Ask the Mother if you need protection, Blaise." She thought she sensed him nodding. They lay down again, back to back like a pair of bows, arched against each other, and then fell into sleep.

PART FOUR

1863

Chapter Twenty-One

RETURN

January 1863, Cattaraugus Reservation, New York

When Delphine had arrived at Cattaraugus a fortnight later, everything looked different. While it had been just short of two years since they had left for the war, Marguerite had grown old and small; Delphine could see that the winters had been hard on her mother. One never imagines that one's mother—the vast, potent whole of her—might shrink as the daughter comes into her own elder years.

The houses strung along the river, tucked into the features of the landscape, were unpainted here on the reservation, and Delphine, having been to the South and then having traveled all the way back north after the eternity of war, saw for the first time that these structures were not shabby, as she had once thought, but practical extensions of more ancient dwellings, built by ancestors back in the earliest days of story. The smells of the village hit her memory like a stick, beating up visual and sensory images from the underbrush of her past: on that morning it was the hot mash of potato peels for the chickens, coffee grounds, eggshells, bean and cabbage trimmings, all of it reminding her of those childhood days of hunger, when she had envied the hens their hot, nourishing meals.

Delphine had gone there as a petitioner, hat in hand, to ask if she could be accepted back into the tribe, to find out what the terms of her return might be. As she approached the full moon of her life, she noted her place among the women of her family. Her daughter, Turtle Dawn, was weaning a toddler, while her mother, Marguerite, was waning, emptying like a bowl, as if preparing to fill herself again for her journey to another realm. After two years of war, Delphine suffered an uneasy truce with being home. She struggled to see where she might belong.

She saw how her maternal uncle Lazarus had learned to be invisible here. When he moved among the white world, he was overlooked, camouflaged. Could she also do that? Delphine admitted with a pang of embarrassment how she had been formed: wanting to be admired, to be valued for the very visible life she had constructed out of travel, glamorous clothing, being a business woman with notorious friends. Was it time to put those notions aside?

Back in the village once more, she felt her natural self began to peek out from behind the corner of the closet she had built around herself. She started to remember how to move quietly through the woods between dwellings, how to feed an animal so it accepted the relationship that defined you both: horse and person, chicken and person, pig and person. She watched how her cousin killed a hen to celebrate Delphine's homecoming, a model of mercy. When words were intrusive, superfluous, she noted how her People gestured instead. Except with children. For them, words, songs, stories flew through the air, balls being tossed from one to the other. *Play. I have forgotten about play.*

The reservation's Thomas School had approached her through the proper channels, sending the administrator, a woman Delphine had attended the school with when they were children, to inquire just a few days after her return from the war. Would Delphine consider helping the children improve their French? Their business skills? Teach them how to dye? Delphine welcomed this as the first sign that her reintegration might not be so difficult after all. Sitting with the Montour women of the house, her hand wrapped around a cup of tea, the woman saw Delphine's face change after she had made her request, and so she hastened to add: "All this can happen after you have settled in, of course." He words seemed to imply *If you stay.*

Delphine had accepted with this proviso: "I'll start when I am fully returned." She hoped her answer was vague enough that she could keep her word. She was determined not to overpromise.

Winter Solstice had come and gone while Delphine was on her journey back to Cattaraugus, and the community had marked its passage with a quiet Renewal ceremony. This would not be a Famine Moon; children were well fed, elders vigorous, nursing mothers had full breasts. Delphine remembered other times, times she would rather leave forgotten. The time after Buffalo Creek had been sold . . . after the Ogden Land Company had divided the riverside community, leveling homes and gardens that had been in family hands for centuries, dividing the scraped land into plots with square lines, with deeds attached to family names from those who had left their ancestors behind in Europe, families who didn't know this land at all. The exchange of money, the pieces of paper, the force of the law secured her People's staggering loss of their homeland. Could anything have made it clearer? They were the occupied, the vanquished, the losers.

Falling back, with all of their neighbors, to the shantytowns surrounding Buffalo's port, Delphine had had a kind of breakdown. Yes, she had a roof over her head, and while there was always a soup pot, corn mush, and bannock on the woodstove in the kitchen, the suffering was palpable in the air. The days went by in a kind of haze, and even though she was the mother of a toddler and able to take care of her daughter's daily needs, she didn't remember much of anything until Blaise came. But Blaise didn't have stability in his makeup either and gave her only the warmth of his body. Two sons and four years later, she barely remembered Marguerite coming to get Turtle Dawn and the boys. Those terrible times passed as a stupor of shock, the fumes of alcohol, a spiral of degradation.

Blaise, a trader, was *métis* like herself, part French, part native. He brought her out of catatonia, out of alcohol and opiate addiction. How? Not with words but with symbols. With a piece of string held up against a work of the European masters, he illustrated the principle of the Golden Mean. With a piece of heavy folded paper as stylus, he made shapes on a stretched hide with ground charcoal and bear grease, shapes that held meaning she could not decipher at first. His hands encouraged hers to take the paper scraper in hand and form the shapes herself. Bird, clouds, water. Language. He reminded her of the many forms of cat's cradle, coaxing her hands alive again, strengthening her nervous system, inviting her to follow him across creeks on log bridges as a way of teaching her about balance. Blaise had midwifed Delphine's first return to herself, and now he trusted her to midwife her own second return, a return to the tribe she had rejected. Their weakness had made her stiffen her heart against her People in their loss of so much of their culture, their homeland. Their loss was her loss.

Her request to meet with the clanmothers was honored, and in mid-January, Marguerite accompanied her to the longhouse where councils were held. No one lived in the longhouse anymore now that families had their own multi-generation homes. Many of the tribe's treasures, their clan's treasures, were held here without fanfare, the objects on the wall alluding to other, more precious things that were stored away—power objects secreted away in bags from eyes that were not ready to see them outside of seasonal ceremonies. Masks, rattles, turkey capes. Things that had been named by ancestors and passed through families and clans.

Once the council had gathered, the head clanmother spoke first: "You have done everything as we would have done it, Delphine, our daughter. Our clansman, your grandson, Katarioniecha, is on his own path. But you are halfway through metamorphosis, a liquid thing, your wings still forming in the chrysalis."

The women of her clan observed her with alert eyes and composed faces.

Delphine heard this judgment on her state with vast pleasure. *They know me*, she thought. And it was true. They knew her well enough that they could name her condition with the precise term: "metamorphosis."

"What you are saying is right," she began. "I ask myself: What is left? I am not a prophet; I do not know what comes next. But I do know that I can no longer be a wanderer, pretending that I belong anywhere, everywhere. I am only halfway to return, but my souls call out to me: Come home. Come on home." Delphine looked at her mother.

Marguerite looked back with all of the presence Delphine had ever asso-ciated with this woman. "If there is anything you want to know from me," Marguerite said, "now is the time to ask."

Pregnant with meaning, the silence that fell seemed to be waiting for Delphine, to discover what she must ask. And then the question arose in her, along with the realization that there would be no more moments to ask this question and have it answered and be witnessed, the very question that had defined her entire life: "Why did you send me away when I was a child?"

Marguerite was silent for a long time before she spoke. "You are right to see that this is the business of the women's council, not simply a ques-tion long unanswered between mother and daughter," Marguerite began. "When your father was nearly assassinated, danger came toward you. Keri-oniakawida had to go into hiding."

The clanmothers nodded, exchanging looks.

Marguerite continued. "There were those who approved of the message of Handsome Lake. And there were those who would betray him and us. Finally, that school, the Thomas School, was the only place I could hide you in plain sight. The white culture was your protective coloration. I told you to take it on and you did, good daughter."

Something shifted in Delphine. A sandbag dropped and light streamed in through its place.

Marguerite went on. "But then the path home was obscured; the trail had grown cold. When you left boarding school and went to Buffalo Creek, and then chose that man to father Turtle Dawn, I thought I had lost you. When I took your daughter from you, and your two sons by Blaise, I thought you would never forgive me."

Time passed so seamlessly, Delphine reflected, remembering how it had felt when Blaise had first arrived to rescue her. The memories of the boys being born and their being taken had fused in her mind. Silence stretched while she teased apart the two skeins of her sons' existences, saw the abyss that Blaise had hoisted her from. For the first time, she brought it all with her now; just as the battlefield had shown her a place where silence did not exist, could not exist, a place where healing could never take place, the

silence of her tribe would now shield her while she continued her metamorphosis.

Will I live? she asked.

It is not known, came the answer.

Delphine continued down her path of inquiry to see what doors might
open.

Courage, she thought.

"You raised my daughter in our tradition," she said to Marguerite, then
bowed her head in acknowledgment and gratitude.

She raised her head and looked at her mother again.

"You let me go deeper and further into that world."

Marguerite had not moved, had not blinked. She answered, Sphinxlike:
"We needed your daughter. We needed to make sure Turtle Dawn was
raised true."

"She is true? While I was sacrificed?"

"You have always had your own path. Your father dead, his people scattered, hiding, afraid. We couldn't see what the white people would do to
us, how they would take us apart. We released you to take that path. You
are strong; you knew where you had to go."

Delphine took a deep, full breath, the first she had taken in perhaps a
decade, and with it felt herself let go of something inside her, some ancient
knot she had carried under her right shoulder blade. Her body realigned
around the adjustment and then her entire nervous system followed suit,
all her musculature shifting into place. Even the eyes she looked through
focused in an entirely new way. *I am home again,* she said in Dialog.

The clanmothers nodded to each other. *Each of these daughters speaks
Her truth,* their eyes said.

Marguerite moved then, seemed to shake herself like a bird in winter,
puffing out her feathers for warmth, for strength, for a display of power.
"When you settled down with Blaise Lazar, I knew you would come home.
I just didn't know how long it would take. It makes my souls happy to see
your return before I die." Her eyes blazed at Delphine, a fire so bright she

couldn't see anything else, as if she were looking at the dark night after a bolt of lightning had splintered the sky.

"We greet you," said the head clanmother, a lean, unbent woman descended from a well-known family of women warriors, from the days when Haudenosaunee women battled beside their men, in the days before the Peacemaker. "We thought of you as our Trojan Horse, Delphine. We still do."

Sensory memories rushed in on Delphine then, a cornucopia of gifts. There were sights and smells—bannock, roasting corn, cedar smoke, pemmican, tobacco—but mostly there were sounds. Sounds of children playing in a waterfall, women speaking to each other in their native language, and then in French when they didn't want the children to understand them, laughing. She heard the silence that heals, that allows thoughts to travel from heart to heart, that allows words to form slowly, like soap bubbles on a June morning, fragile and transcendent, while the sun rises in the bright morning to flicker up the sycamore limbs that hang over a river. The Thomas School hadn't scrubbed these things from the slate of her childhood. Crunching snow. Breaking ice. A woman crying softly beyond the wall of skins that separated the longhouse into family compartments. A jingle dress. It was all there. And in it Delphine knew there was still a self to claim. Yes, there was loss. Discontinuity. But it was all hers. *Mine, my legacy.* Brokenness. An honorable human path.

Delphine attended to her breath, to all of the sensory information that called to her, and she sat with it, digesting it, until silence returned. Then: "I am ready. Tell me how to return."

The clanmothers carefully outlined their plan for her return. The one thing no one mentioned was how her cocoon could survive the winds and freezing cold of winter. No words could speak what they all knew: After three decades away, was true return even possible?

Chapter Twenty-Two

LONGBOW LINEAGES

Mid-January 1863,
Cattaraugus Reservation, New York

"Uncle," Delphine said. "I need your help."

Lazarus observed his niece dispassionately. She needed the salt of his skepticism to create the friction against which her deep history would come alive again. He could see she knew that completing this metamorphosis was her only route. He was the most important man in her maternal line. There would be no other guide.

"You will do everything I say, as I say?" he asked.

"Yes."

"Then let's dress you. Arm you. Set up camp in the deep forest. We will both cook, both gather firewood. I will lead you."

She nodded. Perhaps he would be surprised that she knew how to do these things, had learned them at the sutler camp. She knew how to fight, how to survive in the deep woods.

He continued laying out the more difficult conditions, ones he felt sure she would balk at, especially as she was used to being her own boss. "Where to go, when to make a fire, where to be still for the day, when to persist on our course, no matter your discomfort—all those things you will leave to me to say?"

"Yes. I give you my word. I must learn these things that Threadneedle learned from you when he was a boy."

"You will call me by my true name."

He said it to her once and expected her to remember it. "Kerioniakawida. The clanmothers will give you your real name when you have earned it."

"Do you know my true name?"

"Yes." He nodded. "You are becoming it."

Silently, he opened her pack, taking each thing out, examining each for strength, sharpness, utility. While she watched, he weighed each item with eye and hand, laid aside certain things—a small pair of scissors, several pellets of opium, just-in-case clothing—and then carefully packaged into oilcloth any object that might mildew. Without comment, he accepted her clean rags for menstrual blood, for she was still bleeding on occasion, a bar of soap carefully sealed against rodents' teeth, a jar of bear grease, the fletching tools her mother had given her. When she picked up the pack he had readied, it was heavier for the necessities he had added: cornmeal, salt, maple syrup, strips of cloth, twine and rope.

They closed the door to his cabin, leaving the hearth to cool. She had watched him tuck a coal into a wad of moss, place that inside a birchbark box, then secret it against his person. He said a prayer he did not share with her. Delphine's position as an outsider struck her with renewed force. She had no right to ask how long they would be gone.

Lazarus found the right camp for them, although it took all day. She thought she had become inured to cold and privation during her time following the army. Now it became clear to her that Blaise had taken care of her. She could see that here she would provide her own comfort, from deep inside herself. *I am not soft,* she told herself. *My essence was not corrupted by white culture.* But then a deeper voice pushed back. *But what am I? What is left when I subtract all those things I have taken on as protective coloration?* Finally, the biggest question: *Will I be worthy?*

They bent saplings to the ground and staked them down, then gathered bark for the sides of the wickiup, designed very much in the style of a small sweat lodge. They covered the structure with cedar branches and then lashed on the in-the-grease horse blankets and then, on top, the oiled and waxed canvas they had hauled in with their donkey. Lazarus showed her how to tie certain knots for certain purposes. Delphine struggled to remember what Blaise had taught her, how to improvise a knot on something a rabbit was supposed to do: "In the hole, around the tree, and back in the hole."

While they worked, her hands cracked and bled, and her body frequently insisted that she stop. The sweat dried on her body, chilling her even while she was heated from working. Delphine was always cold, and she shivered violently even as they relaxed by the fire.

As they sat in the glow of the flames, Lazarus took the jar of bear grease out of her pack, held out his hands for hers, and rubbed the orange healing ointment into her palms, across her lips, under her eyes.

After a day or two, she began to cough. He watched her, this uncle raptor Kerioniakawida. He ground rosehips in the evening for her tea and again in the morning before they started to work. He was teaching her how to take care of herself.

Her body was always sore; she groaned involuntarily when she stood to leave the fire at night and when she climbed from her bedroll to start the fire every morning. Lazarus added a yellow powder to their stew. At other times, she watched him scrape inner bark from the poplars to make a powder that he mixed with a small amount of maple syrup.

He doesn't want to lose me, she thought. *He is protecting me.* And yet it was not easy, and she ached from head to foot from her labors. When she went off alone to void her bladder, she often wept and moaned quietly so he would not hear her. It made her feel better, to weep tears of remorse for the things she had done that had brought her here. If she patted her own head, she felt the comfort of a parent for an aching and feverish child.

"You are full of poisons," he said to her one evening. "Yet powerful. We will prepare a sweat lodge."

Her eyes widened, then narrowed. "Isn't it forbidden for a man and woman, alone in the woods, to sweat together?"

Now he laughed for the first time in the entire fortnight they had been together in the woods. "There are no rules for what we are doing," he told her. "Your daughter allows me to see her naked when we do a ritual bath. We alone define how we will be together."

Turtle Dawn lets him see her naked? she thought, wondering. *What is he telling me?* Her mind began to twist on itself.

They gathered rocks—the "grandfathers" and "grandmothers" were easy to identify as the former were square, the latter round—and piled them beside their wickiup. Firewood was stacked and ready; cedar boughs chosen, cut, and placed. They hoisted all their food and supplies into storage in the trees, as well as their sleeping mats and skins, so no animals would chew on their valuable supplies.

"We will not be eating, cooking, sleeping, working," Kerioniakawida said. Then, tenderly, he added, "You are like my child. Your mother has no brothers and only one sister, my mother. That makes me the most important man in your life. Do you understand my responsibility?"

She nodded. She would not say, *Yes, Uncle, I understand at least this much.* No displays of pique would be tolerated. Theirs was a traditional society; any older man in her maternal line would be referred to with respect, with an honorific.

"It will be well done for me to act as your Firekeeper. You will go into the sweat lodge first and I will bring you the stones. When you come out, I will go in to take what is left."

Her eyes widened. "You can do that?"

A single nod said yes. "I can go into the same sweat as you and take what is left. The clanmother showed me the way to do this without danger to either of us. You have stopped bleeding?" He asked this to confirm that there were no secrets between them. He trusted his nose to tell him her state.

Her menses had become spotty in this stage of her life, and with it her desire seemed to have increased. *Does he know that I touch myself to ecstasy and think of Blaise, wonder what he is doing? That I wonder also when Marie moved out of the tent? If she even did?* Delphine was not accustomed to feeling vulnerable and she shut the door on her emotions as quickly as she had opened it.

She nodded in response to Kerioniakawida's question. *Yes, I have nearly stopped bleeding.* She had entered that time in a woman's life when the energy of a man would come into her and balance with his strength the mercy left after her childrearing years. She understood that her element was wood, which would be carefully hardened in the fire—wood become a weapon, a digging stick, the strongest tool that can still be flexible.

He showed her how to gather the starter bundle, what prayers to say, how to handle hot rocks with antlers. They built the fire together, Kerioni-akawida leading, Delphine, his acolyte, following, not an easy role for her.

When everything was ready, Delphine walked the path of cedar into the sweat lodge. It was permitted for her to pour her own lodge, even though it was not the usual way. Kerioniakawida brought her five hot rocks, which he placed in the order they should take according to the four directions, the four elements, and the spirit of the lodge.

The night before, when they were meditating to discover the spirit ani-mal of their sweat, a cougar had entered their camp, recognizable through its signature cough, its whining inquiry. The hairs on Delphine's arms and the back of her neck had stood on end, electrifying her. Maybe this cougar had been watching them all along. They dedicated their sweat to the cougar.

Kerioniakawida went out and the flap came down. Delphine sat in dark-ness. She had been told there would be four phases of ritual within the lodge. She only had to come through each one. In the first, she sang the songs while Kerioniakawida beat the drum outside. In the second, she prayed to the Cougar Mother to strengthen her for her quest. In the third segment—the difficult one—Delphine asked the Cougar Mother to lead her into an examination of conscience. With each segment, fresh rocks came in from the fire, and as she poured water on them she felt her skin expand, her spirit float out of her body to dance around the tent. The moth, the butterfly, the thing in the chrysalis, was liquefying, the worm uncer-tain what it would become next. Death? Certainly death was required to become the next thing: a winged thing. In French, her second language, *les imagines* was the word given to silkmoths.

Kerioniakawida kept the drum going; it spoke like a dancer.

Midway through the third segment, Delphine was afraid she wouldn't make it, that she would have to ask to come out, to break the sacred round. Pressing on, she let the cougar spirit bring images for her consideration, images that would help her reconcile past and future. She revisited her cruelty to her mother, indifference to her daughter, hostility to her husband, neglect of her sons. And grandson, Threadneedle. All of these things she revealed to herself with perfect clarity. And remorseless sexuality. Delphine understood that the Cougar Mother was playing with her, a cat toying with her prey.

Delphine would have to take a fierce grip on her unruly self if she hoped to stay the course. As it was, she was scarcely surviving. She began to doubt the process.

What good will come out of remaining in the sweat? she asked herself.

And then she answered herself: *It is not your place to ask this question, only to remain here.*

She lay on the floor of the lodge, her nose sunk deep in the yellow and withered grass by the edge of the blanket walls. She lifted the edge of the blankets held down with rocks; a small stream of silvery air entered. She pressed her nose into the grass roots, breathed in their green promise of return, life itself.

Isn't this forbidden? she asked herself.

Whatever I need to survive is allowed, she answered, letting the stream of air ignite a fire within her.

Where the grass stubble clung to life, waiting for spring, the smell of earth revived her. It smelled like a woman and woke a blaze in her that suddenly laid out the terms of her metamorphosis. *Surrender.*

Then Kerioniakawida was at the door, opening it to bring in the last rocks.

Delphine was disoriented and wondered if she had been unconscious. Before she could call out to him, Keroniakawida left and the door flap closed her again in this grotto for the final round.

Now Delphine spoke aloud as she poured water on the rocks: "I ask you to heal my past," she told the Cougar Mother. "I ask you to remove the veil from my eyes, so that I see the only path that is open, the right path for me, the blessing of original acts, ones only I can bring into this world." She moaned, wept, gathered herself. *Make of me what you intend, Mother. Whatever you require of me, Mother,* she said, not knowing whether she spoke aloud or silently.

She hadn't lost count: twenty rocks over four segments. When Kerioniakawida opened the flap for the last time, she crawled out. The cold air felt divine on her bare skin. It was, all at once, the coldness of the creek, a plastered wall, a cool river rock, silk. Linen. She had been turned inside out.

She wanted only to lie on the cold ground.

"Conserve your heat," Kerioniakawida warned sharply.

She picked herself up reluctantly. Her skin radiated well-being into the chill air, hardening her nipples. She ran her hands down her flanks. She was silky and … something else. *My skin is an organ,* she realized, listening, smelling, tasting what it sensed. In wonder and in glory, she dressed again in linen and wool, skins and furs, feeling her clothing trap her heat. Now she could see how Turtle Dawn could be naked around this man. The women of her lineage felt safe with this man, who was constant, trustworthy, a backbone. *Have I ever felt this with a man?* she asked herself. *Our shared humanity, our bloodline, makes me inviolable with him.* Then for the first time she realized, *I am the gateway to our descendants,* and she felt her neglect of her sons as a terrible pain throughout her body.

She picked up the drum and played her beating heart for Kerioniakawida's turn in the sweat. She knew she was now past her time of bleeding for the rest of her life. *Will the new wings that lay down my back, tender and motionless, become animate? Part of me come springtime? Volition, like flight.*

Something prickled at her shoulder blades, waiting to be born.

Delphine was shifting poles from east to west, from north to south, taking up her role as a baby-elder in her tribe, assuming the role her mother would soon leave, for her to inherit. She had to be equal to it. She felt herself growing into a new name, a new role, one completely unique to her new self. *It can't be any other way,* she thought. *This is my path. I am who I am. All of my life has prepared me for this.* The next day, after two more infusions of rosehips, she wasn't coughing anymore. Now when she coughed, it seemed like a call for sympathy, for attention: "I am pathetic," it said.

"Today we will make you a weapon," Lazarus said, and then, to remind her, instructed, "Follow my lead."

He led her to a grove of yew trees. "Men in our European bloodlines invented the longbow. I want to see what kind of bow this makes." They found just the branch the yew could spare, asked the tree for permission to take it, and then sawed it out. They thanked the yew for her sacrifice. Delphine would come to understand that this asking and thanking would accompany each of their interactions with the world. They barked and stripped the branch, turned it patiently over the fire, bent it, shaped it into a bow, hardened the ends. He gave her the job of flexing it repeatedly during the cooling and heating cycle. He showed her how to anchor one end against a tree and flex the bow against the base of the tree; her arms grew stronger with the effort.

They cut and rolled sinew. Strung the bow. Kerioniakawida grunted with surprise when he pulled the bow.

Every morning they worked with the bow. He gave her arrows, telling her that she did not have time to learn to make her own, as crafting arrows that would fly true was not just a skill but an art form. When the bow was ready, Delphine tested it. She was strong, but at first she could not even draw the string. *After all this, I am not strong enough,* she thought, defeated.

He modeled it for her, showing her how to plant her feet so they grew into the ground, showing her how he tightened his stomach muscles before he pulled the sinew against the curve of the bow. How the right angles made between his shoulders and his feet gave the arrow torque, moving through the sprung steel of his trunk. How to make herself copy the yew tree's spiral dance, from the inside out. He told her to bind her breasts.

She realized then that she didn't need more strength. She became the yew tree, used her legs, trunk, arm, and eye—the single eye in the space between her eyebrows, which intersected with the energy coming out the top of her head. On the day when she put it all together and she drew and the arrow flew and hit the target that Kerioniakawida had blazed onto a tree with a pitchy torch, nothing needed to be said. With each thunk of her arrow, she waited for his grunt of approval, the only sign that she was making the kind of progress that met his standards.

They set snares for small birds and game. She was keenly interested in this. Her hands fumbled again and again, setting off the snare trigger in a flurry of tree branches. When Kerioniakawida left their camp to gather more wood, she worked on the delicate design of triggers and snares, figured out how much pressure she could use, at what angle to cut the joinery. She began to intuit the dynamics of it, how it all worked together to set off a directed energy flow that could trap the quickest rabbit, the most wary grouse. Lazarus showed her that rubbing herself with the inside of the willow bark disguised her human smell from contaminating the snare. She cut willow, removing her gloves to blow on her fingers, windmilling her outstretched arms until her fingers could feel again. She husbanded their precious supply of bear grease, which she used to keep her fingers supple.

Kerioniakawida went out with her every morning to check their lines. For days, they caught nothing. She watched and learned. She would not give up.

One day she woke in the morning before Kerioniakawida. She rose, started the fire with the small prayer she had found in her own heart, and boiled water. There was something in the day. A quickening. She let her self dissolve. And then she felt herself slide into the next place. She had been there before but always forgot, always lost it, that certainty that she was a creature of the universe, that the universe loved her as much as every other thing in it. What could remind her each morning of the sacredness of life, of being a part of it all? *Ritual.*

She stepped quietly down to the creek, took off her outer clothing, broke ice on a small eddy near the shore, brought the silvery water, pure as sacrament, to her face, twice, to her breasts, twice, to her arms. Sparkling drops flew into the sky, the earth, met the fire within her. The drops hung in the air. Did she imagine a rainbow? *Conserve your heat,* she remembered. She dressed, greeted the morning, and returned to camp to make the morning tea.

That day they found two pigeons in her snares. She gave thanks and then they gutted the birds, stripped off their feathers like little coats, and spitted them for breakfast. He showed her how to offer the offal to scavengers and the pigeons' feathery coats to the fire. *Sacrifice and sacrament.*

He put a pinch of tobacco onto the fire, prayed, then looked at her.

She followed his lead, putting a pinch into the fire, and then inhaled the fragrant smoke offering, raised her face to the sky, and breathed out another prayer of thanks to the pigeons and to creation.

He doesn't need to tell me what to do anymore, how to live a sacred life.

While they watched the two pigeons snapping on the spit, he said, "This is how I met Kristiana, running her trapline in the winter. I thought I was well hidden. She roasted a rabbit, then called me out of the woods, asked me to share her food."

Delphine was startled, trying to picture the girl she remembered, a pale European girl who had not even begun to bleed becoming skilled enough to run her own traplines when Delphine, in her fifties, was just learning twenty years later. "Who taught her?"

"Your daughter, Turtle Dawn."

Then she pictured the Kristiana she knew now, lover of her daughter, founder of Regina Coeli and Cottage, and saw her mother's handiwork, how much that girl had transformed into a formidable woman, a blade of annealed iron, flexible and full of power, like her bow. *What source of strength did she draw on?* She began then to think of Kristiana without jealousy or rancor. She began to understand both the nature of sacrifice and of giving thanks. *I still have much to learn.*

They ate well. Kerioniakawida had brought bags of dried corn, dried venison, dried blueberries, rosehips, and nuts. They skinned and roasted grouse, rabbit, pigeon, and squirrel. He showed her how to brain-tan and work the rabbit and squirrel skins until they were soft. The salt and alum they had brought for the skins dried her hands, so every night she rubbed her portion of bear grease into them by the warm, flickering light of their campfire.

Without protection the winter would dry her hands, but bear grease, he said, was healing. "A woman should be working skins at all times in winter," he told her without judgment. "Then, using bear grease is justified, to work against the salt and alum."

He showed her how to see the ermine so white against the snow, hard to spot except that tiny black tip of the tail. She learned where to set snares to trap ermine and mink, both from wily families with good noses. She learned how to keep the kill in their traplines from being eaten by other predators.

Delphine loved best the nights they sat around the fire working while Kerioniakawida told her stories. When the snows came, they moved inside the former sweat lodge; he made a fire in the middle, opened a vent to let the smoke out. In other circumstances they would not have used the sweat lodge—a sacred and powerful space—as a wickiup, but in this moment it would have been too much of a luxury to build a separate structure.

His stories filled in the blanks about her father, Handsome Lake, and the rest of his family. About Handsome Lake's brother Cornplanter. About the importance of Allegheny and the ancient villages there. His words answered many of the questions Delphine had wanted to ask. She had wondered how he justified bringing along his flat, round drum when a similar instrument might be improvised in the woods. Now she knew; it was a special drum, had its own history, was named. The sound of it echoed all creation, became the backbeat of their stories, drummed them home. She knew now how her people had learned their songs and the cadence of their stories.

The drum was memory. It sung; Kerioniakawida's words followed.

After a time, Delphine noticed her hands had changed. She studied them. They were muscular. She flexed them. She had calluses where blisters had once arisen. They reminded her of someone else's hands. But whose? She always had dirt under her nails, dirt ground into the lines in her hands. She was startled to find that she had changed more since she turned fifty than she had changed in all the years before that.

Will this capacity for metamorphosis follow me through life? she asked, wondering if her mother hid her own great capacity for transformation under a stable exterior.

Had it surprised her mother to find herself a mother again so late in life, mothering Turtle Dawn, Delphine's child? Thinking back, Delphine could not remember there being any apparent perturbation in the still, deep waters of her mother's demeanor. Only time would tell whether Marguerite's gamble of trusting the tribe to raise her two grandsons had worked. Marguerite knew she could not raise the two boys and Turtle Dawn, but had it been a mistake? Now one of those sons was dead: Simon, in the war. Malachi had become a man. Delphine had not told her mother she knew these things. But now she saw that being a mother was past correcting, past amending. Some things were over and couldn't be retrieved.

A full moon emptied; the new moon came again. And they held a ceremony.

When Delphine counted forward, it was the end of February. She used to be able to calibrate her menses against the moon and know where they were on the calendar, but now, without her menses, she had come to rely on different methods. She kept a small stick hidden from Kerioniakawida on which she made marks to keep track of the days. It had been six weeks. For the first time, Delphine felt that return might be possible. *I feel comfortable*, she realized. *Mostly.* She grimaced at the irony of it, a measure of her self-delusion.

Except when they slept, their hands were never idle. They broke dogbane, rolled twine on their thighs. Stripped milkweed, dried the strands, rolled them.

They tied nets for the small silver fish that would be coming up the creeks soon. "Smelt" they called them in the restaurants of Buffalo. She wove an eel trap out of hazel they had collected near the stream. Her hands, becoming so different from her old hands, told her how she was becoming someone much more capable than the old Delphine—someone fashioned in the chrysalis of her life here.

Before bud-break, they pollarded the nearby willow so that the year's shoots would grow straight, for basketry, for the tribe. She also worked rabbit and ermine hides continuously, unhappy with the way they were turning out but determined to improve her technique.

The women of my tribe have secrets—secrets they pass down from generation to generation, she thought. *But I . . .* She never allowed herself to complete this sentence, editing her thoughts when they threatened to imagine a negative future or judge her past harshly.

At night, when she might have thought of nothing but her own discomfort, her boredom, her longing for company other than Kerioniakawida's, he continued to tell her stories, teach her lessons.

"We Haudenosaunee produce a prophet when it is absolutely necessary. The Peacemaker arose when we could no longer be at war with each other and survive. He turned a people who made war on each other into the great nation we have become today.

"Handsome Lake came when the greatest threat, the whites, made it clear they would destroy our People, take all our land as they pleased, drive us into the ground. If only you had known your father! But you have him in you. I gave my life to him, forfeited wife and children to protect him. Became Lazarus, He Who Hides. This is why your return is important. Do you see what I am saying?"

No, she did not, not really.

In fact, she had not known that her return was important to anyone except herself. This gave her much to think about. While her hands did their work automatically, she let her mind wander. When she made a mistake, Kerioniakawida always pointed it out and insisted she unravel and begin again. Paying attention became the ultimate challenge.

She wanted to ask him, "How can I attend to my handiwork and still let my mind unknot itself?" but she knew he would laugh, so she did not ask. Someone deep inside her brought the answer as if on call; she began to see how attending to her work *was* unknotting her self.

More importantly, she discovered how to summon something she could not yet name, something that responded to her requests, maybe even *to her prayers*. She did not know yet what to call *it*, but she knew *it* was there. Something responded when she asked—*prayed*—with pointed timing and specificity. With totems and omens. Even sometimes with a sense of humor, a pointed wit.

She was learning so much but still had so many questions. *I do not even know my own true name!* Kerioniakawida did not call her by her European name, and Delphine pondered the fact that she would be nameless while she completed her metamorphosis. She was beginning to trust this state of having her identity blurred and her own wishes ignored. Soon, she found she didn't even care what parts of her personality were being jettisoned in the interests of her transformation. *Throw it out!* she thought when she noticed some bad habit, some tic of thinking, and she would gesture with a fling of her fingers. This attitude helped seal the necessary deconstruction taking place inside the chrysalis.

Delphine began to notice the particularity of things as the woods now came into sharper focus for her too. This ash tree. This grove of ironwood. This stand of hickory, that one of beech, both of which had been heavy with nuts the previous fall. The prints of animals that came to the seep or creekside: fox, raccoon, heron, yes. Also the principal animals, the predators: wolf, bobcat, otter, mink, cougar. Bears slept through the winter in their caves and under the roots of trees.

After Kerioniakawida pointed out to her the thin stream of steamy breath that arose from the first den they came across, she looked for these spots of deep hibernation herself, pausing, waiting for him to notice so she could point with a nod of her head.

At night, they listened to wolves howling. Kerioniakawida knew each of the packs, knew their principal members by gender and by age. He named them to her so she could picture them. "When the maple buds swell large and red, we will take food to the pups and the nursing females who head up their packs, just as the clanmothers head ours. But first you must bring down your own buck, to be part of the food we bring them. First Food for their pups should have deer meat in it." He had brought in the necessary nuts and dried fruit for them and had been careful not to let Delphine touch them or eat them. "The ingredients cannot be tainted with human energy or smells. It will be one of the pups' first discoveries of the world. Everything must remain wild."

When she killed her first turkey with her bow—her *first* kill with her bow—a big tom who had been doing his display dance to a group of admiring females, Kerioniakawida declared her ready. He had been preparing her for this moment, and over the previous days had thinned her repasts until finally Delphine was only drinking liquids.

That night, as she sat awake tending the fire in her vigil, a raven flew to the edge of the encampment; Delphine recognized the bird as a messenger. She sipped the turkey broth Kerioniakawida had prepared for her and had a vision of the deer herd. In a flap of heavy black rags and raven wings, her spirit flew above the herd, saw where they were browsing. Had he put anything else into the turkey broth? She slept a deep sleep that night, waking naturally hours before dawn.

They rose in the dark, dressed, lit no fire, spoke no words. The dark feathers of the raven glinted in the moonlight as he observed them from the brake.

Kerioniakawida had compounded black paint from charcoal and bear grease. He painted it on her face, in straight lines down her cheeks, one down over her nose, and another down her chin. Then he did his own face, with a practiced hand.

She looked at him and nodded.

They prayed then, asking their buck to give himself to them, promising to use his life wisely. Delphine knew it was the only path that would open for her, once again the narrow gate of her return.

Then Kerioniakawida strapped a rack of antlers to his head, pulled a hide around himself, and bent over, holding two sticks for his forelegs.

Delphine slung her bow over her shoulder and chest, pulled a doe hide over her back and head, picked up the two sticks they had fire-hardened for her forelegs, and followed Kerioniakawida down to the thicket they had chosen to best intersect the buck they had been anticipating, from the herd she had seen in the vision.

Wet and cold, the predawn was treacherous with mud puddles, which broke noisily if you stepped on them, and would freeze your feet if you stepped in them.

In their ceremonial deer dress, they moved like deer, hesitating frequently to pretend to browse or to raise their heads and listen. By midday, streams would be gurgling under the ice, spring's harbinger. But now, apart from the call of the raven, there was no noise but the creaking of trees as they scratched their limbs against each other.

Kerioniakawida settled himself in the thicket, antlers rising above, while Delphine approached the tree they had selected in the middle of the clearing, just as the false dawn announced night's end. A gibbous moon swung low in the sky like a horn cup. Delphine automatically calculated the time: the second full moon—the Hunger Moon—had passed, making it mid-March.

Arching up over the eastern horizon came all the stars that were harbingers of spring, and Delphine reveled in the procession of seasons as their world left winter behind: maple syruping season, bud-break, smelt. And First Food for the wolf pups. Her return, her metamorphosis, was well under way.

She disappeared into the leafy notch of the oak tree they had chosen and pulled her bow up after her. Dawn came. Delphine listened with her skin.

She heard something off to the left. A beaver going home after the night's work, scouting for tomorrow's raw materials. A pair of red foxes going to the creek. Then silence. The vixen barked in the distance, marking a successful hunt, food for her and milk for their kits, tiny and sightless in the den. Her lifelong mate would take what she left him. He knew his role in their matrilineal den.

Then, horizontal movement, slow, blurred through the vertical stripes of the trees. A doe and her sister were stepping through the woods, heavy with their fawns, fat from the apples they had eaten through fall and winter. Now they must browse for what greenery they could find. Noses down, they pushed at the snow to find shoots, moss, the tender leaves of trout lily. Delphine saw as she never had before how beautiful the Deer People were, how peaceful, expressive, beloved by the Creator.

The does entered a willow thicket and then rose on their hind legs to nibble the ends of branches, cutting with the sharp incisors of vegetable eaters. They fell back to four legs, their bellies heavy, in a dance that celebrated the life both within them and without. Cradlemates about to become mothers, they raised their arms playfully to each other, dancing onto their hind legs again, burdensome bellies lightened by play. Delphine would not dream of killing one, and wished them pleasure in their fawns.

And then she stopped breathing. As the does vanished deeper into the willow thicket in the direction of the creek, two males appeared, lifting their heads, listening, smelling, tasting the air for its messages. One was young—three to four years old by its antlers, furry with youth approaching maturity. The other bore eight points, mossy with age, the massive rack heavy on his head. *His majesty,* she thought.

Ask! Kerioniakawida prompted in Dialog.

Him? she thought, wondering how she could ask to take such a life.

And then she did it. She asked the elder buck, *Will you offer your life for my quest, to complete my return to my people, to make my first rites as a warrior, to make a buckskin for a purpose I can't divine yet? I ask you to do this thing together in the world, you and me, to become the next thing. Will you make the sacrifice?* She promised him she would respect every part of his body if he would offer it. She asked the hard question, a pit in the flesh of her fruit: *Am I worthy?*

He moved, turning his broad side to her, then lowered his head to nose the snow aside, to search for the fine blue bunch grass he could often uncover beneath the snow in this place.

She rose smoothly out of her notch, arrow already nocked, easy as mist or water. She drew the arrow back, bow and bowstring an extension of her arm, shoulder, spine, legs, and released.

The buck jumped and fell, its neck twisted at an unnatural angle, its eye already dimming.

Kerioniakawida stood.

The younger buck sprang for the woods, its white tail flagging that it would live another day to take the place of the elder stag Delphine had slain.

Delphine slowly made her approach. She fell on her knees before the beautiful creature, put her ungloved fingers at its nostrils to feel for breath, then whispered her thanks, lifted his antlers to expose the throat, and drew her knife. She inserted the sharp end into the side of the buck's throat and pulled the length of it across from side to side, as she had rehearsed many times in her mind. It was harder to do than she had imagined.

As his blood bled out into the empty gourd she had brought for this purpose, she breathed her gratitude. Then she corked the gourd and stood back as Kerioniakawida lashed the front legs and then the back legs of the stag onto the carrying poles they had used as crutches when they were four-legged beneath their hides. Together they lifted the poles onto their shoulders. She was ready: sixty pounds on each of them for a buck that weighed as much as Kerioniakawida.

They made it back to their camp and were pleased to find nothing had been disturbed while they were gone. They lowered their packs out of the tree, moved them into the still-warm wickiup, and then raised the stag into the tree on the same rope, stopping when it hung at shoulder level. Kerioniakawida unlashed the gourd of blood from the carrying net he had put it in on the end of his pole.

Now the butchering began. She wanted to collapse but would not, and she called on her guardians for a second wind to help her do what she had to do. Together they stripped the guts of their contents, putting the offal at a distance from the camp for predators and scavengers. They emptied the intestines into a bowl fashioned from a burl, soaking them clean. Organs removed, they set slices of liver sizzling in a pan on the fire that Kerioniakawida had struck into life, to serve the two hunters, to restore their strength, and to honor the buck.

I am ravenous, she thought. Kerioniakawida gave her a wad of green to chew, something he had dried and brought with him to season their stomachs to accept the rich meat after their fast.

The buck's antlers were then removed and his skull opened, his brains carefully set aside. Then they ripped a seam up the belly, took the hide off like a coat, carefully cutting the fascia away. The hide was salted, rolled up, and put to one side, for working. And now they butchered the naked animal: ribs, legs, haunches, flanks. Tendon and sinew pulled away from the meat were rolled out taut on a spindle to dry without shrinking, ready to rehydrate when the use for sinew would arise. Hooves, blood, and bones, all of it went into the cauldron set to boil for broth and paste, a gel that would be dried in a sheet and enjoyed as a nourishing treat for children, elders, the sick.

Having eaten their own fill, exhausted and satiated they went to their tent and bedrolls while light was still in the sky, but only after they had lifted everything into the tree, having wrapped it all in an oiled canvas tarp to wait until morning. The cauldron lid was weighted with rocks and the broth was left to cook over the banked fire while they slept.

Tomorrow she would scrape the hide with a special tool Kerioniakawida had given her as a gift. She also had fletching tools passed down to her by Marguerite, who had gotten them from her own mother, the woman who had fled before Sullivan's army while the ashes of life in her homeland smoldered behind her. As preparing a hide was the work of women, she would wait to finish the buckskin until she was home again with her clanswomen, but she could begin the process now, following instructions she had gotten from Marguerite, and with Kerioniakawida's guidance.

The next morning, she rolled out the hide. She hefted a scraper into her hand, shifted it around for the best grip, then began to scrape and cut the meat from the hide. Marguerite had said she would have to alternate hands, as the work was too arduous for one hand alone, and Delphine could already feel the wisdom of this advice. Now she tentatively scraped, noting the angle of the scraper that seemed to work best, but only after accidentally tearing a hole in the hide up near the forelegs. *There is no way to repair a torn hide.* She would put her frustration aside for now, until she discovered the use for the finished buckskin. Blaise had told her once that many rug makers purposefully put flaws into their weaving, a way for the spirits to enter and exit the wool so the rug would continue to have a life.

She firmly put images of Blaise out of her head; she could not afford to distract herself with thoughts and feelings for her mate. She felt a tightening between her legs, a contraction in her womb. Hard nipples would not serve her here.

Now that Delphine had taken her buck, the time for leaving their camp was drawing near. She watched Kerioniakawida putting tools and supplies carefully away, packing the thongs and cording they had made, carefully examining for mold and rot the rabbit and ermine hides she had finished. It was her job to roll them up for storage following the pattern he had set. She could see he was husbanding the food and herbs they had brought to last just so long. She began to intuit that they would leave in about seven days.

To prepare the buckskin she would be finishing with her clanmothers and sisters back on the reservation, Delphine coated it with a paste made of the stag's brain, using a tool her mother had called a spreader. It had no sharp edges, just a broad, flat blade, as if for applying wet plaster to a wall. When the whole skin was covered, she wrapped it tight again and set it aside.

Before they could return home to Cattaraugus, they would also prepare the First Food for the wolf pups and bring it to them, something Kerioniakawida said he had done with her grandson Threadneedle. He told Delphine how two years ago, when Thread was still recovering from his injury, he had asked Kilian to perform the First Food rite for the wolf pups with him.

"It confused the wolves for me to approach with the First Food offering with a different son," Kerioniakawida told her. "How much more confused they will be," he mused, "when I approach this year with a woman—a most unusual woman. One they have seen in our camp." He was referring to the wolves' visit to their camp when the offal was left out after the buck kill. With Kerioniakawida's guidance, she was beginning to recognize them as individuals: the old grizzled matron, her daughter, her mate. The bachelor uncle. The stripling pups from last year's whelping.

On the starry night they were to provide this year's pups with their First Food, Delphine heard several families of wolves calling to each other across the valley floor from their dens. As she rolled the small, fragrant balls for the wolf pups, using parchment to keep her human smell from transmitting itself to the wild food, Kerioniakawida told her again, this time in more detail, how the den was structured like their own tribal culture, with the matron at the head, her daughters coming next in line, and each male going to live with his mate's mother. She heard this as an analogy to her own life and her relationship with her mother and her daughter. She was matron now.

And she would soon be worthy of it. The clanmothers had given her a unique challenge to complete her return. She had already passed her first test, the killing of the buck. Still, she didn't know what she was being prepared for aside from rejoining the tribe as a matron-in-training, to take her mother's place, and even in that she felt unsure. *How can I ever step into my mother's place?* she wondered with skepticism. *And for what purpose am I preparing this buckskin?* Although she asked these questions, she trusted it would all be revealed to her. She just had to be patient and do her job correctly for the formula to work the way it was supposed to.

Sometimes when she lay in her skins unable to sleep, she thought through her new feelings for Kristiana—this woman, another alpha female in their pack, who had transformed, becoming someone who could share power—becoming certain that they could work together, side by side.

What would happen next? With an unresolved war in progress, men she loved still fighting for their lives, their business—Regina Coeli—completely sunk into the war effort, her People having lost their place in the world and now struggling to hold on to their way-of-life . . . It was becoming increasingly hard to trust that the world would right itself.

With gas lighting, steamships, messages sent along wires strung across the landscape, it was next to impossible to believe that the day would be green and fresh again, that she—Delphine, the flawed, the apostate—would ever grow into the kind of woman who could . . . what? She had no choice: she would have to trust that she would be ready.

I need only play my part.

Chapter Twenty-Three

THE PRICE OF AN
OPEN HEART

Spring 1863, Cattaraugus Reservation, New York

When Delphine and Kerioniakawida emerged from the woods, their packs laden with furs and hides from animals they had trapped and processed, a late snow, deep and heavy but lasting only a short time, arrived to hasten the signs of spring. The intensity of the whiteout, the dismaying sameness of the deep cover that laid on the land, blessedly brief, gave way to western winds. One could practically see the buds swelling, feel the earth warming, sense the grumpy wariness of animals as they broke out of hibernation.

Back home at Cattaraugus, Delphine moved in with her mother.

Marguerite needed her daughter's help as much as Delphine needed her mother's guidance, and now with both elder women of her maternal line in the same household, Turtle Dawn—who had moved into Kilian's old house in Cottage—had brought her magnificent stove in a wagon to her mother's house on the reservation.

Nesting Swan, who was just on the verge of speaking, imitated whatever the women of her family were doing, patting bits of dough to fry or bake, rubbing a piece of hide against itself repeatedly, making twine on her small thigh. She was content to rest her head on the lap of any one of the women, all of them being as one woman to the child. Four generations of her female line, one home.

It was the rarest April Delphine could remember, and the work on the buckskin became both background and foreground of all the other work the three women undertook together, interspersed with frequent visits from clanmothers and their daughters to advise and help. They used racks that had been built in their great-grandmothers' time to stretch the buckskin set before the fire. During daylight hours, which began to lengthen, they foraged for cattail shoots, wild leeks, watercress. Delphine took her fire-hardened digging stick and watched carefully as the women in her family showed her how to use it, where to look for the bitter spring nourishment that cleansed the blood.

"This leaf, this root," Turtle Dawn instructed, speaking in the shortened language that suited being in the wilderness. "Good to roast on coals. Sweet like candy." They moved deeper into the woods, where leaf mulch made the ground soft. Turtle Dawn pointed to a colony of whirling leaves. *Mayapple*. "This leaf," she emphasized, "its root poisonous, but strong medicine." Turtle Dawn stuck her finger down her throat to demonstrate its use. She dug her own digging stick in, went deep with her whole weight, and levered up the plant, a white root that looked like a small human, with two legs dangling from a stout root. "Emetic."

When the run of the little silver fish arrived, they took lanterns on poles to the creek and, using nets like the one Delphine and Kerioniakawida had made from milkweed, brought home baskets of the smelt both to eat now, for the nutrients after a long winter, and to dry and store. Soon, when the eels would travel along the banks of the rivers to the south, where their relations lived, they would trade smelt and smoked whitefish for shad and smelt. People to the south prized the salted eggs of the sturgeon, which grew as long as a man and could live for a hundred years in Lakes Erie and Ontario.

Turtle Dawn had been thrilled to find that Kerioniakawida and Delphine had brought home the buck's blood, which she now had drying on metal sheets before the stove at home, the bone and blood forming a gel the children craved each spring. Delphine made sure Swan and Marguerite got their share.

All the while, Delphine sought out news of the war. The Confederates had invaded Pennsylvania. The Union had not had a victory, only draws with heavy losses on both sides, the pattern that had characterized this war up to that point. After Fredericksburg, the need for a decisive victory by the North was being drummed throughout the land. Thoughts of *What if we lose?* were beneath every bit of news passed from person to person. *And if we win, how will we go on as a country?*

When the sap began to run in the sugar maple, she had the pleasure of being at the tapping and gathering, at the boiling, and at watching the fires throughout the night. It was traditionally a man's job, and although many of the men of a certain age were gone to the war, the sugaring fires were tended by both older men like Kerioniakawida and younger men who had refused to take part in this white man's war. Their warriors' prolonged absence was changing things quickly; the women—who were always welcomed at the sugaring fires—now also took shifts, sampled tastes of home brew.

They also drank strong tea brewed with herbs that heightened their senses and gave the words they spoke to each other extra resonance. They told sugaring stories that could be repeated generation to generation, accompanied by a lot of sly jokes and laughter. The camaraderie of those long nights as the sap bubbled and scented the air in the small shack that held the boiling pans made Delphine realize that she had slipped back into a timeless place, away from the sharp arrow of a white person's progress through life. She had taken her place in the universe, one that none could fill but herself, fully awake, dancing on the precarious edge of her lifetime.

In the council meeting, she heard her true name for the first time, one she already knew, as it had been used to describe her by the women in her lineage, by the clanmothers in the rare times she had been at council meetings, and by Kerioniakawida when they had been together in their winter camp. She had taken it as criticism, but now she recognized it as her true name: She Who Hunts. She had always interpreted the words to mean She Who Searches, but now the restlessness of that name made a sharp contrast to the meaning she now understood: her role as an instrument in the focused pace of the hunt.

More at home now in her tribe, she took even greater interest in her ancestry. One question that pressed upon her was this: Should she dedicate herself and the rest of her life to the fulfillment of her father Handsome

Lake's life? She spoke to anyone and everyone who would tell her about him, and she discovered his teachings had been the foundation Blaise had referenced when he'd first helped her stop using alcohol and opium. She began to recognize that her people were still divided over his teachings.

While she had taken great pleasure in hearing her mother finally name Handsome Lake as her father, which had led her to dive into knowledge of her family and their trajectory based on their relationship with this influential prophet, the day inevitably arrived when she began to separate from her father's teachings, yet another necessary step in her becoming fully formed in her chrysalis.

Even as she rejected some of his teachings—for instance, that homosexuality was unnatural—she came to acknowledge that her own family saw gender as a fluid state. Her past and her future were a single thread with no breaks. Good had come from the union of Kristiana and Turtle Dawn in the creation and shaping of her grandson, Threadneedle. Kilian, though none of his blood ran in her veins, was a man who loved all women, and could love all women in a single woman. She considered Blaise, their long love affair, their partnership. Wouldn't he be pleased to see how she had become a Hunter, come into her own, no longer an acolyte looking for her place. While the war had made it clear to her that no God existed, that even the Mother's face was turned away in horror, yet . . . who was it who responded to her heartfelt prayers? *It. It* listened. *It* responded.

Delphine felt the restlessness of spring upon her. Was her metamorphosis complete? She had no one but herself to consult on this question.

One morning, on the cusp of spring, with news of the ice on the canal melting, allowing it to open, she heard a familiar jingle of horse harnesses outside their door. Blaise stood on her threshold, his hat in his hand.

"Blaise! What . . . ?" *Something is wrong.* Blaise had left their sutler tent, often enough, to resupply in Trenton or Philadelphia or even Washington, but this was another week's journey north, pushing hard. "Blaise, come in! I am so . . ." She threw her arms around his neck, buried her nose in his smell, his furs, rubbed her chin on his rough stubble.

He pulled back from her, away, surprising her. "I can't come in, Delphine.

I can't stay here in your mother's house. Where can we talk, alone?" He gestured. "Out here?"

His signals confused her. "Is Thread hurt? Have you just been to Cottage? How could you leave the front?"

"Everyone is fine, Delphine. Kilian is watching the sutler tent. And Thread. When I left, they were both fine."

"Kilian! Thread? Aren't they busy? On the move with this new general, chasing the Rebels north into Pennsylvania? Word came that Philip is heading south with wagons to bring everyone in Newtown to Cottage. Did you stop there?"

He laughed lightly at all her questions, relaxing apparently, but not crossing the threshold into her mother's house. They stood outside on the stoop feeling the spring sunshine, hearing the return of the birds, smelling the trees' blossoms flower before they unfurled their leaves. "Yes, yes, Kilian and Thread are watching the tent. That's how I could get away," he said, his eyes gliding over hers, his hands nervously turning his hat in his hands, looking for a thread to pick up their conversation. "I got onto trains. Lucked out. Got this team in Newtown." With his head he gestured behind him, where his horse and a spare rested, jingling their harnesses. "Rode hard, got in last night." And then he seemed to relax, resolve.

Kerioniakawida drifted by as if from the wings in a stage theater, on cue, and Delphine realized that Blaise had stayed with him in his cabin the night before. Blaise took her hand and pulled her toward Kerioniakawida's cabin, walking fast while Kerioniakawida took the reins of Blaise's horse and led him off, all without a word.

She dug in her heels. "What has happened? Why are you here? Is it Malachi?" She couldn't take it if her only remaining son had died.

He stopped, facing her. "I will explain everything once we are alone and inside the cabin next door. Right? Everyone is well: No one hurt or dying. Everyone in Newtown, everyone in Cottage, Regina, the baby . . . Everyone is all right, Delphine. Trust me. Come on," he urged gently.

She surrendered.

Kerioniakawida had built up his fire. A pot of tea sat on the table with biscuits, two *boules*, last year's preserves, honey—everything prepared for two people who needed to talk.

Now she was wound tight, but she resolved to keep quiet. Whatever it was, he had come all this way to say it. She only had to wait, to listen.

"I don't know *any* way to tell you this gently," he began, then paused. "Marie didn't leave when her ankle healed. She didn't move back into her tent. In fact, she didn't even sleep in her tent."

The knowledge of what he was saying swelled in her, squeezing all the breath from her. She had presumed and now was caught out, exposed: this man, her partner, did not carry on, doing what was his to do, while she did what she had to do. Her life had turned and she had been so intent on her own metamorphosis that she hadn't realized there might be a corresponding turning in him. She had a guilty realization: *Have I thought of Blaise except in passing?*

And then the voice inside her asked, *Have you forgotten that Blaise also has his own path, his own truth to pursue?*

"I don't see why I can't have you both," he was saying.

She startled. *Have I missed something? What did he just say?*

He smiled. How long had it been since she had seen Blaise smile like that?

"You would be—will always be—of course, my first wife. The main one."

Surely he isn't seeing me, she thought. *To be able to say this thing to me.*

"We are . . . We are in the honeymoon phase of our relationship." She had a moment of being confused about who the "we" was. He smiled that smile again. "She is . . . fun. Did you know that about her? You remember. She made us laugh."

Does he expect me to be happy for him? Her ears rang. She faded into and out of the room. She was sharply aware of the tea in front of her, of the fact that Blaise lifted his cup to his mouth, looked off to the side, then directly at her, as he gathered his courage about him to say these hard words.

"She is pregnant with our child." His voice was soft and tender. His eyes sparkled even as he attempted to dampen down his emotions. He reached across the table for her hand.

She couldn't help her reaction. She batted his hand away. "Don't touch me!"

He withdrew his hand. His voice hardened. "I love you, Delphine." Then softened: "And I love her."

He wanted to share his happiness with her, his partner, his best friend throughout their long marriage together: "I am the luckiest man alive to be loved by two such women."

He wants me to be happy for him, to share his good fortune! She was incredulous. *But do I have a choice?* She tried it on for size, this new garment being measured for her.

Is this the will of the Creator? Is this part of my metamorphosis? Moving into being the "first wife"? Now that I am past my bearing years, should I have to suffer the role of watching another woman swell with his seed, nurse his child? See his tenderness for them, his coolness toward me, the counselor now, eventually the crone?

"How could you?" she asked. "How could *she?*"

He took her hand and held it even as she willed herself not to return the current running through his hand, persuading her as he had always persuaded her. "Things haven't been the same between us for a while, Delphine. After Fredericksburg. You left for four months. After the rape." He looked down. "How you felt about it? I felt . . . differently."

"How did you feel?" A great, cool calm was possessing her. *I told him it was not a rape.*

"I felt enraged. I wanted to kill them. And almost did. I wanted to kill you for saying it was nothing, it was pleasure. Saying it was not rape. *Four men.*" She could see him steel himself to say the next thing. "You have taken me for granted, Delphine. It's been a while since you really saw me, took care of me."

Is this true? She needed to take the situation apart to look at it properly. *I thought we had an agreement; it's how we are together.* She had to get away from him. Had to be by herself, to see how she felt.

"You will be staying here with Kerioniakawida?" she asked.

"Who?" he said, and then saw that she also knew Lazarus' true name.

"Yes. If that's what you want." He touched her face with his forefinger. "This can work, Delphine. I don't love her any more than I love you."

His words fell like an anvil on her heart. *Does he hear what he is saying?*

"I can love two women, make two women happy."

She closeted herself in the chest of her feeling. Her eyes blurred with fury, with rage, with grief. She stood abruptly and the chair fell to the floor behind her. "I have to get back, to Mother's," she said. "Come to breakfast tomorrow. A late breakfast. I will be ready to discuss this with you then."

"And you will consider it?"

She gathered herself. She had to know what was at stake. "What if I say no?"

His eyes filled with an indefinable emotion, sparkled as if with tears. Or perhaps a ruthlessness she had never seen in Blaise before. "Please, Delphine . . . Give me this. Give *us* this. All of us. It will be fine. You like Marie. We could all live together happily. The new baby . . . You will see."

She stepped out and closed the door quietly behind her. She took a deep inhale, felt herself breathe, felt herself floating above, outside herself. When she walked back into her mother's home, Marguerite and Turtle Dawn were sitting at the table.

"What has happened?" Marguerite asked.

"Lazarus says that Thread is all right," Turtle Dawn said. "And so . . . ?"

Delphine told them about Marie Tepe. She relived the whole of their time together in the sutler tent, in the yard: Marie, Delphine, Blaise. Thread and Kilian coming and going. The battles. In between. Her friendship with Marie. She saw it all again in her mind's eye. She told them what Blaise had proposed.

"Can you do it, daughter?" Marguerite asked, then paused. "I know I couldn't do it."

"I could do it," Turtle Dawn said. "That's why I told Kilian he is free. Free to love another. I don't prefer that. But I can live with it."

"I don't know," Delphine said. "I think I have no choice. I think he has taken away my choice."

A long silence filled the room. Turtle Dawn rose to put another quarter log into the firebox. They sat in unusual stillness; the three women's hands were never idle. Eventually, Marguerite made a sound to Turtle Dawn, who stood, carried the teapot to the kettle steaming on the stove, then filled it and brought it back.

"These are hard times," Marguerite said. "Unusual times. Blaise is living on the edge of a great slaughter."

"I had to leave, Mother. You know that."

"Yes. I know that. You had to do what you had to do. And he is also free. Free to do what he has to do, free to choose."

Time passed. The three of them, the family's maternal line, drifted into and out of thought. Midday arrived. None of the women were hungry.

"And now I must choose," Delphine said at last.

Turtle Dawn spoke. "You don't have to choose what he has proposed."

"Don't I? If I choose not to include Marie in our family, then he might go with her."

"You have been together many years. Most of your adult life," Marguerite said.

What is she saying? Delphine wondered. *That we have had enough? Or that we should stay together?*

"Blaise is my father, isn't he?" Turtle Dawn asked her mother.

"No. No, I hadn't met Blaise when you were conceived. I told you that."

"He has been with you since before the Duladiers came. Way before I met Kristiana. He is the father of my brothers."

"Yes. You were six." A pause. "I think you remember." Now the realization dawned that Turtle Dawn had been as traumatized as she had been after the loss of Buffalo Creek and their ancestral home, the years of deprivation, her catatonic episode.

"I remember you had my brothers."

Marguerite, her elder, had saved her family after Buffalo Creek had fallen to the Ogden Land Company. Long past her mothering years, she had looked after them all, moved them to their Lenape homeland along the Delaware, ran her shebeen to make a little money. The boys ran wild with their peers in the tribe while Blaise and Delphine were off building the family business. With Wolf Clan in each tribe, the Montour family had been welcome on any reservation that had Wolf Clan members, just as they had been made welcome at Cattaraugus.

"Yes." She thought of those boys, one towheaded, one dark, one dead, one somewhere in the war. Whelps raised by the community, virtual orphans. She wondered how Simon and Malachi had felt about her, about Blaise. "Blaise didn't seem to care much about his boys . . . not as a father. And now . . ."

Turtle Dawn spoke to say the hard thing: "You chose Blaise over me, Mother."

Marguerite raised a hand over her teacup. Both women looked at her, their matriarch. "I had marked you as mine to raise, Turtle Dawn. Before your mother chose Blaise."

"That's not how I remember it," Turtle Dawn said.

Delphine spoke again. "Blaise gave me the life that I needed. No responsibilities except to myself. He—" She choked hard on her next words. "He said that was what he wanted too. Just us. No children. Now . . ."

"Now he wants this child. Wants Marie. And you." With her typical economy, Marguerite summarized the choice to be made.

Maybe this is because he just lost a son? Simon, she thought. "I am going to walk out," she said. "Alone." She rose and grabbed her pack from a hook near the door, then thrust a few things into it. She drew on her leggings and moccasin boots, then pulled on her mittens. "I don't know when I will be back. Blaise is coming over tomorrow morning to talk. Right now he stays with Ker—with Lazarus."

"We have someplace we have to be tomorrow morning," Marguerite said. Turtle Dawn nodded. "The house will be yours."

We will be undisturbed, she means to say. That is the gift that my mother has given me all my life: leaving me undisturbed to become whatever I would become, unhampered by roles like daughter, tribal member, mother. Wife. I have been cut off, Delphine realized. *I have been given the freedom to become who I would be. And I would have cut off Turtle Dawn, but for my mother . . . And* then she thought formless thoughts about being opened by the knife of war, so that she could be grafted back onto the tree of the tribe. *Is it too late?*

Not too late. With this touchstone, her thoughts floated to the surface again to ask, *Is it too late to have my marriage? My daughter? My grandchildren?*

Delphine walked out on the path she knew well, then chose another path cutting through the woods to the south, heading for the base camp she and Lazarus had occupied during her metamorphosis. Her mind was a blur, along with her body, which was moving her through space but leaving her alone to think. She was trying to think with her heart. A dam had given way inside her, the flood sweeping everything before it. *It's true, what Blaise said. I haven't thought of him, of his needs, for a long time. I have taken him for granted, and his support, his love. But isn't that what we had agreed? Under the tent of our marriage, our partnership. Now he has taken that room for himself. For his pleasure. He says it is a big enough tent for three, for four . . .*

She saw the wolves, shadows sliding through the trees. She knew them; they knew her. She stopped, took a stance, threw her head back and howled.

My heart is broken! she told them. *It hurts so much.* She had to put her hand between her breasts to calm the torrent. Blaise's act was tooth, claws. What acts of neglect was she being paid back for? Her heart was prey and predator at once. Like hands that have been frostbitten, after they begin to thaw, her heart burned and throbbed, systole and diastole, each heartbeat a cataract, a convulsion.

Is this necessary, Mother? A necessary part of my metamorphosis? To take so much from me? To subtract the love that has nurtured me all of my adult days?

She looked at the sky. *I am alone,* she howled. *Alone.* She Who Hunts cried out her pain. The matriarch wolf and her daughter threw back their throats and responded. She wasn't alone.

The campfire was going; Kerioniakawida had been there before her, although he had swept away traces of his presence with a cedar bough. Their wickiup still stood, a blanket held over the door with a cedar bough to keep the wind from entering. She knelt at the door, all strength gone from her. She crawled in, found the furs laid out on the sleeping mat, pulled them over her head, and wept. *How could I not have understood what was at stake?* she asked herself. And now that she was alone, she had to admit the pain that pierced her like a thorn, that another woman, a tribeswoman, had performed such a cruel act of treachery. Had she been that desperate? She would never ever forgive Marie.

When she woke, it was dark. She stepped outside. The stars were brilliant, but cold and impersonal. No moon. Kerioniakawida had kept the fire going while she slept, but again he had erased signs of his having been there. She could feel that he was not there now.

Upon waking, she knew she had come through the first stage of this loss, the stage that had made her want to erase herself. Alcohol would ease her, she knew. There were drugs that would erase her pain. But she knew that was not the way that *it* was orchestrating. *This pain is mine*, she told herself. *Given to me by the Mother. This is the final stage of my return, my metamorphosis.* She was able to consider that objectively. She considered that her brokenheartedness—something she had not experienced before—was also a gift from the Mother, the next necessity.

Oh, it hurts; make no mistake. But an open heart, to feel compassion for others' suffering? Yes, necessity. A gift. Pain is the best spiritual teacher.

She had now completed the fourth stage in the sweat, under the eye of Mother Cougar. She saw it clearly; she had been so hard-hearted. She had always felt she had to be hard, to do what she wanted to do in the world.

Is this the price of an open heart? she asked while she curled there in the wickiup, wounded so badly, feeling it deep within, as if she had been punched in the stomach. *Blaise, my lifelong companion? What will be left to me?* But then: *I still have my choice.* She realized then that she had thought it through, had worked it out in her body during the night. *If this is his weapon, his tool to get what he wants, I will turn it back on him.* Now her tears fell, hot tears, tears of rage and betrayal as much as of hurt and loss.

Toward dawn a new notion occurred to her: *I thought I could do it, for Blaise. It seems so just, so fitting. As I pass my fertile years, why not let him have another woman? But I can't.* Rage filled her when she thought of Marie's betrayal. *She broke my trust, stole my man, planned it even as I said goodbye to her, exchanging gifts. She paid me with the saddlebags her grandfather had made for her!* Delphine was furious. When she pictured Marie, she knew she would become violent as soon as she laid eyes on her. *I cannot abide her as a co-wife. Not a woman who is a sneak thief.*

Then a calmer voice rose from within: *I will not willingly cede my place as Blaise's main woman. His partner in bed, on the battlefield, in business.*

An even calmer voice joined in: *He will prefer her. She is younger. She will be nursing his child. He will come to my bed only when he cannot have her. Will come to me for old times' sake. Will come to me to keep the threesome going. But then I will have to see that tenderness in his eyes when he looks at her, and see the look she returns to him, witness their love, and I . . . No, I cannot live that life,* she admitted to herself. *A life of humiliation, fallen from my place at the center of our relationship. He can go live with Marie's people and raise their child. If he can even manage to do that after so many years being a full part of my family.* Her throat closed thinking of the decades she and Blaise had been partners, lovers, best friends. *I am enough for myself. I have my maternal line. But Blaise! He has no one. He left his tribe, his people. Like me. I also forfeited my family! We lived the life of world citizens, cosmopolitans! And now?*

She couldn't do what he asked. He would have to choose between them. He was her man. *He will have to choose.*

A small, still voice spoke her fear: *He will choose her. Marie.*

Yes, she acknowledged, taking it in, hardening it around herself, like armor, an essential piece of She Who Hunts. *Oh, the pain!*

Later that morning, she strode back, found Blaise waiting for her on the settle outside the home she shared with her mother and daughter. She opened the door, invited him in, and faced him, strong.

"Choose," she said.

He tried again to reason with her. He wanted both women. He had come a long way to make this work. "Why not?" he asked. "I want her. I want you. You will see. You like her; I have seen you together. We can make this work."

She shook her head. "I cannot trust her now. She said she was leaving when I left, as soon as her ankle healed. She stole you, behind my back. Sneaking. Laughing at me! There was a time when you could have asked me, told me you fancied each other, and I would have invited her into our bed. Yes, I thought of it. Admit it; you thought of it. And she did too. It was there in the air between us. But now . . . I don't ever want to see her again!" She felt she might go speechless with rage, but the words kept spilling out of her.

"And you!" she shot. "Go." She wanted to throw her cup at him, make him duck. "Don't let me see you around here tonight, Blaise. Leave here. Now. Go to her." She picked up his moccasin boots that he had carefully taken off when he had stepped into the house and, opening the door, she placed them carefully outside.

"Don't do this, Delphine," Blaise said, alarmed.

The chill spring wind flooded into the house, swept into the corners, cleared away the dust and odors of winter. "Leave," she said, low in her throat so he could hear her determination. "I can't share you with her. I could have, at one point . . . But not now. I cannot trust her; I see that now. She took my place in your bed, in your heart, without asking. I cannot forgive that."

She saw it in his face. He was resolved to have Marie. Her heart flopped weakly in her chest, turned over, sunk, leaden. "And I cannot trust you. So you must leave."

She faced him squarely. "We are divorced," she said, in her native tongue. She didn't know where she had ever heard the words before, but they came to her and now she had said them.

He flinched. He knew the words, had known what her putting his moccasins outside the door meant. "Don't do this, Mar . . . Delphine. Don't do this." He tried to cover up almost calling her Marie, but they both knew for certain then that his heart had changed.

She said the words again, kept the door open for him to leave. "We are divorced." Now she could not even see him through the red raging tide of her fury. Of her grief. "We are divorced," she said a final time, now to his back as he went outside.

She bolted the door shut behind him. Hands shaking, she prepared herself some strong valerian tea with hops and a shot of the whiskey that Marguerite kept on hand for tinctures. She gulped them down. Blaise was gone. He had left her without a backward glance. She would steel herself to go on without him. But for now, she crawled under a pile of blankets, calling on oblivion.

Chapter Twenty-Four

COMPLETING
METAMORPHOSIS

*April–May 1863, Cattaraugus Reservation,
Cottage, and Seneca Falls, New York*

One spring day, when all the moths and butterflies were breaking out of
their chrysalides, when the buckskin was as buttery and smooth and supple
as she had hoped it would become—a true expression of the hands and care
of so many of the women of her lineage—Delphine had felt herself emerging further from the shell she had built around herself. She had felt the
armor was necessary to shield the tender, wounded beating heart within,
but now? Painful as it had been, she took her open heart into the world and
found so many individuals to care about, to shed her light upon. She found
reciprocity, comfort, renewal. *I am beloved*, she realized with amazement.

And now, one full moon later, with her pain receding and her rage and
sorrow leaked away, her metamorphosis was almost complete. She was
stronger now; madness would not overtake her as it had when her People
had lost Buffalo Creek. Her new wings lay heavy and satiny on her back,
wet and untried, but she knew they would prove useful in their own time.

Ah, but it was painful becoming fully alive! Her tender flesh, her flayed
heart—what protection would she have now? She felt her colors, her delicate, powerful wings tasting the air to ride. She felt her power, as if she could
visit and harvest from any fragrant flower, bees her companions.

She had the whole world to experience. The whole world and each remarkable human being, each remarkable plant and animal to trade essences with. She left home without a qualm, knowing it was there for her return so long as war, pestilence, white people, wildfire, or famine did not take it. And now, without Blaise, where was home, really?

In Cottage, each dwelling was chockablock with people, the street muddy with carriages and displaced people looking for new homes, looking for respite from the war. The Duladiers from Newtown were among those who had sought and found refuge there. Everything was unsettled, everything changed and changing.

The Army of the Potomac was pursuing General Lee up the river valleys of Virginia into Pennsylvania, but Lee would not be stopped. Even now his army might be running through Newtown, burning their homes, their silk *magnanerie*, their fields. Would he enact a scorched-earth policy once he was in their homelands, in retribution for the homes lost in the South? Delphine saw how good it was that Philip had mounted a wagon train to move the Pennsylvania family to Cottage, out of harm's way. But how long could that last? She allowed herself to imagine the entire continent as a slave-holding nation, with a majority of the people—women, natives, Africans—enslaved to white men and their coldhearted profits. Slaves held in check by violence. Families separated. Chained to machinery.

This was Delphine's first contact with white civilization since her return, she wondered if anyone in Cottage would notice her metamorphosis. She wandered through the town, taking comfort in the heavy sharpening stone and flint that she wore in a pouch at her waist; she carried her own fire. She had been learning to survive alone. But how would that help her now?

And then Kristiana saw her. Delphine had told herself she was only passing through Cottage on her way to catch a train. She only needed to stop at her dye works; Cottage was a way station where she would not stay. She needed one thing only: a length of linen. A shroud.

"Delphine!" Kristiana cried. She ran up to her, gripped her hands, looked her over, head to toe. "How good it is to see you!" Then: "Turtle Dawn told me. You have returned."

"I just arrived," Delphine answered.

Kristiana pulled her down the street, throwing information at her all the way, and then drew her into the light shade of a maple tree in spring, heavy with the scent of its pollen. They were in front of what had once been Kilian's house, which Delphine knew was now Turtle Dawn's home, given to her by Kilian. "We are relaunching Regina Coeli! We have taken it back from my father's clutches."

Delphine did not remember Kristiana ever having spoken so animatedly before. Had Kristiana experienced a metamorphosis as well? *If so,* Delphine wondered, *what had happened?*

"Did Lazarus not tell you? We want to conceive. Have another child." Kristiana's eyes sparkled. She drew a hand over her stomach. "Now that he is back from the woods and you have returned . . ." She smiled. "Perhaps next time I see you . . ."

Delphine murmured her reassurances, reluctant to be drawn into Kristiana's world. *She is a force of nature,* Delphine thought. *No one can resist her.*

"Yes," she said. "Kerio . . . Lazarus was with me all winter. Thank you for letting me have him, to help with my return."

"Yes, yes, I know," Kristiana said, not letting go of Delphine's hands. "And now we need you here."

Is this the price? Delphine thought. *Now that I have returned, I have debts to pay—to my communities, both native and here in Cottage? To Regina Coeli? To my daughter? To all my relations? Including the Duladiers?* Such responsibility ran counter to her nature. She was accustomed to being alone, making decisions alone . . . *And now?* She let Kristiana pull her along, and although she tried to walk independently, it was with a sense of being attached to something bigger than herself, attached through Turtle Dawn. Through Threadneedle. *How am I related to this person?* she quizzed herself.

"Did Blaise stop here?" she asked.

"Blaise?" Kristiana looked blank. "Why would he be here, so far from the battlegrounds? No." She shook her head.

Delphine could not have endured staying in Cottage if everyone knew about Blaise and Marie. She could not bear the pity, the whispers. "I cannot stay, Kristiana," she said simply. "I am on my way south, looking for the army. I came to ask you for a length of linen that I can dye and take with me."

"Turtle Dawn told me," Kristiana said. "She described your time in the woods this winter. Lazarus had shared with me what he needed to do. He said that you asked. That the clanmothers asked." She was still holding Delphine's hand. But now she stepped the length of her arm away from Delphine: "How did they know what you needed to do?"

Delphine gave Kristiana a long look, wanting the younger woman to hear her question and apply it to herself.

Kristiana laughed. "Yes, how do they know? Grandmother Marguerite told me what to do."

So this is the change in Kristiana, Delphine thought. *And it was orchestrated by Grandmother. Of course. Something has relaxed in Kristiana.*

Delphine disengaged herself gently from hands that were pulling her into Turtle Dawn's house.

"We can't do this without you, Delphine." Kristiana's enthusiasm fell away, and Delphine could see now that the younger woman's face looked scrubbed, as if she had been crying for a long time.

Other people, Delphine thought. *Don't turn your back on other people.* Other people's lives also changed violently, churned. Other people suffered. They transformed. Kristiana planned to become pregnant with Kerioniakawida's baby. Again. Life must continue. Life demanded she continue as well. Why? Because she had come through her metamorphosis and now life called out to her. She must respond. "Take me into my daughter's house, then, Kristiana. Where are you living?"

"Please come with me," Kristiana said, glancing at the door they had been standing in front of. "Everyone will be so glad to see you. The linen is yours to take, Delphine. Of course. You are one of the leaders of our operation. I have given you my authority. I have given Thread my shares. But you will see: We have so many things that need to go to the dye works. Here. And in Seneca Falls. We need you to start up your operation again." Then she seemed to recall her earlier promise: "We have kept your dye works operating in your absence. But it is not the same without you!"

Delphine had never seen Kristiana so voluble. "Yes," Delphine responded, simply. "I will return, I promise. But only after."

Kristiana threw open the door to the house. Delphine heard the clatter of sewing machines, saw the operation within. Six machines occupied the center of what had once been the kitchen. Undyed clothing was being taken out to the shack in the yard, where Kilian had once stored his supplies for his field kit, where Kristiana herself had been brought back to life by Grandmother Marguerite.

Turtle Dawn came out of the back room where Thread had once lain in his sickbed. Surprise lighted her face. "Mother! What are you doing here? I thought you were on your way back to the battlefield."

Delphine was suddenly struck that neither her daughter nor Kristiana, nor any of the women in this room (for all of the people in the room were women), knew what war was, what it is like. *They don't know!* Delphine said to herself, understanding for the first time the force that animated Kilian's dispatches.

She allowed herself to consider dispassionately that place where she was going: to the brutality of war. To the revenge that drove men across fields, roaring with rage. To the hatred that allowed a sharpshooter to pick off one man after another, ending his story for all time, his brains splashed over autumn leaves, dirty snow, spring grass, barley heads heavy with grain. Some woman's son, husband, lover. The round of the year ground on, like a millwheel, back to the season where so much had been freighted in the earlier circle. Delphine felt like she stood on the edge of her death, looking down at her feet to see the chasm that opened before her, bottomless, black, beckoning. *Once you have been to war,* she thought, *all of the machinery of nature, all the details of the world are flattened, having lost their depth and meaning. Only we give meaning to life.* Someone had said that, some philosopher ... *We give life meaning with our choices. I have made my choice. And Blaise has made his.* Her heart wrenched as if it were being wrung. She restrained herself from putting her hand on her heart to alleviate the pain there, would not reveal her suffering to these women so blatantly. Enough that Turtle Dawn and her mother knew.

Kristiana and Turtle Dawn invited Delphine into the side room that had been Kilian's bedroom and closed the door. The din in the kitchen faded somewhat. "It isn't easy keeping your head in such a time," Kristiana began, "but we have."

"With each other's help and the work," Turtle Dawn offered.

Delphine was incredulous that these two women behaved as if nothing had ever happened to their partnership. Not the anguish of separating after decades of being lovers. Not the maiming of Thread's foot, not Kristiana's shunning, not Turtle Dawn taking Kilian for her lover, not Kristiana giving Thread her shares. The two women still enjoyed what they had with each other. And the community flourished in their penumbra.

"Mother," Turtle Dawn began. "We need you to open your dye works."

Delphine shook her head. "I have to get back to the battlefield," she said.

"Yes," Turtle Dawn said. "We know."

"After," Kristiana said. "After your return."

Delphine realized then that she had not thought about after, about what she would do when she would not be Blaise's partner any more, when Kilian returned from the war, not a whole man but a scarecrow. *Does Turtle Dawn know?* she wondered. *And Thread?* No one could peer into the future to see how Regina and Threadneedle would fit into life after the war. Delphine could not imagine how the husk of a man named Kilian could be with Turtle Dawn again. *Let it be,* her heart counseled her.

"We need you here, after," Kristiana said. "We need to become a triumvirate; we need you to help us run Regina Coeli . . . from your position as a Trojan Horse inside Wilhelm's factory."

Need. Need. Need.

"Listen to me, sisters," Delphine began. "Surely you must know this: We can't tell what tomorrow will bring."

The two women, a generation younger than Delphine, stopped talking, stopped the onrush of their energy, stopped trying to persuade the older woman. They calmed themselves and began to listen. She saw then that they recognized her as their elder. They didn't need to know the details to see how she had become She Who Hunts.

Turtle Dawn let go of Delphine and reopened the door into the factory room with all of its energy, spewing out garments. White garments that Delphine would give color to, if she agreed.

"I will . . . do my best. To return," Delphine said. "But you must know: Nothing is guaranteed."

The two younger women nodded, as if she had been encouraging them.

"Are you stopping in Seneca Falls, Mother?" Turtle Dawn asked.

"Yes," Delphine responded. "I will see Regina. And Wilhelm. See what I can do to lull him into complacency."

Six yards of linen stowed in her pack, Delphine spent the night in Cottage, studying the situation, considering what Kristiana and her daughter were proposing. *Yes, there will have to be an after.* They had cleverly set into place all of the elements they would need to best Wilhelm, to take over his factory, to relaunch Regina Coeli to a nation of women anxious to put the war and the absence of their men behind them.

Kristiana and Turtle Dawn, no longer lovers, were nonetheless yoked together, pulling toward an approaching flax harvest and the technicalities of coordinating another year of production without Kilian, without Threadneedle.

Later that day, Delphine stopped into Philip's to greet her granddaughter, Swan, now a small girl child who ran to her grandmother and clasped her around the waist, burying her face into the fragrance of her belly. Delphine stayed for a cup of tea, held Nesting Swan on her lap. She took a small piece of buckskin out of her pack and handed it to the child, who took it proprietarily and, standing, began to work again on the piece she had worked on all spring, surrounded by the women of her family, the Montour women. Now she positioned it on the table, turning it this way and that, studying it, imagining what it might become. Delphine spoke softly into her seashell ear about the small bag she could make to keep her precious things in and wear around her neck.

"And I have another gift for you," Delphine said softly to Swan, who turned, hands stilled, eyes attentive to her grandmother. Delphine drew a cord out of her pack and threaded something onto it. It worried Delphine that Swan did not speak yet. She held the child's shoulders with firm hands. "I have put two things on there for you: a brass bullet casing and a turquoise bead."

The child fingered the two charms that hung down in front of her chest. Did Delphine imagine that her lips formed the word "turquoise"?

Delphine spoke softly into the child's ear: "I am counting on you and your friends . . . to put an end to war."

War is bad, isn't it? the child asked her grandmother in Dialog, her expression solemn, scanning for marks of suffering on Delphine's face.

She speaks in Dialog! Delphine thought. Then she responded in Dialog. *Very bad.*

The two oldest Duladier women came into the main room from a walk they had taken together—the sisters Elisabeth and Catherine, whom Philip had yanked out of Newtown before the war reached them. Delphine had to remind herself: *They are respected matriarchs too. Catherine is Philip's wife. This is their home.* It was hard hearing them call Swan "Eliza." No wonder the child was confused.

Delphine knew that the elders of this family must be grieving that they had not been able to raise even one *volte* of silkworms this spring, perhaps the first time they had failed to harvest *cocons*. This discontinuity would have been fatal to a smaller silk production, but the House of Duladier had been through wars before and they had known what to do. They had brought a portion of their eggs with them to Cottage to hatch and mate, so they could collect more eggs. Cottage had plenty of mulberry trees, so they were able to glean a scant new harvest from a few moths. History repeats itself, apparently, to lineages that nurture resistance.

"Twenty-five years in this country," Catherine said, and Elisabeth finished her thought: ". . . and this the first year that we had not been able to complete a season."

Delphine could see the pain, all in their eyes. Now that Delphine was an elder herself, albeit just a baby-elder, she could imagine their suffering. They had had to abandon their *magnanerie*, that beautiful space Philip had designed and Wilhelm built, sanctified and burnished by a quarter century of dreaming their way into metamorphosis. What would become of them, the House of Duladier, Duladier Soie, if everything they had built were looted and then burned? Now Delphine had an answer that would only have occurred to her since Blaise left: they had each other.

As if in response to these thoughts about how the traditions of the silk would endure through future generations, Catherine and Elisabeth, who had been whispering together, now turned to face Delphine. The sisters glanced around the room and, seeing that Philip had stepped out, leaving them alone with just Delphine and the child, Catherine drew a piece of paper out of the pocket in the side seam of her skirt and passed it across the table. Catherine and Elisabeth exchanged glances and then nodded toward Delphine, encouraging her.

"These are the words we use to bring the silkworms through their long metamorphosis," Catherine said.

"To prepare them either to die or to be reborn again," Elisabeth added. "We use these words when a woman labors to bring forth a child, in her metamorphosis, in the infant's becoming, as they separate."

Catherine finished the transmission of knowledge: "And these are the words we say when someone dies, to guide a being into its new state."

Delphine glanced at the text. "O Aspirant," she read, then looked sharply at Catherine over the top of the vellum on which the words had been carefully penned. She understood what she was to do at once. "I will memorize the words," she said, "and then I will burn the paper."

The two Duladier women nodded. *Yes.*

Just then, Turtle Dawn and Kristiana walked into the house and brought their everyday world into focus once more.

Her long absence from Cottage now allowed Delphine to see the shape of the community as it was falling into place. "Show me what you have been doing," she said to Turtle Dawn and Kristiana.

"Come," Kristiana offered. "Let us show you. Philip is just outside, he'll want to join us."

Philip, who walked with a stick now, was waiting on a settle right outside the door. The sound of the screen door banging, the distant hum of the mill below, the beauty of the flax fields waving in the late spring breeze—all of it struck Delphine with force, a smith's hammer on her exposed heart.

She couldn't help herself; she put her hand between her breasts as if to ease the sudden wringing pain.

When Delphine asked about the factory, Philip told her that the Flustys— Maeve and Thomas—had been taking charge more and more, moving between their bleaching greens and Wilhelm on the canal and their fields and operations in Cottage. They had the strength of survivors, having experienced the pain of losing their original homelands in Scotland, and then in Northern Ireland, and now they fiercely defended their way-of-life in Cottage—their right to live their lives at scale, in a village structured by their guild, family, and church. They had built their own modest chapel in the midst of their linen operation, and they never missed a Sunday nor failed to stop and cross themselves in front of the small shrines they had built along the way, like Stations of the Cross but with statues of the Mother sheltered within the roofs of the altars, each one also housing a bowl of flowers and the stub of a candle.

"Their devotion to the Virgin Madonna echoes our family's devotion to the Black Madonna," Kristiana said. "Yes, we still keep it secret . . . but the Scots-Irish weavers must intuit our devotion, just as we intuit your family's devotion to Mother Earth, as everything about you as a People tells us, without words." Did Kristiana know how her words poured over Delphine's heart like an emollient? They were approaching one of these small shrines on their way down the street from Philip's house. "Thus I not only tolerate this but pray here myself."

That Kristiana prayed aloud disoriented Delphine a bit. She hovered to the side of the roadside shrine, looking at every feature of it. This carved statue of a woman, a child at her breast, was not repellent to her but reassuring. It held the resonance of the Virgin's earlier model, the Black Madonna, puissante and indomitable to be sure, but faithful to those who made their devotions to Her. Kristiana's voice was fervent in her wishes that all would come out right for all of them, and that each man would return home safely from the war. They broke away and continued down the street.

"My prayers are always the same," Kristiana said. She looked at Delphine pointedly to see if her elder would reciprocate some information about her own devotions.

Delphine could see that Kristiana's devotion had been rekindled by war and its inevitabilities of maiming and ruin, death and destruction. Even Kristiana saw now: We are all in the hands of the Scales, perhaps of the Mother, perhaps of the Creator. *It*. But Delphine's own devotion to *it* was too fresh. It was too difficult to explain how the loss of her belief in a god had brought her to this conviction. How those who had been at Fredericksburg had come to believe that the Mother had turned away from her children, appalled and wounded.

Abandoned and bereft, Delphine had plumbed this presence, *it*, who still governed the world of incidents and co-incidents, creating intimate signposts along the path to help a person keep her way. To keep from falling off the World. And *it* satisfied, sustained and intrigued her.

Philip, who had recently spent all his time preoccupied with organizing wagon trains to bring their extended families—Duladier and Montour—from Newtown in southern Pennsylvania to Cottage, New York, seemed rudderless once everyone had arrived and settled in. Delphine wondered if Philip had begun to feel stifled, impotent as he approached his mid-sixties. "Philip," she began, "How are you doing?"

He seemed to know what she was asking and filled her in with details. Yes, Tom and Maeve not only had the weaving and bleaching operations completely in their control, they were mentoring the younger generation, holding meetings each night to teach them how to resist the factory model.

Delphine had heard Tom speak before. "Resistance is an ancient and honorable tradition," he and Maeve told their followers. "It rises up in every generation." The young ones, particularly Regina, listened, trembling at the edge of both their own adulthood and the war's outcome. To civilians, the distant war paralleled the wars they did experience: the war against the factory model for their own way-of-life seemed as much a losing battle as that of the Union against the Confederates. And the war for women's rights had much more immediacy than the war to free slaves, as few of them knew slaves firsthand, while women's lack of substance felt like slavery to many.

Philip's hands shook as he lit his pipe. "Who else could tell the young ones how to make a life for themselves in such times if not Maeve and Thomas, this couple who work beside us daily, who have suffered so much and not been bowed? Who else knows what will work, what will not?" Philip puffed away contentedly, in no hurry, perhaps forgetting they still wanted to tour the operation with Delphine.

Observing this new Philip, retired and happily so, Delphine wondered if she would ever know the luxury of being a contented elder. Back in Cattaraugus, sheltered within her clan, Marguerite was preparing to die, yet she seemed to be at peace with her mortality. Delphine could not help thinking she might have seen her mother for the last time.

Death was thick in the air. Even Kristiana knew the significance of the length of linen Delphine now carried with her. It symbolized the possibility that someone—someone they loved—might die in the war. If they all survived the war, the length of linen would be Delphine's shroud when she died. Or maybe she would use it for her mother. She only knew that she needed to take it with her, along with the buckskin. She had to be prepared to face death like the woman she had become. Remembering the first few words she had read on the vellum Catherine had given to her, she knew she must not only be ready to give her own life but also be ready to ease another person's exit from this life into the next.

Delphine was possessed of a powerful sense of being in the right place in the right time, of every detail hitting a bull's eye. Every thing was woven to every other thing.

Now that she had a good idea of how strong Regina Coeli's counterinsurgency was to Wilhelm's juggernaut, she felt confident that the women of Regina Coeli had a vision that could yet win the day.

Catherine had given her a prayer than began "O Aspirant . . ." and now on the long, slow trip down the canal Delphine worked on etching those words into her lips, her heart, her mind. She could have taken the train, and if she had she would be there by now. And she had been in a hurry, hadn't she? But she had since surrendered her own sense of timing to *it*, knowing that the drum that drove the raveling and unraveling would work better if she did not interfere with her puny and shortsighted will. She understood now that the prayer she had been given was really instructions for a spirit caught between the land of the everyday and the Next Thing. How to survive metamorphosis. She had survived it, just barely, and now she must live it. The responsibility of flying was hers to command.

She allowed herself to fall under the enchantment of the season. The swoon of May lay upon the land and rose up from the still waters of the canal every morning. As evening fell, a mist crept over water and land alike, like a spirit lizard inserting its feet into every crevasse, making the imprint of their watershed visible in its footsteps. Lilac trees and wild roses, heads heavy with rain, arched over the banks. The meadows were establishing their clans: in this season, buttercups, daisies, clover, Indian paintbrush, red-orange and yellow. These would give way to tiger lilies, sweet pea, chicory. Whippoorwills exchanged calls across particularly smooth stretches of canal, and at night the fireflies began their irregular twinkling—random to humans, music to their species.

And yet all of it was being torn with both hands in the name of war. Her slow procession through the landscape was both soothing and rending to her heart.

Even before she stepped off the boat in Seneca Falls, she learned that a new class of dyes was sweeping their world, developed by a chemist from the coal tars produced as a byproduct of the gasworks that not only lit Wilhelm's *manufacture* but that was beginning to light up whole neighborhoods like candles on a Christmas tree. "Aniline" they called the dyes. Bright, colorfast, cheap. Out of this derangement, was it possible a new type of human being was being born? She didn't know what to think of these new dyes any more than she knew what to think of who they were all becoming. Her gift for prophecy was not as developed as Kristiana's or even her mother's; she had only questions . . . and a stalwart trust.

In mid-May, Delphine stepped off the canal boat and headed for her dye works, in the building where Wilhelm had his factory along the canal in Seneca Falls, where the Declaration of Sentiments, the document that had magnified the call for women's rights, had been read and then sent around the world just fifteen years earlier. She observed the stone laundry and bleaching house being completed at the edge of the canal, satisfied that she would have the satiny product to dye right at hand, fresh from the bleaching greens. *After.*

In an upstairs room of the facility, she took out the length of linen Kristiana had given her and pondered the ways it wove together all the strands of her lineage, both native and European, even as it kept their individual strands intact. She used all her turmeric to dye the shroud a bright saffron yellow, the color the ancient Druids had used to honor their chieftains. She made notes which dyestuffs she would have to replace, after. She was out of nearly all her materials, but the inventory of raw ingredients in the storeroom at Kilian's house in Cottage would continue to accrue: onionskins, dried beets, cochineal, indigo, madder, marigold, all lined up and labeled the way Kilian liked it, alphabetically. Too, the women from her tribe continued to collect materials from Buffalo's produce depot for a business run by women from their tribe; they now saw how it could help support a decent life off the reservation.

As the linen soaked, Delphine felt the change, ready to try her wings, to be the family's spy. She had been afraid that it would be too difficult, but now it looked as though it would be easy. She had her buckskin, all the tools that came with being an elder—flint, grouse wing, cedar, sharpening stone, tinderbox—and now her length of linen, dyed saffron. Wilhelm would be no match for her.

When the linen was finished—dyed, set with mordant, put through the wringer—Delphine tucked it inside her bag and was just on her way out the door of the factory when Wilhelm called to her: "Delphine!"

Piss-poor luck, she thought. She turned slowly, pasting a smile onto her face. "I thought you were busy," she said by way of a plausible excuse for not going to see him. "I didn't want to bother you."

"Could you come into my office for a moment?" he asked. "I have a request," he added with a rakish grin. "Unless you are in too much of a hurry."

She followed him to his office and entered, but she did not take a seat. She put her sack of damp linen on the floor beside her like a sandbag, her body language suggesting she had just a minute to spare. "What is it, Wilhelm?" she asked.

"Could you close the door?" He did not take a seat either but hovered two body lengths away from her.

"If this is business, why would I need to close the door, Wilhelm?" She touched the dagger in the scabbard that hung concealed at her waist, ready if necessary.

"A little bird told me there's trouble in Paradise," he said, expressionless but watching her like a raptor watches a meadow for movement. When she said nothing, he added, "Blaise stopped by on his way back to the battlefield. After seeing you. To settle some accounts."

Still she said nothing.

"He tells me you have divorced him. Tells me that he's giving up running a sutler tent, giving up his share of the dye works, moving to Akwesasne, back to the Mohawks. Isn't that where your people originally came from?" he asked, all innocence. "The original Montour?"

Was her silence unnerving him? He took a step toward her. She would not back away from him but stood her ground.

She knew what he was doing: attempting to throw his net over her, to ensnare her in his scent, his physique, his wealth. Truth be told, she never could stand Wilhelm's smell, which for her had always been a fatal flaw when choosing whether to reciprocate a man's attentions.

His voice was husky, almost a whisper. "I am only a decade older than you. If we put our business together—and our lives—no one could stand before us. We could dominate the clothing market when we come out of this war. We could take over Regina Coeli and scores of other businesses that will be up for sale—a fire sale—after the war."

She adjusted the straps on the burden basket she had designed out of canvas and leather to carry her necessities, then picked up the sack containing the damp shroud, indicating that she had heard enough of what he had to say.

He stepped up to her and took hold of her upper arm. She knew he was feeling her bicep and the side of her breast. She remembered her promise to Kristiana: to go along with their plan to lull Wilhelm into complacency. She hadn't expected to be facing him until after the war, but now the time was upon her. Rather than put her dagger into him, she smiled with what she hoped was a promising smile. She wanted to put her hand on his, as Blaise had trained her when she and Marie practiced combat. She could draw this man in and then flip him over her shoulder and onto his back.

"You know how long I have desired you," he said, putting all of his earthy, pulsating energy into the touch of his hand on her. Then he stepped back. "Consider my proposal."

"I promise you," she said. "I will."

After she left the factory, she found she could not control her shivering despite its being a lovely early summer's day. She went down the banks of the canal toward the bleaching greens and bathhouse where Maeve and her daughters would soon be setting up their finishing operation. She put down her things and lay on her back, emptying her mind and calming herself until the shadows told her that the sun was beginning the descent from its zenith.

That night she stayed at Regina's house, let herself fill up with the certainty and comfort that came from seeing Regina's baby, her great-grandson, Blake. Her grandson, Threadneedle, had engendered a son through this Duladier woman, this girl Regina, Catherine and Philip's daughter. Their families were joined yet again. Kristiana and Lazarus. Turtle Dawn and Kilian. Now Regina and Threadneedle.

None of these Huguenot people—Shadow People they were called, the Duladiers—had seemed real to her when they had first arrived over two decades ago. She and Blaise had passed through Newtown often enough, to see her mother, to ask for something, to check on their children, but their stays were always brief. They left money. They left supplies. And then they left. They always left.

After Delphine and Regina had finished their dinner of soup, with Blake asleep in his mother's lap, his head fallen back from her breast, his mouth hanging open, a drop of milk still on his lower lip, Regina began: "I didn't know you very well, Delphine. Before . . ."

"I knew you well enough to love you then, Regina," Delphine said, reaching across the table to squeeze the younger woman's hand. Delphine had stopped in Seneca Falls last September, after Antietam, with Blaise. And while Blaise negotiated with Wilhelm, for money to buy supplies, for uniforms to restock their inventory of Zouave uniforms, for trading tobacco and dye formulas and who knew what else, Delphine had found Regina going into labor and had helped her bring the baby, her great-grandson, into the world. She and Regina would always have that bond. She was able to say, genuinely and with a completely open heart, "And I love you even more now. Like a daughter."

Why had it never occurred to her before that Blake was named after Blaise? That Blaise was, through the tangle of many marriages, the great-grandfather of this infant, and the baby's name honored that bond? She shuttered her aching heart. Blaise would have his new family, among the Mohawk. Delphine would not have to witness it. But now she had this keepsake, from her grandson, Threadneedle—his son, Blake, like the mystic poet. *De facto.*

As Delphine prepared to leave Regina's house the next morning, she bound her breasts and tried on a small size of the male Zouave costume she had taken from the factory's inventory. She would return to the battlefield, where she belonged, but this time in the disguise of a man. If she was no longer welcome on the battlefield as a *viviandière,* she would go as She Who Hunts, but with the marks of her gender masked from common gaze. She knew what to expect from war. If dressing as a man was her only chance to go back, she would do it. Dressing as a man was also the only way she could face Marie and Blaise, if they were still there. In the sutler tent. In her bed. And so she boarded a train as "Mr. Montour," and no one questioned her, a green soldier going to the front in a brand new uniform.

Chapter Twenty-Five

I NEED THIS...
FROM ANYONE

Early July 1863, Gettysburg, Pennsylvania

*And so, like the snake awakening in spring sheds his skin
and begins to move quickly,
when Lee uncoiled his troops
and flowed northward into Pennsylvania
along interior valleys, the Union was not only taken
by surprise but alarmed.
Lee was heading for their homes!*

Delphine returned to the battlefield for her grandson, Threadneedle. It took all the courage she could mount to return here, without Blaise's support, and with the possibility that she would have to witness the new couple's happiness in the midst of the gruesome intimacies of death particular to war. She hadn't returned for Kilian, whose doppelgänger concealed a ruined wreck of a man, his company's Fool, alive only because Thread kept him so. He was worse than useless, except in the surgeon's tent. Don't-ask-him-to-boil-water-for-coffee Kilian. And yet the mutilations of war brought out the healer in him, no matter his emotional state; he was apparently irreplaceable in the surgeries. But yes, she would bring Kilian out, along with Thread. For her family, all of them.

Delphine had spent the last six months preparing herself for whatever came next. She was going to pull Thread and Kilian out of the war and back home, even it meant they would have to dress as women or hide out in the woods like Lazarus for the rest of the war. Now it was She Who Hunts who made the choices: they would not fight in this war any longer. She knew this in every bone of her body, with complete certainty: She didn't know how it would end, just that it *would* end.

It was night by the time she found the sutler tent. She gritted her teeth as she approached, then stopped to listen outside the canvas flap for sounds within. She opened the flap and found Blaise there sorting inventory by lanternlight. Alone.

"Delphine." He turned to her, empty-handed.

"Blaise." She couldn't meet his eyes. "I just came to get a few of my things. I'll . . ."

"Delphine. I sent Marie home, to her family. She's . . . gone."

She looked around. She saw no evidence of Marie. "Blaise. I . . . I don't know."

"You don't *know?* I choose you, Delphine. Us. Isn't that what you wanted?"

"Blaise. Why? What is it that *you* want?"

"Delphine." He began speaking in French, the language of his family, the *trappeurs*. The *voyageurs*. "She is dry where you are . . . moist. She is sterile where you are fertile."

"You are talking nonsense, Blaise. She is pregnant. With your child! How is that sterile? I am past bleeding. I am not fertile anymore."

"No. No, I am not talking nonsense," he placed himself directly in her path, held her gaze. "I came back here, ready to pack up and leave for Akwesasne, to start again. I was shot, Delphine. A stray minié ball. The surgeon said it came this close to the main vein going to my heart. I nearly died." He lifted his shirt and showed her the wrappings around his chest, just below one nipple. "And I *saw*: Marie is a stranger. I don't know her family. Your family is my family. Has been my family. My story is with you. I can't start again. You . . . stimulate me. Your ideas. Your drive. Your honesty. Marie . . . she . . ."

Delphine was taken aback by this declaration. "She stimulates you! And more, she attracts you. You will miss her."

Blaise paused. "I do," he said. "I do miss her." A shadow passed over his face. "Marie will be fine. Her family will raise the child." He swallowed. "I am just the father. Her brothers will be the child's actual fathers, introducing him or her to the tribe, their clan. Marie . . . she will be far away." He seemed to collapse into himself. "Out of sight, out of mind." He gave her a wan smile. "Isn't that what they say?"

Delphine tried to push past him. "I . . . I have to see Thread and Kilian. Please . . . I can't talk with you about this now, Blaise. Can't even hear the words you are saying." Her voice was rising. Soon she would have to shove him if he didn't move.

"I'll take you to them. I know where they are camped."

Their horses were grazing side by side, tethered near the sutler tent, same as they had ever been. *But it would never be the same. Nor should it be,* she thought. *We would have to start all over. And I don't think that is possible.*

"Did Marie ride Brushfire?" she asked, but before she let the notion upset her, she realized that someone would have needed to ride her horse so he would not get persnickety. "I've changed, Blaise," she said as she jumped onto Brushfire.

He gave her a sharp look that said, "We'll see . . . ," meant to remind her how well he knew her.

From a brake close by the men's camp, Delphine and Blaise crouched, watching. The men of their company were dancing and kiyi-ing to drums. Their boys—the men of their People—did this before each major battle, and now the white farm boys they'd gone to school with, hunted with, brought in the hay with, did it as well.

The drums had their effect. Delphine and Blaise, huddled together in the brush, listened to each other breathe until Delphine's breathing told Blaise what he needed to know. He brushed her stomach, now hardened by her winter's work, found the drawstring and pulled it, releasing the fly that allowed a man to piss without taking down his pants. The linen was smooth and soft as skin, but nothing like the silk that Blaise knew how to pull down in Delphine, rough and tender at once, familiar and piercingly new, just invented fresh in response to this yearning.

Just the warmth of his hand on her leg left Delphine trembling, then convulsing around his fingers. "I don't want you anymore, Blaise!" she gasped.

He laughed.

As the drums beat in a rhythm that compelled the young men to dance, Blaise reached behind Delphine and pulled her to her feet. There was no need to be quiet now, the young men totally captured in their own ecstatic snare. He pushed her back against a proximate tree, and then Delphine turned, her belly rubbing against the smooth, glowing bark of a beech. *I need this*, she thought. *From anyone.* She felt his fingers inside and out of her, and then as he breathed into her ear and nipped her neck, he stepped inside her legs and moved his phallus over her parts, in her, over her, drawing sounds out of her that she knew revealed how he was reaching her, bringing her to this pitch. When he thrust himself into her, she stood on one leg, lifting the other out of her pants in a balletic move as if she were opening herself to him further, then wrapped that leg around him to press into him more firmly. Feeling his whole length inside of her, she froze with the power of penetration that came after having been deprived of it for the entire winter and spring.

It was summer, full on. She arched and he paused. Her first orgasm would send her to her knees if he did not hold her up. He waited to thrust again, bringing them both to the ecstasy that war gives coupling, an ecstasy they could approach and let take them over, approach and let take them over, until the false dawn and exhaustion sent them inside, fleeing the cold dew that settles down on the land before the real dawn wakes the birds.

On the way back, they shared one horse, tying Bucephalus to come behind Brushfire. Blaise kept one of his hands on Delphine's breast, knowing that she kept pressure on herself against the saddle horn, and that when they arrived at their tent they would know what to do with each other's bodies—for who was what and which was whose?—before they fell into a deep, rapturous half-sleep before sunrise.

When it was over, she turned to him. "I don't know, Blaise," she said. "This joining doesn't mean anything except that I needed this." *From any man*, she meant. *Now.* He listened with all of his skin to her words. "But after . . . ?" she said. "Don't count on it. Thank you, but I am not yours anymore."

"After will come soon enough," he said. "And then we shall see." He pulled her into him, spooning, and they fell deeply, dreamlessly asleep.

Chapter Twenty-Six

MOCKINGBIRD IN
PEACH ORCHARD

July 3, 1863, Gettysburg, Pennsylvania

In any other year, it would have been haying time. The dew was quickly vanishing, pulling up off the land in sheets of transpiration almost visible to the naked eye. Clouds were gathering in the early July sky, and by late afternoon they would build to thunderheads. But it was the battlefield, and even though the rye would go to waste in the surrounding fields, each and every man knew that here, in Gettysburg, where the roads all came together like a spider's web, they would fight a decisive battle. Everyone was in his or her place. As they hunkered together in a peach orchard laden with a heavy harvest, the juice of the fruits dripping down their chins and off the ends of their elbows, Threadneedle told Kilian this:

"My People and our history have always been marked by peach orchards. A Dutch governor on Esopus Creek once hanged a clanmother who dared to harvest the ripe tree that the governor had built his house near, declaring the tree to be in his backyard now. Typical of a white man—particularly a military white man!—he thought to claim for his own what had been the Lenape People's tree for the tree's entire lifetime."

Kilian had heard this particular piece of history before, but he loved to listen to the same stories again and again, as every story was told differently by each storyteller.

"The clanmother knew full well what she was doing, as did the governor.

He hanged her—a clanmother!—as an act of war, and a war did in fact start and end in that place. The War of the Esopus we call it. And for a century—a century, Kilian—no Dutch were permitted to settle in the Delaware watershed on what is now the New Jersey side of the Hudson. That's how we feel about our clanmothers," he concluded. "And about our peach orchards."

Kilian remembered another story about mature peach orchards, told to him by Grandmother Marguerite and then again by Delphine. The mature peach orchards along the Montour family's Susquehanna homeland had been savagely cut down when Sullivan's army invaded the valley of Thread's maternal line seventy-five years earlier. In the place where the Montour family's history was written in the stones and ridgelines rimming the river.

Thread leaned back on his elbows, his long hair braided to keep it out of the way. Legs spread out before him, he was looking at the sky, a little smile on his lips. A flock of goldfinches lilted by on their way to the thick heads of thistle that were scattering their pollen and summoning finches to feast. The year had reached that season where every creature called to its mate, every flower to its pollinator, every thistle to its goldfinches, and black cherry trees to blackbirds, all in a drunken orgy whose clamor shook the forested edge.

A bird sang from a nearby tree.

"Mockingbird?" Kilian guessed as the bird ran through its repertoire. Thread sat up and clapped Kilian on his upper arms in acknowledgment of his lucky guess.

"You have been a fine brother to me, Kilian," Thread said. "I am counting on you to be a superb uncle to my son." The two men were still half-drunk from the night before, a drunk that was still pleasant, that had not yet degraded to a hangover. The ripe peaches in which they indulged for their breakfast would draw yellowjackets when the sun fell upon the orchard, but now, in the chill of the morning, with light flickering through the trees, the grass, the peaches, their company? All was perfection. Stasis.

Kilian took refuge in the clerk. "We are cousins. And will always be brothers to each other. Because I am Blake's maternal uncle, I will always be like a father to your children. May you and Regina have many more." As Kilian said these things, he reflected on how their relationship had changed during the war. *Why does Threadneedle always seem like the elder—his twenty years and a handful to my thirty years plus?* He had often heard their mothers refer to Threadneedle as an old soul, and in fact all the women seemed to confirm this. Kilian wondered why he had taken it upon himself to come along on this war to protect his younger cousin? At this point, almost two years in, it seemed a ruse—nay, a curse—that he, Kilian Sechinger, son of Catherine, lover of Turtle Dawn, and father of Nesting Swan, had brought upon himself.

Thread reciprocated the compliment with his characteristic warmth. "And may you and Turtle Dawn be a happy couple, for ever after."

Kilian wished this for himself nearly every night, at least the ones when he fell asleep conscious rather than exhausted from hours in surgery attempting to sew young men and their fathers back into a semblance of normalcy. *A crazy quilt,* he had begun to tell himself when thinking of their torn bodies. His previous life seemed so distant, the thought of seeing Turtle Dawn again was beginning to seem a thin fable. He couldn't convince himself to imagine that he would be immune to the cleaver of the battlefield. But still he wished it. To be with Turtle Dawn once more, to be clasped in her arms, between her legs. To stay there until morning, feeling the silk satin of her long back, her flanks and belly.

Thread surprised Kilian out of his reverie, leaning toward him with a glint in his eye. "I called our ancestors last night, Kilian, after our dancing, between midnight and dawn, when most everyone was sleeping."

The salt of sudden tears stung Kilian's eyes, feeling like a heavy sweat, strange in the early morning. "And . . . ?" he ventured.

Thread lay down on his back, pulled his brimmed hat over his face as if he were going to nap, and crossed his booted ankles. "I called them—called our ancestors, Kilian, to come to me." He lifted his brim for a moment, to give Kilian a direct stare: "*Our* ancestors, Kilian."

He meant the Celtic stock, the Druid lot.

"And suddenly they were there, checking me out, seeing who had called.

A small band, four or five, their cloaks whipping around them. They must have been on horseback from the way they wheeled around to look at me. Or riding a dervish." Thread grinned, but there was no amusement in that tight grimace. "And then one revealed his face to me as he took in mine. Face to face, inquiring. Right out of the lands of the Standing Stones they were, Killy. I can't say I recognized his face, lean and lined, a chieftain's age. But I shall never forget that face, shall always yearn for another glimpse of it."

"What did he look like, Thread?" Kilian asked, enraptured.

Thread, who was not much with words, challenged himself to express what he saw in that face. "His eyes. Alive in some way that we've lost, with tearing ourselves from the places where we were the Original People, tearing ourselves from our layered stories, our collective memory, our dells and streams, our medicines, our totems, our salmon, our oaks. They knew who they were; that was apparent. Clear and sharp, his eyes looking to see who *we* had become. Who was calling."

The mockingbird was now mimicking a sorrowful tune—perhaps the mourning dove? And then a battlefield barrage started up to their left. It was beginning.

Kilian had to know, and so before he rose he asked casually, "Were they coming for us, do you think, Thread?"

Thread sprang to his feet, along with the rest of their company, ran to an orderly who had appeared, then returned to Kilian with their orders. "We'd better get our horses, Kilian. They're moving us. They're going to want us mounted."

"Here?" Kilian looked around, bewildered at the low-slung branches heavy with fragrant fruit. "Horses? In the peach orchard?"

"They've seen Jeb Stuart riding in toward the battle. He's shown up at last; his scout just arrived." Thread was talking about a Confederate cavalry officer known for his caprice, who had been missing for the better part of a month. Thread's mouth twisted in a grimace as he said, "Our scouts have his position." And then his expression changed to pure glee. "They want us to divert him."

Chapter Twenty-Seven

ACCEPTING
THE MANTLE

July 3, 1863, Gettysburg, Pennsylvania

Delphine wound buckskin strips across her breasts, pulling them tight. Then a corset of linen, heavily reinforced with whalebone, that smoothed her lines and gave the illusion of manly substance under her linsey-woolsey shirt.

"It will be too hot for that shirt," Blaise observed, tossing her a linen shirt that looked too new and fresh to belong to a soldier.

Delphine put the shirt on the ground and worked her foot over it, staining the linen against the mud floor of their tent.

"Here," he said, putting a smear of mud on her cheek, and then swiped some over the seat of her pants, bringing heat to both of them. He smiled.

No! she almost shouted in response, and then, "No," she said more calmly but still firmly. "Maybe never again." *You need to know that. But thank you for the servicing.* Then she slid out the tent flap and headed for the peach orchard, where Kilian and Thread's company were bivouacked. Still early, with the dew on the grass wetting Delphine's feet and ankles, the sultry, sensuous heat of summer was already rising off the meadows. A red sun just glinted over the horizon.

She could smell the ripe white peaches the soldiers were eating as she approached.

Then, just before she reached them, as her eyes were searching to pick out their company and Thread and Kilian, a flurry sent everything into chaos. Men who had been lounging on the grass under the trees were running. Dread mixed with excitement spread like a miasma over all.

"What's happening?" she asked a man rushing by.

"Our scout brought in a report that Jeb Stuart's cavalry is approaching from the north. The men in the company who have mounts and can ride are being sent out."

Delphine whirled and ran back to the sutler tent.

Blaise came out with a questioning look as she was throwing the saddle on Brushfire. "Our company is being called out to meet Jeb Stuart's cavalry," she explained.

"Stuart's finally arrived?" To the terse nod that Delphine gave him, Blaise asked, "You're riding with them?"

"Yes. Scouts have reported his approach over north." She jerked her head in that direction as she mounted.

"Away from the valley?"

"At the far edge." She drove her heels into Brushfire and took off for the company's tents, where she found Kilian and Thread already mounted with the group of young men from Cattaraugus and Newton who had enlisted together. This company distinguished itself by being mostly made up of men with mounts; many of the soldiers were natives who could ride like centaurs. Thread had his hat off and was waving it like a flag. Mounted men gathered around him.

"Where is the bannerman?" Delphine shouted to Kilian.

"Dead," Kilian shouted back, immediately recognizing her even in disguise. "You want to carry it?" He jerked his head back toward his tent. She saw the pole and crimson banner leaning against the side and turned her horse back to pick it up. She thrust it into the tack all in one motion.

"Let's go!" Thread shouted, and the pounding of horse's hooves and young men's jubilant battle cries drowned out any individual exhortations.

They rode hard, five miles out, following Thread to a high meadow ringed by trees. The fields were planted with blue rye ripening in the heat of early July.

Thread motioned them into the shade of the trees at the edge of the field.

They didn't have long to wait. Stuart's cavalry rode out at the north end of the field, Stuart brandishing his saber, rousing his men while their horses resisted the tight rein they were held under. He rode a massive black stallion, his fabled vanity on display in the form of a black ostrich feather foaming above his head from his helmet like his own personal storm cloud.

Thread stood in his stirrups. "This war must end, and we are the ones to end it, here on this battlefield. Take back our honor!" he shouted, saber high. Cannons boomed out to their right, where the main battle had begun. "Stuart is mine," he growled and, lowering his saber like a lance, he kiyi-ed their war whoop, which was echoed across the company. They thundered over the field toward Stuart's company.

The heat of the day suffused Delphine with a rare and heady exulta-tion. She had never understood how exciting it would be to cross sabers with another human, the clanging and roars reduced to her grunts, her counter-parries. Delphine had been working with a staff since she was a girl; training with Blaise in the saber had been no different except for the sound and slide of steel.

"Give no quarter, Delphine," Blaise had taught her. She was giving no quarter!

"If you ever lock sabers, you must not hesitate to kill your opponent, or you will be killed. Know this, Delphine." He had looked into her eyes as they pressed their arms and shoulders into each other along their crossed sabers. "If you find yourself in a saber fight, you must kill your opponent within the first few seconds. Because if you lock arms with a man, Delphine . . ." He had grunted and thrown her off balance. "Strong as you are for a woman, you will be the one to die."

But that was then. She had been annealed in the hard winter with Keri-oniakawida. She focused on the thrust and the slice, on defending herself from being skewered. She could do nothing about what came from behind. The men in her company had watched her training during her time as a *vivandière*, shouting encouragement, offering advice, and now she fought for them, and for Blaise, for herself, for Thread and Kilian, cutting and chopping to either side of Brushfire. She gasped when she realized she had cut through Stuart's cavalry and was out the other side. Her company's standard rippled in the air above her, scarlet against a cloudless blue sky. Groaning men in blue and in gray were already on the ground, one holding a shoulder, another with an ear dangling from his head.

Thread's horse had been shot out from under him, crushing his bad foot, and he struggled to emerge from under Bucephalus, rising awkwardly as Stuart himself galloped up, saber above his head like an avenging angel.

Before an astonished Thread could even draw his saber, Stuart opened him up from groin to clavicle, then rode past, on to his next victim.

And then Kilian was there, beside Thread, easing him down to the ground, looking around in supplication, his cries for help soundless against the clamor of battle. Those who still had horses were riding off for the woods. As Delphine galloped toward Thread, Kilian sprinted off for the cover of the woods, his eyes white as a spooked horse as he glanced back over his shoulder and then disappeared.

Delphine threw herself to the ground and slapped Brushfire on the rump to send him away before she flattened herself on the rye, precious minutes passing as Thread bled out on the ground.

The Rebel cheer rent the air, then Stuart gave the command to move out. The thunder of hooves marked their departure from this small sortie, an appetizer to whet their hunger for the more important battle, which cannons announced was well under way.

Delphine was alone in the field with dying men and horses. And Thread-needle.

She ran to him, knelt beside him. He made sounds that were difficult to hear, but there was no question he was in pain, his bowels steaming in a shiny heap beside him. His eyes were filled with the shock of what had happened too quickly to absorb. His blood became a steadily broadening puddle under him, his life draining away. She looked at the terrible cavity under his shirt, at his dark hair, at the dreadful pallor of his face. His beauty. And then Blaise was squatting beside her, for strength and witness.

Delphine pulled a plug of opium out of her kit.

"Don't waste it on me, *Gran'mère*," Thread said, all his life gathered in his eyes. Declaring their relationship with that one word, one she had shortshrifted for so long, he called Delphine into being. "I knew you would be here," he said. "I dreamed it. I told Kilian to go! And Mother is here. Here, with me."

Delphine bent near his face to watch his last breath.

He opened his eyes partway, panting. "Tell Regina . . ." He could no longer keep his eyes open. Blood trickled out the corner of his mouth. His hand clenched and unclenched like a woman in the last stage of labor. "Tell Regina, tell Blake, after . . ." The bowstring that had been Thread relaxed.

Delphine had not prepared herself for the black abyss that opened and then swallowed her. Later, much later—she couldn't tell how long—she felt Blaise's arm on her shoulder, his voice calling her name gently. She stood, Thread's body curled on the rye beside her. She looked at the sky and prophesied: "Thread, I will avenge you in a different coin than this."

She bent down, grasped a handful of rye and soil, let it fall. She gulped. "Thread," she began. *He is still here, as much as he was before.* He was there, witnessing her words after his sudden and violent death, perhaps wondering what had happened to tear him so suddenly, so violently, from life. "I call upon Grandmother Marguerite to be your guide as you begin your journey." She felt her mother's presence so powerfully. "I accept the mantle of Grandmother myself. I honor you, Grandson, in your death." She gathered herself with difficulty after saying this harsh truth aloud. "I pledge . . ." There, she had control of her voice again. "I pledge that I will make your life resonate." She paused again, feeling that control. She was the elder here; there was no other. "I vow to use the sharp edge of your death as a sword. For us all."

The words having been spoken, she allowed herself to fall back into an oblivion from which she could send this image of Thread to whomever was on the receiving end back home. Folded over her knees, watering the soil, the trampled rye, with her grief, she sent the message in Dialog. *Turtle Dawn. Kristiana. Regina.* She called to them. *There will be no turning back now. Nothing will ever be the same. Thread is gone. Kerioniakawida! Your son Katarioniecha is gone from his body.*

I am bringing him home.

Chapter Twenty-Eight

LINEN AND BUCKSKIN COCOON

July 18, 1863, Newtown, Pennsylvania

At Kristiana's behest, Lazarus had tracked Delphine and Blaise to Newtown. He had asked the couple, who had so reverently brought Thread's body back from war, to please wait twenty-four hours while he brought Kristiana over, so they might be preside over their son's proper funeral rites.

While Kristiana wandered through her childhood home, walked the streets and alleys of the deserted village, abandoned like Vesuvius by families in the midst of daily life, and then settled in to their beautiful *magnanerie* on some Duladier business, Blaise and his elder, his mentor, sat around their campfire on the brow of the hill above the village so Lazarus could hear firsthand the story of his son's death.

Blaise began in a stream of words that gained force as the scene took shape before them. "The divining foretold this. I asked the fire and was answered. Fire and blood, yes, but this time would be different . . . for me."

He glanced nervously at Kerioniakawida, who nodded, his eyes fixed on the middle distance in front of. "Tell me everything, so I can see it," Kerioniakawida instructed Blaise. "Don't leave out any details."

Blaise took himself back into that day, less than a fortnight ago. "When Delphine told me that the boys from the 23rd had saddled up and left the peach orchard, I filled my saddlebags with everything that could be needed—medicine, her buckskin, her linen shroud—and galloped off, letting my horse follow the scent of Brushfire. She told me the direction and I found them right away. Katarioniecha must have led me there," he mused.

"By the time I arrived, he lay on the ground, his guts beside him in a heap, his last breath coming from him. He said, 'Tell Regina, tell Blake, after . . .

"Then: no more.

"Delphine was sending the message to all of you, her forehead pressed to the ground as if the earth itself were a drum that would carry the news.

"She chanted and raved something like 'Red-winged blackbirds and grasshoppers foretold the killing season with their rasping,' and 'We won't hear from Kilian for a long time.' She telegraphed all of us, naming her recipients—Kristiana, Regina, Turtle Dawn, you—and told all of you aloud, 'Know the exact moment: Thread has fallen. Kilian fled.'"

Blaise looked at Kerioniakawida for confirmation that he and Kristiana had gotten his message, but his spiritual mentor was focused, as if in a trance, and did not respond visibly. Out of his long association with this family, Blaise knew his role; he rose to place two more logs across the fire, with intention, so they would not smoke. He sat again and waited until he felt he could pick up the thread of the story.

"When Delphine rose, she moved as if in a mesmerized state, yet sure-footed, strong, tears wetting her cheeks though she had no time for hysteria. I moved to help her, try to see in advance what she needed. You know her: she would try to do it all herself."

It seemed to Blaise that Kerioniakawida nodded. *Yes, he knows Delphine.*

"We dragged Thread's body first to the edge of the woods, removed from sight. The main battlefield across the ridgeline continued to resonate with cannon boom and rifle volley, the hoarse shouts of men charging. Or cheering, impossible to tell at that distance. To us there in the dappled woods, off to the side of a field, it sounded soothing, like waves breaking on pebbles of the shore." He glanced at the man, Thread's father. "A shore your son was departing from. Delphine, she would not let his spirit depart in a confused state. She was prepared to guide his canoe off that beach and into the water."

Blaise thought about what he was about to describe, wondered if

Kerioniakawida would censure them for it, so unfortunately parallel it was to how their People honored an animal in its death.

But a human? Did we do right? he wondered.

"I didn't want to be there, watching Delphine grieve our grandson, preparing his body, beginning his funeral rites. I scarcely recognized her. I have never been comfortable watching someone become whole—you know that. Have never chosen to attend a woman in childbirth. But Delphine?—She talked in a stream to Thread, to his spirit wandering on the battlefield, perhaps disoriented.

"I listened myself, in that way you have taught me. I would swear to it: I heard his spirits asking questions. *How did I get unhorsed? How did Stuart just ride by me? Kilian . . . ?*

"She spoke to your son as she never did in life, tenderly, with an open heart, comforting him, strengthening him for his journey. She made him promises, promises that she anticipated would help him accept his state, be resigned to his death. She promised that she, this woman, his grandmother, would take care of the loose threads. His mothers, his wife, his son, Blake."

Emotion welled in Blaise.

"Can you believe that? She was promising to look after Regina! There was a time not too long ago when I couldn't have imagined my wife caring about the well-being of Regina. But she is changed. The winter with you in the woods . . . her return. The shock of me and Marie. But Regina? Remember, she had coached Regina through her labor with Blake, and it made sense. Watching her escort Thread through his death, I saw Delphine has transformed into a woman who knits things together that might otherwise come unravelled."

Blaise took a great breath and expelled it forcefully before he could continue.

"She spoke to her daughter, Turtle Dawn, to her mother, Marguerite. She was in the presence of a host of people. She invoked you. 'Kerioniakawida,' she said over and over, and I realized I knew nothing about what happened between the two of you over the past six months. She spoke to you as she has never spoken to me. As I speak to you, as a man, as a spiritual guide.

When you and I last spoke and you learned why I had ridden all the way to Cattaraugus, what I had to say to Delphine, about me and Marie, you were steadfast, and I thank you for that. You did what I asked, watched over her.

"Now I see what has become of her. She was preparing for this, to become the woman who could do this, for all of us."

Blaise was getting to the hard part. He didn't want to forget anything, because he and this man would never go over these details again. He knew that.

"'Where am I?' I asked myself. I could see I was invisible to her. As I watched her carefully clean the great cavity of Thread's body that once contained the entrails that had spilled out of him like a nest of shining snakes even before he was dead, I felt as if it were my core that had been eviscerated. A great empty place yawned inside of me. What had I done to earn this premature feeling of my own evisceration? Other than pleasure myself, while Delphine was ... what? Transforming?" Blaise laughed a bitter laugh, cynical at his own shortsightedness.

Lazarus roused from the place where he had been holding himself. Turning to Blaise, he gave him an absolution that Blaise felt was hardly deserved: "You were on your own journey, Blaise. You were also searching for the Next Thing." Kerioniakawida's voice was so low when he said the next thing, Blaise wondered if he had said it aloud. "And then you took that minié ball."

Kerioniakawida's compassion flowed over Blaise like a healing balm. After he had allowed himself to feel the relief, the gratitude, and, yes, completion, he found the strength to continue, to say the hard parts that he was afraid would bring the tribe's judgment down on him, and on Delphine.

"She removed the organs that had kept him alive and placed them in a natural bowl in the earth she dug to the side of his body. Just as if he were a buck, she stripped his entrails of his last meal and then carefully rolled the emptied gut away. I knew my role then. I took the offal to the rye field, to the predators, the site of the battle that was so short it hardly deserved a name. Threadneedle Field, I have named it to myself.

"I asked myself and I still ask myself: Where and when did she learn this art? I thought I knew this woman, my wife, better than any person, and certainly better than any woman. My own eyes were blurring with tears and sweat, with the shock of witnessing what no man or woman should bear to see. And it was being done by a woman I had never truly seen in twenty-five years. One I did not even know existed."

Time passed and the stars whirled overhead in their seasonal procession. Kerioniakawida seemed almost transparent to Blaise, insubstantial. Blaise cleared his throat of unspent emotions to continue.

"After Delphine was done eviscerating his body, we moved Thread from the edge of the forest to a clearing, wrapped him in a horse blanket, and brought him under cover of battle to our sutler tent. He was clean and bloodless, though he still dripped liquids from the process of decomposition that we hastened to halt."

Blaise looked at the man known as Lazarus, He Who Hides. "Are you sure you want to hear this part, every detail? She did it; we did it. We managed to bring his body back here for our funeral rites tomorrow. But do you want to hear every detail?"

Blaise could feel Kerioniakawida observing him. He felt rather than saw his nod, heard it in Dialog: *Yes, every detail.*

His last meal?

Yes.

Peaches.

Kerioniakawida made a sound and squeezed his eyes shut. An owl hooted nearby. "Thank you," he said. "Now if you would continue."

"At this point, in our sutler tent, she seemed to see that I was there for the first time, acknowledged me as her helper. You practice the art of invisibility, Kerioniakawida. How else could you survive the ridgeline you walk between Peoples, with a death sentence hanging over your head? You know that palpable feeling when you are visible again.

"'Salt, Blaise,' she said and I brought it, a whole bag. As if we were preparing to tan a hide. From her kit she produced a small surgical saw, which she used to carefully open several holes in Thread's skull. She then removed a piece of bone big enough to enter with a spoon to take his brains out, into a bowl."

Blaise thought to himself, *I will never forget that sound of a metal spoon scraping against the inside of his cranium.* Then he looked toward He Who Hides and told him, "I will never forget the sight of the organ that had made your son, my grandson, who he is, who he was." Both men were fully aware that these details of Threadneedle's death would never be spoken again.

"'Do you understand what I am doing, Thread?' she asked his disembodied spirits, who had been torn so violently, so unexpectedly, so—" Blaise lit upon the word he had been searching for. "'. . . unceremoniously, from his body.' I must bring your body home for those who already begin to mourn you. Your mothers, Turtle Dawn and Kristiana. Grandmother Marguerite. Your father, Kerioniakawida.' Each name came out as a gasp, as if someone were punching her repeatedly in the diaphragm. At the mention of your name, she stopped to sternly staunch her tears, pinching the edge of her eyes where they meet her nose, her mouth twisting into a masklike rictus. She remembered to name the Huguenot family as well—the Duladiers who would be mourning him. 'Your Uncle Philip,' she said. 'Aunt Catherine. Kilian.' She looked around as if aware for the first time that Kilian had gone, fled into the shadows of the woods."

And now Blaise seemed to become aware of where they sat, this place, Newtown, where these two families' story together began, on the Delaware, the seat of the Montour family and the Lenape People. Near the *magnanerie* where the Duladiers had first come to rest on this continent, asking the Lenape, the Montours, for an introduction to their new homeland.

"She reached into the bag of salt with her hand, then smoothed the handful over the inside of Thread's body. As if she were preparing a goose to roast. 'Regina,' she intoned. 'Baby Blake.' As she said the boy's name, I wondered if Regina and Thread had named their son after me. The sounds are so similar. 'Am I to grow into one of the most important men in this boy's life, as his matrilineal great-grandfather?' I asked myself."

Blaise paused as if waiting for Kerioniakawida to deny his role in the family, to question the place Blaise had found for himself. Then he soldiered on. As if swimming upstream. How else could he go on but in perfect faith?

"The heat had become unbearable. The flies gathered, determined to feast on flesh.

"Her hands moved in the bowl, crushing, mixing. 'The herbs, Blaise,' she directed.

"I lugged over the entire box.

"'Also the kitchen box,' she said.

"I was hurrying. We both knew this was a race against time.

"Her hands never ceased moving. And when the mixture was ready, she rubbed mashed brain over the interior of Thread's body. She pulled the herbs out of the box of her medicines, throwing some to the side, arraying others and adding them to the medicine. 'I need you to crush alum, Blaise.'"

Now Blaise was thoroughly reinhabiting the scene, as if he were there again, at Katarioniecha's deathsite. He could feel the older man's satisfaction at where and how they had here arrived together. Blaise continued on, encouraged.

"I got the small mortar and pestle and crushed some alum, calculating how much of the mineral would be required to seal the internal cavity of Thread's body.

"'Another bowl, Blaise,' she instructed. 'And water. I need you to keep the flies away.' Her voice was flat with the effort of containing her emotions. The strangeness of the scene fell over us: We were preparing our grandson, to carry him home as if he were slaughtered game.

"By now I was starting to understand my role better. I waved to keep the flies from laying eggs that would become maggots even as she made the cavity unpalatable for them. Earlier I had built a fire, a fire I still don't remember kindling, which then snapped as surely as this fire, working its way toward becoming coals. As if it built itself there in the yard of the sutler tent.

"She glazed and then cauterized the interior where the salt had been laid in. The brains were doing their work, but they needed time. And we had no time. The alum would serve. I passed her the mortar bowl of the crushed mordant.

"She smoothed the alum over the cauterized salt and brains. I brought her a clean bowl of water.

"She washed her hands.

"I threw the slop away from the tent. 'Here flies. Come here,' I called.

"Do you see, Kerioniakawida? We were out of our minds, in another place where minds and sense and time scarcely count." Blaise was asking for his elder's blessing on the way they had conducted themselves, but Lazarus was not only their elder and spiritual guide, he was Threadneedle's father. Blaise was still uncertain how he would react. He only knew that whatever way this information struck Kerioniakawida, their elder's response would be as original and authentic as what he and Delphine had done.

"At the time, I hope you understand, Delphine appeared more sane than ever. She was focused, doing her best work. She brought her faith and peace to the ritual, not howling, not born in the chaos of anger or vengeance.

"When I returned with the clean bowl, she began throwing in ingredients from her medicine kit. Some things I recognized: precious spices, repelling herbs like wormwood and wolfsbane, herbs from her kitchen, including thyme, oregano, lemon balm, marguerite, angelica—things I had last seen blooming outside our windows in Cattaraugus. She pulverized bay leaves she had traded at great cost to keep the moths out of our food and clothing. She gathered bundled and tied pine needles, lined them up precisely, enough to make a burden basket, and broke them neatly into short pieces to add to the bowl. When the bowl was full, she threw them all into the mortar.

"'Grind this, Blaise.' She passed it to me, without a glance.

"I was a whirl. Picture it." Blaise waved his hands like a conductor, as if drawing an invisible tableau in the air. "The sounds of battle parse the hills and fields, distant music. An incoming tide of sound, drawing the pebbles onto the shore, hissing them out to sea. Poetry, Kerioniakawida. This is what I need to tell you. An orchestra of sound escorted our son onto the path of his journey."

Blaise never spoke like this, of poetry, but these were not ordinary times. He allowed and invited spirit to inhabit him. He scanned the sky to the east. Dawn could not be far off. The moon was setting in the west while Jupiter marked its place in Virgo. Orion the Hunter grazed the horizon.

"She prayed aloud for witness and she prayed for strength as she stuffed the green mixture into the hole in Thread's skull. When her knuckles made sure every round of that bowl was full, she carefully replaced the section of bone she had removed. She stuffed more of the mixture up his nostrils and into his ears with a tool I readied for her. As she filled his mouth, I got a needle threaded with sinew for her to carefully sew his sweet young lips shut. Now we are both openly one heart, one pair of hands, one witness . . . you understand?"

Blaise could not help himself now, and he wept. He wiped snot from his nose with one fist, snuffed, spat, and then continued.

"She emptied what was left in the bowl into his cavity, grabbed for a few more ingredients—precious sage, sacred tobacco—and then began to sew his length." Blaise's voice grew hushed.

"After, in the after, I quietly gathered what remained in the two boxes of herbs and brought her the pot of hot water, the folded golden linen shroud, and the buckskin she had tanned in anticipation. In anticipation of someone's death.

"The man Threadneedle, Katarioniecha, lay before us as if he held a great secret, his lips sewn shut, his ears and nose sealed with the herb mixture, his anus plugged with the stub of a candle.

"Delphine washed him now, carefully wiping eyes, nose, mouth, cheeks, those same ones we had both kissed when he was a child, after he had hurt himself, before we sent him back out into the world to develop calluses. Our prodigy.

"'Who is left to take over Regina Coeli? None but we who are aging.' I spoke in that sacred channel to all of us, at this moment of grieving.

"Thread, who had been given many gifts, now wandered adrift, cut down in the midst of his life. What would his legacy be? What gifts would we harvest, after?

"I began to wonder then if I should take up my role as the tribe's man— even though I am only a part of the Montour family through marriage. *Should I be doing the rites that the Montour men would do in this circumstance?* I asked myself. Delphine was doing the rituals and saying the prayers women have been performing for uncounted millennia. It settled upon me then that I was that designee, the mantle falling softly over my shoulders, firm as a grandfather's hand. I hope I did right, Kerioniakawida," Blaise said softly, looking still for permission and approval for what had already been done. He stood and added two more logs carefully, the last they would need before dawn.

"I took up the drum, which was probably last played by Thread, and began the grieving kiyis, the chants that told you, 'Your son has died.' I chanted with all my heart, as if an entire drum circle surrounded me. I sang out every emotion in me, not only for me but for you, He Who Hides, Kerioniakawida, in whose place I was singing, and also for Turtle Dawn, Thread's mother, and for Kristiana, who bore Thread. I sang out for Delphine, who had taken up her role as Grandmother. I sang. For all of us."

Blaise's story was coming to an end and he drooped from fatigue and with the exhaustion of completion.

"And here's what's true, Lazarus. Deep in my belly, like a water drum, I sang for my son, Simon, whose spirit might still have been wandering six months after his violent death, this motherless child, lost before setting out on his journey. *You will hear me,* I called him.

"*Wee-saw-say-hay-noo,* the Thunder People, heard me. They growled with a storm to mark this dawn . . . like no other dawn.

"Pinches of tobacco went into the fire to open up the channels of communication with the spirit, just as you have taught me, Kerioniakawida, and, through the spirits, to our family back home. The pauses in my rhythmic drumming, my kiyi-ing, became fragrant. Threadneedle's death song. Katarioniecha's death song. Our grandson's death song. Your son. Simon's death song. Go, it said. *Leave on your journey. We are complete.*

"When I dropped to the ground, drained, I saw that Delphine had wound Thread's body in the linen shroud she had been preparing. She had torn it into strips, wet the strips in salty flour water, and bound his body tightly, legs together, arms over the chest cavity. Thread's body. Finally his head disappeared into the saffron linen strips that hardened as they dried. You will see. Tomorrow.

"And then I witnessed something I had only seen and heard once before, that first season when the Duladiers burned their *cocons*. Here—right here! you were there!—on the brow of this hill.

"Delphine sewed Thread's shrouded body into the buckskin she had prepared, a cocoon from which he would emerge a winged thing.

"'O Aspirant,' Delphine intoned, having memorized the words Catherine had given her for this moment. 'Do not be afraid. The door is opening to the light. Do not be afraid but go forth.' The portal that Threadneedle had inhabited in his life opened, as he began to pass into the great mystery of death. Her prayer continued with instructions on using the breath— anatomical instructions in making it through the gates from death to life again. You remember that night, so long ago, Kerioniakawida. When they burned the silk here, where the Duladiers used to have their midsummer fires. Where we used to light the signal fires for our People."

The older man stirred then and rose. "I am going to get Kristiana," he said. "I will be back before the sun sets." He placed his hand on Blaise's shoulder. "You did exactly what you should have done, exactly right, just as I would have done if I had been there." Blaise heard him move off along the brow of the hill, heard his horse whinny as he mounted up and left.

Alone, Blaise had a moment before he had to begin making the preparations for Katarioniecha's funeral rites. He wondered, *Is it the same with us, Delphine and me? Threadneedle is dead. We too must go forward. We must not be afraid. We must go through the door into the light.*

She must take me back into her heart.

Chapter Twenty-Nine

BURNING THREAD

Late July 1863, Newtown, Pennsylvania

Kristiana was waiting, in the Duladier *magnanerie*. Thought it had been short ride away from Newtown at Philip's Pavilion on Neshaminy Creek, where she and Lazarus had been staying together since they'd heard the news, they had spoken as they rode side by side through the meadows, along the path. "Remember the time he was stung by a bee on his nose when he was smelling a flower?" Kristiana and Lazarus had smiled poignantly with each other remembering this. Lazarus had brought her back to life there at the fish camp, in the Pavilion, with tea and bread and pemmican. Potatoes and salt cod. The stinky civet scent of sex. She consumed the smells, pushed away the substance. As if she could eat! As if she would ever eat again.

In Newtown, when Lazarus went off with Blaise, she found lanterns in the *magnanerie* and wrote.

What if each battlefield were ringed with mothers, wives, sisters, waiting to see if their warriors would live another day? If all the women followed their men from battle to battle, could war proceed?

If mothers were not sending their sons to war, what might happen? But there were mothers who sent their sons to war! Tainted women? Women who thought they had no choice? Whose men demanded their faithful blind following? Did they justify their action with patriotism? My country, right or wrong?

But if they could hear those boys weep and call for them, how could a mother, wife, sister condone war if she witnessed this?

No wonder boys come home from war with broken spirits when they have to put on a daily face that says, "That didn't happen." When it did happen. "Everything is back to normal." When it isn't. When it never will be normal so long as their mothers, sisters, wives, and daughters have no idea what their sons, brothers, husbands, and fathers have just been through.

She heard Lazarus open the front door of the *magnanerie*, she wrote one last thought that would not be suppressed:

Fathers know. Why don't they stop it? Those who stand to profit, those who stand to lose, how can these things measure against the loss of sons, of even one son?

She remembered Thread's small, earnest face raised to ask a question in a piping voice. Those narrow shoulders, that vulnerable neck, those arms clasped about her neck in love, in trust, in fear. She still could not believe she and Turtle Dawn had allowed him, still a boy, to go into that deadly ring. Was it right to defend property? To defend the abolition of slavery? To defend one's autonomy against another's? At the risk of losing one's young life?

There is no honor or glory in war.

Kristiana flung her arms out wide, throwing away these chimeric thoughts that played and replayed in her head incessantly. "Stop!" she shouted. "You must begin to live in this moment, Kristiana."

Lazarus came in to the atelier where she sat writing, bent over her shoulder, closed her notebook, caped the inkwell, and took her to the narrow bed in the *magnanerie* that was meant for a single *maîtresse*, locked in the dreaming.

Next day, they burned Thread's body on the hill in Newtown, where their midsummer fires used to be. They had all been there when Catherine had had to burn the *cocons* from their first silk season. They had been tainted with both tangible and intangible disharmony. None of them would forget this spot, marked now with Thread's remains. Their Lenape band would never forget either, as this was where the first signal fires had been lit, long ago, telling their People either to flee or to gather with their weapons.

Chapter Thirty

THE DARK THING IN ITS LEAFY BOWER

August 1, 1863, Seneca Falls, New York

Regina rose from her bed of grief. A knock at the door.

It's my landlady. She wants to take the baby. The baby. My baby. Thread's baby who is hiccupping with his loss. The loss of his mother.

"Your baby misses you," the woman said. "Give him to me and I will comfort him." She held out her arms.

The landlady looked for fresh diapers. Nearby was a pile of soiled ones, sour and covered with the yellow feces of an infant who ingests only his mother's milk. She removed his diaper, and Regina sensed she was supposed to stand nearby and act as if she cared. The baby's rump was red with rash, burned with the ammonia of unchanged diapers. He screamed with pain, with loss, with hunger. She lowered herself into her chair at the table, head bowed to the page to show her landlady that she couldn't care … not until she finished writing. She heard the door click closed, the baby's cries receding as he was comforted by a maternal body. Only then could she pick up her pen again.

That night, I saw the moon like a sickle descend and take his life and others, reaping the battleground like a harvest.

It may be hard, even from a distance of fifty years, to come right up against it again. It may be hard to ever trust that bland sky, that

treacherous sun, that innocuous laughter, when—at a young age—I met
the dark creature that lives inside the day, that sits in its nest in a leafy
bower, poised to tear the illusion of tranquility aside and scream, scream
deep into the well you may be fortunate enough to have fallen into.

Independence Day. Unpacking picnic hampers. Children jumping in
and out of the pond, shaking diamond droplets into the air. Later, incen-
diaries crack the sky, chrysanthemums of light and color. And then sleep,
in our nests of eiderdown.

Amen to all that. To peace. To balance.

All the while, the dark thing crouches in the deepest shadows.

Mother, I pray that my children and grandchildren will not have to
inherit that legacy, part of the human condition, part of earthquake, war,
famine, and pest. Turn your face to us once again, Mother. Aren't the
children inheriting enough woe, without the loss of your tender concern?

She rose and stood at the window. From next door came the sounds of
everyday life: a child calling from another room, the clank of cutlery, the
soothing sounds of her landlady rocking and singing to her baby, Thread's
baby.

She turned to the table, where her notebook sat closed, where the inkwell
yawned open. The landlady had left a basket. Regina pulled aside the cloth
and found two yeast rolls, two eggs, a paper of bacon.

She walked to her stove, crumpled a paper she had thrown there, placed
two thin sticks from the woodbox over the paper, and lit it. As she watched
the fire catch, she carefully placed three larger sticks over the burning mass
and then remembered how this was done.

She would boil water. Wash her hair. Go through the steps of washing
nappies for Blake: grate flakes of soap into the boiling kettle, wring and
rinse in cold water. Snap them out and hang them on the line with the
wooden clothespins her landlady kept in a tidy bag near the clothesline.

She would see where to enter life again. How else could Thread's death
make any sense, ever? He had left her this legacy of everyday life.

I will never be in bed again in the daylight, she vowed, weeping into the eggs she was beating with a fork. She couldn't face cooking the bacon—its congealed fat that would melt in the heat and then harden again, ruining her skillet—no! She shoved it back into the paper. Meat, pork especially, was too raw to consider.

She poured the eggs into the hot skillet, which flashed with the contact, eggs salted with tears. She could see that this was a privilege she could claim, a gift from Thread, that she would spend the rest of her life working to secure the rights of half of the population, the half that brought life into the world. She was the portal through which Blake had been born. She put her faith into that unseen Mother of them all, who made nightmares turn into the stuff of dreams. She would use her life as only a Regina, a queen, could. However she pleased.

Chapter Thirty-One

DEBILITAS

Autumn equinox 1863,
Finley Hospital, Washington, D.C.

The army doctor flipped through the pages on his clipboard. The patient was bound in a straightjacket; some subjects were more comfortable this way.

Few of them were as damaged as this one, and not all as lucky, to be held in the arms of this hospital, where men could recover before being asked to return to their lives. Or, often enough, to the battlefield. This one would not return to the battlefield. He had been broken, permanently. A danger to himself and others, the question was whether he could enjoy the life he had before, after his invisible injury.

The doctor conducted interviews with Civil War veterans under mesmeric trances, a new method that sought to heal them by reaching the deeper levels of memory. This subject, Kilian Sechinger, thirty years old, went willingly into the trance state. His diagnosis, the doctor noted, was "debilitas," an indeterminate diagnosis that says nothing about external wounds.

The doctor began by having the patient locate himself in the hypnotic state in the usual way, by visualizing his feet even though his eyes were closed, then traveling up his body to describe his clothing, and finally looking at his hands, still in his mind's eye. The doctor asked him about his family, where he grew up, and how he happened to enlist in the war—all standard protocol for entry into the trance.

"Tell me what's going on around you," the doctor prompted.

"I'm walking away from the Valley of Death. Everything is . . ." The patient began to make choking sounds.

"Remember that you can't be harmed," the doctor reminded him.

"I know I can't be harmed. But I don't particularly want to go back there and see." The patient was convincing.

"Did you take part in a battle? Did you—"

The patient interrupted the doctor with a raised voice. "Yes . . . I know where you're trying to take me and . . . I don't want to think about that." This patient apparently imagined that he could set the terms of his recovery.

"Okay, then what happened after?" The doctor was pressing. "You had run away, hadn't you? After that battle. You left. Did you desert?"

The patient's voice returned to a monotone. "No. It was all chaos. There was no desertion. We were running like hell. It was a rout." The patient's voice took a steep rise in volume. "I don't want to talk about the battle."

The doctor's voice was soothing. "All right. That's fine. Let's go to the next important time for you. Tell the story as it happened."

"After I ran away from that terrible place, that killing ground, I saw a light through the woods. I walked up on the porch, looked in the window. I walked into her cabin. And she was sitting there by the fire. She looked up at me and her hand went to her mouth, like she was going to scream. But I went up behind her and I put a chokehold around her neck and my other hand over her mouth. And I told her that I would kill her if she screamed." The doctor could tell: the patient was reliving this scene. They were where they needed to be, doctor and patient, in the moment.

"Who was this woman? Did you know her?"

"I had never seen her before."

"What happened next?"

"She was alone there. At least I think she was alone. Maybe there was a baby. Or an old man. I don't even know."

"Was she a Southern woman?" The doctor was trying to find out which direction Kilian had run, north or south.

"No. She was one of us." The doctor flipped through the pages of the chart, located the patient's last name, Sechinger, and concluded that this man had probably run to southern Pennsylvania, which was full of Germans, seemingly all related to each other, and speaking the same language, worshipping the same God.

"Did you know where you were?" he asked.

"Somewhere not far from where I used to live. We have family in that part of the state."

The doctor nodded, his presumptions confirmed. "Why did you do that to her if she was from the North? Was she a threat?"

Now the patient fell into a rhythmic monotone, as if he were reciting a tone poem. "I knew that if I was going to survive, she was going to have to help me. And I didn't know if she'd be willing to. I wanted to let her know that I was going to be in charge now. And she was gonna do what I wanted her to. Because I could have anybody coming and looking for me. And they would be looking for me. We had soldiers from both sides coming through that part of the world all the time. And how she wound up in this little island of serenity in the midst of all this insanity I didn't know. But what I did know was that I had to have it. She had to help me. And the only way that I could make her help me was to make her help me." He stopped suddenly.

"What happened next?" The doctor, an army doctor, found that he was genuinely curious about this story that had taken place *off* the battlefield.

"She calmed down. She served me some food, turned out the lights, and then I took her to bed."

The doctor was used to stories of rape when deserting soldiers left the battlefield. "So, you slept with her," he stated euphemistically. "And then?" He expected to hear about the woman weeping, begging perhaps, but no, not in this case.

"The next morning, we set it up. She showed me where the cellar was, and we practiced what I would do, what she would do. I'm pretty sure I was out of my mind. I was out of my mind. And she was frightened. And I wanted her to be. And she should have been afraid of me. Because I would have killed her."

"Did you ultimately leave this woman?" The doctor was trying to find out how long Kilian had stayed in that cabin until the soldiers found him and brought him to the hospital for evaluation and treatment.

"Leave her? No."

"You stayed with her for a longer period of time?"

The patient seemed momentarily confused. "Well . . . I am with her now. I plan to stay with her the rest of my life."

"You don't plan to go back home to . . ." The doctor flipped through his chart. "Dawn?"

There was a long pause. Finally the patient asked, as if to himself, "How could I have gone back to Dawn?" The doctor looked on as the patient considered his own question. "Elizabeth and I, we are bound to each other. Fate gave us to each other. What happened to me, there on those battlefields . . . I couldn't do that to Turtle Dawn. Elizabeth . . . she succors me. She spreads her wings. I cannot live without her. My father, he brought Turtle Dawn here. To see. That I am pledged to another."

"That must have been hard." The doctor's voice no longer sounded clinical. He hadn't heard this story before. "To find your true love in the midst of the battlefield."

Kilian shook his head to imply there was nothing he could do in the face of inevitability. The doctor had interviewed this young woman, Elizabeth—eighteen years old, according to her own report, although he had his doubts if she were that old—to find out if she were a prisoner of war. Had she been held against her will? Had she asked him to release her? She was already pregnant, and her neck was ringed with black and blue marks from his choking her. She brought Mr. Sechinger peace, she told the doctor. She loved him, she said. The doctor noted that Philip Sechinger, the patient's father, had pledged to take care his son, to help the couple make it, after.

For Kilian now there was only Elizabeth, the girl he had found the night he had fled, crazed, fearful of the cleaver that descended from the heavens, fearful of them finding him, taking him back to that field where the cleaver still descended, reducing men, horses, wheat, boys to rubble, to butchered pieces, to chaos flying into the void of the voice, the voice of the bull, bellowing from the heavens, for ... what? Retribution. But retribution for what? The possibilities were too many to enumerate.

That was the first night he had tried to choke her, after he had taken her, hard, from behind, bucking her up off the bed. When he had released her, her gentle hands persuaded him to relax, to sleep.

Only Elizabeth could get him to let go of his muscles, the ones that choked off visions of the moment that Thread had ...

Kilian suckled at her breasts as if he were an infant; she put her body and soul squarely in the way of the cleaver, which couldn't touch him when he was in her. She shielded him from retribution, from the red eye of the bull—his roar, his thundering hooves—her wings, her golden wings, shielding him from the moment. As he was choking off her life, she flooded with ecstasy and he released her. He floated off with her on that golden raft.

Only Elizabeth could give him another moment. In another time. Send a breath to him from all his ancestors, from Thread, from his sister Regina, a gift of the Madonna, She of the honeyed hive, bottomless bounty. *Salve Regina.* Hail Holy Queen. She took him to a place he'd never been and yet had dreamed of, had grown up knowing was possible, to a place where no war existed, a place where love and peace supplanted hatred and chaos. A place where everything existed simultaneously, and yet a place where he could let go of the world, live in the moment. Where Thread's belly wound would knit together. In a parallel world. "Not" become "knot." Elizabeth was a font of mystery, full of sunlight.

She sang to him, old hymns from the Old Country, from Hesse, from a simpler time:

And every man 'neath his vine and fig tree
Shall live in peace and unafraid,
And into ploughshares beat their swords.
Nations shall have war no more.

The doctors had queried Elizabeth, but then let her be after Kilian had promised he would marry her as soon as they released him. She was a drug; he had to have her. They let the couple use a room so he could take her again and again as he had that first night, savage, weeping. Her crooning, singing, stroking. Him tearing, plunging like a ship through an illimitable abyss. Elizabeth extended her wings, floated him in the liquid amber of her hive. Took his blows. His choking off her air. She found ecstasy and pleasure for both of them there.

"You could hurt the baby," the doctor had told her.

"Kilian comes first," she told him. "He is my pole star, given to me in a time of darkness."

∞

Part Five

∞

1864

Chapter Thirty-Two

THE DANGER
OF KEEPING SECRETS

February 1, 1864, Cottage, New York

When Kristiana walked into Philip's house, a rattle of teacups greeted her as the assembled principals of Regina Coeli—Philip, Catherine, Regina, Delphine, and Maeve—jumped to their feet to fuss about her, take her cloak, find her a chair by the stove, a cup of tea. The green velvet folds of her gown revealed the curve of her belly.

"Tell me again when you are due, Kristiana?" Catherine asked, moving her shoulders as if to suggest that she was not so far along in old age that she could not remember what it was to bear a child.

"This summer," Kristiana smiled, although she regarded Catherine with some surprise, as though her old adversary showing up at this table, at this time, was an act of malicious fairies. "Are you happy here in Cottage, Catherine?" she inquired politely.

Philip bit his tongue to stop himself from blurting out something that would reflect his anxiety about these two women getting along, now that his wife had become a permanent resident of Cottage, a village Kristiana had founded.

His daughter Regina, her strawberry blonde hair pulled into a complicated set of braids Philip recognized as one of the traditional Duladier styles from an earlier generation, stayed seated with Blake. The baby boy, who had celebrated his first birthday in the fall, was nursing vigorously and alternately slapping and stroking his mother's breast with a proprietary air. His grandparents—Catherine and Philip—hovered over him even while pretending to be about other business. Not the most attentive mother, Regina seemed grateful to anyone who asked if they could spend time with Blake. She hid it well from the family but seemed to resent motherhood and the demands that an infant stole from her efforts to organize women to secure their rights. Despite their age, Catherine and Philip frequently took the boy in for weeks at a time, just as they did Eliza when the child was much smaller, and now again. With Turtle Dawn sequestered in mourning and Eliza still not speaking, leaving the child alone all day with her grieving mother would have been a disservice to both.

Isn't it strange how differently people grieve? Philip thought. *Thread's natural mother is pregnant and thriving while his adoptive mother is sunk in grief.*

Delphine, who had been standing looking out the window, had turned as Kristiana came in. "Kristiana! Look at you: all apple-cheeked. The snow is sticking, isn't it? At last. Where is Lazarus?" *How can I call him that when I know his true name?*

Kristiana removed her bonnet and brushed the snow off it. "I don't really know. His heavy boots and goose-feather jacket were gone off the peg, so he clearly dressed to be out in the snow. But he was very mysterious last night. I left Cattaraugus early this morning." She shrugged her shoulders. "He was long gone. The snow had covered his tracks."

Philip took Kristiana's hands and chafed them between his own. "Come sit down, Kristi. Put your hands around a hot cup of tea."

Even though he was her uncle, Kristiana resisted Philip's babying her and moved past him to stand over Regina, who was tucking her breast back into her bodice. Kristiana held out her arms to Blake, to hold her grandson in her lap. While she played pattycake with Blake, who cackled in delight, she stole a glance at Delphine. She had known this woman most of her life and yet had only just become close with her after the war, a war which was still going on, although without this family. Their war had ended with Gettysburg.

Kristiana smiled tentatively and addressed Delphine. "Grandmother Marguerite's death was very peaceful. I sat all that day at Lazarus' house, burning candles, praying for my second mother, my spirit mother." She held Delphine in her eyes, then sat and squeezed her arm before accepting a cup of tea from Philip. She opened up her gaze to include Catherine. She told her in Dialog, and anyone else who was listening: *I recited 'O Aspirant' to help her to pass with guidance from both families.* "And now that we are resident in Cattaraugus," she said aloud, "our child will be raised Montour." Kristiana's composure implied that her conceiving this second child with Kerioniakawida, on the heels of Threadneedle's death, would balance them all in the great scales of justice.

With Kristiana's help, Delphine had been able to pin down the date of her mother's death. In fact, her sense that Marguerite had been there, on the battlefield, to guide Threadneedle had been accurate. Her mother had died at the end of June.

Kristiana spoke again in Dialog, reminding them all that she had been *maîtresse de la soie* for a dozen years, by invoking that spiritual message board they all shared to touch down with her mate, Lazarus, deep in the woods. *Mon tour. My tower. The further our family gets from that time when our maternal line took that man's name, the more mysterious it becomes.*

Delphine's eyebrows raised at Kristiana's presumptions: *Our* maternal line?

Catherine began chattering like a squirrel about how their family had grown with all the new babies, but then she stopped, as if suddenly aware that their numbers had also shrunken now that Threadneedle and Marguerite were counted among their ancestors.

As if to cover his wife's insensitivity, Philip spoke: "It seems an age ago that our family first came to Newtown, but it has only been twenty-five years. Marguerite must have been sixty at that time. Your female line ages well." His eyes flicked to Delphine, who smiled back.

Swan was playing on the floor with empty wooden spools, humming to herself.

Philip continued, not expecting a response: "Our silk operation wouldn't have succeeded without your mother's help. It was Marguerite and Lazarus who saved Catherine from those bastards from Grasse."

"We were girls then . . . ," Kristiana remembered.

"Does anyone know here know for sure whether Wilhelm led those men to you, Mother?" Regina ventured.

Philip answered, "He did give testimony against Catherine to the investors. That we do know."

Delphine sighed deeply, as if she were explaining a simple thing to a weak-minded person. "We *do* know for sure. Marguerite and Lazarus were there. They told us, long ago, when it happened. Do you not know about this?" she asked, incredulous.

"We know," Kristiana said. Although she was trying to show everyone that motherhood came naturally to her, she passed Blake, sound asleep from their horseplay, back to Regina.

An uncomfortable moment passed as they each remembered that time, when Kristiana's success had come out of Catherine's failure.

Catherine spoke out of the silence. "I wish that we could all forget about that time. It was so long ago. I have no wish to see Wilhelm again, but that should not affect anyone else's relationship with him."

"Even so: who is he?" Delphine challenged. "Really. Lazarus and Marguerite have always said that Wilhelm was there, in Newton, when you and Regina the Elder were being attacked by those two blackguards, Catherine." She said the word like a man: *blaggards*.

Another long silence followed. Bright-red spots appeared on each of Catherine's cheeks as she gazed at her lap.

Regina sucked in her breath as she grasped the import of what Delphine was saying. She was the only one among them who didn't know the details of that day, and the realization hit her like a bludgeon. "Madonna! Did they have anything to do with Regina the Elder's death? And you, Mother!"

Catherine looked up at Philip in mute appeal.

Delphine, always plainspoken, said, "Lazarus told me. My mother told me. One of them raped Regina and passed cholera on to her and from there to her children."

Regina's chair skidded back on the planked floor as she stood. "This is so hard to hear! Why haven't you told me this before?" She passed the sleeping toddler to Maeve. "Is this why he was shunned? Because those men attacked both of you?"

Her parents' silence inflamed her.

"You had no right to keep this from me!" Regina's face blazed. Philip shifted uncomfortably, as if wondering why he was left to face this alone, for certainly Catherine would not speak in her own defense. And neither Lazarus nor Marguerite were there to explain. Regina put her face in her hands. "Oh! I feel like such a fool! I let myself be taken in by that man!" She turned to Philip. "Father? Did you think I would not be able to bear the truth?"

Phillip turned to his wife.

Catherine touched her daughter's arm. "I am sorry, Regina. Please forgive me. I was too humiliated, I think. And it seemed my shame to bear, not to pass on to anyone else. When could I have told you that would have made things turn out any different? I often asked that of myself. I am telling you now."

"But if you had told me earlier, then . . . we . . ." She couldn't finish what she wanted to say to her mother: that if her mother had confided in her long ago, they might be intimate, like many mothers and daughters. Keeping important secrets blocked intimacy. They had both learned this too late.

Delphine said, "Marguerite told both of us, me and Turtle Dawn. We don't keep secrets like that. A man like that would be put to death among our people, not just shunned." Then she added, "Mother and Lazarus castrated the other one who survived."

As if trying to ease the tension he could feel, Blake held out his hands to Philip, who lifted his grandson from Maeve's lap onto his own.

Regina had an urgent need to hear the whole truth spoken. "Did Thread know?"

Delphine and Philip nodded their heads.

Delphine spoke for the Montour family. "It's dangerous keeping secrets from the men. Especially secrets that concern men. Marguerite finally told him when he came down to Newtown, before the war. That's when Thread stopped helping Wilhelm, stopped working with him."

Regina said bitterly then, "Kilian must have puzzled it out. Don't you remember how Kilian is always puzzling things out? He takes this fact and that apparently unrelated fact and just holds them in his mind and heart until he sees their connection."

Catherine would not say, ever, that Kilian had pressed her for information about his real father, who he was.

The stove cooled. Swan was humming. Philip passed Blake, his head lolling in sleep, back to Maeve; he rose and opened the firebox to throw in three gnarled quarters of applewood. He would not tell his daughter that Kilian had been told the truth when she hadn't. "Why?" she would ask. Because men like Philip were there to protect their women from these things. He still felt a stab of guilt that he hadn't been there to protect Catherine; and look how that had harmed her, all her life.

Kristiana spoke up now. "The question before us is this: Should old men be forgiven?"

"If they repent, make good, and change their ways!" Regina responded, her words echoing throughout the room. *We are talking about you, Kristiana! He's your father and yet you have behaved just as badly!* she thought to herself. *Do you even know who we are talking about when we speak the terms of forgiveness?*

Maeve Flusty, intuiting that this had changed from a business meeting into a family meeting, pushed her chair back. "You know he's here now—your father—visiting your folks in East Dayton," she told Kristiana. "Something about a hunt. Getting a posse together? Speaking of which, I've got to get back to Tom and his string." She passed the sleeping Blake to Philip. "But I bring you a message from Tom. And from me."

She stood so that—though a short woman—she towered over them.

"We had a good autumn last year for bleaching. The days are short, it's true, but the sun was still strong, to the end of October. And I can tell you this: Wilhelm's got those infernal machines of his weaving twenty-four hours a day, by lanterns at night. And each floor has only one stove. It's not enough. Also, his dormitory of bunk beds for the girls has only one stove, and no one keeps it going during the day. There's thin soup on that stove all day and night. But bread only on Sunday. Our spies inside tell us when the nights turn colder they find ice in the wash buckets in the mornings. Consumption is taking hold among the girls, who cough at night under their thin blankets in the same room as those who are healthy. The pounding sound of the weaving machines never stops. I could hear it all the way down at the banks of the canal. And his girls tell my girls."

Kristiana lifted her head, overwhelmed by the murmur of thoughts coming through in Dialog from her family's heads: *Unacceptable. How do we stop the man?* "I'll speak with him when he comes in from hunting. I'll confront him."

Maeve tsk-ed. "He hasn't changed his ways. Just as Regina said, has he made good? Has he said he's sorry?"

Philip looked skeptical.

"He settled money on Blake," Regina said. "He sends money for women's rights. And you are telling me that this is the same man who threatened Catherine? I ask it again: Can old men be forgiven their crimes? Let's ask it in Dialog and perhaps we will get a larger response."

They all held their breath. They had never known Regina to speak in Dialog. Who would have taught her, a child who was not called by the silk? Thread?

Can old men be forgiven their crimes? she asked in that ancient channel.

Maeve paused by the door on her way out. "What is this Dialog you all seem to talk about?" She looked down, busy buttoning her coat.

Regina, who was closest to Maeve, said, "I will tell you when we have a chance to be alone, Maeve." The older woman, having known this family for some time, was satisfied. She went out into the snowstorm, hooded and wrapped with woolen shawls.

The family sat contemplating how tradition sometimes appears as if by magic, without training, without personal transmission. Just as this child had received the tongue of fire from Regina the Elder, now she spoke in Dialog for the first time, with all the assurance of a trained silk *maîtresse*.

And then an answer came: *If they experience remorse. If they make amends.*

Kristiana nodded at Regina, then said to the others around the table,

"I want to make peace: Blake is Wilhelm's great-grandchild." Next to her, Blake had woken up and was noisily banging a spoon on the table and singing accompaniment tunelessly. "The child I'm carrying is his grandchild too. We are family. If he will hear me—if *you* will hear me—we should merge our companies."

Philip, holding Blake back from launching himself onto the table, looked at Regina. He set Blake on a rug on the floor but continued to watch him like a hawk.

Regina, bolstered by her success in Dialog, spoke with confidence. "I don't know. You heard from Maeve how he is running his company. All for the war effort, he says. But will things change when the war is over?" She looked at Kristiana, who sat pensively in the corner rocking chair, its rhythmic creak known to every woman there down to her bones. "Perhaps you are too emotionally involved in this, Kristiana. What if he will not change?"

Delphine was now their elder, and when she spoke, everyone listened carefully. "Kristiana, I am moved"—they all noted how she placed her hand between her breasts—"that you are carrying Lazarus' child again. This feels like it could be the beginning of a new era for all of us. Thread's baby, Blake, playing here on the floor, still at his mother's breast. Lazarus' baby here in your womb." She paused. "Maybe old men can be forgiven their sins. If . . ." She emphasized this last word, then shrugged. She didn't need to spell out the terms of forgiveness, did she? Not when their common store of wisdom had spoken through Dialog. Remorse and resolve. Then: "Philip, I am starving. Do you have anything to eat?"

Philip startled as if caught napping. "I have a wonderful lamb stew, plenty of carrots and potatoes." He brought down bowls and spoons and ladled out a generous portion for Delphine, all the while watching out for the baby. With the lid off the pot and the contents being served, the fragrant odor spread throughout the room: bay and garlic, rosemary and red wine.

Kristiana moved to a chair at the table and, Philip having delivered a bowl for her, tucked into the stew. With a sigh of grateful satisfaction, she put down the spoon for a moment to say, "I want a chance to be a mother this time." Her voice thickened as if she were going to cry. Each one of her partners looked either amazed or uncomfortable. She recovered and continued: "I want another chance. I don't want to run Regina Coeli! I want to be a mother. Be a wife to Lazarus. God knows we both earned it."

Now a look passed between Philip and Delphine.

Philip spoke what everyone was thinking: "Who is going to run the business, Kristiana? Now that ..." *Now that Thread is dead* was the obvious unspoken implication. "That is what we are here to discuss."

Delphine stood to make her announcement. "Kristiana and I have reached an agreement. I am taking her place." The two women smiled at each other. "She is going to be raising her baby with Lazarus. On Cattaraugus Reservation."

Kristiana nodded assent, spoon working at her bowl again, mouth full.

"Turtle Dawn, Philip, and I," Delphine continued, "will run—are running—Regina Coeli. Our next meeting will be a business meeting, with Maeve and Tom Flusty present as full partners. Turtle Dawn is already preparing sketches for the catalog," Delphine lied.

Philip was all admiration for Delphine's brass. In fact, Turtle Dawn was still sunk in grieving for Thread and did nothing but paint, oils that took forever to dry between layers.

Delphine continued, "And I will bring swatches for this season's colors." A general murmur went up, one of surprise and pleasure at this news. "When shall we have the next meeting? I am returning with Regina to Seneca Falls on the train today."

"What about this spring, then?" Philip put in, but no one answered, as the meeting was breaking up in chaos, with people gathering their things to take their leave.

Delphine asked Philip: "What about Kilian?"

The milling stopped. People put their hands out to whatever piece of lintel or furniture happened to be at hand.

"He is coming home," Philip said. "With his wife, his young bride, Elizabeth. She will have their baby this spring also. They are married. I have the certificate."

Everyone looked at Delphine to see her reaction. "Turtle Dawn knows," she said quietly. "He has given her his house, and his shares of Regina Coeli."

Kristiana asked then, "That girl? The one he found in a cabin in the woods when he fled the battlefield?" By tacit agreement, none of them would say the name of the place where such tragedy had befallen their family. "How old is she exactly?" Kristiana asked.

"Fifteen," answered Philip.

Kristiana's eyebrows went up.

"He found her after he fled the battlefield, after Thread told him to run," Delphine added.

"Is he cured?" Regina asked, her eyes red and brimming with tears. She swiped at her nose. Catherine handed her a handkerchief.

"No," Philip said. "No, he will never get over what he saw. The man who is coming home is not the Kilian we knew. It's best you all realize that."

They looked at Delphine, who had been there, on the battlefield. And after. "We saw it happen, slowly but surely. I wanted to tell you, but . . ." She didn't know what to say to excuse her lack of communication. "You all must have read it in his dispatches. Kilian was too tenderhearted for war; he could not leave, and he could not stay. So . . ." She did not want to state what was painfully obvious: that when Thread had died on the battlefield it was the last straw for Kilian's sanity.

Catherine, who had said little throughout the meeting, had the final word as Kilian's mother: "Perhaps this Kilian is the man who was there all along. We just never knew him."

Chapter Thirty-Three

DEATH OF A
WOLF MATRIARCH

February 1, 1864, Cattaraugus Reservation, New York

The snow lay deep and pristine in the woods. Last week's thaw had frozen again, leaving a crust on top, making it hard for animals or humans to walk on it once the day warmed. Silent, not even whispering, but signaling with hand motions, the men followed a trail compacted by snowshoes and boots. The posse of locals were about serious business, men's business. A pack of wolves had been seen slinking around the edge of Dayton, lean and hungry, counting the days until the sheep dropped their lambs.

Wilhelm, who happened to be in town visiting the Shafers, had volunteered to join in. He borrowed a repeater rifle, spent the afternoon cleaning it, and shot it off twice to see how it sighted.

They had ridden off late the afternoon prior so they could be up before dawn and into the woods. They knew they would be on reservation land; they would have to be cautious.

"If the Indians find us, no telling what could happen," Wilhelm had grimly reminded the others. He was related to natives, so the men of the Shafer posse listened to him.

They stayed in a small hunting cabin at the edge of the woods. They kept the fire going all night but let it die out when the predawn came. The hunters got up in silence, just as the moon was setting, and took no coffee or tea. By design, no one had worn anything bright. They marked their faces with charcoal, under the eyes and down the nose, to blend into the winter landscape. They muffled anything that jingled. They carried pemmican in their packs, wrapped tightly so the animals wouldn't smell it. It had been prepared with sunflower meal and oil from the Montour Mill. The Shafer women had guided their men through the preparation, drying thin strips of venison by the hearth, then steeping them in a savory concoction of maple syrup, black pepper, wine, and garlic before drying the strips again on racks before the hearth.

The group stopped for a rest about an hour into their hike, at that time of night when the deepest sleep, the sleep of dreams, reigned. They passed around a canteen of water bound in leather. Wilhelm wanted a smoke but denied himself. In those earlier times in Newtown, those innocent times not long after they had arrived, twenty-five years ago, he had been the one to get up and milk the cows.

He remembered the night Philip and he had brought home Blaise Lazar from Marguerite's shebeen. They had walked through woods like this, all of them lit by earlier tankards of ale. Wilhelm had started a fire in the forge, crept into the house for a precious jar of preserves and a spoon to share. That had been the first time he had heard about the Lenape and their matrilineal tribal structure. He had been disgusted and outraged. Women in charge? It still made his blood boil, proof of the basic wrongheadedness of the natives on this continent. What kind of primitive culture could have come up with counting descendants through the women's line? Letting women own the land? He still felt it, one of the things that was wrong with this world, with this continent that natives called their homeland. They would stop calling it their homeland when every square mile of it had been built upon, when every resource—timber and river, coal, herds of animals—had been put to good use instead of let lie fallow!—Good timber reaching its full maturity, falling and rotting into the soil.

Someone passed him a plug of pemmican. He bit off a piece and chewed it, passed the rest on. The moonlight had been blue that night in Newtown too, turning the snowy scene into a moonscape before it set.

———

Holo woke to a familiar smell. The humans were early. Her pups were tiny, mewling beside her. Too early for First Food. She was hungry, though. On the other side of the pups, her mate lifted his head, smelled, then trotted out of the den to urinate and explore.

Holo's mother lifted her head in the corner, opened her eyes, sniffed deeply, then stood in alarm. *Something's not right,* she growled. She went out the door to join her son-in-law. *Yes, the humans were here. And something else . . . What was it?* They were learning this smell. *The smell of old stick fire. Yesterday's.*

They didn't dare howl to alert the other dens. *We will go. Slip by the humans. Wake the others.*

Wilhelm stretched. He was too old to be out in the woods in midwinter at this time of night.

Then he saw them: dark shapes gliding by at the edge of the woods. He would never have noticed but for the glint of a yellow eye turned in his direction. He raised his rifle to his shoulder and fired. He heard a *yip!*, then crashing through the woods as the others fled. "I got one!" he yelled, surprised. He hadn't expected the wolves to come to them. He blundered through the deep snow where a dark form lay. "Light a torch!" he yelled. "When dawn comes, we'll track the others back to their den."

A torch was brought. He had a sudden vision of the midsummer night they had called in the wild silkmoth, *la Phalène,* that his wife, Elisabeth, had needed to further their breeding program. A Newtown memory. What a strange time for these images from long ago to bubble up!

"It's a female," someone said, turning her over with his boot.

"An old female," someone else said.

Wilhelm froze. The old wolf opened her eyes and looked directly at him. "Thread," Wilhelm whispered beyond all reason. In the light of the dying wolf's eyes, he saw his grandson. He had been told what had happened, but he hadn't been able to think about Threadneedle dying on the battlefield at Gettysburg. He couldn't. He wouldn't let himself. But he smelled his grandson here, now.

A rough hand on his shoulder spun him around: Lazarus, He Who Hides. Thread's father. Wilhelm was momentarily confused. He had heard . . . the man was living up here now, on the reservation, his daughter with him. Again.

His group had been ambushed, surrounded by men his age, hard, tough men. *All their young men are gone to war too,* Wilhelm realized suddenly. As their rifles, knives, and hatchets were confiscated roughly, the men in Wilhelm's posse yelled out questions: "Don't they speak English?" "What are they going to do with us?" They didn't know these men, but Wilhelm did. He may not have known them as individuals, but he knew them as a People. How had they known the Shafers and other men from South Dayton would be in the woods?

Then Wilhelm remembered something, a weapon to use: Lazarus hid himself because he had killed a white man. He pulled his arms free, pushed his fingers into Lazarus' chest, and spoke loudly, no need for caution. Now that he had slain his wolf, they could leave the woods. "This man is wanted for the murder of a white man. I know him!" Yes, he wanted revenge for this red man's despoiling of his daughter Kristiana. The extraordinary being who had come of the union, Threadneedle, his grandson and heir, was dead. The Almighty's verdict on the union.

Lazarus grabbed Wilhelm roughly by the upper arm, then put him in a chokehold. "You old fool," he hissed into his ear. "Do you want the pack of you to disappear?"

Wilhelm stopped struggling and experienced a moment of chiseled clarity.

Lazarus saw it happen and released him. "What have you done, you *dummkopf?* You've killed the matriarch of the pack. Like Marguerite. You understand? If we don't get you out of here, the wolves will tear you apart."

The howling started. The men twisted against their captors. The ridge behind them was alive with wolves. And there, to the left, from that distant ridge, a response.

Holo's mate came back. Her mother was dead, killed by a fire stick. By a man who smelled like one of their humans, but also more: like other things that only men knew. Fire sticks. Tobacco. Other things having to do with fire. The stink of men from town.

Holo was confused. Her pups were awake, sucking at her, frightened. She would mourn her mother later. She was the matriarch now and yet still breeding; it was unheard of. Their numbers had been dwindling lately. That fall, a trap, carefully concealed, had killed her father. Two from another den had been killed with a fire stick last spring when they had taken a lamb!

Her mate waited patiently. Holo was frustrated. She had only the information he brought, as she was unable to get up herself, see for herself, smell and listen for herself, go to her mother's body. She would, later. But now? She lay back down; the pups had to nurse.

"These men . . . are your clan?" Wilhelm asked quietly, lowering and regulating his voice to counterbalance his rising panic.

Lazarus made a sound of assent. "These men are my clan. Wolf Clan," he said pointedly. "The young men gone to war, same as yours." Lazarus waited a beat. He would have liked to wait longer before speaking what he had to say, and yet there was no time. "I am not ready to die," he said. "I don't like having to help you. But you are family: I am Thread's father and you are his grandfather. We will get us out of the woods, all of us. But you must leave us—and the wolves—in peace. I want your word."

Wilhelm quickly relayed this information to his men, asking for their agreement. Turning back to Lazarus, he said, "You have our word."

"Release them." Lazarus turned to address both his clansmen and the Shafer party. "Now run, if you want to leave these woods alive!"

Wilhelm repeated this to his company. "Run! But stay close to the others."

"Throw your pemmican on the ground as we go," Lazarus instructed. "Stay together!"

The pups were fed, sleepy but not happy about their mother removing her warmth. Their oldest brother from last year's litter, disgruntled but willing, curled his body around this year's litter. He didn't want to miss the action outside, but he knew his job. His mother was the Word.

Holo came upon the kill site and looked down at her mother's body. It had not been a kind death, her body ripped, a large hole in her gut. The body was still warm, the smell of blood and feces powerful. Holo wanted to tear out the throat of the men who had done this. Her pack would have to leave their ancient homeland, take a dangerous trip farther north in midwinter, passing close to human settlements. They had to flee—that much was clear. But now? It couldn't be worse timing. They had been betrayed. She would have her revenge.

The plan came to her as if her mother were telling her these things. They would have to travel at night. Stay off the paths. Find food near human settlements. The pups were too young for the trip; she would have to kill them. Something awful and ancient twisted in her as these cold realities cracked open. This is the way it would have to be; it had been done before.

She would go into estrus again, once they'd reached a safe place. Have more pups.

It was cold comfort. Their lineage, broken.

But for now, blood would flow. They would feast on the hearts of their enemies. For a moment she felt something like regret. How long had her tribe been brothers with the humans? But many generations ago, a new breed of humans had pushed into their humans' territory, cutting the forest and pushing their human brothers deeper into the woods. Pushing their wolf sisters out.

She didn't understand it, couldn't figure it out. And then she realized there was nothing to figure out. She was all rage when she walked away from her mother's body, when she told her mate they would have to kill the pups.

Her brother and his mate would have to kill their pups as well. His mate would recognize the ancient truth in that inevitability, as her mother would also have passed on to her what had to be done in times like these.

The plan was in place now: Holo only wanted blood for blood. Her mate fell in beside her, followed by their oldest daughter, oldest son, and their mates. Her brother and his mate howled from the far ridge. They had heard. They were on their way. The humans ran ahead, near the edge of the woods. The wolves ran flat out, yipping to each other. *We will get one.*

These new humans, the ones who broke the ground with metal—did they taste as bad as they smelled? These men with their fire sticks took too many, too much, didn't kill cleanly. Even now, her mother lay with her entrails still steaming on the snow.

She smelled their human stink before she saw him, the last in the straggling line of runners. He would be the sacrifice; it was only right. He was a peaceful human, kept himself clean, respected the deep forest, but he had killed his own. She had smelled it on him, along with the smells of the animals he had taken. He was a trapper. She was closing in then, her pack reporting back with yips: Only old men were here in the forest, running for their lives. Where were their sons and daughters?

Yes, the father, from the Old People, must pay. Her pack would let the others escape; someone must be left to say the wolves had gone, their ancient compact broken. They would leave their homeland and then . . . what? Would their humans wither? When they called, no one would answer. Holo's pack and her brother's wife's pack would go north, where their kind would be safe. They could no longer stay here, where a matriarch could be murdered!

She saw him, smelled him, yipped to the others.

Lazarus shoved at the slowest of his clansmen: "Go!"

Lazarus turned to Holo, opened his arms. When she severed the artery at his neck, he was looking into her yellow eyes. The last thing he saw: her judgment, her mercy.

Chapter Thirty-Four

RESURRECTION, AFTER

March 21, 1864, Cottage, New York

Philip was about to give up when the door opened a crack and then he was inside.

Turtle Dawn closed the door behind him and then looked around, her back still against the closed door, as if seeing her cottage for the first time, with its clutter of canvases and piles of dirty clothing. After another long silence, she said: "How can I help you?"

Philip sighed. "I'm having a devil of a time."

"What are you going to do?"

"I've had no choice." He spread his hands as if defending himself, showing that he held no weapons, no hidden cards.

She started by saying, "Does it make any sense at all, now—," and then changed her mind. She knew Philip had had no choice. Everyone involved in Regina Coeli had been diverted and stopped cold: Thread dead, Killy mad or at least changed, Kristiana fostering Blake after her miscarriage, which, close on the heels of Lazarus' violent death, drove her nearly mad with maternal longing. She now understood how Regina, after Threadneedle's death, had taken on a mission for the rest of her life, one that precluded raising her own son.

And Philip? He indeed had no choice but to follow through on the strategies set in place by all of them, before . . .

"Her father's venture in that *manufacture* in Seneca Falls," he said, despising the man so much he couldn't bring himself to say Wilhelm's name. "He has one hundred machines, weaving and sewing, going night and day. He set up a coal gasification plant to light the floor. He has a laboratory working with the coal tars, my spies tell me."

"Everything Kristiana doesn't want," Turtle Dawn breathed.

Philip continued as if he hadn't heard her. "Delphine and Blaise have their dyeing operation in the same building. That man tried to take over the dye works, but Delphine wouldn't let him. We have had to buy another small building there so we can cut the linen when it comes in from the bleaching greens. We send out those pieces into the homes of the women we have recruited and then take the finished garments from them, which we give to Delphine to dye before we ship them direct from Seneca Falls."

Turtle Dawn put a hand out to stop him. "You've been doing all that, while . . ."

"Yes," Philip said. "We have been doing all that. While the war has been going on, while everyone here has been blasted into their corners, as if from a shotgun." Philip sounded angry. "While you have been in mourning." There. He had said it. "Someone had to keep it going."

He breathed and his voice returned to its normal timbre. He took another breath so he wouldn't stop saying what he needed to say. "Your mother—thank God for Delphine! She has taken over where Kristiana left off." Another breath, as if he were a long-distance runner pulling across the finish line. "And that is why we still have a company. A company with a future to discuss."

"Kristiana!" Turtle Dawn shouted with an anger she knew she could not allow, an anger she must tamp down. "I hate her. She started all this."

"She didn't start the war, Turtle Dawn."

"Oh yes she did," Turtle Dawn said, gulping air. "She started the war in the family."

Nesting Swan, who had been gaping at them from the floor, started to wail, frightened. Turtle Dawn scooped up her daughter and walked briskly to the other side of the room, cooing comforting sounds to her, telling her the lie "Everything is all right," even though every cell of Turtle Dawn's body, including the milk she still gave to the child, said differently: *Everything is not all right.* Everything . . . was loss, was sorrow, the Void. Nesting Swan, nearing three years old but still not speaking, understood these things perfectly well. The child told her when they spoke in what the Duladiers called Dialog.

"Gran'père," Turtle Dawn modeled the name for the child as she walked back across the room to Philip. "Gran'père Philipe." She jiggled Swan on her hip, kissed her neck, breathed in her scent for comfort, before handing her to Philip to take to his home for the day. And then to Philip: "Tell me more."

"Yes, it's a few stops along the canal, to the terminus at Tonawanda and back home here. Have you really never been there to his factory in Seneca Falls? He's set up a big bleaching green for himself there, farther down the opposite bank from ours. He patterned his washhouse and yard after ours. His yarn is principally coming from Scotland into New York Harbor, shipped up the canal to Seneca Falls. He still maintains his flax fields. I don't know why." He said this last bit quietly, as if to himself.

"Is he using power looms?" she asked, speaking just loud enough for him to hear.

He glanced at the child in her arms and realized Nesting Swan had fallen asleep, mouth open, neck slack. He took the child and laid her gently down.

"He's installed two steam-powered looms, dobbies, and he has two jacquard looms. The town already has a scutching mill; we both use it. He's doing cotton as well as linen. Blends. His production—and ours—has fallen fifty percent since . . ." Not one of them would speak the name of the battle that had swung the war to their side but at such a high price to their family.

He sighed again, more deeply now, as if before drinking a bitter medicine that was required for his own good. "And I'm keeping Flusty and Thread's string of weavers going."

"For whom? Who will buy this linen?" she asked rhetorically. Now she said the words that couldn't be said until this moment: "Does it make any sense at all? Wilhelm has all the linen he needs, and more."

He laughed wryly, a dry laugh, like something that would come out of a puffball if you stepped on it, full of seed, bitter as sulfur. He had no choice. "I've canceled our subcontract with that devil. He says he doesn't need us anyway. Calls us traitors and turncoats. Listen to me, Turtle Dawn. While everyone is diverted with the war effort, let's take our own linen production and produce the line you've designed for us. This is our chance!"

"During the war?"

"Yes, right in the middle of the war."

"Have you spoken with her?" She meant Kristiana, their putative partner.

"Regina has given Blake to Kristiana to raise." He looked at her oddly. "Didn't you hear? She's still living in Lazarus' house. At Cattaraugus Reservation. Kristiana wouldn't be denied her second chance to raise a child."

Turtle Dawn's mouth twisted. She blew out a large breath of exasperation, and with that release her face cleared. "It makes me so happy to hear that family are living on the homestead at Cattaraugus, even though Grandmother has died." She looked at Philip with something lit in her eyes. "If you see Kristiana, tell her Swan misses her. Tell her for me."

"I will . . . send a note." Philip picked up his hat, turned it in his hands. "Are you serious about helping?"

"Yes. I'm ready. Time is hanging heavy on my hands. The painting?" She gestured to canvases stacked in every corner. "It's not enough."

"I need help with the drawings. So we can put out our new catalog."

"Tell me." Turtle Dawn leaned forward, a new light in her eyes.

Philip put his hat down, sat again, and began to talk. "With Regina up there in Seneca Falls and Kristiana sequestered, I need help bolstering the Flusty string. The bleaching greens. It's our seed corn, Turtle Dawn. The bleaching greens. That's where the hand and the sheen all come together— right there." He gave her more details, painting a picture of resurrection, of purpose on the other side of after.

"Turtle Dawn," he said, before he closed the door behind him, a limp Swan in his arms. "I'm not sure the Flusty lasses will accept you. I don't know how they feel about . . ."

"Working with an Indian woman?" she said. "We'll see. With Kristiana out of the picture, my mother and I are the majority stockholders of Regina Coeli. If they want their jobs . . ."

Philip reflected on how much this woman had changed.

"I have power; they will need to respect me! Besides, they're not blind: the designs will draw them in. And I'll take Swan with me. Who can resist her?"

"Even so," Philip said, "Tom and Maeve are the best of our people but also the worst: Closed-minded. Clannish. Insular. They keep to a small community, with no exposure to the larger world in which they live."

Turtle Dawn had little experience with such intolerance. She was no longer sure she could win them over. She wasn't even sure she was willing to. Who wanted to work with bigoted, small-minded people?

"How soon?" she asked.

"Now. This spring," Philip answered.

Two months later, Philip, stumbling along a passage in his home one dark morning, stretched his arms out, but Catherine having died suddenly the night before, his arms remained empty save for a bar of light that shone through the window from the low dawn.

Chapter Thirty-Five

SONG FOR WEAVING TARTAN

June 22, 1864, Cottage, New York

Philip had one more thing to do before he left on the trip up the canal with Kilian's new bride, Elizabeth, to show her the business, to see where she could find her place: he had to be blunt with Maeve and Tom Flusty. "With Kristiana out of the picture and Thread gone, Turtle Dawn, Delphine and I are your bosses." He looked at his shoes and then back up, directly at them: "And I am old."

Tom and Maeve both shuffled their feet the way country people do when they are uncomfortable but don't want to be rude.

"If ye are old, what are we?" Tom said.

"Middle-aged," Philip said and they laughed. *They can laugh because they still have plenty of time,* Philip thought. *At my age, just a few years makes a large difference.*

"You took Regina in when I asked," Philip began.

"And look what happened!" Maeve said hotly, ignoring Tom's attempts to stop her with a sharp elbow. "Our Fiona's gone and become a suffragette."

"Is that so terrible?" Philip asked gently. "You are both people of principle. Maeve, I know about what you've been doing at the bleaching greens in Seneca Falls, after your workday is over. I know about the organizing your girls have been doing with Regina, with the women who do our piecework.

The pamphlets you pass out, the meetings you hold—you needn't hide it from me. You should know by now we feel the same way."

Maeve ducked her head, stubbornness beneath her apparent humility.

"Don't you see what it's come to, Philip?" Tom asked. "The young ones want to be in the city. My daughter and my wife!" He glared at Maeve. "And your daughter! All are in the thick of things, while we . . ."

"Are stuck here on the farm, Tom?" Philip asked quietly. He didn't know where to begin to address the difficult thing he had to ask them to do. Maeve and Tom were not racist the way Catherine had been. He wanted to ask bluntly if they had even bothered to learn anything about the Montours. Instead, he turned the question around: "We know so little about you, Tom and Maeve. And we have offered you a partnership in Regina Coeli. What did you do before you came here? We've all been so preoccupied over the last—what? Six years? When did you come?"

"It's seven years, Philip," Tom replied. "Fiona was ten when we arrived off the boat, twelve when we heard about Cottage."

"Yes," smiled Philip. Kristiana had been twelve, Kilian eight when the Flustys had gotten off their ship near Trenton, New Jersey. *So much can happen in those few years between girlhood and womanhood,* he reflected. Then, recalling where he had been going with this chatter, he said, "Can you come for dinner tonight? I leave for the canal trip with Elizabeth tomorrow."

They couldn't say no. Not with Philip so recently widowed.

"What can I bring?" Maeve asked. "I have brown bread and butter. And I have soup on the back of the stove. I'll put carrots and barley into it and call it done."

"And I have a chicken to roast."

"Is anyone else coming?" Maeve asked shrewdly. Philip didn't want to blindside them, but he was hard-pressed to admit Turtle Dawn would be there.

"Elizabeth is packing for our trip tomorrow. Kilian won't come. So . . . I was thinking of asking Turtle Dawn and my granddaughter. Swan." He was having more and more difficulty calling his granddaughter Eliza. He raised his eyebrows as if to say, "Is that all right?"

Maeve and Tom glanced at each other.

Philip knew they loved Swan, as did everyone else in the village. She was a regular fixture, going about with whomever had her for the day—Philip himself mostly, but also Regina or Delphine when they were in town. Swan had gone around with Lazarus too, but now he was gone.

"You and Turtle Dawn can get to know each other better over dinner," Philip wheedled, and he could see that Tom and Maeve understood the reason, though he could also see that it made them uneasy to consider making conversation with a native woman.

When Tom arrived carrying the soup pot, Maeve behind him with a plump loaf of bread wrapped in a towel, Turtle Dawn and Philip had already spread the table with swatches of dyed linen and Turtle Dawn's drawings. Maeve unwrapped the bread from the towel, a piece of linen with red stripes at either end and a heart embroidered in the center. She placed the loaf next to the bottle of beer Philip had brought up from the cellar.

"That chicken smells good!" Tom said in a too-hearty voice. He put the soup pot on the stove and peeked into the firebox, which was snapping and crackling strongly, then glanced at the beer on the table.

"Help yourself, Tom," Philip invited, though Tom was already pouring the frothy beer into a tankard. He took his first deep draught, then sucked the drips off his mustache.

"Leave the door open, Tom," Philip instructed as Tom turned to close the door. A delicious wind carrying the heady fragrance of wild black cherry blossoms swept through the house, taking the smell of roasting chicken out the window Philip had opened on the opposite wall, beyond the table where he and Turtle Dawn were conferring.

Maeve opened the oven door to check the chicken. "Want me to baste it, Philip?" She was already reaching for the brush and the bowl with the glaze.

"Come look at these first," Philip said. Maeve got a look on her face that her husband recognized. No one instructed Maeve on when and what to do in a kitchen—any kitchen. She basted the chicken, closed the oven door, then wiped her hands on her apron before she approached the table to see what the others were looking at.

"Hello, Maeve," Turtle Dawn said shyly. "Tom."

Tom covered the awkwardness of the moment by bending down to where Swan was plaiting grasses. "Did your Gramma teach you that, little missy?" he asked kindly, without condescension. Everyone knew not to expect an answer from the girl. The Duladiers continued to worry that she still wasn't speaking at age three, but whenever one of them brought it up, Turtle Dawn and Delphine warded them off with vague reassurances.

Turtle Dawn gestured to the swatches, an open invitation to begin discussing their plans.

Maeve turned the linen swatches over in her hands and then began arranging them in various combinations: indigo with acid green, indigo with red, red with acid green. She took up the swatch dyed brown from onionskins. "What makes this brown so rich?" she asked.

"Delphine says it's a drop of cochineal," Philip said. "She never gives away her formulas; she keeps them in a thick notepad either with her or under lock and key."

"So this is what Delphine does with the linen I send her from the bleaching greens," Maeve said, wonder in her voice.

Turtle Dawn looked at her with astonishment, then at Philip. "Have you never seen our garments before they are shipped out, Maeve?"

The woman shook her head gravely, intoning, "Nay."

"I think we just stumbled across one of the few benefits of the factory system, Tom," Philip said with a trace of irony. "Everything under one roof? Everyone sees everything!"

"Have you never been in the factory, Maeve—our new building?" Turtle Dawn couldn't believe she was asking this, for Maeve's bleaching greens were just across the river.

Maeve shook her head.

"No, me neither," Turtle Dawn admitted shyly.

This admission seemed to astonish Maeve. "Never?!" she exclaimed. "And you, an owner!"

"That's where we cut your linen, on tables there, into the patterns of our outfits," Philip said. "Then your girls take the bundles out to the women who do the piecework sewing."

"I've seen the bundles," Maeve said stoutly, not willing to be made a fool of by anyone. "But they are as white as when they left the bleaching greens."

"That's when your girls pick up the finished garments and take them up to Delphine's for dyeing."

Philip saw that Maeve had a question in her face.

Turtle Dawn anticipated what was puzzling Maeve. "It just didn't make sense for us to send the pieces back here to Cottage to be sewn. This is all new just this spring. You haven't been to Seneca Falls again since you left there last autumn, right?" She went on, to mend the older woman's pride, "And I have never been there because I can't see the sense of wasting all that time, leaving here, just to see the *manufacture*."

Maeve looked at her sharply to see if she were being made a fool.

"Haven't you noticed?" Turtle Dawn said. "I work on our designs and our catalogs. Everything I do is right here."

"Hmm!" Maeve observed sharply and picked up a swatch. "And what is this cochineal I keep hearing about?"

"That's the red dye that Wilhelm Shafer brings up from Mexico. It's from a little beetle that feeds on cactus."

Maeve took up the red swatch again and fingered it. "Well, my land," she whispered to no one in particular. "A beetle."

"I'll bring back news to everybody when I return from my trip up the canal," Philip said. "But really, come this summer, when Maeve is down in Seneca Falls again, Turtle Dawn, you need to come down there to see it with your own eyes."

Their attention now turned to Turtle Dawn's designs. "Take a look at these and tell me what you think, honestly, Maeve," she said, pulling pages out of the stack and engaging Maeve in talk of peplums and hidden button plackets and gores.

Maeve slowly began to reveal that she knew more about the garment industry than what they knew of the couple's past. "When Tom and I were in Glasgow"—she said it "Glassgoo"—"I worked in the factory. We made fancy dresses for ladies in London and Paris. We had just gotten married when things started to go bad. Tom's brother? He lost an arm there, in one of the machines. And then shortly after, I lost our first baby."

Turtle Dawn shot her a sympathetic look.

Maeve nodded. "Ay, it was hard." She wasn't sure whether she should say what had happened next, but, she pressed on. "Then, well . . . Tom was fired for being an agitator."

Tom continued the story. "We just packed up and left. Left it all behind: family, tradition, the cemetery where all our ancestors lie buried."

"Life is hard for immigrants," said Philip. "Life is hard."

In the silence that followed, they all remembered that Philip had just been widowed. But few can see into the intimacies of a marriage like Philip and Catherine's. The couple had lived apart for most of the last ten years, five hundred miles and a world of differences separating them.

"But then, one day," Philip started again, "you lift up your head and see! You have been in Paradise all along."

Turtle Dawn had never heard this kind of talk from Philip, not in all the years she had known him. But then, hadn't they all changed? The deaths, the war . . . no one was the same. She seized the moment to change the subject: "What do you think of this combination of colors, Maeve?"

"I like this," Maeve said, picking up a plaid, so different from the other swatches. "It's so much like our tartan."

"Yes. That piece is yarn-dyed rather than garment-dyed. It's a blend of linen, wool, and a bit of silk."

"Are you thinking of doing more like this?" Maeve asked.

Tom hovered closer, sensing the women were veering toward something that interested him.

"I don't know," Turtle Dawn said softly. "I don't know what to do. I was hoping you and Tom might give me your opinion." She shuffled through her pages until she came to a design with a tartan skirt, a jaunty hat with a cockade, and a black velvet vest that fit tightly over a white blouse with a lacy jabot. "What do you think of this?" She jabbed her index finger toward the skirt.

Maeve picked up the paper and looked at the design as if it were already real, as if her Fiona could wear it. "It's been so many years since our people wove our own tartans," she mused. "The Brits had us weaving tweed for them, and it was all forgotten."

Tom was looking over his wife's shoulder. "Tartan?" he asked. "No one weaves that by hand anymore. They brought in the big machines, the jacquards and Italian knitting machines. They can weave anything. But no, no one weaves these complicated designs by hand anymore. It's not 'cost effective,'" he said, putting all the irony of his breed into two words.

They were all thinking the same thing: *Threadneedle*.

"Thread was heading toward re-creating all those historical patterns and could have figured it out," Tom said, risking the sensitive subject.

"Could you?" Turtle Dawn asked Tom, her heart in her face. "Could *you* figure it out?"

You could see it in Tom's face: he was fully realizing that this woman, this native woman, was Threadneedle's mother, just as much as if she had borne him.

In the background, Philip was clacking stoneware bowls out of the cupboard, gathering spoons to serve the soup. He pulled the chicken from the oven and brushed it one more time with the glaze.

"I have done," Tom said. "It's how I learned, apprenticed to a tartan weaver. But it takes time. No one wants to do it anymore. No, it's true: You can't build profits into the time it takes to weave tartan, they tell me."

Turtle Dawn knew that they did not need to extract profit from the fabric of one skirt in their catalog. She smiled and turned to Maeve. "Do you still know the songs?" she asked.

Maeve was visibly taken aback.

"Among my people," Turtle Dawn added, "certain tasks go better with the songs we sing as we work."

Maeve smiled ruefully. "You know more about my bleaching greens than I do your designing. Or Delphine's dye pots." *Or your People*, she thought to herself.

"I admit it," Turtle Dawn acknowledged. "I work at my table with my window open. I think I know all of your songs," she laughed. Turtle Dawn began to sing one of the songs in Gaelic.

All of the adults were surprised when Swan piped up, joining her mother in the traditional Gaelic buttermilking song they had heard repeated so many times.

To cover their shock at hearing Swan sing when she didn't speak, Philip squatted down in front of her. "Will you come to the table, my lass, and have a bit of Maeve's soup and bread?" he asked.

Swan nodded and whispered, "Yes, I will, Gran'père," and put her arms around his neck to be lifted.

Chapter Thirty-Six

THE FORGE OF AN ETERNAL FIRE

July 4, 1864, Cottage, New York

Why was it a surprise to Philip that Kilian accepted Turtle Dawn's written request to sit for a portrait? He should not have been surprised; everything was shifting, as when a stream will jump its banks and start a new channel during a spring flood.

Nevertheless, Philip set out with Elizabeth for the slow trip down the canal to New York City, resolved not to worry about Kilian. On the canal, Cottage and all its cares would be left far behind them. He would focus on the matter at hand: bringing his new daughter-in-law, seven months pregnant, more fully into Regina Coeli. They would take the train back to South Dayton and be picked up in a coach in time for Elizabeth to settle back in at home, work on sewing the baby's layette, and wait.

"Come in, Kilian." Turtle Dawn opened the door wide to let in this man she hardly recognized, the old Kilian hiding behind his scars.

He ducked his head and came through the door, squinting, and removed his hat.

"Would you take off your boots?" she asked gently. It was past mud season and yet thick clods of clay clung to Kilian's rubber work boots. Turtle Dawn remembered his small-boy pride when he was first allowed to wear rubber work boots like his father, and a lump rose in her throat. She had barely glanced at the boy then; he had been insignificant compared to what she and Kristiana were exploring together as young women.

Looking at him obliquely now, she realized he was indeed a changed man. A different man with a different wife. *Who is his true wife?* Turtle Dawn thought. *Me or her? He asked me first.* Then: *But what of the long-dead Eugenia, Kilian's first wife?* She knew that the marriage of Eugenia and Kilian was not one of true soul mates; Kilian had told her so. But none of this mattered anyway, not now. Turtle Dawn saw it clearly etched in his face, in the heaviness of his body: she could not be wife to this man.

Turtle Dawn had seen her once, Kilian's white wife, when she was down at the Flustys' with the string of linen weavers. Turtle Dawn could see immediately that the pregnant girl belonged. Maeve introduced Turtle Dawn, identifying her as a major partner in Regina Coeli, the designer of the clothes that were occasioning all this activity. Turtle Dawn looked into the girl's eyes to see if she had heard any gossip about her relationship with Kilian. Turtle Dawn took stock of the girl's reaction: she seemed happy to meet her, was cowed by her presence, and, most importantly, did not seem surprised that one of the partners of Regina Coeli was a native.

As Kilian took off his boots, Turtle Dawn sat next to him on the settle by the door, Swan in her lap. She had prepared the child for this meeting. She watched closely, examining this man called Kilian, who now seemed bigger if hollowed out in his chest, frightening in his ferocity, and clearly a man for whom death had become an everyday occurrence. It was hard to see this change where only a gentle, compassionate, and trusting soul had resided before. In his socks, he squatted down in front of them and took the child's hands in his. "Did your mama tell you I'm your papa?"

Swan nodded.

Turtle Dawn gestured him to the house clogs, which he slipped into without comment, and then he stood, arms flapping slightly, waiting for direction. She situated Kilian by a window, instructing him to be comfortable, but didn't offer tea. She and Philip had put two windows into the pitched roof, one on each side, to capturing the rich light of midday all year round. Before turning back to him, she quietly put a cup of water, a brush, a palette with a few squeezes of paint, and some sheets of newsprint in front of Swan on the floor.

Turtle Dawn worked quickly, starting with a study in charcoal pencil, aware that Kilian might never sit long enough to allow her to translate his portrait into paints. Now she could study him objectively, hand, heart, and eye working together to render a portrait of this man she had known since they were children, a man transformed into a dangerous bomb in less than two years. A man who was now—she had to grit her teeth to admit it—patterned after her own People's men. A warrior. But with significant differences.

What others had told Turtle Dawn appeared to be true: Kilian seemed monochromatic, flat, but there was something else, something just under the surface. He was not moving through life, rote as a machine, but seemed more to be struggling to hold himself together, as if he were a volcano in danger of erupting in a blast that would destroy everyone and everything within miles. She could see how he held his jaw clenched, how his nostrils flared, his eyebrows arched, an effort that she couldn't help but admire. It reminded her of the way her People had respected the silent endurance of a prisoner being tortured, before the Peacemaker, hundreds of years earlier. Thread's death, she understood now, was an eternal fire that was reforging Kilian into someone else. They had each made their uneasy peace with that metamorphosis. After.

Kilian broke the silence first. "What's her name again?" he asked in a voice scratchy from disuse.

"Nesting Swan," she said.

"Nesting Swan," he said thoughtfully. "Yes, I recall."

Turtle Dawn spoke in Dialog even as her eyes flicked toward her subject and back to the vellum where her hand moved, translating lines. *So you want to tell me what happened, Killy? He was my son.*

Kilian answered in Dialog. *Fathers and sons. Mothers and sons. Two mysteries to complicate life.* A non-answer, and Turtle Dawn decided not to press him further.

A half hour passed. The light was changing. A bare branch tapped urgently on the window. The child sang to herself as she painted.

Then, abruptly, he cried out her name: "Turtle Dawn!"

"Don't," she blurted, stopping him.

But before she knew it he was out of his chair and they were against each other's bodies. This was not love but lust and violence, and Turtle Dawn wasn't going to have it. She had never been raped and never would be, ever, not by a man she loved. The child shrieked as the two well-matched adults struggled against each other, pitching into cupboards and screaming at each other not to use weapons, to at least play by some rules the other acceded to. Turtle Dawn screamed for time out, for applying the rules of amnesty, for the sake of the child, who was looking on in terror, and after several moments of violent drama, finally, finally, it ended. The studio lay in a shambles, Kilian on his back, pincered between Turtle Dawn's legs while she rocked her hips, riding him, crooning to both him and Nesting Swan, who was now encircled in her mother's arm, pressed into her breasts, and being soothed by the rocking while Kilian wept, not softly or furtively but like a calf who has lost his mother, bawling openly, eyes blinded, wordless keening, coming to life again only to find that hard thing a blade around which he would never fit, the reality of Thread's being dead.

Much later, the three spooned together. While Swan slept and Kilian breathed into the fragrance of Turtle Dawn's neck, she asked, "What will happen now?"

He startled, as men will do, snuffling awake from a small deep sleep back into the moment. "Let's let the future take care of itself, Dawn. Can we?"

What could she do but agree with such a sensible response? She was not her mother, Delphine, incapable of sharing her mate. From the beginning, she had been willing to share Kilian with another woman. But would his bride accept her?

Chapter Thirty-Seven

NEW BREED

November 1, 1864, Cottage, New York

Six months after Lazarus' death, Kristiana arrived back in Cottage with all the bravado of a martial band, the trees playing the French horns and oboes, the wind piccolos and fiddles. Her carriage was drawn by a matched team of black horses, a strawberry roan hitched behind. Blake peered out at the world from his seat beside his grandmother, a thick ruff of wolverine fur hooding his face.

With her habitual vigor, Kristiana engaged a couple of young men to help her unload the carriage into her old house, where they soon had a fire going in the woodstove. Word spread quickly through Cottage, along the main street and below, along the creek in Milltown: "Kristiana is back!" The founder of both Cottage and Regina Coeli hadn't visited the village since she had lost her pregnancy shortly after Lazarus' death.

The first person to visit Kristiana was, of all people, Elizabeth, Kilian's new wife, with her baby boy, named after Philip, strapped to her chest. She brought a loaf of freshly baked bread, some of summer's sour cherry preserves, and a round of cheese in a beeswax rind. "I hope you didn't come for Philip's funeral," the girl said after she had introduced herself. "You missed it. It was last week."

"Did Kilian take it hard?" Kristiana asked. While Catherine had vanished overnight into her death, Philip had hung on, struggling for breath, all summer.

Elizabeth, still standing at the door with her satchel full of gifts, cut her eyes and head sideways as if Kilian might be approaching. "He's . . . shut himself away. Won't come out. Won't eat. I . . ."

"Come in!" Kristiana said then. "What am I thinking?" She opened the door wide and indicated the settle, where Blake was quietly untying a shoe with all the absorption toddlers bring to a small task. Kristiana accepted the parcels from Elizabeth's arms, and the two women, a generation apart, took seats at the kitchen table.

Elizabeth loosened her clothes and put Baby Philip to her breast to nurse. "I'm trying to figure out what their relationship is to each other," she said. "Blake and little Philip."

"The babies are cousins," Kristiana said. "Blake's mother Regina and Philip's father Kilian are brother and sister." She smiled. "But of course you've figured out that much so far."

"Ah, yes," said Elizabeth, newly come into this family whose relationships and twined lineages felt so complicated to her: Natives married to French Huguenots, who themselves had spent the last century in her family's Hesse, Germany. Natives who themselves had Huguenot bloodlines. Natives with bloodlines from several tribes. Ach! She would untangle it eventually. She couldn't imagine how unsettled she would have been among this extended family without Philip's tutelage.

"I'm sorry for the state of things," Kristiana said, changing the subject. "I've just arrived, just finished unpacking. But this . . . being here . . . it is heaven."

"That's what Father Philip said not too long before he died. On our trip up the canal."

Kristiana smiled mysteriously. She had been on that trip with Philip many times.

"It was right after Mother Catherine died," Elizabeth continued. "He had said, yes, life is hard. But once in a while you look around and see that everything is perfection. That you are in Paradise."

Kristiana's face clouded. "I've had a very hard year. First Threadneedle, my son. Then Lazarus, his father, and also the father of the baby who died before it could be born." She said these things as if she were schooling this young mother in elementary familial tragedy.

The stove glowed as it expanded from the heat.

Kristiana felt as if she might burst open like a ripe persimmon from the emotion of coming home, with her son's son Blake. Their Lenape family still living in the Delaware Valley used to send a bushel of the wild fruit north to arrive at harvest time and be made into a pudding, because Lazarus had cherished them. But it had been a while since things were settled enough to trade and barter. From all the feelings that were flooding through her, just from being in this house where so much emotion had been freighted during her years married to Turtle Dawn, raising Threadneedle, incubating Regina Coeli's success, she felt as though she might break open and spill her seed.

Loss. How it transformed the landscape.

She mused darkly on how she had introduced Kilian into their cozy nest, forgetting that she and Turtle Dawn were estranged when Kilian's intimacy with Turtle Dawn had resulted in Swan. "How is Swan?" she asked. "Is she talking yet?"

"Oh, yes. After the dam broke, she never stopped. Chattering or singing, our little lark." Then, shyly, "I enjoy being her stepmother."

Kristiana had wondered if Elizabeth knew that Kilian was Swan's father, but now it was confirmed. "You know, then."

"Yes." And then she seemed to collect herself, to figure out what to say. "That kind of thing is common in my country. A man has a child—or children—with a woman he does not marry. Kilian told me Turtle Dawn refused him. That was my good fortune."

To deflect this revelation that seemed to take Kristiana aback, the girl Elizabeth drew something from her satchel and turned to Blake. "I brought you something," she said. "From your Gran'père Philipe." Blake looked up with keen attention. "He wanted you to have this." She lifted a small carved horse from her coat pocket and galloped it through the air to Blake, who lifted it from her and continued to rock it through the air around him. "Ach, I want another child right away. But we have plenty of time, of course," she said, then blushed as she remembered that Kristiana had lost her baby, her husband dead. Killed by wolves!— what a savage country they lived in. She had just gotten off the boat from Hesse and arrived at her godmother's abandoned house as the civil war came to Pennsylvania. She had no one to turn to when Kilian had found her. Her salvation lay in paying close attention to what was at hand: this family and their business. "Who does Blake look like?"

"He looks like his father, Threadneedle. My son with Lazarus," Kristiana said. It saddened her to think that perhaps the Duladier family's story would leave Lazarus and Thread behind. He Who Hid and He Who Breaks to Heal. *Not if I have anything to do with it*, Kristiana told herself fiercely. *They will not be forgotten.*

"He's a Montour," she said proudly to Elizabeth. "We shall see if anything of Duladier comes out in him as he grows older," she added wistfully. "A new breed. The best of both, designed to settle this country. That's what they said of Thread."

Elizabeth looked at Kristiana as a thought suddenly occurred to her: "Are you staying here this winter?"

"Yes," Kristiana said, rising to pull the kettle to the point of the stove just above the firebox. "We have a lot of work to do. Now tell me," she said, settling down again, "who of the family is here in the village right now?"

"You're fortunate," Elizabeth said. "Everyone came for Philip's funeral rites." She ticked them off on her fingers. "Regina, Delphine, Maeve, Turtle Dawn ... No one has left town yet."

"Can you take a message to all four of those women for me?" Kristiana asked. "I want to have a meeting tomorrow morning. In Turtle Dawn's atelier, down below. Please."

With Baby Philip fed and bound sleeping against her breast, Elizabeth heard the urgency in Kristiana's voice and, feeling that this was what her father-in-law had prepared her for—for the family, for the business—she didn't hesitate to play her part. She pulled baby Philip close, bundled scarves and shawls around herself, and hurried out into the November day, bleak and sharp as an axe, pleased to be the message bearer.

Chapter Thirty-Eight

WEAVING THE FUTURE

November 2, 1864, Cottage, New York

Houses had changed hands.

When the men went to war, and Turtle Dawn moved out of the home she once shared with Kristiana, and she and Nesting Swan moved into Kilian's house, she had thought she would still be there, settled in, when Kilian came home again. After.

She hadn't imagined she would live there alone.

Kristiana and Turtle Dawn's original home, the one styled loosely after a longhouse, located on the western end of the main street and above the mill town where most of the Scots-Irish lived, had been briefly converted into a warehouse and workshop for the resurrected Regina Coeli. The house where Kristiana and Turtle Dawn had reared Threadneedle had been shut up for months until yesterday, when Kristiana had returned to take up her life there with Blake.

Meanwhile, Turtle Dawn had established a design atelier in a long, bright room that had been a lumber warehouse in the former mill town of Slab City, with a pitched roof and skylights open to the south. It was sided in maple boards that had been left behind when the mill was abandoned. Neighboring villages presumed that some of that land would eventually be returned to farmland and some would eutrophy into beaver swamp. None of the buildings were considered valuable enough to salvage the materials so—to Regina Coeli's advantage—many buildings had been left standing empty.

Turtle Dawn and Delphine had just started to warm the atelier for their meeting when Kristiana walked in.

This is the moment of truth, Kristiana said in Dialog, a form of communication they used little these days, an artifact of their silk heritage that seemed increasingly unnecessary now that the family was all working together in the same town. She and Turtle Dawn and Delphine arranged chairs in a semicircle around the stove. Blaise and Kilian came and went with armloads of wood, which they stacked in beside the stove while Turtle Dawn fussed, setting up a station for Nesting Swan with her doll, a collection of fabrics, and a small strawberry basket that held her few sewing supplies: linen thread, a crewel needle easy to thread, a set of small shears, and a pincushion shaped and colored like a plum, plump and silvery as Swan herself.

The girl's continuous singing, her way of bringing her world into being, was augmented with exclamations at Elizabeth's arrival. Baby Philip was strapped into Threadneedle's old cradleboard. Then, behind her, Regina stepped in, Blake bundled up to his eyes. Blake: so much like the Montour side of the family—raven hair, slanted black eyes, a flat nose with wide nostrils, and a lovely rose flush on golden skin. Sturdy and sensitive. Attentive and grounded. So like his father, all agreed.

Without much ado, Threadneedle's cradleboard, Baby Philip in it, was hoisted into the air and hung from a low rafter. Maeve and Tom Flusty entered with two of their older daughters; the girls headed back into an anteroom with the two children, Blake and Swan, having prepared some entertainment for them. The women took their seats at the table. Maeve and Tom found bench seating behind Regina. Soon Blaise and Kilian came back in from hauling wood to the stove and seated themselves as well.

"Kristiana," Delphine began. "You are our visionary. Why don't you lead off with your observations?" She handed Kristiana the traditional talking stick, which they had adapted from the Haudenosaunee branch of the family.

Before she rose from her seat to begin, Kristiana took a moment to listen to the torrent of the fire catching in the stove, to the chickadees (*chicka dee dee dee!*) outside on the spruce trees, from which snow drifted as the birds settled on their branches in the thin morning air. The sky outside, bleached pale indigo, was embellished with golden-hued clouds, a topography in the sky that mirrored the elements below: distant cumulus, high cirrus, evaporating morning fog. The steady thrum of the mill marked the community's industry, a continuous seasonal throb of transformation.

Turtle Dawn was impatient to hear what Kristiana foresaw for them. And yet she deeply believed that her own work that had predicated their future, now the established ground of being of Regina Coeli. Her designs were celebrated along the coastal cities of their continent as well as in the capitals of Europe. She enjoyed imagining two women admiring each other's outfits, knowing that their label Regina Coeli marked not only the garments but also who the identity of these richly imagined women, their customers, were. Their company's label had become a symbol for a population of women after the Civil War for yes, though the war ground on like many wars, people, especially women, had begun to pick up life again.

Regina Coeli symbolized a future they envisioned for themselves, for a new People, one that melded the best of bloodlines. This new race of humans would countenance no war, no slavery. Everyone would enjoy parity and the chance to excel based on hard work, on merit, on expressing one's individual voice. Their new society, paid for in blood and privation, would be based on community rather than the sacred rights of the individual to do whatever they wanted on their own fenced property. Regina Coeli, founded by women, run by women, for women, had become an imperishable banner, for the rights which could no longer be denied women. Now that the issue of slavery was being put to rest, their men would come home and grant their wives the same parity that native women took for granted. Who had maintained their farms and households while men were away?

Turtle Dawn couldn't wait to pull out their latest catalog, which featured tartan skirts deeply split to accommodate ease of movement, a line of messenger bags in a choice of leathers—cowhide, pony, and buckskin—some with silver chasing. In some designs, the linen was overprinted with silk-screened motifs: branches, leaves, *toile* scenes from summer gardens. The patterns used for cutting the garment pieces to size were in the corner of the atelier, hung together on a horizontal pipe near the cutting table.

Turtle Dawn's interrogation of European ways of looking at the world, the development of her art as a calibrating instrument, had indelibly changed her. She thought of herself as a visionary just as much as Kristiana was, a discovery that had lain like an unripe egg in her until everything had changed. It had happened in a moment: Threadneedle's voice had rung through her like a bell: *Now! Now you must live life fully, Tante Turtle Dawn, one hundred percent!*

Kristiana broke the expectant silence with a deep breath. Lifting her long trunk out of her chair, she opened with this statement, issued in a quiet voice: "We will continue to resist. We will not go the way of the factory town, of Lowell. We will not use steam engines, we will not decimate forests, we will not dig for coal."

Tom Flusty couldn't help himself and rose to his feet, fisted arm raised in the air.

"And yet I am not recommending we take an 'either/or' approach," Kristiana counselled. "I am asking each of you to add your thoughts as I stimulate our collective vision. Please, speak up with your ideas as I lead us there, to look together." She waved one hand in the direction of east. Thread was not there to see how it mimicked the gesture she had made at the stones, so long ago, when she had maimed his foot to prevent his going to war. In the years since, they had all seen Kristiana use this gesture to conjure visions they had come to trust.

"Our factory in Seneca Falls—which we will soon take full possession of—is already the best place for our dyeing operation and our bleaching grounds. What else belongs there?" She quickly vetoed one hypothetical option: "We will not use weaving machines that require steam to run. We will only use wood and coal to heat the factory floors for workers. Never to run machinery," she repeated, then paused. "Are we all agreed?"

Delphine sat alongside Turtle Dawn, mother and daughter, their lineage now the heart of Regina Coeli. When she spoke, the undisputed head of Regina Coeli, everyone listened: "I have also had visions in which I see this other way, the way we have been preparing for ourselves. Kristiana speaks true when she says we must be both/and, not either/or." She laced the fingers of her hands together to illustrate the strength of this interweaving. "The factory is good for certain things: shipping, dyeing, bleaching. Regina and Maeve and their girls are using it to get the word out to women, to encourage our sisters—native and white—to support each other."

Turtle Dawn accepted the stick from her mother. "Here, in Cottage, we will advertise for more weavers." Maeve nodded vigorously. "Our design function is strong as ever, if not more so!" Turtle Dawn looked around the room, noting who seemed to agree. "I like it here," she said. "This is my People's homeland. Perhaps it is becoming yours. Small farming communities just like this one are dotted across the landscape from here to Buffalo. To Seneca Falls. Small communities where farmers grow, pull, and rett flax. Spinning flax to linen thread? Right here on the farm, with our best spinning jennies."

Tom stood and added another two quarters of wood to the stove, which glowed cherry red. He had never seen Turtle Dawn so voluble.

She continued. "But braking and scutching? We must do this for our farmers. An entire wagonload of dried flax in bales weighs little, around fifty pounds. If we bundle the dried harvest and send it from the proximate rail station to the villages, we can brake, scutch, and hackle in a central location and then send finished stricks of linen thread, ready to spin, back to the farmers' wives who grew the flax—those who want the income from spinning."

"And who will not want that extra income?" Kristiana put in. "It will be an essential part of their total household income without taking a woman from her home."

"We could either pay them in cash or in shares of ownership in Regina Coeli," Blaise said. His comment received nods, ayes, and some looks of puzzlement. He could see that this form of ownership would need some explanation, for some.

Turtle Dawn took the stick back from Kristiana. "We must have more linen to meet our orders. Some of you have not seen my designs yet." She smiled. "If we have to order thread from Ireland or Flanders, then I say we do it! It's clear that we have to put all of our efforts into this one company:

Regina Coeli." She paused, looking around, first at Regina, then Kristiana, and finally Delphine and then pointedly at Blaise, before continuing in a low urgent voice. "The war hasn't broken us. Remember: He Who Breaks to Heal." She paused so all of them could recall the meaning of Thread's true name. "War has made us stronger. Let each village that joins us in this cooperative effort become a partner, become another Cottage, where craft—the marriage of hand, heart, and eye—create a life and a living we can all enjoy, one that builds community rather than breaking it, and breaking it for another's profit."

Head down, Kilian bit his nails. Elizabeth brought a fussing Philip down from the rafters and bowed her head over him as she unlaced him from his cradleboard, loosened his swaddling clothes, and opened her bodice, quieting the baby.

Blaise reached for the talking stick from Turtle Dawn. "Where is the wind?" he began. "Where should we best locate the mills to use wind power to process all of our flax into neat linen stricks we can return to the villages for spinning? I have been thinking about this and believe I have been led to an answer, just as Kristiana was led to create good farmland out of swamp, once she had installed miles of drains."

He had their attention and pressed on, drawing the geography with his hands for them all to picture.

"The lake plain that comes off Lakes Erie and Ontario, as we all know, is ideally suited for growing fruit. Here, on the rolling hills of this plateau that head south to the Alleghenies, in these wide river valleys, we have ideal land for farming. For dairy. The escarpment rises steeply off the lake plain before it continues on to these hills. The wind here, at the edge of the escarpment, is stiff off the Great Lakes, and relatively continuous. Somewhere proximate to us, we could locate our processing. Maybe a daisy chain of processing mills. We have to assess it." As he felt questions rising up against his vision, he waited for another gust of confidence to carry him further.

Kristiana reached for the stick to speak. "Who else would like to speak?"

Regina and Maeve both stood, glancing at each other uneasily, as they hadn't prepared anything to say. Regina took the stick Kristiana handed her.

"Of course you are right. Organizing young women to take in piecework and spinning goes hand in hand with organizing them to fight for our rights. But I see a larger problem. Philip and Kilian took care of all our accounts. Philip did our billing and kept our books. Our inventory? Well, it is haphazard now. Which one of us is really suited to take all of this on? I will be secretary to Mrs. Jocelyn Gage." A murmur went up from the table, as this was news to most of the group. Jocelyn Gage was one of the triumvirate of women leading the fight for women's rights. Being secretary to Gage was a plum position for Regina. "But that is calendars, words, and writing, not keeping records and accounting. I can't do it. Who will?"

Attention turned to Kilian, who was suddenly taking a great deal of interest in picking lint off his pant leg. Baby Philip began to howl then, and Elizabeth stood, attempting and failing to quiet him for a few moments before Kilian surprised them all by reaching for the infant, taking the baby in his arms. Baby Philip calmed as his father pulled him to his chest and walked him around the room, humming resonantly.

Elizabeth now accepted the talking stick. "I am not used to this kind of family," she started. "But Father Philip took me under his wing to explain the business to me. Just as Mother Catherine showed me the proper way to keep a home."

A few eyebrows were raised and glances exchanged. What had Catherine known about keeping a home, the sheltered silk *maîtresse* forced into an early retirement? Elizabeth fidgeted. "I am good with numbers. Kilian cannot travel out. I think you can see why." She clearly alluded not only to Kilian's condition but to Baby Philip as well. "Father Philip and I went through all the ledgers. He gave me a description of each of our accounts, which I noted." She hesitated, seeming surprised to find herself standing and talking with such assurance. "I cannot imagine it would be difficult to add inventory, shipping, and billing to my duties. As my time approaches," she glanced at her stomach, "I would like to train a clerk to help me maintain systems."

She sat down hard. Kilian scuttled to her side, handing over Baby Philip to be nursed again. The couple made a small refuge between the two of them, bending over their child and toward each other, their closeness keeping out curious eyes. Kilian's arm emerged to hand over the talking stick.

Their acknowledged leader, Delphine, took it. "Is anyone really surprised that, between us, we seem to have the capacity to envision it all?"

Tom Flusty stood, Maeve staunch by his side. Delphine walked the stick to the couple. "How happy I am to hear you all speak a truth I can live with—*we* can live with," he amended. "Especially after this struggling back and forth between us . . . Maeve and the girls going to the bleaching greens each summer in Seneca Falls . . ." He exchanged a poignant look with Maeve that spoke volumes about intimacies between a couple married that long. "And so we are agreed that our final challenge is weaving. If everything else irons out, we just need to be sure we will have enough cloth to meet demand."

Maeve stepped into the curve of his arm to continue speaking their single mind. "We believe in Turtle Dawn's designs. We are going to need a vast quantity of cloth. The vision you have all laid out is costly—windmills up and down the escarpment, imported thread if need be, trains going to and fro, and . . ."

Tom, overcome with the significance of it all, wiped tears from the side of his nose. Maeve's strong arms wrapped him as his shoulders began to shake. They all felt it—the enormity of what it all meant, the vastness of what they had lost to get here. They thought of the war, and they thought of Thread, their weaving prodigy. Tom regained control and spoke then for all of them. "We will do this in our lad Threadneedle's name." He made it this far and tucked his head back into his wife's capacious bosom.

Regina, Kristiana, and Turtle Dawn's faces each registered the raw emotion that flooded there in the shock of hearing Threadneedle's name invoked.

Maeve found her voice. "I can't think of a greater tribute to Threadneedle. And to Philip. To Lazarus. We will go up against the factory town, with their ghastly steam engines and clacking machinery and gasworks and long hours for low wages!" She paused, letting her words sink in, even as her heretofore hidden gift for oratory revealed itself. "But let us allow this to grow only as fast as t'will. I want no dreams of empire. Each village, as it comes into our union, our guild, our cooperative effort, must come in at its own pace, in its own way. Just as retting has to take place in each locale, in its proper season, in the way that works best in that place, let us grow this venture naturally, without hierarchy. Or too many rules and laws . . . beyond mutual respect," she added. "In our experience"—again she cut her eyes at Tom, who was unhunching his shoulders and regaining his solid stature—"if we hold fast to our human values, are generous, humble, and honest, everything will turn out right."

Tom grasped the stick so they were both holding it. "That's not to say things will never go wrong. We will not be immune to life's hardships and tragedies."

The sound Maeve directed to Tom spoke to the many secret hardships they had endured. She said, "Tom and I are going to be celebrating our fiftieth anniversary of marriage."

"And neither of us travel well . . . ," he added.

"But we thought this spring we would take the boat over to Ulster and Edinburgh . . ."

". . . and talk to some people."

Maeve finished: "While we are gone, we need to have some new homes built. For the people we bring back. New workshops. New looms."

Delphine gestured for the stick.

"With Philip gone, who can lead these building projects? More homes, more weaving spaces, more looms. All that here, Cottage. Windmills for braking and scutching closeby, up north along the escarpment overlooking the lake."

Kilian unfolded himself like a praying mantis, joint by reluctant joint. He took the talking stick without looking at anyone. "Blaise, Philip, and I worked together for years. I am asking you, Blaise, if I could work on the building projects here—and I *can*!" Now he looked out at them, ran his hand through his thinning hair, and dropped his head again. "Could you, Blaise, help me plan, locate, and build the mills?"

Kilian's words were met with a murmur of approval.

Delphine tentatively took back the stick from Kilian before handing it to Blaise, who strode across the room to grasp it firmly. "The mills are my idea. I have been thinking on them for a long time. In Thread's name, my grandson, I would be very pleased to organize this for us! I have spent time in the villages all along the escarpment, as a merchant trader. Our families have occupied these lands for generations, and millennia. Our People," he looked at Delphine, "have a great need for employment. This could be a beginning, for having a business, together, both our People and yours."

Delphine took the stick back again, grinning broadly at Blaise.

"Has everything been said?" she asked.

Regina stood, reluctant, and held out her hand for the stick.

"I know I have behaved like a headstrong, foolish young girl at times." She let some moments pass while she gained control of her voice. "We have all paid a high price to arrive at this moment. Over time, you have each taught me invaluable lessons without uttering a single precept. In a short time, I won and lost the love of my life. I think you will all agree . . ." She paused again and seemed to take strength from some source within her. "We each loved him in a different way. Completely. Wholeheartedly."

Kilian stood suddenly, his body rigid. "Sister!" he shouted. "I should have taken his place." Elizabeth stood and, wrapped her cloak around him, walked him to the door, murmuring, singing, Baby Philip between them, his cradleboard abandoned, hanging from the rafter.

"I pledge not to impose my single vision on our venture," Regina concluded. "This is the main lesson you have all taught me. Not a one of us knows how this all should turn out. And yet, together, we see our way." Blake burst through the anteroom door just then, the Flusty girls in his wake. As Regina sat, she accepted her son into her arms.

Turtle Dawn felt her own consequence in this moment and spoke. "These designs will be celebrated along the coastal cities of our continent, as well as in Europe," she said lifting her sketchbook in the air. "These designs will be celebrated along the coastal cities of our continent, as well as in Europe. From Cottage, New York, to the world! Please, gather around to see our newest line."

The shareholders and founders of Regina Coeli stood, and some stretched with satisfaction while others clustered around Turtle Dawn's cutting table to look at her design pad, to fondle swatches, to admire colors, to disperse among them equally the joy of their resurrection.

Epilogue

His daughter having rejected him, Wilhelm had nothing except his hold-ings, what he had built. And he had built it all for her. After Lazarus was killed by the wolves, Kristiana had sworn she would never forgive him. And so, with a cool head and feeling himself at the end, with no options, he had decided to take his life. With his lawyer he wrote out a will that left his factory to his daughter, and then he sat alone to compose his own eulogy.

> *I have nothing to confess.*
> *I am the future. The world is going my way.*
> *You are quixotic trying to hold it back, a travesty.*
> *I blame my early training as chief cultivateur for our silk venture.*
> *Life and lust rise and swell beneath my fingertips.*
> *What can I do about that?*
> *I have enjoyed myself, taken pleasure where I found it,*
> *made money where I saw potential.*
> *The little people only beg to be taken advantage of in*
> *a predator-and-prey world.*
> *It is ridiculous to pretend otherwise.*
> *Time and history are on my side.*
> *You can't tame the machine, make it do your bidding,*
> *stop its headlong fling with latent resources.*
> *The machines feed our collective greed.*

War? Our natural estate.
I have no remorse. I am grateful to be able to take my own life.
I am a martyr to the future.
I have had a good life, a full life.
I have had two wives, both of whom loved me for a while.
I have had a daughter who loved me for a while.
I have had a grandson who loved me for a while.
I need nothing else.
I have but one regret:
That I did not take my share of Catherine
when we had her spread-eagle
on the bed in the magnanerie.
But I had wanted her to bring herself to me.
There, now you can all feel justified in driving me to this end.
There's not one of you who doesn't have
these feelings I am confessing to: Greed. Fear. Desire.
You shunned me because I act on my feelings,
brought them out for everyone to see.
I am easy to despise. But mark my word: I am the future.
You will go down with your chivalric, outdated, and quixotic values.
Stop the machine? Stop progress? You might as well stop time.
It is you who are finished.
Your way of life, your vision, is finished. Phut!"

A single gunshot sounded throughout the factory, silencing all who heard.

Afterword

The first two novels of the Textile Trilogy, each based on a fiber, are fused style to substance, silk being sensual and electric, linen being difficult to process but long-lasting. The theme and style of each novel reflects the substance and qualities of the textile: *Burning Silk* mimics silk in its pleasure with the sensory world. *Linen Shroud* deals with conflict and the losses we suffered as a people who had higher hopes for what would occur after Contact between native and European Peoples.

The concluding novel of the Textile Trilogy, *Oil & Water* invites the reader to the first oil wells on the planet in western Pennsylvania and New York and pits two visions of the future against each other: synthetics and authentics. These novels have been written at a time when the petroleum and other extractives, along with the chemicals that have been developed, have taken our species down a century-long destructive cul-de-sac. How do we devolve the consequences of what has occurred?

All of the damage that the nineteenth century wrought and the twentieth century nailed into place, can be remedied, if we have both will and vision. Earth herself has proven to have strong powers of regeneration. Will we die as a species because we cannot moderate our consumer culture, the glut of which is choking us?

We already have the positive elements of reconstruction in place.

Mixed-blood cultures have long been acknowledged for their vibrancy—a blend of dissimilar people producing new cultures, like la *Créolité* which ranges over the Caribbean and the Gulf of Mexico, where food, music and dance, dress and even religion are born freshly out of the mix of racial types. In *Burning Silk* and *Linen Shroud*, we see how the *métises*, of native and European stock, could have harmonized the disruptions of colonial conquest had they been allowed to continue on their path toward creating a new People. Instead, a different breed of European pioneer took charge, one that styled native peoples as savages to justify land grabs. To our loss, these conquerors applied a policy of extermination rather than diplomacy.*

These European colonizers failed to appreciate that the matrilineal societies they first encountered among Eastern tribes are not hierarchical like their own Judeo-Christian-Muslim patrilineal cultures. This single difference caused much misunderstanding, for matrilineal cultures are not the inverse of patrilineal, with one gender dominating the other. Parity between the genders, each gender with its particular role, harkens back to pagan forebears in Europe before Roman conquest, but it was not recognized or understood by the European conquerors of the Americas. With their patrilineal blinders on, Europeans could only see the native men sent to negotiate with them as rulers, the final word. They could only see the earth itself as a resource to own and portion out into private reserves rather than commons to share and use sustainably.

In addition to the serious disruptions they created on this continent, much of which we are still dealing with today, Europeans did bring some constructive aspects of their way-of-life to the Americas. In *Linen Shroud* we see how communities were organized into guilds around craft cultures that included textiles, basketry, tanning, and pottery—the more decorative and practical products of daily life—similar to how some native cultures structure their societies. While one cannot overlook the fact that the guilds were part of a caste system that held individual initiative in check, they were nonetheless preferable to a more destructive force: the factory town. During the nineteenth century, and again, starting in the 1960's, utopian communities have risen up against the industrial model, hoping to reimagine and

---

* For these atrocities, we offer the deepest apologies to our native brothers and sisters.

restore possibilities envisioned for this new nation. Historians on the side of the victors, the mass culture, have long ridiculed groups who fully imagined another path forward. The so-called Luddites, saboteurs, and hippies have been grossly misrepresented in our formal histories.

And yet the values and practices espoused in the Sixties and Seventies have infused our mainstream culture. Freshly re-imagined architecture, food, medicine, education, birth, and death have been agents of transformation. Resistance has been resurrected as an honorable path. The best of the traditional ways, the ones we evolved with, are being restored.

We no longer have the luxury of time to explore more dead ends, as we did in previous eras. With solar technology now coming fully of age, taking its place alongside water and wind to generate the energy of commerce, will we be able—creatively and with full engagement of our will—to sequester those parts of modernity that allow us to invent and thrive while jettisoning the synthetic industrial world, including the "miracles of chemistry," whose petrochemical consumer products are, in fact, killing us?

The idea that individual rights should be privileged over the common good is so pervasive in the short history of this country that it will take great efforts to change the tide. War, as a route to dominating extractive resources, can be seen differently, the potential damage to all cultures involved—victor and victim—stepped around with human tools like diplomacy, international law, gun control, mediation.

But perhaps we had to be brought to this point in order that we might listen to the whispers of our hearts. What compromises can we live with? What must we do so our species doesn't have to die, taking this beautiful, diverse world with us? I believe this: What we have imagined can still occur.

The typefaces used for the cover and interior are
Adobe Jenson Pro with Duc De Berry display.

The book and cover design are based on an original design by David Bullen.
Composition and layout by Nancy Austin.
Susanna Tadlock served as the production manager.